DESCENT: LEGENDS *of the* DARK

Terrinoth: an ancient realm of forgotten greatness and faded legacies, of magic and monsters, heroes, and tyrants. Its cities were ruined and their secrets lost as terrifying dragons, undead armies, and demon-possessed hordes ravaged the land. Over centuries, the realm slipped into gloom…

Now, the world is reawakening – the Baronies of Daqan rebuild their domains, wizards master lapsed arts, and champions test their mettle. Banding together to explore the dangerous caves, ancient ruins, dark dungeons, and cursed forests of Terrinoth, they unearth priceless treasures and terrible foes.

Yet time is running out, for in the shadows a malevolent force has grown, preparing to spread evil across the world. Now, when the land needs them most, is the moment for its heroes to rise.

ALSO AVAILABLE

ARKHAM HORROR
Wrath of N'kai by Josh Reynolds
The Last Ritual by S A Sidor
Mask of Silver by Rosemary Jones
Litany of Dreams by Ari Marmell
The Devourer Below edited by Charlotte Llewelyn-Wells
Dark Origins – The Collected Novellas Volume 1

DESCENT: LEGENDS OF THE DARK
The Doom of Fallowhearth by Robbie MacNiven
The Shield of Daqan by David Guymer

KEYFORGE
Tales from the Crucible edited by Charlotte Llewelyn-Wells
The Qubit Zirconium by M Darusha Wehm

LEGEND OF THE FIVE RINGS
Curse of Honor by David Annandale
Poison River by Josh Reynolds
The Night Parade of 100 Demons by Marie Brennan
Death's Kiss by Josh Reynolds

PANDEMIC
Patient Zero by Amanda Bridgeman

TWILIGHT IMPERIUM
The Fractured Void by Tim Pratt
The Necropolis Empire by Tim Pratt

ZOMBICIDE
Last Resort by Josh Reynolds

The GATES *of* THELGRIM

ROBBIE MACNIVEN

First published by Aconyte Books in 2021

ISBN 978 1 83908 098 2

Ebook ISBN 978 1 83908 099 9

Cover art by Jeff Chen.

Map by Francesca Baerald.

Distributed in North America by Simon & Schuster Inc, New York, USA

Printed in the United States of America

9 8 7 6 5 4 3 2 1

ACONYTE BOOKS

An imprint of Asmodee Entertainment Ltd

Mercury House, Shipstones Business Centre

North Gate, Nottingham NG7 7FN, UK

aconytebooks.com // twitter.com/aconytebooks

This book is dedicated to Adela,
my one-and-all.

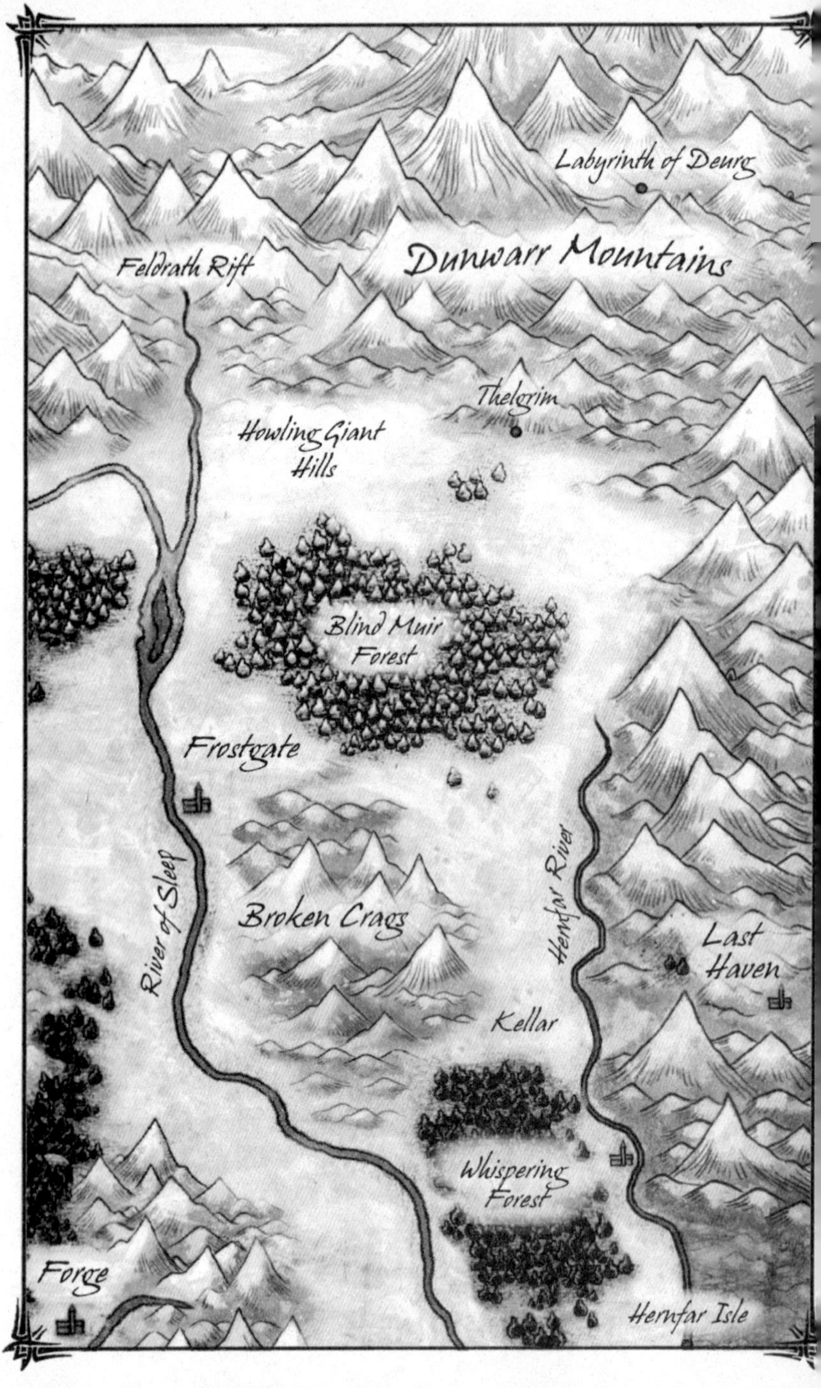

Labyrinth of Deurg

Dunwarr Mountains

Feldrath Rift

Thelgrim

Howling Giant Hills

Blind Muir Forest

Frostgate

Hemfar River

River of Sleep

Broken Crags

Last Haven

Kellar

Whispering Forest

Forge

Hemfar Isle

PROLOGUE

"Stay close," Tiabette told Sarra.

She knew it was a stupid thing to say, because right now she was clutching Sarra's hand as tightly as possible. The little girl had no choice other than to stay close.

In truth, Tiabette knew she was saying it for her own benefit as much as her daughter's. 'Stay close' had become a sort of mantra over the past few months, all the way from their home west of Kellar, on the long, brutal trek through the Howling Giant Hills, west seeking shelter in the icy streets of Frostgate, and then north-east and beyond to the edge of the world. 'Stay close' sometimes felt like all Tiabette had, the only form of control she could still exert in a life that, otherwise, had been wholly taken away from her.

"I'm tired," Sarra complained. Tiabette did her best not to snap back at her.

"Not much further now, sweetheart," she said, keeping her eyes fixed ahead.

She didn't think she could carry Sarra in her arms again. In the months spent on the road with the other refugees, trying to outrun the Uthuk warbands that were spreading like the plague through eastern Terrinoth, she'd seen incredible feats of endurance from parents battling to keep their children alive. She felt as though she'd carried Sarra across half of Terrinoth herself, through cloying mud and swampy tracts and thorny, cutting forests. In Frostgate she'd given up the leather of her shoes to mend her daughter's – she had walked barefoot ever since, the soles of her feet long since reduced to pads of tough, numb skin. The two of them had come so far, yet, despite it all, she wasn't sure she could carry Sarra another step. If she fell now, she knew she wouldn't be able to get up again.

"You always say not much further," Sarra complained. Tiabette closed her eyes for a moment as she walked, trying to keep her voice level.

"This time I really mean it. Look. You can see the end, right there. It's getting closer, with every step."

She opened her eyes and pointed forward, over the bowed heads of those trudging in front. Beyond them the Dunwarr Mountains rose like a vast curtain wall, sheer flanks of gray and purple soaring up to jagged parapets of snowy white. It seemed as though they had been set to guard the heavens themselves, framed by a cloudless sky that arched overhead from peak to flanking peak like some vast, azure vault.

"We're really going there?" Sarra asked, following Tiabette's gesture. Directly ahead, further along the rocky path that the caravan had been following through the foothills, stood something that glittered gold and silver in the distance. From far out it looked like a wall set into the base of the mountainside, a smooth block carved by cunning artifice into the jagged lower face of the peaks. Tiabette knew that it wasn't a wall though. It was a gate.

"We are," she reassured Sarra, managing to smile down at her. "And we're so close now we can even see it! So not much further!"

How many times had she said those words lately? How many times had they been a lie, told as much to herself as to her daughter? Now, finally, they were coming true. Just a little further.

The caravan trudged on. There had been about a hundred of them when they'd first left Frostgate three weeks earlier. Now there were half that number. Some had broken off and gone to Highmont as they had skirted past the southern edges of Blind Muir forest. Others had turned back or dropped by the wayside. Some had simply disappeared overnight. Tiabette tried not to think about those.

She'd learned quickly how to survive on the road. You couldn't trust the people in the caravans. All of them were desperate, and desperate people did desperate things. The ones that offered to help, they were the worst of all – they always wanted a favor in return, or were just searching for the weak and vulnerable behind the guise of kindness, sifting for prey amidst the lost souls cast onto Terrinoth's roads by the war that had gripped the baronies. They were like wolves, stalking in amongst the flock, always watching, always hungry.

She'd discovered that to her cost when an elderly man who'd looked after Sarra on several occasions while she'd been bartering for food, had robbed her while she slept. Now she avoided the helpers, avoided those with the distant stares, and the ones who muttered constantly under their breath. She spoke to no one, and instructed Sarra to do the same.

"Stay close," she urged her once more. Sarra clung on,

though Tiabette could see how her small steps faltered. Not now, she silently urged. Not when they were so close.

The gates were more clearly visible now. Tiabette tried to focus on them, seeking anything that could help take her mind off the stiff, trembling exhaustion in her limbs or the aching pit of hunger in her stomach. She could see an arch of carved rock rising above the huge entranceway, its sheer size only becoming apparent the nearer they got. Towers and ramparts had been carved directly into the steep slopes to their side, seemingly spouting fully-formed from the rockface, so well designed it was difficult to tell where mountain ended and fortress began. The gates themselves stood partially open, the sunlight gleaming brilliantly from the burnished metal cladding them. Tiabette realized, as the caravan drew gradually closer, that they had been fashioned in the likeness of two huge Dunwarr warriors, standing back-to-back, as though warding off surrounding foes in the midst of the mountain pass. Even with the entrance still at a distance, the sheer scale of the architecture almost made her falter and lose her footing.

She realized that the track, for so long a rutted, stony pathway winding unevenly through the foothills, had been replaced with a more solid road of carefully-laid, interlocking cobbles, worn smooth by the passage of countless feet. The valley was likewise constricting ever more sharply on either side of them, its flanks rising above to block out the sunlight while leaving it shining down upon the great gate ahead of them, making it gleam like a beacon in the gloom.

"Will we get to see the dwarfs, Mam?" Sarra asked her. "The ones who live under the mountains?"

"Yes, sweetheart," Tiabette said, too distracted to reply properly. There was a change in the movement up ahead, or rather, a lack of it. The family of five directly in front of them – a husband and wife, their parents and their infant son – had all come to a stumbling halt, blocked by a covered wagon carrying sacks of supplies.

Something, somewhere down the line, had stalled. That in itself was hardly unusual. It seemed that every hour a cart would throw a wheel or one of the oxen would falter and fall. The whole procession would then shuffle to a halt, as people argued and cursed one another. Eventually whatever had caused the delay would either be fixed or simply hauled off the roadway and abandoned, and the ponderous line would get underway again.

Tiabette usually kept to the side whenever there was a halt. Tempers always rose, and she'd seen enough blood spilled in thoughtless anger over the last few months to know it wasn't worth getting involved in the crowd that always gathered around whatever was causing the obstruction. Today, however, was different. Today the end was in sight, achingly close. After everything they'd been through, to be able to see the gates themselves – it was too much.

She felt her anger flare.

"Stay close," she repeated, keeping hold of Sarra's hand as she led her off to one side, into the cold lee of the sheer slopes flanking the road. She was trying to get a better view of whatever had caused the caravan to stop, but others had already had a similar idea. Bodies blocked the route up to the gates, voices rising as a sense of agitation swept through the huddled groups of refugees.

"Why are we stopping?" Sarra asked, standing on her tiptoes as she strained for a better view.

"We aren't," Tiabette corrected her, leading her along the side of the road. From Kellar to the very base of the Dunwarrs, she hadn't struggled half the length of Terrinoth just to be stopped by some fat sutler's broken wagon axle.

The press of bodies grew rapidly denser. The gates were soaring just ahead now, the scars of a thousand sieges visible in the huge, elaborately crafted metal bands that protected the entranceway. The voices around Tiabette were rising as well, competing with the shouting now audible from ahead. It appeared to be coming from the gates themselves.

There was no obstruction, she realized, not on the road anyway. The caravan had met another that appeared to have been stalled right in front of the gates themselves. A short slope led up to the final approach, and the raised elevation allowed Tiabette to see over the heads of those crowding in front.

The gates were still open, but the route through them had been blocked. A solid phalanx of Dunwarr warriors stood like a wedge between the two halves of the entranceway, the mountain sun gleaming brilliantly from burnished helmets and metal-banded shields. One of their number had come forward, taking up a position a few paces ahead of the front ranks. She seemed to be in conversation with a gaggle of refugees, presumably the leaders of the caravan that had arrived just before Tiabette's. Their voices were raised, but the hubbub of the intervening crowd masked their actual words.

"They're going to bar the gates," an old woman in a ragged shawl next to Tiabette exclaimed. "They're going to lock us out!"

"Nonsense," snapped a heavy-set man dressed in a fur-lined, red merchant's tunic, glaring back at the woman. "The Dunwarr have been accepting refugees for months. They wouldn't just stop today!"

"You can't know that for sure," called out another voice, unseen amongst the gathering.

The claim drew out more voices, rising and melding together in an angry, confused outcry. Tiabette felt the same rising swell of panic that was infecting those around her, twinned with the desperate hope that she was mistaken. Surely something like this couldn't really be happening.

"What's going on, Mam?" Sarra pleaded, tugging on Tiabette's hand. She shushed her, trying to follow what was happening at the gates. One of the refugees, an elf, was throwing his arms up angrily. He turned and stormed back towards the crowd, as several of the human delegates seemed to try to push past the dwarf they'd been conferring with.

There was a general, swaying motion amongst the bodies around Tiabette. She felt herself being thrust forward, shoving, jostling refugees beginning to force those at the front up the slope and towards the Dunwarr ranks.

"Hold on," Tiabette shouted to her daughter, trying to keep her close. It seemed as though the crowd was going to surge up into the dwarfs, heedless of their presence barring their way.

That was when a voice rang out, deep and commanding. It was accompanied by the single peal of a mountain horn, unseen, echoing sharply down the valley.

The dwarfs ahead reacted immediately. Shields were brought up and slammed together, creating a fearsome, echoing report that sounded from the slopes on either side. At the same time, the second rank shifted. Tiabette caught sight of crossbows being raised, poised between the overlapping shields of the Dunwarri in front. They were loaded, the wicked tips of the quarrels gleaming.

A wail went up from the crowd as those at the front urgently began to push back against the ones shoving forward from behind. Sarra screamed as she was almost dragged from Tiabette's grip. She clung onto her daughter with both hands, pulling her in close as they were both nearly lifted from their feet by the diverging currents driving the crowd.

There was another horn blast, ringing through the cold, clear air. People around Tiabette were crying and screaming now, total panic overwhelming the refugees as the sound of vast, rumbling hinges rose above the discord.

With another shuddering crash, the Dunwarr phalanx moved. They took a step back, shield wall staying intact and crossbows never wavering. Another step, then another, the darkness beyond the doors slowly swallowing them up. As they went, the vast gates began to swing steadily shut, the sunlight catching the scarred metal.

"No," Tiabette shouted as she was driven further back by the crowd, her hopes plummeting as a sense of absolute helplessness gripped her. She tried to free herself from the press, but it was no use. All she could do was cling on to her daughter and attempt to shield her from the shoving, stumbling, shouting mass.

With a crash that seemed to shake the very mountain peaks above them, the gates of Thelgrim slammed shut.

CHAPTER ONE

The man named Slevchek slammed his fist into the table, spilling ale and scattering coins across the scratched, sticky timber.

"Cheat," he bellowed, glaring furiously at Raythen. The dwarf returned an equally fierce look, his single, dark eye glinting in the sallow candlelight of the taproom.

"Piece of advice, manling," he said. "It's not clever to accuse someone of cheating at cards when they've just beaten you. It makes you look like a bad loser which, I'll grant, you probably are. But, for future reference, if you're going to sling mud do it while you're ahead. The second round we played, perhaps, or the third, while you were still winning. It makes it more believable, more honest-looking."

Raythen wasn't sure if anything he'd just said had reached Slevchek's admittedly small brain. The heavy-set merchant was practically steaming with fury, his fists bunched, jaw clenched, ruddy complexion turning an even uglier shade of puce. His compatriots, two other human traders sitting to his left and right, seemed caught between their desire to back up their friend and their aversion to making a scene in the middle of the bar.

In Raythen's private opinion, it was a bit late for that. The taproom beneath Skellig's Inn had gone deadly quiet as carousers turned their attention expectantly towards where Raythen and his fellow gamblers were sitting. The dispute had been rumbling all evening, as Slevchek became ever-more drunk and belligerent. He'd mocked Raythen's early setbacks, then reacted with increasing outrage as the dwarf had first won back his losses, then started steadily building on them.

Of course, the oafish human was quite correct – Raythen *had* been cheating. Nothing especially nuanced, but naturally the pack was rigged. Raythen had a few duplicates he'd palmed, with a backup Barony Queen concealed beneath a platter of half-eaten poultry wings he'd been deliberately taking his time with.

"Never trust a Dunwarr when it comes to gold," Slevchek spat across the table, cuffing drool from his chin stubble. "Especially a one-eyed, one-handed one!"

Making such a remark toward a dwarf would normally have seen the human's skull smashed by a bar stool or an axe, but Raythen had heard it all before. Besides, he was no ordinary Dunwarr. He smiled.

"Come now, manling, we're three apiece. If I'm cheating, I'm not doing a very good job of it," he said.

"You've won all the big bets," whined one of Slevchek's companions, a sniveling, sunken-eyed little man whose name Raythen hadn't bothered to remember.

"I wasn't the one who started raising the stakes," he pointed out. "That's down to you three gentlemen."

He could feel the attention of the rest of the bar on them, a fact Slevchek and his friends seemed oblivious to. Right now, that was the only variable Raythen felt vaguely uncomfortable about. He could keep these three idiots going all night, but what if someone else intervened? What if one of the other patrons had seen the trick before, or just possessed a keener eye and a clearer head than the human trio. He'd noted the presence of two elves earlier in the evening, and one of the bar servers had been staring at him for the better part of an hour, even before Slevchek's outrage had started to draw a more general crowd. He feared it wasn't because of his good looks either.

"The hand," Slevchek exclaimed, gesturing furiously. "The hand is fake!"

Raythen made a show of sighing heavily.

"We've been over this," he said, making sure he was speaking loudly enough to be overheard by the rest of the taproom. "Yes, the hand is fake. No, I've not stuffed cards or coins in it. Look."

He grasped the wooden prop with his other hand and unbuckled it, removing it from the sleeve of his green cloak.

"Solid fairoak," he said, tossing it across the table. "Inspect it for yourself. Again."

Slevchek snatched the carved object and squinted at it, blinking rapidly as he tried to focus through his inebriation. He let out a grunt of frustration and tossed it to the accomplice on his right, who turned it over in his own hands, searching for some sign of duplicity.

"If you're quite done, I'd appreciate it back," Raythen said, holding his good hand out. "Perhaps we can also stop insulting and harassing an old dwarf and get back to the game? Unless you manlings would rather call it a night?"

"I want my money back," Slevchek barked, hitting the table again as his friend reluctantly passed Raythen his replacement limb.

"You can win it back," the dwarf said brightly, refastening the hand. "What do you say to one more round? All or nothing?"

"Liar," Slevchek bellowed, attempting to rise from his seat but falling back into it instead. He fumbled at his belt and drew a long, lean bullock dagger, the candlelight winking from its slender blade. "Give me my money!"

Raythen reached out with his good hand and snatched the front of Slevchek's jerkin. Ignoring the knife, he hauled him forward so he was planted firmly against the table's edge, knocking over a flagon of ale and scattering coins and cards as he did so.

"I didn't lie about the hand, you stupid manling," he snarled. "It's solid. But I do just happen to have a third one, and it's currently pointing a loaded hand bow at your manhood, underneath the table. So, settle down, smile, and play one more round, and you won't be spending the rest of the night trying to pluck a quarrel from the only treasure that really matters. Agreed?"

Raythen fixed Slevchek's eyes with his own, their faces inches apart, the stink of unwashed, intoxicated, idiot manling almost more than the dwarf could bear. He saw the slow, pained realization in Slevchek's bleary gaze, giving way to the spark of outrage.

"Choose your next words very wisely, my friend," he urged. This was the decisive moment, the one he'd been expecting since he'd first offered the three merchants a game. Either Slevchek would accept what was happening and would be walking out of Skellig's unharmed but with a lighter purse, or Raythen was about to be forced to make a hasty exit of his own with the money he'd made thus far. The ace up his sleeve – not quite literally, in this case – was the false hand he sometimes employed to confound opponents. An extra sleeve was sown into his heavy green cloak, concealing his real arm and hand while the focus of those across from him remained on his wooden prosthetic. His finger tightened fractionally on the hand bow he was grasping below the table.

Play the odds right, and nine times out of ten you'd come out on top.

"Raythen," said a voice, shattering the moment.

Still gripping the front of the merchant's tunic, both Raythen and Slevchek look up, slowly. While the dwarf had been trying to get his point across, a hulking bear of a man had approached their table. He was clad in a fur-edged cloak, his head shaved, a huge, bristling moustache drooping down almost to his chest. He loomed over the table, looking pointedly at Raythen.

"You're late," he rumbled.

Raythen let go of the tunic abruptly, letting Slevchek slump back in his chair. With practiced speed, he began to unload and conceal the crossbow beneath the table, all the while smiling up at the big man.

"You know, Cayfern, I was actually early. Couldn't find you anywhere though, so I thought I'd entertain these fine fellows until I spotted you. I suppose I lost track of time. My apologies."

He finished with the hand bow as he spoke, slipping it into his rucksack. Cayfern grunted. He seemed oblivious to the attention much of the bar was giving him – the big human was practically a minor celebrity in parts such as these, a well-known face in the taverns and inns that crammed their way along Frostgate's icy streets.

"Well, if you still want a job beyond tavern pickpocketing, I suggest you come with me," he said. "Now."

"Absolutely," Raythen said, rising and offering a short bow to the merchants. "Duty calls I'm afraid."

Slevchek rose unsteadily to confront the interloper, and Raythen couldn't help but smirk as he saw the man's anger turn to dismay as he realized he barely came up to Cayfern's chin.

"I would sit down if I were you, Slevchek," Cayfern said. "Enjoy the last of your ale and go home quietly to your wife."

He extended a hand to Slevchek's shoulder as he spoke, patting it. Slevchek once more fell back into his chair.

Avoiding making eye contact with anyone else, Raythen swept his winnings into his sack, slung it over his shoulder and followed Cayfern through the taproom into a small space through the back of the bar. It had once been a pantry, but its shelves were now empty and thick with dust, the only sign of its former use a few old sacks of meal still heaped in one corner. A single table and four chairs filled the cramped space, lit by a lonely, festering tallow candle. Cayfern sat across from the door, his chair creaking beneath his weight.

Raythen hesitated before taking the seat opposite. They were not the only two in the room. A woman was already at the table, looking decidedly bored as she passed a small stone shard between her fingers. She was dressed in an embroidered golden coat that turned to long, flowing pleats below the waist, worn over a silken white shirt with flared sleeves. Her hair was long and dark, plaited down her back and held away from her forehead by a red and gold wrap. Bangles and charms decorated her wrists, and a carved bone staff was propped casually against the chair behind her, topped by a shard of blue tanzanite that seemed to shimmer like the ocean depths. Her face was lean and sharp, like a hawk's. Raythen could practically feel the sorcery bleeding off her.

"I didn't know we'd have company," he said.

"Sit," growled Cayfern.

He obeyed. The woman slipped the shard she'd been toying with into the pocket of a bag strapped around her waist. Raythen looked at her directly.

"Can I be the first to say what an honor it is to be in the presence of a runewitch?" he asked.

"You know me?" she replied, her accent thick. If she was surprised, she didn't show it.

"Every adventurer worth employing has heard of the great Astarra, Greyhaven's finest protegee," Raythen said, smiling at her.

"I dislike you already," the sorceress said. Raythen laughed. Being disliked was hardly a break from the norm for him.

"Astarra, this is Raythen, formerly of the Dunwarr city of Thelgrim," Cayfern said. "He will be joining you on the expedition."

"Will he indeed?" Raythen asked, turning his attention

back Cayfern. "That's good to know. Last I heard, Raythen had only expressed mild interest in finding out why the great Cayfern had put out a call in the bars and taverns of Frostgate for Raythen to join him."

"I know you well enough, dwarf," Cayfern said. "I know that when you start preying on fat, drunken merchants in Skellig's, it means your coin pouch is empty. My employer is offering to change that. You'll take the job."

"That all depends," Raythen said.

"The money is good."

"That's a start, but I was rather wondering about the company."

"If you know of Astarra, you will know of her abilities," Cayfern said, nodding briefly to the woman.

"Exactly," Raythen said. "And I suspect those abilities probably don't come cheap. So just what sort of task is dire enough to see your mystery employer paying out to hire a runewitch? And, more importantly, who else are we still waiting for?"

"I was wondering that myself," Astarra said.

"Four chairs," Raythen added, nodding to the last, unoccupied seat. The room had clearly been set up for the meeting, and he knew their host well enough to be certain he wouldn't have accidentally set out extra spaces.

Cayfern said nothing. He was a well-known facilitator in the northern Baronies, a go-to between the rogues, malcontents and bravados that populated places like the Free City of Frostgate, and those who wished to employ them anonymously for work across Terrinoth. Raythen had been contracted by him four times previously, though whether the person actually paying him had been the same one or a different client each time, he had no idea. What mattered was that Cayfern always paid up in full when the time came. He clearly chose his employers carefully, and in this sort of business, that counted for a lot.

The facilitator didn't answer Raythen's question. Instead, he looked pointedly past him, towards the door. Raythen twisted in his chair as it opened.

A tall figure stepped inside, forced to duck under the mantle. By the dirty light of the candle, his immediate appearance was nightmarish. He was achingly gaunt and pale, his skin seemingly stretched too tightly over a jagged skull. His ears came not to one point, but three, and his eyes were black as fresh pitch, sunken into his bony face. He was clad in raggedy, dark robes, and had manacles fastened around his wrists and throat. His only visible ornamentation was a large, strange-looking key hanging from his waist.

Raythen reached for the axe under his cloak as Astarra surged to her feet. Only Cayfern didn't react, and when he spoke it was without concern.

"Welcome, Shiver."

"What in the name of Kellos's holy flames is this?" Astarra demanded, lifting her staff. Her eyes had gone wide, and her knuckles white where she gripped the arcane conduit. The figure that had caused such a reaction – a deep elf, Raythen realized – looked at her without a hint of emotion, though he felt the temperature in the pantry plummet, as though a window had just been opened directly onto the icy streets outside. His breath started fogging in front of him.

"This is the third member of the expedition," Cayfern said,

as though it was the most obvious thing in all of Mennara. "His name is Shiver. Like the rest of you, he was chosen specifically by my employer."

"He's a dark sorcerer," Astarra snapped, apparently sensing the interloper's aura. "What are you, creature? A necromancer? A slave to the Ynfernael?"

"You are Cayfern?" the elf asked the big man, ignoring Astarra. His voice was hoarse and scratchy, as though unaccustomed to use.

Cayfern nodded. "That I am. My employer thanks you for answering his call."

"I do not know your employer," Shiver said. "But I have seen you enough in my dreams to know this path is the one I am bound to tread."

He grasped the back of the last unoccupied chair and pulled it out with a long, slow scrape. Astarra was still on her feet. Her staff had started to glow a cold blue.

Raythen cleared his throat and reached over to his false hand, beginning to unbuckle it.

"I can do magic too," he said pointedly, removing it and freeing his real hand, which he placed flat on the table next to the other. "See? If we're going to have a sorcerous duel in a tiny closet, I should warn you both, I won't hold back."

Cayfern laughed. Astarra looked from Shiver to Raythen, but the tension was broken. Slowly, the light of her staff started to fade. Raythen noted that he could no longer see his breath either.

"Aren't you going to chastise the elf for being late?" he asked Cayfern. The manling ignored him, though Shiver turned his black gaze on him.

"I was waylaid several times," he rasped. "Waking visions."

"Oh, well that's alright then," Raythen said. "Perhaps Cayfern can get on with telling us why we're here, and I can get on with rejecting his offer of a job with either of you two."

Cayfern looked pointedly at Astarra. She sat, though she kept her staff in one hand.

"I don't work with dark sorcerers," she said, looking hard at Shiver. "I have learned enough over the years to know that death stalks all those who do. No good will come of it."

"Shiver is not a dark sorcerer," Cayfern said. "My employer does not pay those who dally with the unnatural arts."

"He feels like one, and he looks like one," Astarra pressed.

"And I look like a completely trustworthy, honest Dunwarr ranger, but I'm not," Raythen snapped, beginning to lose his temper. "Now, I didn't come to this … lovely establishment in this wonderful city just to sit and debate the philosophies of magic. So, could we please get to the point. Cayfern?"

The facilitator looked at him silently for a moment before starting to speak.

"A month ago, Thelgrim, ancient city of the Dunwarrs, closed its gates. Since then, there has been no contact whatsoever with the inhabitants. No one has entered, and no one has left. All lesser entrances and exits into the mountains also appear to have been closed. The city has been sealed off."

"I had heard that the Dunwarrs had grown silent," Astarra said. "But if you want to know why, perhaps just ask the Dunwarr sitting opposite you?"

Raythen scoffed.

"I can assure you, if I was in any way privy to the thoughts of Ragnarson and the other short-sighted fools who rule that place, I would not be here right now," he lied. He had no intention of elaborating on his knowledge regarding the king's mindset. "I haven't set foot in Thelgrim in almost twenty years."

"None know why the city has been shut off," Cayfern said. "My employer has asked far and wide, and has received no satisfactory answer. That is why he has brought you together–"

"No," Raythen interrupted. The trio all looked at him. He kept his eye fixed on Cayfern.

"If your master thinks I'm going back to Thelgrim, he hasn't done his research," he went on. "I thought you knew me better, Cayfern."

"You have unfinished business there," the manling said. "That is why you will go. And this…"

He planted a bulging leather purse down on the table. It clinked heavily.

"That's just the initial payment," he said. "My employer promises more once the contract is completed. It'll be enough that you don't have to spend your evenings robbing drunken oafs in stinking, dirty taverns in Frostgate."

"Maybe I enjoy doing that," Raythen said, not moving to pick up the bulging pouch. "What's the payment in?"

"Honest Dunwarr silver," Cayfern said. "My employer vouches for it."

"I'm sure he does," Raythen said.

"And just who is your employer?" Astarra asked, seemingly unimpressed by the offering on the table. Shiver, who hadn't said anything since sitting down, nodded once. Raythen had been wondering the same thing all evening, though he'd done this enough times to know there was no point in asking a professional facilitator like Cayfern. Whoever they were, they had a lot of dwarven silver for a start, and an interest in Thelgrim, but not the personal contacts necessary to find out what had actually become of the subterranean city. Raythen had been trying to think of a match for someone like that, and so far, he had nothing. That, in his considered experience, didn't bode well.

"My employer will remain anonymous," Cayfern said. "All you need to be sure of is that they can pay, and pay well. I will attest to that."

"Forgive me if I don't find that overly reassuring," Raythen said. "Not while you still haven't told us what he actually wants us to do."

"He wants us to go to Thelgrim," Astarra said, as though Raythen was an idiot. He smiled condescendingly at her.

"To what purpose exactly? Knock on the great gate, ask how Captain Lyssa Svensdottir is and whether old Ragnarson is in good health, then saunter back here to collect our riches? Come on! What else is there to it, Cayfern? Tell us the whole story."

"Once you have entered the city, you will proceed to the headquarters of the League of Invention," Cayfern said. "There is an item there which my employer would have you collect and return here with."

"I knew it!" Raythen exclaimed, slapping his palm on the table. "I knew you wanted me to steal something!"

"Not steal," Cayfern said, stoically. "The League know you are coming. You are to ask for Mavarin, and he will provide you with what you need freely."

"And just what is it we're going all the way to Thelgrim to collect?" Astarra asked.

"It possesses magical properties," Cayfern said.

"A runebound shard?" Astarra asked. Raythen noted a pulse of light that ran through her staff as she spoke the words.

"Yes," Cayfern said.

"Which one?" Astarra demanded, the need in her voice obvious.

"I do not know," Cayfern admitted. "I was not informed. But my employer wants it retrieved from the Dunwarr. He has already struck a deal for it, and merely requires its collection. Bring it here and you will all be paid, and paid handsomely."

"I have no need for coin," Shiver said abruptly. The deep elf had been a silent, brooding presence since taking his seat, but now he clasped distressingly long, black-clawed fingers on the table and fixed his unnatural gaze on the facilitator. "Your master sought me out, so he must know this."

"My employer tells me that this may be of greater interest to you." Cayfern removed something from the pocket of his furred cloak, planted it on the table and slid it slowly towards the elf.

It was a lock, heavy and edged with rust. At a glance, it seemed wholly unremarkable. Shiver looked at it for a while, his black eyes unreadable, then slowly reached out and grasped it daintily between forefinger and thumb, as though it was some strange, slightly disturbing insect. He held it before his eyes and then, to Raythen's amusement, sniffed it, before placing it back down as carefully as he had picked it up.

"There are more?" he asked in his cold, dead voice.

"Two more, both of greater significance than this," Cayfern said. "If you get the job done."

Shiver said nothing.

"I'm not working with him," Astarra reiterated, as though the deep elf wasn't sitting right there.

"Then that is your loss," Cayfern said, with an unconcerned shrug. "Both in the present, and in the future. My employer informs me that they likely have further tasks to complete after this one, tasks involving more runeshards. You could learn a great deal from them. Their power is, by all accounts, formidable."

Raythen recognized a bluff when he saw one, and right now Astarra wasn't doing a very good job at it. Cayfern, he knew, was better at those sorts of games.

"If the contract is of no interest to any of you, I will tell my employer as much, and they will reiterate their call for interested parties to make themselves known," the big man said, picking up the sack of silver.

"I'll consider it," Raythen said. It was getting late, and he was in no mood for more distractions, not tonight. "In fact, I'll take the job. But I'm going to need a bigger down payment than the… relatively generous one currently on offer. Your employer clearly appreciates my abilities. They won't find another Dunwarr dwarf in Frostgate with the skills I possess. No one is better suited to this task."

Cayfern looked at him, face unreadable in the guttering light of the tallow candle. Then, he reached into his cloak and drew out another pouch, tossing it onto the table with a clink.

Good at bluffing, but not that good. Raythen nodded and offered Cayfern a smile.

"I'll take the job."

"As will I," Shiver said. Raythen realized he'd slipped the old lock into his robes without him noticing.

He looked left, at Astarra. The sorceress was glaring at Shiver but, slowly, she forced her gaze back to Cayfern and composed her expression.

"Tell your employer," she said, "that the runewitch accepts their terms."

"I will," Cayfern said. "There will be no signed contract. You are expected to be back here with the shard by the first full moon following the Feast of Flames. I will be waiting for you."

"That gives us just over two months," Astarra pointed out.

"Which should be enough time to journey to Thelgrim, retrieve the shard, and return," Cayfern said.

"And if we can't gain access to the mountains?" Astarra asked. "What if we're delayed?"

"Don't be."

"I'll hold onto these for the time being, just for safe keeping," Raythen said, breaking the silence that followed Cayfern's words. He reached across the table and grasped the two pouches of silver. To his surprise, neither Astarra nor Shiver tried to stop him. He forced himself to keep a straight face as he secreted them in one of the concealed pockets of his rucksack. This was going to be easier than he'd expected.

"Well, it's been a pleasure catching up, Cayfern," he said, nodding to the human. "But I should really get back to the bar. I promised Slevchek I'd let him win back his losses."

"You really think that's wise?" Cayfern asked. Raythen rose and offered him a short bow.

"Would I be worthy of this great undertaking you've tasked me with if I said no?" He looked at the other two.

"It's a pleasure to meet you both, and I look forward to

becoming further acquainted over the course of our little expedition. We're going to have all sorts of fun, I've no doubt."

"Tomorrow morning, outside," Astarra said coldly. "I'm leaving with the dawn, whether you're there or not. I don't want this to take any longer than it has to."

"Don't worry," Raythen said. "I think we all share that sentiment."

CHAPTER TWO

Raythen snatched onto the outer sill of the window, doubled over, and was sick against the side of the wall. It left him in a rush of choking, stinking, stomach-churning bile, burning at his throat. He resurfaced, gasping, still clutching onto the window.

"By Fortuna's lucky dice," he managed weakly.

"Did you even sleep last night?" Astarra asked from behind him, her voice riven with disgust.

"It's just a little ritual," Raythen lied, looking at his reflection in the grimy window and cuffing strands of sick from his bristling, black beard. "A tradition. Every time I set out on a new journey I spew my guts up against a wall."

He felt his stomach lurch again and, unseen by Astarra, screwed his eyes tight shut. He was willing away the churning of his insides, the cold, clammy sweat, the pounding in his skull. He was in no fit state to embark on a month-long trek, back to the city that had already taken so much from him. But damned if he would admit any of that to his new companions.

"I'm fine," he said, opening his eyes and forcing himself to take a deep, slow breath, followed by a swig of tepid water from the skin at his hip.

"I didn't ask," Astarra said. Raythen turned to look at her, forcing himself to put on a smile.

"Not a morning person, are you?" he said.

"Apparently neither are you," Astarra pointed out. She was shielded from the cold wind blowing along the dirt street by a heavy mantle of mottled leonx pelt, the white fur a contrast to the long, black braid of hair that hung over one shoulder. Her staff was strapped to her back, its blue tip shimmering slightly as it caught the dawn.

"Where did you spend the night?" Raythen asked her as he hefted his rucksack and settled it onto his stout shoulders, tugging at his muddy green cloak to free it from the straps.

"In one of the bedrooms upstairs," Astarra said. "And you?"

"Under one of the tables downstairs," Raythen said. "I think…"

He reached up and tentatively probed at the side of his head, hissing as he felt the lump that had formed there overnight. Everything after leaving Cayfern had been a blur. He remembered another bout of cards, though he had no idea if Slevchek had been involved or not. There were patchwork recollections of shattered glass, shouting, a stool hurtling through the air. He'd come to beneath a table in the corner of the wrecked taproom. The first thing he'd checked had been Cayfern's silver and the coin he'd won – all intact. That was what mattered. He'd forced himself to leave a few pieces with a stony-faced barmaid attempting to clear up the damage, before stumbling out into the weak dawn light.

"The question is, where is our third, gallant companion?" he wondered out loud, turning away from Astarra to survey the street.

Frostgate lay before him, gray and bleak in the gathering light. Summer still ruled over this corner of Terrinoth, but it had long lost its luster. Raythen knew that soon the traders, merchants and mercenaries would be returning to the infamous Free City, seeking shelter and coin as the northern routes became impassable and the rivers iced over. The number of inhabitants would quadruple in the space of a few weeks, and a whole new settlement of yurts, tents and shelters would spring up beyond its walls. Raythen always made sure he was gone by the time the weather turned – he had too many enemies fond of Frostgate to risk being around at the height of the season.

"The elf is already here," Astarra said, causing him to look back and follow her gaze.

Shiver was standing in the darkness of the alleyway that ran down the flank of Skellig's, as still and silent as a revenant. Raythen almost jumped, unable to mask a scowl. He wasn't used to being taken by surprise.

"Where in Fortuna's name did you come from?" he demanded. Shiver stepped forward into the muck of the streets, his tattered robes trailing in the frost-hardened dirt.

"You have sick on your boots," he said, without answering Raythen's question. The dwarf looked down and realized he was right. Without bothering to wipe them clean, he smiled and reached up to clap his hand on the deathly figure's shoulder.

"We're going to be friends, you and I," he said. "I can tell."

Shiver showed no reaction, other than to slowly look down at Raythen's hand until the dwarf removed it from his shoulder.

Astarra strode past them both without a word, headed for the gate.

"Looks like we're getting underway then?" Raythen called after her, checking his pack one more time and taking another slow breath to calm his stomach. "Honestly, if I was in Thelgrim and I knew we were coming, I'd shut the gates too."

Shiver had set off as well, manacled hands in front of him, tucked into the long hems of his sleeves. Sighing, Raythen began to follow.

The mountains surged on either side, climbing towards the heavens, their white peaks shining in the sun while all about their feet lay in shadow.

They stood before him, a woman and her child, bowed with exhaustion. Their clothes were ragged and dirty, their hair tangled and greasy, their eyes hollow, their cheeks starved. They stared into his soul like shades damning their own fate, and the fate of those who had led them to this. They said nothing.

Slowly, the child raised an arm and pointed, past him, up at the mountainside. He looked but saw nothing. When he turned back, the mother was pointing too, in the same direction. Neither had taken their eyes off him.

He heard a sound, low and soft at first, but rising rapidly. It was water, he realized, the sound of water rushing and surging. It grew and grew, until it was a raging, roaring torrent. But he couldn't see it. He looked all around, turning in a circle, searching frantically. It sounded as though a flood was sweeping down the valley, yet there was no sign of it, nothing beyond the thunder in his ears.

He realized abruptly that both the woman and the child were gone. Then, the water hit him.

Shiver surged to his feet with a gasp, his heart racing. Around him the forest lay quiet. Dawn was only just beginning to show itself between the branches, a soft, pallid light lending color back to the mossy boughs and thick, hanging ivy. The undergrowth rustled nearby and a flitwing took flight, chirruping as it darted back up into the canopy.

He sighed softly. For a moment he had forgotten where he was. But, as the vision sloughed off and his heart eased its pounding, reality returned. He had spent the night on the southern edge of Blind Muir forest, beneath the boughs of a great silverbark tree. His back was still sore from where a knot of roots had dug into it. He stretched, feeling aching muscles ease and bones pop.

He was soaked, he realized. His robes, his skin, all of it was drenched, as though he'd been caught out in a thunderstorm while he'd slept. He grimaced. Despite the wetness, he felt no chill.

He'd been right to take on the task. That was what he'd been telling himself since they'd left Frostgate, the week before. Regardless of the company, the memories had been leading him here, along the path of the Aenlong, Empyrean magics that he had been cut off from for so long. And the memories didn't lie.

He knew a part of him had been afraid. That was why he hadn't used the lock until last night. He was worried he'd made the wrong choice. Worried he had once again been misled by hope. The locks had all pointed towards answers, and it had been so long since he'd had any. So long since he'd known anything beyond his penance.

He was on the right path though. It had been a vision, not a memory, that the key had unlocked. He had seen the Dunwarrs. The rest, he could not yet explain. The path would show him though, in time.

He looked down at his feet and saw the lock the human had given him. The key was lodged in it, turned to the right. He hesitated, then reached down and grasped it. As he picked it up, the rust marring the lock began to spread. A thousand years passed in the blink of an eye, as it ate away at the metal, gnawing and crumbling it, until the last of the dust was carried away by a breeze that gently rattled the branches of the silverbark behind him. He was left holding only the key.

He tied it around his waist once more. He was tired, but the time for rest had passed. The other two would be looking for him, likely hoping he wouldn't return. That didn't worry Shiver. In their place, he'd have felt the same way.

"Just where do you go some nights?" Raythen asked as he sat by the fire. It had been over a week since departing Frostgate, and the trio had not long passed north of Highmont. The road was becoming decidedly narrower and more rutted, and patchy fields and wooded outcrops had started to give way to wild heathland and rugged hills as they traveled further north and east. Blind Muir still lay to the left of where they had pitched up for the night, a dark, brooding mass that seemed to watch them constantly.

Shiver said nothing as he sat, cross-legged, picking at a bowl of porridge Astarra had cooked up.

"He goes into the forest at night, like all evil things," Astarra said, not deigning to look at the elf. "I have seen him. Blind Muir is cursed. All know that."

"He probably just doesn't want to risk you murdering him in his sleep," Raythen pointed out to the sorceress.

"I rest better alone," Shiver said, tersely.

Raythen didn't press the matter. Since leaving Frostgate, he'd learned a number of valuable things about his companions, not least of which included the fact that the gaunt, ragged elf was less of a sinister presence and more a miserable loner. An aura of fear was convenient when it came to shunning others, and Raythen had no doubt Shiver used it to good effect. It certainly had Astarra fooled – she was convinced he was just waiting for the opportunity to cut their throats, drain their blood and sacrifice their souls to some Ynfernael demon.

For her own part, Raythen suspected the runewitch was even more powerful than she was letting on. He had seen her employ her magics for the first time when they'd come across a caravan paused where the road crossed over a stream. One of the carts had tipped in, wounding a mother and catching a child in the current. Astarra had summoned the energies of one of her stones, the Deeprune, and commanded the waters, shaping them as a potter might shape clay and forcing them to surrender the small girl back into the arms of her mother.

Raythen would have been impressed, if he hadn't been forced to stop Astarra attacking Shiver moments later. The elf had gone to assist the woman injured in the accident, turning his strange, chill elven magics to sealing up a gash on her arm. Astarra, it seemed, had thought he was draining the life from the poor individual.

Once he'd managed to convince her to back down, the refugees had shown their gratitude with a gift of some bread and oats. It was the third such group they'd encountered in the past seven days, each one seemingly more miserable and bedraggled than the last. Toiling columns of wagons and carts clogged the road, creaking and laden down with all manner of possessions, not to mention people – the old, the young, the infirm. Those who still could, trudged alongside them, heads bowed with exhaustion.

Raythen knew this road wasn't the only one troubled by such processions. He had noted the rise in numbers of refugees, from the last job he'd done in Dawnsmoor all the way to Frostgate, where sorry clusters of homeless, destitute families huddled desperately around sputtering fires in the cold streets and alleyways. He'd seen displacement before, many times, from those fleeing Riverwatch after the great festerskin outbreak, to the dispossessed abandoning the Borderlands during the raiding season. He'd never known these sorts of numbers though. It was as if all of Terrinoth had been forced to take to the road with only what they could carry on their backs or heap on a cart.

From what Raythen had seen, there were no unifying demographics either. Many of the refugees were human, but he had spotted the features and heard the accents of every barony as far south as the great woodland of the Aymhelin. There were orcs and dwarfs among them too, a few Hyrrinx catfolk, even elves. All brought with them stories of unrest, of bandit attacks and Uthuk raids and, most persistently, rumors of a great battle that had been fought against the demon-worshipers in Kell or one of the other eastern baronies.

Wordlessly, Shiver rose from beside the fire and stalked off. Raythen caught Astarra's glare and couldn't help but smirk.

"Why do you hate him so?" he asked her. "Is there some past history between you two that I know nothing of?"

She shook her head defensively. "I saw enough promising students at Greyhaven destroyed by the lure of the darker forms of magic. I told you, I know one when I see one."

Raythen grunted noncommittally. Secretly, he was glad Shiver had departed for the night. He'd been wanting to talk to Astarra for a few days, and had been trying to gauge when best to do so. He had questions about her involvement, and he wanted them answered before he started putting any more trust in her.

"I've been troubled by something for a few days now," he said, his tone casual as he glanced at the runewitch over the fire. "Since that night in Skellig's, actually. It's had me thinking, day and night, because I reckon it's important, but I just can't quite figure it out. Just what do you want in Thelgrim?"

Astarra didn't reply, gazing stoically down into her porridge.

"You didn't take the silver," Raythen continued. "Didn't show any interest in it. Neither you nor the elf have even asked about it since I took it all. He at least was offered something else, though I've no idea what he wants with a collection of old locks. Probably something terribly sinister and esoteric. You though, Cayfern offered you nothing else, yet you still took the job."

"I will not discuss this with you," Astarra said tersely.

"Don't fancy killing time?" Raythen asked, with a hint of mockery. "I suppose you can just talk about how much you distrust Shiver all evening if you need to."

"My reasons are my own," Astarra said.

"I always follow my instincts," he told her, deciding to change tack, be more direct. "And right now, they're warning me more about you than about our raggedy deep elf. That's quite something."

"And perhaps mine are the same," Astarra snapped, finally looking at him. "You think you are so much cleverer than those around you, Dunwarr, but your imagined intelligence is nothing but low cunning. You took the silver only after cajoling from the facilitator. You've spoken multiple times of the fact that you have no desire to return to Thelgrim, despite it being the city of your birth. Why is that? Why do you hate, or fear, a place that was once your home and remains the seat of your people? What are you going back to?"

Raythen refused to bite. Astarra had hit upon a flurry of hidden wounds with her words, and he wasn't going to give her the satisfaction of knowing it. He bit his tongue.

"Why have the gates of Thelgrim been closed?" she asked, clearly intending to take over the role of questioner. He glowered at her, doing his best to keep his cool.

"If I knew that, I could have collected my full payment in Skellig's and never left its sordid delights," Raythen said. "And if all goes according to plan, you'll never have to know why I left the city in the first place."

"As long as it doesn't interfere with our task, it doesn't concern me," Astarra said. "That's a form of thinking you would do well to embrace."

"If you're planning what I think you're planning, I'm going to stop you," Raythen said. "At least until I'm back at Skellig's with another few pouches of silver."

"And just what am I planning?" Astarra asked.

Raythen smiled at her without warmth, knowing that she was still trying to draw him. He wasn't going to let this escalate any further, not with accusations that could break the group apart before they had even reached the mountains. It wasn't the time for that, not yet.

"I suppose I'll have to wait and see," he said, leaning back against his pack and drawing up the hood of his cloak.

On the tenth day, Shiver sighted the Dunwarrs. They were too distant for Raythen and Astarra to see at first, but by the early evening they were all able to pick out the glimmer of the lowering sun, painting the far-off, snow-capped peaks a soft pink.

The road took them north, past Blind Muir and the township of Fallowhearth, where they spent one uncomfortable night in a grubby little tavern. The brooding woodland that overlooked the town was left behind as the hills grew ever steeper and craggier. On the eighteenth day they sighted a watchtower overlooking the road from a rocky mount. Part of its upper walls had collapsed, lending it a crooked air. Black-winged hookbeaks flocked from its deserted parapets, their cawing sounding mournfully over the rolling moorland.

"That marks the northern border of Upper Forthyn," Raythen said, as they passed beneath the cyclopean sentinel. "We're beyond the baronies now."

They'd barely gone past the tower when Shiver came to an abrupt halt. Astarra, as usual, was in front and either didn't notice or didn't care, but Raythen nearly walked into the back of the elf.

"Have you seen something?" he demanded, moving round so he was in front of Shiver. In the past two weeks he'd found himself growing more and more reliant on the elf's wickedly sharp senses, envious every time he thought of just how much he could achieve in his own line of work if he had those sorts of abilities.

Shiver didn't reply. Raythen quickly realized that the elf was not, in fact, detecting some distant threat or presence, but appeared to be in a trance.

"Astarra," Raythen called carefully. The human finally came to a halt and turned back.

"What's wrong?" she demanded.

Rather than answer, Raythen slowly raised a hand and clicked his fingers in front of Shiver's face. The elf didn't react. He was staring blankly into the middle distance.

"He's frozen up," Raythen said, as Astarra doubled back to join them. "He just stopped in the middle of the road."

There was a soft rattling sound. Raythen frowned and looked down. He realized that Shiver's hand had started to shake, disturbing the manacles clamped around his slender wrists.

The shaking grew worse, spreading across his whole body. The elf's eyes fluttered, and he began to emit a low groan. A sense of foreboding gripped Raythen – he hadn't seen anything quite like this before, though it reeked of unnatural magics to him. Slowly, not wanting to trigger any sudden reaction, he grasped the haft of his axe.

With a crack like thunder, power exploded around the deep elf's body. He lunged, both Astarra and Raythen throwing themselves back instinctively. Pale energy blazed in Shiver's eyes and around his wrists, pulling him taut and rooting him to the spot, arms outstretched. Through a surge of panic, Raythen realized that the light had coalesced as ghostly chains, connecting the manacles at his wrists and throat and wrapping tight around his body, binding him in place.

Shiver screamed. The noise was hideous, primal, a wail that spoke only of loss and devastation. Astarra had her staff up, an arcane word on her lips. Raythen snatched her wrist roughly.

"Wait," he shouted over the sound of Shiver's anguish.

Astarra snatched herself free, but stopped her incantation, the spell unfinished.

Shiver's scream died. The power began to fade as rapidly as it had appeared, the chains binding him disappearing. He stood, shaking once more, seemingly even more frail and gaunt than before.

"What, in the name of Fortuna, was that?" Raythen asked aloud. Slowly, he let go of the axe in his belt.

The words seemed to snap Shiver from his trance. His eyes refocused, and the shaking stopped.

"What dark sorceries did you just unleash, elf?" Astarra demanded. Light was still pulsing from her staff.

"It was… a dream," Shiver said, slowly and carefully, as though unsure of himself. He clasped his hands before him, his expression grave as he took in the roadway, the tower, the mountains beyond it, as though he was only just seeing them for the first time.

"You were awake," Raythen said.

"They come whether I'm asleep or not," Shiver said, his tone growing uncomfortable as he appeared to understand what had happened. He looked down and grasped the key hanging at his waist, seemingly checking it was still there.

"Was it a vision?" Astarra demanded. "A prophecy?"

"No," Shiver said. "The opposite. A memory."

He pushed past them both. Raythen didn't try to stop him – it was the first hint of anger he'd gotten from the elf since they'd met. He found it as disturbing as the waking vision that had gripped him. Not for the first time, the dwarf wondered just what he'd gotten himself in to. Glib rogues, thieves, devious merchants and collectors of stolen goods were the sorts of individuals he knew, the ones he was comfortable dealing with. Astarra and Shiver were, in their own arcane ways, very different to his usual company, and he didn't like it one bit.

Without looking back, Shiver began to walk down the road, calling out as he went.

"Come. Night is not far off, and this is no place to stop."

CHAPTER THREE

"You will unlock the gate," she said, her voice like poisoned honey in his ear. "You will unlock the gate, and kill them all for me. Am I clear?"

Shiver said nothing. The pain redoubled, searing into his wrists and his neck, making his back arch as he fought against it.

"Open the gate," snarled the voice. "Open it as you have opened a hundred before. You know you will, so why delay and prolong your suffering?"

Shiver tried to fight it, as he had done every time, but he could not. It wasn't just the pain, though it felt as though it was searing his very body. It was her claws, digging into his mind, forcing him to obey. Right now, he could no more resist her than a puppet could resist its strings.

With trembling fingers, he raised the key.

"Shiver!"

He opened his eyes, and realized they hadn't actually been closed. Raythen was looking at him.

"Thought we'd lost you again," he said, smiling without any warmth.

"I'm fine," Shiver said, wishing he meant it.

He'd almost slipped again. He'd seen that memory before, lived through it more times than he could count. It was returning with increasing frequency though, and had been ever since setting out from Frostgate. He didn't know yet whether that was a good thing or not. All he was sure of was that he was on the path that had been set for him.

He began to walk, thankful of the fact that Astarra was well ahead on the road and didn't seem to have noticed how he had come to a halt. He knew that losing control the way he had the first time had done nothing to help his standing with either of his companions. In truth he didn't care what they thought, but he feared Astarra. Her anger, her drive, seemed absolute.

"So what's the deal?" Raythen asked, walking alongside him. "With these memories? I mean, we've all got them, so why the magical song and dance?"

"I don't have them," Shiver corrected. He had no desire to engage the dwarf in conversation. Ever since setting out, the thief had been probing at both of his companions, searching out their strengths and weaknesses, alternating between them. Shiver had known his type before. He didn't intend to make the mistake of becoming friends with him, and he certainly didn't intend to share the shrouded nature of his past. So much was still hidden from him, memories stolen away by the dark mistress he had served. Raythen didn't deserve to know about any of that.

"You know, I searched out where you were sleeping once,"

Raythen said. "Found you curled up in the roots of a silverbark, the night before we left Blind Muir behind.

Shiver looked sharply down at the dwarf as he continued.

"You were speaking. I thought you were awake at first, but you were talking in your sleep. That, or it was another kind of trance. It was all in elvish, but I understood a few words…"

The dwarf trailed off, clearly baiting Shiver into asking what he'd said. He wondered if Raythen really spoke any of the elven tongues, or if he was just trying to bluff a reaction out of Shiver. He suspected the latter.

"You shouldn't have found me," Shiver said. "Seeking me out after dark can prove… dangerous."

"Well, that's not exactly encouraging."

"It isn't supposed to be."

The dwarf lapsed into silence, much to Shiver's relief. He tried to forget about the memories of the last few days, mentally repeating one of the well-worn mantras that helped anchor him in the moment. It would struggle to stave off his waking visions, but it at least calmed his mind in between the periods when they struck. *Atali nametha ren.* The path is the purpose. *Nameth hatala.* The path goes on.

The path did go on. The Dunwarrs towered above them now, a hundred jagged peaks resplendent in the afternoon sun. The road had carried them up into the foothills, to the very feet of the mountains. Shiver could feel the lightness in his lungs and the coldness in the air, defying the strength of the sun – they were high above the baronies now, Upper Forthyn at their backs, the sprawling moorlands lost to a purple haze. Their destination was close. According to Raythen's estimations earlier that morning, they would be at the gates of Thelgrim before nightfall. When Astarra had pointed out to him that the gates themselves were likely still shut, he'd looked at her as though she were an idiot, before chuckling.

"Don't worry, there are other routes in besides the big doors. That's what you brought me along for, isn't it? I know of a hidden port right by the gates."

They carried on in silence for a while, before the dwarf spoke up again.

"What are the locks for?" he asked. If Shiver had cared for human mannerisms, he suspected he would have sighed aloud. He said nothing, continuing to trudge along the path.

"I don't mean to pry," the dwarf went on. "But you must understand my professional interest. I've had a lot of experience with locks and keys. I don't often find people with locks that don't guard anything, or keys that fit them all."

"How do you know it fits them all?" Shiver asked. "You have only seen me unlock one."

"But getting the runestone from Thelgrim will see you with two more," Raythen said. "Which means they come with their own keys, you have to find their keys separately, or you're carrying a big ring of keys under those rags and keeping them all very, very silent. Or the one key you've got fits them all."

"Any one of those could be true," Shiver pointed out.

"But only one can be the most likely," Raythen replied.

"You ask too many questions, Dunwarr," Shiver said. He was doing his best to remain detached from the conversation, wary of playing the dwarf's game, not wishing to give in to negative emotions. Raythen was testing him, he knew, looking to see if there was anger beneath his reserve.

There was.

"Knowing when to ask, and when not to, is an important skill," Raythen said.

Shiver realized that Astarra had halted up ahead. She was standing on the edge of a pile of boulders, heaped beside the road, gazing off into the distance. Shiver and Raythen joined her. He saw immediately what she was looking at.

Their destination was in sight. A narrow valley lay stretched out before them, its sides like sloped walls of rugged stone. At its far end the sunlight glimmered, caught by bands of steel. Shiver picked out the vast gates, set into the mountainside of a great peak that seemed to rise to the very heavens themselves.

"How good it is to be home again," Raythen said with obvious, dark sarcasm.

Shiver's eyes didn't linger for long on the distant gates. He was drawn to the valley beneath. There were people there, hundreds, if not thousands. He could see the wisps of smoke from campfires and the shapes of tents and shelters, humped irregularly on either side of the roadway.

"Are those people down there?" Raythen asked, squinting and raising a hand to shield his good eye.

"Yes," Shiver answered, feeling an upwelling of sorrow he sought to swiftly suppress. Now was not the time for either anger, or sorrow. "More refugees."

"They must have been gathering there ever since the gates were closed," Astarra said from up on the rock. "The Dunwarr have abandoned them."

"They should count themselves lucky," Shiver heard Raythen mutter under his breath.

"I hope you know a way in that they don't," Astarra said to the dwarf.

"Well let's go and find out, shall we?" Raythen said.

The path led them down into the valley, in amongst the people crowded there. The makeshift encampment washed over Astarra as she led the way. Dirty, disparate refugees filled the space between the cobbled roadway and the valley sides, huddled in small groups and extended families. The muddy wagons and carts that they had hauled across Terrinoth had been transformed into makeshift shelters, canvas coverings rigged up as tents and pallets turned into lean-tos. The mountain air was clear no more, thick now with the smell of cooking and woodsmoke, animal dung and unwashed bodies. The murmur of conversation melded with the crying of children and the lowing of tuskers and oxen, filling the craggy space with the sounds of a people dispossessed and abandoned.

The sorry enclave filled Astarra with equal parts determination and anger. They needed leadership. She could see it in the lost, fearful gazes that followed her as she moved between the ragged shelters and stalled carts. They needed someone to challenge the injustice that had left them stranded here. If they had someone with power – her power – they would not be allowed to whither of starvation and exposure. She would not have allowed any of this to happen.

This was the reason she had to continue down the path she had chosen, the night she had abandoned Greyhaven. The place was cloistered in every sense of the word. She still remembered the fury of her tutors and the dire words of

Master Veta, one of the university's Lords Regent, who had tried to reason with her the night she had almost killed Master Loach.

"There is far more to the Verto Magica than markings and stones," the orc had warned her. "You cannot master runecraft without knowing that. You will never reach your true potential if you leave behind the learning within these walls."

Well, she had left it behind, along with all the hidebound myopia of that august institution. Already she was so much further forward than she would have been if she had stayed at the university. She had mastered three different shards and was learning more every day. She had great power already, the sort that could make a real difference and could stop suffering like this.

She just needed a little more.

She approached the gates, trying not to let the others see how she marveled at their size. She had heard tales of the Dunwarrs and Thelgrim, of course, but she had never seen either, never been this far north. It thrilled her. There were so many parts of Terrinoth yet to be explored, so many secrets to be uncovered and new abilities to master. And always, there were the runestones, the secret to her future. If she could claim the stone they'd been sent to retrieve, even just for a short while, what secrets could it teach her? The possibilities were tantalizing. They made even her current company acceptable.

The others were lagging behind. She paused, glancing back irritably. Raythen was standing by looking at Shiver, who was in turn glancing left and right, seemingly scanning the crowded encampment for someone or something.

"What's he looking for?" Astarra demanded of Raythen. The dwarf shrugged.

"He wants to ask someone what happened here."

Astarra's frustration flared. She didn't have time for this. She was impatient to enter the mountain, to discover what awaited her and attain the power of the runestone they were there to collect. The sight of the refugees and their desperate conditions had only quickened her resolve. Perhaps, with the runestone, she'd be able to convince the warden of these gates to open them once more.

"I think it's quite obvious. The Dunwarr shut the gates. They've been out here ever since."

If Shiver had heard her, he wasn't listening. He moved off the roadway and in amongst the shelters. People recoiled from his gaunt visage and hurried to get out of his way.

Astarra did her best to remain composed. She'd told herself over and over that she needed these two – or at least the Dunwarr – if she was going to make it in and out of Thelgrim alive. The elf though, he reeked of darkness and death, and it wasn't just his grim appearance. She had known foul magics in her time, had come far too close to them on a few occasions. They offered power, but at the cost of control. She'd seen the misery they caused.

She and Raythen followed in Shiver's wake, drawing even more murmurs and looks. She was about to snap at the elf to stop and explain himself when she realized he appeared to have found what he was searching for. Or rather, who.

A woman was standing by a sutler's cart, a loaf of bread in her hands. She looked tired and afraid, her clothing threadbare and her hair unkempt. A small child was hiding behind her skirts, staring with terror at Shiver as he asked them something.

Astarra strode towards them, intending to rescue the pair from the deep elf, but Raythen arrested her with a firm grip.

"He knows them," he said. "Let him ask his questions."

"How could a horror like him know a simple refugee family?" Astarra asked. "They don't look like they know him."

"Well, them knowing him is a different thing entirely," Raythen said.

"They shut the gates in front of us," the woman was saying, a warding hand keeping her child back as the other clutched onto the bread. "I don't know why. There are rumors, but no one really knows. I don't know anything about the water either."

"What does he want with her?" Astarra hissed. They were beginning to draw a crowd, a fact that appeared to make Raythen even more uncomfortable than it did her. She had no doubt the dwarf was used to doing his business unnoticed, and had presumably intended to smuggle them past the gates without attracting any attention. The realization that things weren't going according to expectations made her nervous.

The woman was shaking her head. Shiver reached into his robes and drew out something that glinted in the cold shadows harbored at the valley's bottom. The woman hesitated, then took the coins. Shiver turned away from her and looked at Astarra and Raythen, as though noticing them for the first time.

"What in the name of the Turning was that?" Astarra demanded of him as they headed back to the roadway. "Why are you questioning random women and their children?"

"They weren't random," Shiver said tersely. "Their names are Tiabette and Sarra. I've seen them before."

"How?"

Shiver glanced at her, as though considering his answer, before responding.

"A vision."

"I thought you said you didn't have visions?"

"I didn't," Shiver said. He came to a stop in the road, looking past Astarra at the gateway soaring like some monolithic idol above the huddled masses in the valley.

"I asked her how the gate closed," he said. "She was here when it happened, with the first refugees. The Dunwarr blocked the gate and then barred it. They didn't give a reason."

"Hardly a revelation," Astarra said.

"What did she say about water?" Raythen asked. "At the end."

"It was part of what I saw," Shiver said. "But she couldn't tell me anything more."

"Well, I hope it was worth it," Astarra said. "Because you've got the whole camp taking an interest in us now."

"And they know we've got money," Raythen added darkly.

The crowd watching them was continuing to grow, voices rising amidst the press.

"We should leave," Raythen said, low but urgent. "This could turn ugly."

"I thought you knew a way inside?" Astarra said.

"I do, but I'd rather they didn't. If they see us vanishing into the mountain, what will happen? At best, they'll follow us, and we're suddenly responsible for a thousand hungry refugees breaking into Thelgrim."

"The way in is not at the gates?" Shiver asked.

"There's one route in there," Raythen said. "A small sally port halfway up the rockface beside the right-hand door, accessible by a path you'd think would be too sheer to climb before you tried it. But if we take that now everyone will see us. Whatever the reason the gates were barred, I doubt their keepers will appreciate us showing these people a different way in. We need to double back and take to the mountainside."

"Fine," Astarra said. "Lead on."

"It may be better if Shiver does that," Raythen pointed out. "At least until we're clear of the camp."

If the elf was insulted, he didn't show it. Astarra and Raythen followed him as he led them back along the road, back to the great gates. Eyes wide, those who'd been massing around them hurried to clear the way.

CHAPTER FOUR

They doubled back along the road, until they'd lost sight of the valley and its destitute inhabitants.

"Will we be able to find the entrance before nightfall?" Astarra asked Raythen. She was unhappy at the time lost, but Shiver had left them exposed. As they'd left the encampment, she'd almost feared being accosted by the more desperate among those abandoned outside the gates.

"If we hurry," Raythen said. "Better to get inside and spend the night in the tunnels than out here anyway."

"Why is that?" Astarra asked as they halted on the roadside.

"Mountain superstition," Raythen said evasively. "And, more importantly, it wouldn't surprise me if some of the fine folk we've just seen follow us and try to lighten our purses while we're asleep."

"Your view of the world is very bleak, Dunwarr," Shiver said, to Astarra's surprise.

"Just trying to stay alive," Raythen said, a little bitterly. "Which begs the question, why am I here in the first place? Come on."

He led them off the road and up the mountainside. It was less sheer than the valley had been, though Astarra still found herself struggling after a hundred or so paces. The slope was mostly rugged scree, treacherous underfoot. She couldn't see any obvious route that Raythen was taking as he forged ahead. Frustratingly, neither of her companions showed any sign of difficulty as they took the slope.

She forged on, using her staff to assist the climb. By the time Raythen came to a halt her heart was beating hard and her thighs were burning. She reached up to wipe sweat from her brow, realizing as she did so that the ground they were standing on was more level than it had been.

Raythen had found a track. From the road it was indiscernible amongst the crags and rocks, but up on the mountainside itself it was visible, a faint thread that wound its way along the slope.

She looked back the way they had come, seeing the road stretching out, far below now. The valley was visible, hazed by distance, the gates a far-off gleam. The sun was going down, setting the tops of the vast mountains alight.

It was a spectacular view, unlike any Astarra had ever seen before. A part of her wished she could linger and take it in, watch as the vivid brilliance drained little-by-little from the purple and gray slopes and flickered from existence behind the snowy peaks. But Raythen was already moving off along the pathway, seemingly unconcerned with the natural splendor of his home.

She chastised herself. She hadn't come all this way to stand and stare. The runeshard called to her, another step on the path she'd chosen for her life. Power would not be won by idleness. She looked briefly at Shiver, who was also gazing out at the sunset, then walked past him after the dwarf.

The shadows lengthened, creeping over the moorland and the hills below, reaching slowly, steadily up the mountainside, stretching out to grasp at the trio struggling along its flank.

The path took them higher. Astarra pushed through her tiredness, determined not to falter in front of the others.

The last of the sun was fading when Raythen brought them to a sudden stop. The slope around them had changed – the path had taken them above the valley where the gates were set. Now a sheer drop fell away to their left, down towards the road and the encampment, while to their right the cliff face continued to rise, stern and uncompromising. The flat ground between them was only wide enough for single file, a fact that didn't seem to trouble either the dwarf or the elf. Astarra dared snatch a glance over the edge, and immediately regretted it. The encampment was lost in the darkness that had bled up out of the valley below, the only sign of life the pinprick illumination of cooking fires.

"This is it," Raythen said. He didn't even seem to be out of breath. Silently, Astarra cursed the extent of dwarven stamina.

"The rock marks it," Shiver said, looking even more gaunt and sinister in the twilight. Astarra wondered what he meant, then noticed the short pillar of stone rising from the cliff to their left. It was a little, craggy spur, incongruous enough, but it was clearly what Raythen had been looking for. The Dunwarr was already busy inspecting the face of the cliff to their right, running his fingers over the unyielding surface and muttering something under his breath.

Astarra resisted the urge to ask just what the dwarf was looking for. She waited. With the sun gone the wind had turned chill, knifing through the valley and tugging at her pelt. She focused on Raythen, rather than the drop to her back, wondering if he'd be able to find what he was looking for once true darkness had fallen.

"Is that what you're seeking?" Shiver asked. He'd moved a little further along the track and was now indicating a part of the rising cliff that looked just as unremarkable as the rest of it. Raythen said something in his native tongue. Astarra doubted it was complimentary.

"Light's playing tricks," he added, shifting to Shiver's side. Astarra joined them, and realized immediately what they had found.

There was a crack in the rock face, running up in front of them. It could have been naturally made, were it not for the perfection of its placement. Due to the sharpness of the angle someone passing along the track, especially in the direction of the gates, would likely have walked right past it without noticing. Even knowing what he was looking for, Raythen hadn't been able to immediately spot it – it had taken Shiver's razor senses to locate it.

The crack led into the mountain.

Astarra realized she must have been staring, because Shiver spoke to her, his tone explanatory.

"Fashioning the rock like this is a common Dunwarr attribute," he said. "They are able to hide passages in plain sight, if the nature of the face allows it. Great expertise in the bending and crafting of stone is required though."

Astarra said nothing. A part of her wanted to snap

petulantly back at the elf, as she had done a number of times since they'd been on the road together, but even in her tired state she realized that would be churlish. Instead, she looked to Raythen, who was already moving into the crevasse.

The darkness within seemed absolute. Dunwarr could see well enough underground, and a deep elf like Shiver even more so, but she had no intention of delving into the mountainside without some form of illumination. As Shiver began following Raythen she reached to the head of her staff and unfastened the blue tanzanite orb. Beneath it, wedged into the staff's reactive carved tusker bone, was the Deeprune, one of the runebound shards she had mastered. The power of the ocean depths had served its purpose, for now. She removed it carefully and secreted it in her waist pouch, before drawing out a different shard.

Unlike the Deeprune, which seemed to have been worn smooth by the crushing weight of the seas, this stone was jagged and scorched black, like a splinter of volcanic rock. Its name was the Ignis Shard, and it was hot to the touch.

Astarra lodged it into the bone tip of her staff, then retrieved the volcanic rock that twinned with it from her pouch, fixing it into place on top. She could already feel the staff heating up in her grip, the elemental fury of the Ignis's hot, broiling core drawn by the stone.

"*Kellos lathara hem,*" she murmured, raising the staff and letting the last of the anger and frustration she'd felt in recent days flare through it. The Ignis Shard ignited, an orange flame sparking and flaring into life around the volcanic rock, dancing like a firefly in the twilight.

She saw Shiver look back, his pale face picked out by the

sudden illumination. The fire burned in his black eyes, his expression as stoic and unreadable as ever.

Astarra advanced into the crevasse. At first, she was forced to go partly side-on, the cold, hard rock seeming to close in on her like vast and unyielding jaws. After a while though the space started to open out, eventually becoming wide enough to walk two abreast.

"What was this used for?" she asked, her voice echoing weirdly up the tunnel. "Smuggling?"

The flickering light of her staff picked out the stonework around them – it wasn't rough like the cliff they'd left behind, but seemed to have been worn smooth in places, as though something had passed through the rock that had left it leveled off.

"It's part of the defenses," Raythen called back. "But yes, someone who might have fancied getting in and out of Thelgrim unseen could have used it in the past. If they didn't mind the risk."

"Risk?" Astarra asked, not sure she wanted to know. Raythen didn't reply.

The tunnel grew larger and more regular, though the strange smoothness remained. Eventually they came to an intersection, three tunnels branching off, two uphill to the left and one, narrower, descending away to the right.

"We'll stop here for now," Raythen said, indicating the space before the junction. "I don't fancy treading the Hearth Road without getting some rest. Especially as we've no idea what we'll find when we reach it."

"No idea?" Shiver queried, his voice a soft, dire rattle that seemed to echo down the branching tunnels.

"Well, unless you know why the gates have been sealed?" Raythen said, looking back at him as he hefted his pack off his back and onto the tunnel floor. "Perhaps everyone's been slaughtered by your kin? There are plenty of deep elves in these parts, and few with a good word to say about the city of the Dunwarr."

"I have no connection with any," Shiver said. "They are not my kin, or if they were, they have not been for many centuries."

"You're not going to skulk away down a tunnel to sleep?" Astarra asked the elf as he sat with his back to the wall, wondering whether he was telling them the truth about the local clans. He looked at her with his soulless eyes, gleaming in the sorcerous firelight.

"I do not intend to sleep."

"That doesn't make me feel any better," Astarra said, sitting down against the wall opposite him and drawing her pelt close. She was cold and tired, and in no mood to endure the elf sorcerer's disconcerting habits.

"It does me," Raythen said, settling down with his head propped against his pack. "Means neither of us have to keep watch."

"How far to the Hearth Road?" Astarra asked him, trying not to think about Shiver watching over them as they slept. "And how long does it take to reach Thelgrim?"

"From here, a little over a day's travel," Raythen said, noncommittally. "It's a subterranean passage that will take us straight from the gates to the city itself. We're on schedule."

"Assuming we're not delayed when we reach our destination," Astarra pointed out. "You said before you don't know anything about this League of Invention."

"They're one of the minor associations seeking guild status," Raythen said. "There are dozens of them in the city. I never had any dealings with them."

"Well, that's about to change," Astarra said. She glanced at Shiver. The elf was looking away down the tunnel they'd come through, unblinking and silent. She watched him for a while longer before grasping her staff and murmuring a thanks to Kellos.

The light of the Ignis Shard faded and died, leaving them in darkness.

Shiver waited until the breathing of the others had become slow and regular. He stood in the darkness for a while, utterly still and silent, watching them both. Then, when he was certain they were asleep, he padded along the tunnel to the right.

As he walked, he placed his hand on the rock, letting his fingertips glide along the worn stone. He could feel immense power here, primal and rooted deep within the mountain. It was the threat Raythen had mentioned, but it was far off now, settled and still.

He walked further. It felt strange to be underground once more. He could only assume that he had been born beneath the earth, had grown up in the tunnels and passages that many deep elves called home. He had few memories of his childhood – like everything before his freedom, it was opaque, hidden from him no matter how hard he sought it.

He had hoped that journeying into the mountain would help recover some of what he had lost, but he didn't dare seek it directly, not with the other two still so close. Putting together the pieces of the past was like reassembling a mirror that had been shattered into a thousand pieces. Each shard was razor-edged. Placing them back together could be dangerous.

He recalled the woman he'd met in the valley, the one he'd seen after opening the lock. Tiabette. Hungry, cold, desperate, like the hundreds – likely soon to be thousands – abandoned before the gates of Thelgrim. He had wanted to tell her to leave, to escape the danger hanging over the mountains like a shroud, but what good would such words have done? To have come all this way, she couldn't turn back again, alone but for her child, with little food and money and the long road south beset by bandits. It would have doomed her, just as it would have any of those sheltering before the gates.

It wasn't her place to go back. It was Shiver's place to go on.

As he walked, he wondered about the other elves who inhabited these spaces beneath the mountains. He had told the others that he had no ties to the local clans. He hoped that was true. It was difficult to be wholly certain, given that his past was a patchwork of memories, incomplete and fractured. He knew little – or could remember little – of the deep elves of the Dunwarrs, certainly regarding how they related to his own kin further south. All deep elf clans made their homes beneath the mountains and tended to be nomadic in nature. Beyond those aspects though, and a shared, universal hatred of the Ynfernael, there were few ties of commonality that bound them. Shiver had little idea what to expect if they happened across one of the local daggerbands. He disliked such uncertainty, though he considered the odds of encountering them low. Deep elves and dwarfs rarely found common ground, and these tunnels were very much the territory of Thelgrim's Dunwarr guilds. The rock was redolent with their presence, fashioned by their hands.

He stopped abruptly, his soft footsteps faltering in the dark. Memories assailed him, of people like Tiabette, lost and abandoned and crying out for help. He offered them death instead. Their screams seemed to echo through the tunnel, rising up to a piercing, soul-chilling cacophony.

Not now, he thought desperately. He sought one of the mantras he had long ago learned, trying to focus his mind on the simple purity of repetition. He faced one of the tunnel walls, arms outstretched and hands planted against the smooth stone, his head bowed.

Atali nametha ren. Nameth hatala. Atali nametha ren. Nameth hatala.

Slowly the screams faded, echoing away into the oblivion where they belonged.

He straightened up, and realized he was shaking. That had not been a new memory – he could only gain those from the locks, or entering a deep, meditative state in a place of great significance to the Empyrean. No, the screams, the pleading, the death, those had all been with him for a long time, unlocked years ago. In a sense they had never left him.

He stood still for a while, letting the shivers subside, drinking in the total silence, the stillness of the mountain that surrounded him and wondering if, ever so distantly, ever so faintly, he could still hear a scream, echoing away through the tunnel.

He turned and rejoined the others.

Raythen descended carefully along the downward-sloping tunnel, side-on, his boots scuffing on the rock underfoot. He'd had a rough night, unalleviated by stale bread and a strip of overly salted pork for breakfast.

Food was running low. He'd been planning on buying, or stealing, more from the encampment in the valley, but of course Astarra and Shiver had ruined that plan. He wondered, in particular, how the sorceress was faring. Both Raythen and Shiver were well-suited for the underground, in their own ways. Darkness did little to impede their sight, and Raythen would easily find sleep stretched out on cold, hard bedrock. They needed less sustenance than the human, and possessed a keen, instinctive sense of direction. Astarra possessed none of those advantages. Raythen found himself wondering whether she'd turn back, and wondering whether he should encourage her to do so. Her determination – at times bordering on a very Dunwarr-like stubbornness – had impressed him so far, and he had no doubt the runes at her command were formidable. He just wasn't sure he wanted to be around when she was goaded into fully using them.

He'd led them through the mountain, doing what any good Dunwarr would do and not stopping to think. He kept moving, trusting that deep-seated intuition, hoping it would lead him on the right path.

And it had. He could see light ahead now, not the pale gleam of daylight but the flickering, fiery glow of torches, not dissimilar to the light cast by Astarra's sorcerous staff. He'd been looking out for the sign of flames since stepping into the crevasse on the mountainside, silently praying to Fortuna that, after so long above ground, his Dunwarr sense of subterranean direction hadn't deserted him.

The narrow, sloping passage he was taking came to an

end. Ahead lay another tunnel, running left to right. It was unlike any of those they'd traversed so far – its walls were not untrammeled rock, but had been planed smooth and carved with thousands upon thousands of runic inscriptions, tiny, intricate lettering that ran from the cobbled floor all the way to the arching roof. The entire space was wide enough to have marched fifteen Dunwarr warriors shoulder to shoulder down its center, and tall enough to have fitted the twisting spire of a shrine of Kellos within it without scraping the ceiling above.

"Another tunnel," Astarra said from behind Raythen, looking past him. "I thought you were taking us to the city, Dunwarr."

"Thelgrim is not a city as you know it," Raythen said, stepping into the wide passage, gazing from the rune-carved walls up to the long, arched roof. "It is buried deep within the mountain's core, a day's journey beyond the entrance commonly considered its gates."

"So, this is the route through the mountain?" Astarra asked as she followed him out, looking left then right, taking in the grandeur of the buried passage without verbally acknowledging it to Raythen.

"This is the Hearth Road," he affirmed as Shiver joined them, his eyes on the dwarf rather than the glory of their surroundings. "And only one thing is missing. People."

The great, subterranean roadway was deserted. Raythen had never known it to be like that before. It was the arterial route linking Thelgrim with the outside world. Normally it would have been busy with trader's wagons, supply caravans, armed patrols and heavily-guarded convoys carrying precious metals and rare artifacts between the city and the world beyond the Dunwarrs. Right now, however, absolutely nothing stirred for as far along the tunnel as Raythen could see, in either direction. The only movement was the flickering of the great, slow-burning torches that sat in braziers every few dozen yards, the only sound the breathing of Raythen and his companions. It was disconcerting.

"The gates are closed," Astarra pointed out. "Why would anyone be using this road anymore?"

"They are more than just gates," Raythen said, trying not to lose his patience with the human. She was out of her depth here, in every sense, and it was beginning to show.

"The gates are an outpost," he continued. "There are markets, stores, a barracks. Many traders from across Terrinoth don't even travel down the Hearth Road to Thelgrim proper. They do their business there, then depart. It's more convenient for them. Some even think the gates *are* Thelgrim. But even if they were shut to the outside, those who inhabit them would still come and go to the city along this route."

"Then perhaps the gates haven't just been sealed," Astarra surmised. "Perhaps they've been abandoned."

"I've never heard of that happening," Raythen said, dismissing the possibility as further evidence that Astarra had no knowledge or understanding as far as the Dunwarrs were concerned. "What sort of disaster could have prompted that?"

"There are many," Shiver said. Raythen looked at him sharply. The deep elf had been even more silent than usual since they'd penetrated the mountains. Raythen had been wondering just how much of it was familiar to him. He'd claimed not to be from the Dunwarrs, but as a deep elf, places like these were hardly unusual. He certainly didn't seem as out-of-place as Astarra.

"You speak as though you know what's happened here," he said to him. "That makes me uneasy, and I don't like feeling uneasy. Care to enlighten us?"

"There are echoes," Shiver said. "The pain of abandonment. We will find nothing of use at the gates."

"Cryptic nonsense," Astarra said.

"We can't know anything for sure until we reach the city," Raythen said, seeking out a course of action before another argument could flare. "I've also had more than a few... encounters with Captain Bradha, who commands at the gate. On the off chance that she's still there, I'd rather we go in the opposite direction."

"Our goal is in Thelgrim," Astarra said. "So, to Thelgrim we will go."

CHAPTER FIVE

They set off along the Hearth Road, following it as it delved its way deeper into the mountain.

Astarra had never seen anything quite like it. The vast, drafty halls and the towering cloisters of Greyhaven had possessed an austere majesty, but no scriptorium or grand library could prepare her for this place. Had it been built above ground, the precision and care applied to every inch of the mile after mile of stonework would have been incredible. The fact that it had all been burrowed from the solid, unyielding bedrock of the Dunwarrs was almost beyond belief.

"What do the walls say?" she asked Raythen as they walked, noting how, despite speaking aloud, there was no echo, no phantom repetition caused by the great subterranean passageway.

"The usual nonsense," Raythen said. "A history of the mountains, of the city, traced all the way back to the old myths. A litany of kings and guild-masters. The sorts who write the histories. Or order them to be written, anyway. Wouldn't want to be the poor mason-apprentice who had to do all the chiseling."

He laughed, not sparing the walls a second glance. Astarra wondered how he could be dismissive of such a wondrous place. She supposed that familiarity bred contempt. She'd seen awe and amazement in the expressions of young scholars setting eyes on Greyhaven's pillars for the first time, yet it was a place she herself had come to hate. She rarely thought of home either, of the apple orchards and the small, thatch-covered farmstead, of the fields of swaying corn that surrounded it, and the rutted woodland track that led to the marketplace of the nearest market-town, always bustling and often, in her memories, dappled in summer sunshine.

It felt like a different world from the fire-lit, stony stillness that now surrounded her. Yet with each step, Astarra felt her determination grow. If she was to become a true runemaster, worthy of the legacy of even Timmoran the Great, she knew she would have to travel from one end of Terrinoth to the other, and possibly beyond. Here beneath the Dunwarrs, on the edge of all she knew, the progress she was making was more immediate, more real than it had felt in months.

That which she sought was almost within her reach.

She realized that the torches ahead had gone out. A stretch of perhaps a hundred yards had fallen into darkness, a fact that didn't seem to concern the other two.

"The braziers have to be restocked from time to time," Raythen said, as though sensing her hesitation. "Part of the Masons' Guild is almost wholly dedicated to keeping the Hearth Road alight. Seems like they're slacking."

Astarra said nothing. The darkness of the main tunnel itself didn't overly concern her – she could see the next lit braziers ahead, like beacons in the cloying shadows that lay between them. More worrying were the side-tunnels that lay within the unlit section.

There were secondary routes connected to the Hearth Road all along its progress. Some were just bare rock tunnels, like the one Raythen had led them down, but others were carved archways that seemed to lead into smaller subsidiaries of the Hearth Road. Raythen had explained that some were nothing more than storage cupboards and way stations along the road, but others did connect to the warren of tunnels and passages that seemed to dig and twist their way all through the mountain.

"Some are uncharted," Raythen claimed, apparently without concern. "No one knows how far or deep all of them run, except perhaps a few long-beards in the Miner's Guild, and even they're probably just lying to get the younglings to buy them more ale."

Astarra had watched each passage entrance carefully as they went by. The darkness of many seemed absolute, and she couldn't shake the sense that there were eyes gazing back at her, unseen from beyond the archways. A sense of foreboding had started to creep over her, making her skin prickle and her heart beat faster. The confidence she had felt when first taking in the sight of the Hearth Road was in danger of guttering out.

She ignited her staff with a word and a thought, waking up the reactive material. The light it gave off seemed to do little to ward away the shadows they had stepped in amongst.

There was a change that only dawned on Astarra as she

walked further – the soft sound of footsteps made by the trio had grown quieter. One of them had stopped.

She turned sharply. Shiver was standing a dozen paces back, in amongst the shadows. He was facing the blackness of one of the passageways, remaining perfectly still.

Raythen came to a halt beside Astarra and looked back at the elf too. She noticed the Dunwarr's hand had disappeared inside his heavy cloak, as it always did when the dwarf seemed uncertain. He was grasping one of his weapons, she was sure.

"Shiver," he called out softly. The elf didn't respond.

"Perhaps he sees something," Astarra said. "Or maybe he's having another of his trances."

The memory of the one the elf had suffered on the road had stayed with her. It was the scream, more than anything. The noise had been horrific, chilling. It was the sound of a soul that was lost and damned, of that she was sure.

Raythen seemed frozen, unable to decide what to do. Astarra called out sharply, finally drawing the hint of an echo from the precisely carved tunnel.

"Shiver!"

The elf looked at them both, so sharply that Astarra almost jumped. The black eyes, once more reflecting the firelight of the staff, held hers. Slowly, he raised one long, pale finger to his lips.

That was when Astarra heard it. The faintest of clicks.

"Move," she snarled, shoving Raythen and throwing herself in the opposite direction. A projectile slashed between them from the darkness of another of the conjoining passages, a dart that clattered off the far wall of the tunnel.

"*Talatha ignis,*" she shouted, grasping her staff in both

hands. The flames that coiled about its head surged, sweeping down its length and setting it wholly ablaze.

The light illuminated their attackers just as they leapt from the surrounding tunnels. They were tall, pale and painfully slender, clad in close-fitting leathers and dulled metals. Their raven hair was bound up in topknots, and their eyes were mostly dark.

Deep elves. Astarra didn't have time to feel outrage at the treachery that had befallen them. She swung her staff at the first attacker to lunge at her, a shrieking assailant wielding a pair of long daggers that gleamed in the firelight. The elf ducked beneath the blow with horrifying agility, and before Astarra could recover the twin daggers were scissoring at her exposed throat.

"*Ignatus*," she cried out, throwing herself back in a desperate effort to avoid having her neck laid open to the bone. The fire that had engulfed her staff surged, flaring up with conscious anger and catching the elf as he moved in for the kill.

The elf stumbled as the flames caught his arm and back, his battle-scream becoming a howl of agony as the heat seared his flesh and ignited his clothing. Astarra kicked out at him, afraid a reflexive slash from one of the blades would still catch her. He staggered and flailed at the flames, the twin knives clattering as they fell to the roadway.

Something slammed into her side, driving her over. Her staff slipped from her grasp, the fires dying the second they broke contact. She sprawled, trying to right herself, and realized Raythen and a deep elf were all-but on top of her, locked in a death-grapple. The Dunwarr had one strong hand clamped around the elf's slender neck, while the elf was trying to dig a dagger through Raythen's cloak and into his flank.

Astarra twisted, her legs pinned by the pair, trying to reach her staff. Another dart cracked off the roadway right in front of her, almost pinning her wrist to it. She heard Raythen hiss with pain, a counterpoint to the ugly choking sounds the elf was making.

It felt as though her arm was going to burst from its socket. Anger gripped her, a terrible fury that burned as brightly as the Ignis Shard. She wasn't going to die here, in the darkness beneath the mountain, led blindly to her fate by some treacherous, fell sorcerer. She hadn't tamed three separate runeshards and sought others from the Traitor's Wastes to the Ru Steppes just to have her throat slit in the shadows.

A single finger touched the side of the staff. The reaction was instantaneous. The fire reignited with a roar, blazing brightly from end to end.

"*Ignis meldaris,*" Astarra roared, binding the flames into a ball of burning fury and dragging it from the fused shard of volcanic rock tipping the staff. She hurled it at the elf straddling Raythen, the discharge of magical energies strong enough to tear him from the Dunwarr's grasp and fling him hard against the far wall. The impact must have forced the air from his lungs because he didn't scream as the fires engulfed him.

Raythen got to his feet, panting and clutching his side. Astarra scrambled across the road and snatched up her staff again. Her hands remained unburned, the fire unable to harm its summoner as she swung it up and turned to meet the next attack.

Except, there wasn't one. The Hearth Road was empty once

more, but for Shiver. He was still standing across from one of the side tunnels, though now there was a body sprawled in front of him. It was a fellow deep elf, and it looked as though it had just been hauled from the depths of a mountain glacier. It lay on its back, hands raised, fingers bent and frozen, entirely covered by a thick layer of bristling white frost.

"Traitor," Astarra barked, advancing on Shiver. Adrenaline had given way once more to raw anger, potent enough to make her staff glow white-hot and cause its flames to coil and twist about her, fury made manifest. Shiver faced her, standing his ground and raising one hand.

A blast of bitter cold struck her full on, as though a gale from the highest peaks of the Dunwarrs had suddenly been summoned to the mountain's core. The shock of the icy blast stole her breath away and caused her flames to gutter and retract.

"Back down," Shiver snarled, his jaw clenched. Ice was blossoming across his raised hand, beginning to physically encase it.

Astarra's anger redoubled as she realized he was drawing on the Turning without so much as a conduit. She thrust her rage into her staff once more, reigniting its flames, the flicking wrath twisting and guttering as though in a storm.

"You led us into this place," she hissed, her head beginning to pound as the focused strain took its toll. "You led us here so your kin could slaughter us, or worse."

"If they were my kin, would I have stolen the soul from one?" Shiver demanded. Astarra's eyes darted to the brittle corpse at Shiver's feet. The split-second's distraction caused her flames to sear away once more.

Shiver pressed the sudden advantage, taking a step forward. Astarra felt the chill biting to her core. It was agony. She tried to refocus but couldn't. There was nothing now but the cold. It felt as though the deep elf was turning her very soul to ice.

Abruptly, the sensation dissipated. The elf had lowered his hand, ice crunching as he flexed his fingers. Astarra was left shivering and panting, her breath frosting in the now-frigid air.

"I didn't betray you," Shiver said, his own breath short as he recovered from the surge of magical energies. "I sensed them just before they attacked us. I was about to warn you."

"But you didn't," Astarra snapped. She smacked the base of her staff into the road, causing newly formed ice to cascade and shatter. "Do you really expect us to believe it's just coincidence that we've been attacked by deep elves?"

"Did I blame you for the interest the bandits took in us on the road from Frostgate?" Shiver demanded, his voice now as cold as his magics. "They were all human. I am not responsible for the actions of every elf in the Dunwarrs. I have no ties with the deep clans here!"

"Regardless, deep elves on the Hearth Road doesn't bode well," Raythen said, before Astarra could respond, moving in between the pair. He sounded in no mood for an argument. She noticed the pain on his face, underlit by the fires still consuming the corpse of the elf she had blasted off him.

"You're injured," she said.

"Barely," he grunted.

"Show me your side."

Raythen glared at her for a moment, then removed his hand and pulled his cloak back. The leather of his tunic was dark just above his hip, the blood gleaming in the firelight.

"Can you heal that?" Astarra demanded of Shiver.

"You trust me to?" the elf retorted.

"I'd say it'd improve your standing," she said.

Shiver looked at Raythen, who shrugged. The elf hesitated, then spoke.

"Unlace your jerkin."

The dwarf grumbled something in his own tongue, but did as Shiver instructed. The elf approached and slipped his hand over the bloody wound, closing his eyes.

"I was expecting it to be cold," Raythen said, surprised at the elf's touch. Shiver said nothing, though his manacles rattled slightly as he began to shake.

Astarra watched carefully. The sight of the elven magics at once angered and awed her. Like many practitioners, her abilities required the runestones to work – anyone could utilize them, with a little training, but their power didn't extend beyond the particular effects specific to that shard. Astarra possessed three – the Deeprune, the Ignis Shard and the Viridis Seed, each one acquired in desperate, deadly circumstances and truly mastered only after years of study and experimentation. The power of the runes, often untapped by more inexperienced wielders, was immense, but it didn't compare to the abilities of those who could reach into the heavenly energies of the Empyrean, or even those like Shiver who could access the Turning without a locus. Their skills were innate, unshackled by the specifics of the shards. It was a kind of power Astarra knew she would never possess.

"That's all I can do for now," Shiver said, withdrawing his hand. The stab wound in Raythen's side had ceased bleeding and was scabbed over.

"My energies are spent, for the moment," the elf went on, his tone almost apologetic. Astarra noted he seemed even more pale and drawn than usual, and he was still shaking slightly. She felt a surge of satisfaction. It seemed he hadn't snuffed out her own magic quite so easily after all.

"Well, it's better than nothing," Raythen said, peering at the wound for a moment then beginning to lace up his jerkin once more. "We should keep moving. If the elf clans are attacking travelers on the Hearth Road, then the gates really must have been abandoned. I haven't heard the like since the last Deep War, and that was when I was still a youngling."

"Do you think they might have attacked Thelgrim?" Astarra asked, casting her eyes back to the smoldering remains of the elf she'd immolated. "What if the city has fallen?"

Raythen scoffed. "Thelgrim is the most secure place in all of Terrinoth, runewitch. The clans don't have the numbers to take it, even if they wanted to. The deep elves and the Dunwarr keep themselves to themselves most of the time. Something bad must have happened if they're attacking people on the Hearth Road."

"That, or they recognized one of us," Astarra pointed out, looking back at Shiver. "And had a score to settle."

Shiver didn't appear to be listening to her. She was about to repeat the accusation when he spoke.

"More are coming. We need to go."

"Agreed," Raythen said, beginning to move up the tunnel. Shiver checked him.

"That's the direction they're coming from."

"They're coming from Thelgrim?" Astarra asked.

"Yes," Shiver said. "And they're not deep elves."

As he spoke, Astarra detected what the elf's ears had already picked up. The sound of iron-shod boots, tramping in unison along the Hearth Road.

"Into the side tunnels?" she asked urgently. She ignited her staff as she spoke, feeling the fiery wrath of the Ignis surge through her, melting away the bitter chill of Shiver's magics.

"You want to risk bumping into more of those dagger-wielding cutthroats?" Raythen said, glancing from the roadway to the dark arches looming on either side of them.

"They have not gone far," Shiver said. "I can still sense their presence."

"Then the only way is back along the road," Astarra said.

"Perhaps," Raythen said, sounding despondent. "But if we want to reach Thelgrim, this was bound to happen at some point. Trust me, I'm looking forward to it even less than you two."

The oncoming figures had entered the light of the nearest lit braziers. The flames gleamed and shimmered from helmets, shield rims and axe heads. Astarra realized she was watching a cohort of Dunwarr warriors, fully armed and armored, marching down the Hearth Road towards them.

The urges to run or to fight flared up inside her, warring with one another. She knew both options were foolish. Raythen was correct. The plan had never been to attempt to enter Thelgrim covertly. As far as they were aware, the Dunwarr were awaiting their arrival, or at least the League of Invention was. Right now, trusting that to be the case suddenly seemed dangerously naive.

She stood her ground, glancing sideways at Shiver. The elf was leaning with one hand against the tunnel's rune-carved wall. He seemed spent. Raythen was stepping forward so he was in front of both of them, hands on his hips, facing down his oncoming kinsfolk. Astarra counted about fifty – too many for even the Ignis Shard to overcome.

"Well, this is quite the greeting party," Raythen called out over the sound of the tramping boots, the noise of the oncoming dwarfs rising to a thunder that seemed to fill the whole tunnel. Astarra planted her staff before her, keeping the rune alight but focusing on not letting it surge. Ahead of her Raythen was framed by the advancing phalanx, the gleam of their armor reduced to a dull, faceless glitter as they entered the stretch of tunnels where the braziers had failed.

With a crash, the Dunwarr came to a halt. Their shields slammed together, forming a barrier of steel as the second rank presented a row of primed crossbows, quarrel tips bristling.

Silence followed. It was all Astarra could do to keep the flames of the Ignis in check.

Raythen raised both hands and, slowly, began to clap.

"Very impressive," he called out over the serried wedge of warriors. "Consider us thoroughly intimidated. But if you were looking for the elves, we've already driven them off. Except for this one, that is. He's with us. At least, I think he is."

There was no reaction from the Dunwarr host. Astarra risked a glance at Shiver. The deep elf appeared to have composed himself to a degree, standing away from the tunnel wall, his hands clasped before him. He showed no reaction to being faced with a wall of Dunwarr steel.

"You need to patrol the Hearth Road more regularly if you consider this good enough protection for those traveling it," Raythen went on.

At last, his words drew some sort of reaction. There was a clatter of armor as two of the front-rank Dunwarr broke the shield wall momentarily, making way for a figure who strode out to face Raythen.

"You are either very bold, or very foolish, to return to Thelgrim," the warrior said. She was wearing gilt-edged pauldrons and a cuirass over a knee-length surcoat of shimmering scale mail. Her finely-engraved half helm hid the upper half of her features, and two plates of long, red hair hung over her shoulders. She carried a short sword and a heavy shield emblazoned with the embossed, snarling head of a slope-tusker.

"Captain Bradha," Raythen said. "How wonderful to make your acquaintance again. I was starting to wonder if we'd even get an opportunity to catch up, what with the gates standing abandoned."

"You and your companions will accompany us to the city," Bradha said, her voice terse. "The king will wish to see all of you."

"Well then, I'd best offer you a proper introduction," Raythen said, full of faux joviality. "These two upstanding subjects of Terrinoth are Astarra and Shiver. We're traveling to Thelgrim on business, and we'd appreciate not being detained or abused."

"Thelgrim is closed to the kind of business you peddle," Bradha said, before turning back to her phalanx and raising her shield.

With flawless precision the block split, creating a channel through its middle. She looked back at Raythen, then at Astarra and Shiver for the first time.

"This is not a request," she said.

Astarra hesitated, but Raythen was already walking past Bradha to the heart of the Dunwarr formation. He looked at her.

"You shouldn't test Bradha's patience," he said in a stage whisper. "Fortuna knows, I've found that out the hard way."

Astarra sighed and let the fire of the Ignis Shard die. She and Shiver both began to follow Raythen, the ranks of the Dunwarr closing around her.

She just hoped this was all part of the rogue dwarf's plan.

CHAPTER SIX

"This wasn't part of the plan," Raythen said over the tramping sound of Dunwarr boots. "There's really no need for an armed escort. I'm not expecting King Ragnarson to stand on ceremony."

"Trust me, he won't," Bradha said. It was the first time since setting out together that she'd risen to Raythen's bait. As happy as he was to have provoked a reaction from the Gate Captain, he didn't much like the hint of relish in her voice.

He was telling the truth, to an extent. Ideally, he'd have gotten into Thelgrim unnoticed and retrieved the runestone from the idiot inventors without concerning the city's hierarchy with his presence. Of course, that was always going to be a long shot trailed by two figures as out-of-place as Astarra and Shiver. He kept glancing covertly at them as they were marched along the Hearth Road together, silently willing them not to do anything stupid, at least as long as he was still with them. Astarra seemed as close to furiously lashing out as ever, and he was surprised Bradha's cohort hadn't filled Shiver with crossbow bolts on sight, especially if the deep elves had resumed their raids.

Now that the Warriors' Guild had them, they were going to have to do it the hard way. He'd tried to wring information out of Bradha without making it too obvious, but she was as recalcitrant as she'd ever been. It seemed Raythen still hadn't been forgiven for the merry chase he'd led her and her warriors on through the Deeps, or the blow he'd dealt her escaping from the undercroft of the Dunwol Kenn Karnin. He resisted the unwise urge to ask her if he'd left a scar.

Thelgrim, at least, didn't seem to have been overrun by a surge of deep elves or wiped out by some sort of cataclysm. Raythen supposed he was glad of that, even if a deeply buried, bitter part of him wished the city of his birth would be annihilated by some titanic cavern collapse. What could have caused Bradha to abandon the outer gates though? He'd asked her as much and received nothing but a warning glare.

Ahead of them the Hearth Road was coming to an end. The precisely carved tunnel dipped, beginning to widen out into a vast cavern, a cavity at the core of the mountain so huge that Raythen was barely able to discern either ceiling or walls.

Within it lay Thelgrim. Raythen actually heard Astarra's gasp over the thumping of boots. Cynic though he was, he couldn't blame her, not this time. There was no sight in all of Mennara quite like the greatest city of the Dunwarrs.

It filled the cavern from end to end – in a way, it was the cavern. The towering walls and the vast stalagmites that studded the well-worn floor had been crafted and fashioned into buildings great and small, burrowed atop one another into the core of the mountain.

The soaring space would have spent eons in stygian darkness, but the genius of the Runescribers' Guild had ended the eternal night of the Deeps and brought light to the Dunwarr's depths. Crystal starglobes adorned the distant ceiling, their wan light catching the precious stones buried in the countless stalactites and refracting their natural luminescence down onto streets carved from the bristling rock below. They lit up the gems and crystalline sediments that in turn studded so much of the cavern's sides and floor, the natural wealth of the mountain that had been crafted around them. The array of brilliance made the whole city glitter, like one vast, precious geode, the sublime heart of the great mountain range that had given the dwarven people their ancestral home.

"Keep moving," Bradha snarled. Raythen realized Astarra had come to a halt, stunned by the sight of the great city that shimmered and glimmered below them. He managed to make eye contact with her, giving her a warning look. She started forward hastily.

The edge of the city lay before them, beyond a stretch of road that ended with a plunging chasm. A single bridge spanned the opening, the only way from the Hearth Road into the city. Raythen, of course, knew plenty of other routes from elsewhere in the cavern, especially through the deeps on the northern end, but it seemed today he'd be walking in through the front door.

At the far side of the long, slender bridge loomed another set of gates, built into a fortress formed from a single great stalactite. Its arrow slits and crenelations seemed to glare down at them as they approached, stepping onto the bridge.

Bradha barked an order and the Dunwarr broke step,

standard practice when crossing over. A host of boots pounding in unison did nothing for structural integrity. Raythen was shoved between two burly warriors as the column narrowed out for the crossing. He didn't mind – he never much fancied being able to see over the edge and into the utter darkness of the chasm. The elders of Thelgrim had ordered it formed after the Third Darkness, as a last line of defense. It had taken the Masons' and Miners' Guilds over a century, but the work had been completed. Fool's legend claimed it ran all the way to the core of Mennara itself.

"So, you think the old Dunwarr himself will be happy to see me?" Raythen asked Bradha as they fell into the shadow cast by the fortress. In truth he was goading the captain in an effort to take his mind off what he suspected lay ahead.

"Do not speak of King Ragnarson like that," she responded. "Or I will take my short sword to your tongue and think nothing of the consequences."

Raythen smiled to cover his nervousness, but didn't say anything more. He knew well enough not to test someone like Bradha. In fact, he was surprised he hadn't earned a beating from her already.

A horn sounded from up ahead, ringing sonorously through the great cavern. There was a thump and a groan of heavy hinges as the gates before them began to open. Raythen was struck by how much it looked like a huge maw, yawning wide at the end of the bridge as if to swallow them all. It wasn't a comforting image.

They were marched into the fortress. A cobbled entrance hall awaited them, lit by braziers. The column reformed after exiting the bridge and came to a halt at its center, the crash of the final, heavy footfall resounding in the confined space. It matched the boom of the gates as they slammed shut at the same time behind them, making the fires in the braziers shiver.

In the silence that followed, Raythen began to applaud again.

"Really, spectacular precision," he said. "Just how long does the Warriors' Guild spend practicing its marching? It can't be easy, putting one foot in front of the other, over and over again."

Bradha turned and snatched him by the shoulder, hauling him in close. Her eyes burned with anger behind the intricately carved rim of her helmet.

"Say something," she snarled at him under her breath. "Go on. Say something more. Anything. Give me an excuse to break your nose."

Raythen forced himself to smile as he fought the battle of his life to hold his tongue. He raised both hands, and Bradha let go, shoving him away.

"Front rank will reform on me," she barked at her warriors. "The rest of the column is dismissed!"

There was a clatter as the seven Dunwarr at the front took up positions on either side of Raythen, Astarra and Shiver. The gates at the far end of the hall had started to open.

"Whatever happens, say nothing and do nothing," Raythen said urgently to his two companions as the rest of the column broke up. "Even if it seems like a matter of life and death. Just let me do the talking, the thinking and the acting. Let me do everything. Is that clear?"

Astarra nodded, while Shiver remained as opaque as ever.

"Is that clear?" Raythen repeated with a snarl, his one eye fixed on them. He knew he was showing weakness, which he hated to do, but right now his nerves were giving him a degree of focus. He wasn't risking them messing this all up, not when they were already so close to failure. If they put a foot wrong, none of them were going to get a second chance.

"Yes," they said together. Raythen couldn't keep the relief from showing on his face.

"Move," Bradha said. They set off once more, beyond the hall and out into Thelgrim proper.

The ancient city of the Dunwarrs didn't seem to have changed in the years since Raythen had last visited, but then he doubted it had changed in the past few centuries either. The street beyond the gateway fortress was wide, set between two stalagmites that were so vast they would likely have accounted for half the city of Frostgate each. Houses and stairways had been carved into their sides, row upon row, layer upon layer, dozens of dwellings, shops and taverns that looked out on the roadway from small, square windows and doorways chiseled into the refashioned, reformed bedrock. Dunwarr masons prided themselves on the unparalleled ability to craft the living stone of the mountain into a tiered city without disrupting the natural patterns of the rock. Thelgrim was their masterpiece, a place where it was impossible to say just where the structures finished and the mountain began.

Raythen had seen all of it before, but one thing was noticeably different this time. Normally the Southgate, the wide street directly off Thelgrim's southern entrance, would be thronging with people, not only Dunwarr but traders and visitors of all kinds from across Terrinoth. The spaces to the side of the roadway would have been crammed with makeshift stalls and haggling booths, with foreign merchants selling all that Thelgrim so often lacked – silks and fine cloths, fresh meats and fruits, timber and parchment – in exchange for the rich, raw bounty of the earth. Instead, there was nothing. The edges of the street were deserted, and the wider avenue was little better. The few denizens he could see, almost all of them Dunwarr, hurried by without even glancing at the unlikely trio and the warriors flanking them, their heads bowed and eyes averted.

He resisted the urge to ask Bradha a genuine question about the lack of people, knowing that, at best, she'd tell him nothing. Right now, they were prisoners in all but name, and he feared that their circumstances were only set to worsen.

The route led them deeper into the city. Thelgrim's streets were a maze that ran between and around the rocky outcrops, great and small, that constituted the city's foundations. As they went Raythen noted not only the scarcity of Thelgrim's inhabitants, but also the fact that many stores, shops and wayhouses were boarded up. It was as if the city had been abandoned, or its population shut up inside their homes. He'd seen similar fates befall many other places in Terrinoth, caused by war, plague and strife, but never had he known it to befall mighty, immutable, enduring Thelgrim.

The only question was why?

Their route took them along a narrow street between two rocky buttresses. Overhead arched a span of stone, Dunwarr-crafted. The sound of rushing water betrayed its purpose – it was part of the Deeprun, the subterranean river that gave the city life. After first settling beneath the mountain, the Dunwarr had fashioned a mighty aqueduct that ran through the cavern, redirecting the flow into the Blackwater, the great lake that lay at the cavern's center. As it passed through the city, tributaries from the aqueduct provided running water to taverns, workshops and even ordinary homes.

The lake itself came into view as they left the street, an expanse of water surrounded by the looming outcrops of city-rock, dark and seemingly bottomless. The only ripples that disturbed its glassy surface came from the waterfall that marked the end of the aqueduct, and the churning of the mill-wheels along the far bank, where a host of workshops and smelter halls stood hard on the lake's shores.

The bastions of industry paled into insignificance next to the main building dominating the embankment, the Guild Hall. It was one of the few freestanding structures in Thelgrim, not built into the flank of a rock formation but laid stone slab upon stone slab, up to a great sloping roof lined with countless squares of black slate. It was supported by ten pillars, each carved with magnificent precision to appear like ten huge Dunwarr, lifting the weight of the roof upon their arms and shoulders. Each titanic figure represented one of the ten guilds that ruled over much of life in Thelgrim, and had done since the old noble lineages fell by the wayside.

For all its size and grandeur, the Guild Hall was neither the largest nor the most intimidating structure overlooking the Blackwater.

Bradha led them on the near side of the lake. Past the nearest stalagmite, their destination became clear. Raythen had expected as much, but he still cursed under his breath as the others took in the sight.

They were bound for the Dunwol Kenn Karnin.

Astarra fought to maintain her concentration.

She had never seen anything like Thelgrim. The sheer size of the cavern alone was stunning. It seemed larger than the mountain it was buried beneath, its scale difficult to fathom. One of the Dunwarr guards had actually shoved her earlier when she'd almost come to a complete stop staring up at the ceiling. The strange orbs and the light they cast upon the thick, jagged crust of gemstones and geodes created a glittering, multi-hued constellation, a heavenly map born out of Mennara's rugged heart. It was the most beautiful thing Astarra had ever seen, so much so that she hadn't even considered rounding on the dwarf who had pushed her.

The Dunwarr seemed wholly unaffected by the wondrous sight, including Raythen. Astarra had feared what would happen when the patrol had first encountered them on the Hearth Road. Since first meeting him, she'd assumed that Raythen, clearly a thief to the very core of his being, was wanted in Thelgrim. He'd have stolen something and been banished or, worse, they'd still be hunting him. If that was the case however, the reaction of the dwarf captain hadn't made sense. The Dunwarr hadn't exactly seized them and shackled them on sight, even if they also hadn't left them much of a choice in accompanying them to the city. Regardless, they were now at their mercy. She could only trust the original instructions about the League of Invention.

She fixed her eyes on what she assumed had to be their

destination. Beyond the black lake stood a structure that towered above even the tallest of the surrounding stalagmites. It had been built into several rocky buttresses that rose up from the cavern floor, forming a stronghold of parapets and bastion towers that looked out over the waters and the aqueduct that fed them.

This, she assumed, was the final fastness of the Dunwarr, the heart of their realm and the seat of their rulers. The realization that she was about to be brought before King Ragnarson of the Deeps wasn't an especially reassuring one. She just hoped Raythen knew what he was doing.

They were marched along the side of the lake, leaving behind the last of the dwelling places carved into the cavern's jagged floor. Those in themselves were marvels to Astarra. She had never envisaged anyone living on top of one another the way they did in Thelgrim, where tiered rows of buildings were cut into the flanks of the rock pillars and stalagmites, tapering out towards the top. Part of her had assumed the city would be a crowded warren, some sort of vast underground burrow where people were crushed together. There was none of that here though. The houses were neat and ordered and the streets that wound between them, for the most part, were wide and open. The twinkling stone-light cast by the orbs high above completed the impression that they weren't actually underground at all. It was a world away from the pitch-black, claustrophobic tunnels and crevices Raythen had initially led them through. That was a relief, though she was loathed to admit it.

The only thing that seemed to be missing was the people. She wanted to ask Raythen if it was normal for the streets to be so quiet. The Dunwarr she did see either hurried past or stared from the small windows and door arches of their homes. She wondered if the seeming abandonment had something to do with the shutting of the main gates. But if so, what? Had some sort of plague befallen the city? Some prophecy of doom? Had the deep elves besieged them, or fought a great, slaughterous battle that had left Thelgrim partially depopulated?

The citadel seemed unwilling to share answers on the matter. It glared down at them with stony dwarven distrust as they approached its gates. She heard orders, barked in the rough Dunwarr tongue, ringing out over the battlements. There was the slow, heavy clanking of chains as the portcullis ahead of them rose, the doors behind it swinging inwards to expose a fire-lit entrance hall.

"I hope you know what you're doing," she hissed at Raythen. He glanced back at her with an expression that was hardly comforting.

"Hold your tongue and don't set anyone on fire, and we'll be fine," he growled back at her.

She held her staff a little tighter. They were ushered in through the gateway, then halted in the entrance hall. More Dunwarr were waiting, not just warriors but others in tabards emblazoned with the golden livery of the mountain. Several hailed the captain and exchanged a short, sharp conversation before one hurried away up a set of spiral stairs cut into the bedrock of one of the outcrops the citadel was built upon.

"You will come with me," the captain said. She had drawn a torch from a holder lining the wall, slinging her shield across her back.

"Well, we've followed you this far," Raythen said. The

captain didn't so much as look at him, but motioned Astarra and Shiver forward.

The elf hadn't uttered a sound since crossing the span into Thelgrim. Given what had happened on the Hearth Road, Astarra wasn't sure she even wanted to be in close proximity to him. The deep elf attack had shaken her, and she found it impossible to believe he wasn't in some way responsible. He'd shown no desire to resist the dwarfs so far though.

They were pointed towards a series of steps that delved down into the rock of the citadel. A narrow passageway, its stairs worn and shrouded in musty shadows, twisted downwards until it reached a long, low undercroft, lit by a single brazier at the far end. The walls were lined with doors studded with iron grates. It didn't look like the royal hall Astarra had anticipated. Her hopes plummeted, replaced by an indignant anger.

She turned on the dwarf captain as she followed them down, the light of her torch making her armor gleam and shimmer.

"You intend to imprison us?" she demanded. "This is a jail, isn't it?"

"This is only the upper dungeon," the captain said. "I assure you, there are far worse places where you might be held. Your stay here will be only temporary, one way or another."

"What's that supposed to– ?" Astarra began to say, but Raythen cut her off.

"Will he come in person?" he asked the captain.

"I couldn't say," she responded, advancing down the undercroft and pointing at one of the heavy-set doors. "You know him better than I."

Raythen shrugged his shoulders, about to step through into the cell beyond. Astarra grabbed his arm urgently.

"I've trusted you this far," she said. "Tell me this isn't what I think it is."

"That's what I was wondering myself," Raythen admitted, loud enough for Bradha to hear. "I was about to ask the good captain the same thing. Is this really the kind of hospitality the Dunwarr are now offering their visitors? Imprisoned in a cell with barely a word?"

"If I was imprisoning you, I wouldn't let you keep that staff, for starters," the captain replied, stepping into the space and fixing her torch into one of the brackets. "And I wouldn't leave this unlocked. Wait here. You will be called upon. If you need anything, one of my kindred will be outside."

Raythen looked back at her and nodded. Astarra glanced at Shiver, but the elf was as unreadable as ever.

Face set, she ducked into the cell after him.

"What did you do?" Astarra demanded of Raythen the moment the captain had departed. "Why are they treating us like this?"

"Honestly, I thought it'd be worse," Raythen said. Astarra hissed with frustration, pacing the whole length of the cell before turning sharply back to point an accusing finger at the dwarf.

"We've just been imprisoned in all but name because that captain recognized you. At the very least you should have told us you were wanted in Thelgrim!"

"I'm not wanted," Raythen said, with a bleak smile. "That's the whole problem."

He sat down on the bench that ran along the wall of the otherwise empty cell. Astarra continued to pace, her swift footsteps soft and urgent on the bare stone floor. This wasn't the sort of welcome to Thelgrim she had been anticipating. It was as though they already knew she had designs for the runestone. Was this all an act of treachery by Raythen? And what about Shiver? She glanced at him as he stood in the far corner, arms hugging his body.

It seemed the elf was having similar thoughts, because he was the one who broke the silence.

"You are not who you seem," he said. Astarra halted and looked from him to Raythen. The dwarf glanced at Shiver briefly before looking away and shrugging.

"Who among us is?" he responded. "Certainly not you, elf."

"My past is a mystery to all, including myself," Shiver said. "But yours you deliberately conceal. You portray yourself as a thief, a rogue, but that is not the truth."

It was the first time Astarra had heard Shiver interrogate either of them about anything. She wondered if it was an indicator of the dire nature of their situation.

"It is the truth," Raythen said, not looking at the elf. Astarra realized she was seeing something else she'd not yet witnessed – the dwarf was genuinely uncomfortable. "I've never denied my nature to either of you this past month."

"Perhaps not your nature," Shiver said, black eyes glinting in the firelight. "A thief, yes, but you are more besides. That is what you have concealed from us. From everyone beyond these walls, I suspect."

"You never told us why you didn't want to come back to Thelgrim," Astarra added, picking up her own train of thought. "You wanted us to assume it was because you were some kind of petty thief. But a Dunwarr captain doesn't seize a thief with a fully armed patrol twenty years later, escort them to the heart of their city then leave them in an unlocked cell with a human and an elf sorcerer."

Raythen sighed before speaking, his voice heavy with frustration. "I've got a past here. More than just… petty theft, as you put it, Astarra."

"A past that you wanted to avoid by not coming back," Astarra pressed. "But why? What do the rulers of this city want with you?"

"It's what they don't want with me," Raythen said, finally fixing his one, fierce eye on his accusers. "I didn't wish to return because I'm the son of the King in the Deeps. My father is Geirmund Ragnarson, ruler of Thelgrim."

CHAPTER SEVEN

Shiver said nothing, letting the words sink in as he considered them. Astarra was not so measured.

"You're the heir to the Dunwarrs, and you never thought to mention it to us?" she shouted. The tip of her staff had ignited, the fire drawn forth by her anger.

"I'm not the heir to anything," Raythen snapped. "You'd know that if they'd taught you anything at all about the Dunwarr at that worthless university you ran away from. Then perhaps you wouldn't be gawking at everything you see in the Deeps like a newborn youngling."

"The ruler of Thelgrim is elected for life by the city's guilds," Shiver said, as Astarra visibly vacillated between fury and confusion. "It is not a hereditary position. Ragnarson was a prominent member of the Blacksmiths' Guild, though he has been king now for so long that some forget the elected nature of the role."

"I'm the heir of nothing," Raythen repeated coldly. "Except perhaps a mind-numbing existence beating away at an anvil for the next few hundred years."

"How did you think you'd get away with this?" Astarra asked incredulously. "How could you expect to walk into Thelgrim when you're the king's son?"

"His only son too," Raythen added. "And yes, I did expect to walk into Thelgrim. What I didn't expect was to find the Hearth Road abandoned and the city apparently half empty despite the gates being shut. It's not difficult to go unseen in the trader's caravans and the market places, even with characters like you two. I could have slipped away to the League headquarters and been back with the stone in no time. It wouldn't even have taken us a whole day in the city."

"Yet here we are," Astarra said. Shiver considered reaching out and quelling her staff's fire, but he didn't want to risk angering her even further. He had sensed more to Raythen almost since the beginning, but he had seen no need to pursue it, until now. He knew better than any that the past was immutable. Whatever Raythen had previously done to incur the wrath of Thelgrim and its king, it needn't define his future.

"This isn't a problem," Raythen was saying, tone at once angry and defensive as he faced down Astarra. "They won't keep us here for long."

"Then why are they keeping us here at all?" Astarra asked.

"My father will want to speak to me," Raythen said. "That's all. We'll be on our way soon enough. Just let me do the talking."

"You've been saying that since we set out," Astarra snapped. "Look where we've ended up? A dungeon in a Dunwarr citadel!"

"You don't know anything about my father," Raythen said. "And I know more than I'd care to. If you think you can argue your way out of here, be my guest. But you won't scorch your way out. Stone doesn't burn."

The words drew Astarra's attention to her ignited staff. She closed her eyes, took a breath, and the fire simmered and died.

"We are still no closer to establishing why Thelgrim has been cut off, or why the streets are empty," Shiver said, silently thankful that Raythen had managed to restore a degree of calm to Astarra. "I believe doing so to be a priority. You should ask your father when you see him."

"Honestly, I half thought all this was because he'd died," Raythen admitted. "But it seems not."

"So, our plan is just to wait and let him have a little catch-up with his father?" Astarra asked incredulously.

"Right now, something along those lines would seem most prudent," Shiver said. "We are in no position to further antagonize our hosts."

He'd been silently weighing his options since the Dunwarr had accosted them in the tunnels. The entire venture was under threat, but he knew better than to completely abandon the option of diplomacy. He'd seen where that led to enough times before.

In truth, he was still recovering from the attack on the Hearth Road, and not only physically. He had sensed it coming, but a part of him had doubted it was actually going to happen. The souls he had felt around him had been kindred spirits, even beyond the simple fact that they were fellow deep elves. Somehow, he knew them. He thought they were just going to watch the strange trio pass. He hadn't anticipated any sort of attack, let alone the furious assault that had befallen them.

He could still feel the soul of the one he had killed clinging to him, fading but still present, like a slow chill that worked itself all the way into the bones and couldn't be shaken off. It had happened so fast. The flash of steel in the dark, the glittering of eyes, black like his own. The response had been reflexive on his part, a warding hand, a word that only truly belonged in the coldest, deepest glaciers of the far north.

The elf had hissed a word of his own as his heart had stopped beating and his lips had frozen shut.

"Daewyl."

Shiver tried to banish that particular memory, tried to forget the chill he had summoned, the death he had inflicted. He had no use for such a memory. It had been self-defense. Just as it had been self-defense so many times before, and as it would be so many times again.

"Shiver!"

He looked up, sharply, and wondered at what point he'd sat down with his back to the wall. Both his companions were staring at him, and Raythen had risen from the bench. He tried to make sense of what happened, but could not.

"You fell," Raythen said, answering the question Shiver didn't want to ask.

"It was a memory," he said, using the craggy wall to haul himself back up. Raythen took a step towards him, then seemed to think better of it.

"You seem to have a lot of memories," Astarra said.

"Not enough," Shiver said, wincing slightly as he regained his feet. "That's the problem."

"Why are you here?" Astarra continued. "What do the locks mean? Why are they so important that you would risk coming to Thelgrim when it seems like the Dunwarr must be on the brink of a war with the deep elves?"

"The locks are… arcane in nature," Shiver said, not wanting to be drawn but sensing that, after Raythen's revelation, Astarra was in no mood to leave her other companion's secrets undisturbed.

"I think we could work that one out ourselves," Raythen said, unable to resist a flash of sarcasm.

"They grant you particular powers?" Astarra asked. "Premonitions?"

"I've already told you," Shiver said. "Memories, mostly. I have to unlock them, one by one. I seek them all over Terrinoth."

"How did you lose the memories? Why do they matter so much?"

Shiver didn't answer. A sudden numbness gripped him, and his thoughts fled away for a moment. He heard the rattle of his manacles, and realized he'd started to shake. He tried to reach out to the Empyrean, but he found himself unable to grasp even the small trickle of Empyrean magic that was available to him. It was as though an invasive force had turned the energies of the great ether into quicksilver – it ran though his fingers, refusing to form, refusing to become something he could grasp and turn tangible.

He felt suddenly sick. The numbness was growing worse. He slumped back down against the cell wall, a moan of pain and fear slipping past his lips.

"Something's coming," he managed, forcing himself to fix his eyes and focus on Astarra and Raythen. "Something terrible."

•••

Raythen was about to try and haul Shiver up onto the bench when he heard the sound of boots ringing through the undercroft outside.

"What's he saying?" Astarra was asking urgently. Shiver was mumbling something, his eyes rolling back. To Raythen it looked as though he had gone into shock. At first, he'd thought it was a response to Astarra's questioning, perhaps even an act, but he could feel the same thing creeping over him now, growing stronger as the approaching footsteps rang louder.

It was a strange blankness, as though some cosmic entity had suddenly called into question whether or not any of them actually existed. It made him feel at once hollow and insignificant, and brought on sensations of panic he hadn't had to endure since he'd been a youngling. One glance at Astarra told him she had started feeling it too – the grip on her staff was white-knuckled and shaking.

He knew what this was. Bad news.

The sound of the boots halted abruptly outside the cell door. It swung open without a sound, revealing Bradha the Shield at the head of a band of Dunwarr.

Raythen stepped back from the entrance as the captain came in, followed by one of her armored Warriors' Guild brethren carrying a small velvet pouch carefully before him. Next came two more Dunwarr, twins clad in formal leather jerkins stamped with a gold leaf design depicting the mountain and the jewel at its core – Thelgrim. They were both bald, but their beards were snowy white and braided into twin forks, one with a silver clasp and one with gold. Their expressions bordered on disdain as they took post on either side of the doorway, behind Bradha and the other warrior.

The last Dunwarr to enter was the tallest. He was wearing simple boots and breeches and the heavy leather smock of a member of the Blacksmiths' Guild. The humble pretense was cast into doubt by the circlet of shining, brilliant gold that sat upon his brow, and the ringlets in his white beard. It had been laboriously braided and beaded with hundreds of intricately cast little golden tokens, so that in the firelight it seemed as though the imposing dwarf wore a breastplate of glorious silver and gold. His eyes, like Raythen's, were flinty and gray.

"Hello, Father," Raythen said.

"That is not how an outsider addresses the king of Thelgrim," Bradha snapped, but the tall dwarf raised his hand. He hadn't taken his eyes off Raythen.

"Captain Bradha has served as the commander of the gates of Thelgrim for the better part of a century," King Ragnarson said, his voice like mountain rock cracking and grinding its way down a shale slope. "Along with captains Svensdottir, Svensson, and my two advisors, Korri and Zorri, there is no dwarf anywhere on Mennara who I would trust more. Yet even then, when she told me that my son had returned, I did not believe her. Even now, looking at you, I struggle."

"Well, I have put on a few pounds," Raythen said. "Lost a few assets. None that matter though, I promise."

It took every ounce of will and experience to keep his voice calm and level. His heart was racing, and he could feel his hands quivering, despite his best efforts to appear relaxed. He'd been anticipating this moment since he'd seen Bradha and her brutes tramping down the Hearth Road towards him.

He'd played out his father's likely words and his own reactions dozens of times as they were marched through Thelgrim, and all over again as they sat waiting, his thoughts festering. But somehow, all his preparation hadn't been enough. All his wiles, his wit, all his experience dealing with the hardships Terrinoth had flung at him over the past twenty years, were at risk of flying away, leaving him as a shaking youngling once more, a beardless child quailing before the wrath of his father, the king.

"Why?" Ragnarson demanded. His tone wasn't angry, not yet, but it was as cold and as hard as the Dunwarr peaks in midwinter. "Why have you come back?"

"Why else?" Raythen asked, determined not to break so easily. "Silver."

"There is none here for you. You have never been part of my inheritance."

"Believe it or not, it's not your silver I'm seeking."

"Then just who did Captain Bradha catch you in the process of robbing?" Ragnarson demanded, nodding past Raythen at Astarra and Shiver. "These two?"

"They are my companions," Raythen said, forcing himself not to bite so soon. He glanced back, and saw that Astarra had gone pale, though she was still on her feet. Shiver was shaking uncontrollably though, curled up in the corner of the cell.

"If you want to talk, take away that Null Stone," Raythen said to Ragnarson, nodding towards the warrior carrying the velvet pouch. "Otherwise, I'll say nothing more."

"A Null Stone," Astarra said abruptly, apparently finding focus. "There's a Null Stone in here?"

Raythen watched Ragnarson frown slightly, clearly trying to gauge just who and what Astarra was. He gestured curtly to the warrior with the bag, who in turn shook a small runeshard marked with a square symbol onto his palm.

"I will have none of your sorcery here," Ragnarson said.

Raythen wondered how much being in the stone's presence was affecting the king and his fellow, silent interrogators. If it was, his father made no sign of discomfort. He was just as Raythen remembered him.

"That null void has completely severed the elf sorcerer's connection to the Turning," he said, trying to change tack. "It's no better than torture. Remove it."

"You should have considered that before helping an Ynfernael worshiper infiltrate the mountain," said one of the white-bearded Dunwarr to Ragnarson's right with the golden clasp – Korri – his voice edged with spite.

To Raythen's surprise, Astarra responded before him.

"He isn't an Ynfernael worshiper," she snapped. She was pale, but she stood tall as she stepped towards the gathering of Dunwarr before the door. Captain Bradha unsubtly let her hand drop to the hilt of her short sword.

"Remove that stone," Astarra went on, her eyes full of threat.

"You do not address the King in the Deeps like that, outsider," growled the advisor with the silver-clasped beard, Zorri.

"He's not my king," Astarra retorted.

"If you want the stone removed you will surrender your staff, for a start," Korri said.

"You can take it from my bloody corpse, Dunwarr," Astarra exclaimed.

"We've done nothing," Raythen said loudly to his father, moving to stand between Astarra and the royal delegation. "You have no reason to imprison us, and no right either."

Ragnarson glared for a moment at Raythen, then, suddenly, struck him with the back of his hand. Raythen took the blow, its unexpectedness stinging more than the strike itself.

"I thought you'd stop taking me for a fool when I ordered you to leave this city," Ragnarson said. "I only regret I didn't formally banish you before the Guild Council."

"As I recall, I was the one who chose to leave," Raythen said bitterly, facing down his father.

"An arrangement that served both of us," Ragnarson said. "And now you return, slinking in the shadows of the Hearth Road, consorting with demon-worshiping deep elves, and worse, stealing from the tombs of our hallowed ancestors."

Raythen caught himself in the midst of his reply.

"I've stolen nothing," he exclaimed, outraged. "Nor have my companions!"

"Lies," barked Korri, stepping towards Raythen before Ragnarson's sharply raised hand stopped him.

"Where is the Hydra Shard?" the king demanded, his voice now low with threat. "You will tell us, or you will fester here beneath the horror of a Null Stone until it is recovered."

"The Hydra?" Raythen repeated incredulously, wondering what in the name of the Ancestors was really going on. Just what had the three of them walked into? "Father, I have no idea! I didn't even know it was gone!"

"For once in your life, stop lying," Zorri snapped.

"You expect me to believe that, with the mountain gates shut and the whole city sealed off?" Ragnarson said.

"We didn't know why the gates were closed," Astarra spoke up, glaring past Raythen at the king. "No one outside Thelgrim does. There are thousands of refugees beyond your gates right now, starving to death!"

"A necessary evil, until the device is retrieved," Korri said. "If the recent influx hadn't brought so many beggars and thieves to our city, perhaps it would still be where it belongs, in the tomb of the great Deeplord Holburg."

"If the Hydra has been stolen, none of us had any hand in it," Raythen repeated. Anger had overtaken fear, the rare fury of being wrongly accused. "You have no proof, nothing but your own blind hatred."

"Your presence here is proof enough," Ragnarson said. "You reappear, a known thief, after twenty years, in the wake of the most treacherous, disgraceful act of robbery to have ever befallen Thelgrim. You have taken me for a fool far too many times before, my son, but you will not do so again."

"This is absolutely ridiculous," Raythen said.

"Tell us where the Hydra is," Zorri demanded.

"I don't have the Hydra," Raythen shouted. His father's appearance, the effect of a Null Stone and the unexpectedness of the accusation was all too much for his reserve. He was angry, and he wasn't thinking straight enough to either craft a lie or come up with a better way of talking himself out of the situation.

"They should be disarmed, my king," Korri hissed.

"Whoever comes for my staff first, dies," Astarra said loudly. "Null Stone or not, you have been warned."

"There is no need for any of this," Raythen said, thoughts racing now as he tried to regain control and chart a way out.

"If someone really has stolen the Hydra then we can help you. We can track them, find them."

"I see you still enjoy playing games, my son," Ragnarson said. "I suspected as much. The Null Stone will remain here, just outside the cell door. Perhaps, given time, it will help convince you to give up your childishness and tell me where you have hidden the Hydra."

He looked past Raythen at Astarra, continuing to speak.

"You may keep your stick and your trinkets. The Null will render them worthless anyway. I am leaving Captain Bradha on the door. Try to escape and she will kill you. I will return when you are ready to admit to your crimes."

"Well, this is a first," Raythen said bitterly as Ragnarson prepared to leave, his frustration getting the better of him. "Arrested for a crime I haven't even managed to commit yet."

The king said nothing. The twins followed him out, eyes lingering on Raythen, followed by Bradha and the guard. There was a heavy thump as the door closed behind them, followed by the rattle of keys and, finally, the resounding thud of the lock.

CHAPTER EIGHT

Astarra closed her eyes. She felt sick and weak, but she stayed on her feet, trying to fight back against the horrible pall that had fallen over them all.

After the Dunwarr left, Raythen had sat down heavily on the bench. He was still there, his head in his hands. Astarra couldn't find the words to comfort him, so instead she mastered her thoughts, looked at him, and asked him a question.

"What is the Hydra Shard?"

Raythen didn't answer. He didn't even look up.

She tried once more to reach out to the Turning, to the invisible magical power that infused all of Mennara, but she found herself grasping at nothing. It was as if a hard barrier had been conjured up between her and the runeshards that allowed her to access the Turning. It was unyielding, and there was no way to find purchase on it, no way to crack it or break it down.

She had heard stories of Null Stones, had even sought one herself, in far off Sudanya. The trail had proven long-dead, a fact she was now thankful of. Stories had spoken of the void shards inscribed with the Null marking created in the Turning, how their unique design drained magical properties rather than enhanced them. She had assumed the other tales associated with such stones – of horror and madness – were just that, the stories of the ignorant, of those who didn't understand runemagic or the miracles they could bring about.

She would never doubt them again. The stone didn't feel so much like a void. It was a direct barrier, walls set all around her, claustrophobic and suffocating. And if it felt that way to her, a runewitch who relied on the shards in place of a direct conduit, how much worse must it feel for Shiver?

The elf had at least stopped his shaking and sat up since the stone had been removed from the cell, but he showed no sign of snapping out of the trance he'd slipped into.

Astarra actually found herself feeling sorry for him, which wasn't an emotion she'd expected. He seemed so vulnerable suddenly, so hopeless. A part of her scolded herself for her weakness, but it was natural. Right now, he was suffering, and Astarra liked to believe that she never stood idly by when that was happening, regardless of who was in pain.

"Raythen," she said, reaching out and putting a hand on the Dunwarr's shoulder. He started and looked up, as though he'd forgotten Astarra had been standing there the whole time.

"We've got to get out of here," she told him. He stared at her for a second, seemingly only just remembering where he was, before shaking his head.

"The door's locked and Bradha's outside."

"You really expect me to believe a locked door is going to

keep you anywhere?" she asked, trying to instill some fight in the thief. "You still have your pack, your weapons. You must have plenty of ways of breaking us out."

"When I was a youngling, I saw Bradha the Shield hold one of the passages in the Deeps alone for half an hour against a combined raiding party of orcs and humans," Raythen said. "She eventually filled it with so many dead bodies that they couldn't even get at her. I can unlock the door, but if you want to take her on – without your runestones – then you're doing it yourself. And even if you can bring her down, what next? We're in the Dunwol Kenn Karnin, for Fortuna's sake. The Fortress Within the Mountain. We're not walking out."

"We'll think of something," Astarra said, trying her best not to sound desperate. "You could wear her armor? Pretend you've been ordered to take us out."

Raythen let out a short bark of laughter.

"Don't believe everything you hear about in the stories, runewitch. Tricks like that fail ninety-nine times in a hundred."

"That's the Null Stone talking, not Raythen," she said, but he shook his head.

"You're no rogue, Astarra. I am. And you know how I've lived this long? Picking my fights."

"We've got to try," Astarra exclaimed, changing tack. She pointed at Shiver. "He can't stay here like this. Look at him!"

The deep elf was lying propped against the wall, his eyes glazed. Astarra was sure she could see the faintest glow of copresence around the bonds, and while she had no idea what that signified, she doubted it was good.

"My father thinks I'm guilty," Raythen said, only glancing at Shiver. "Trust me when I tell you that I speak from experience.

Nothing is going to change his mind or convince him to let us go, not until the Hydra is recovered."

"What is the Hydra?" Astarra asked again, hoping for something, anything, that might galvanize the Dunwarr into action. It was clear the encounter with his father had shaken him to the core. It had left her worried as well. Up until now he had been their guide in Thelgrim, the only one who seemed to have a clear plan. That didn't look to be the case anymore. She knew she had to keep him talking, reignite some kind of spark.

"It's a shard incorporated into an ancient relic, a device created by the Runescribers' Guild in the Third Darkness," he said, gazing up at Astarra. "I thought you of all people would have heard of it."

"I know the legends," Astarra said. "But only what outsiders and the libraries of Greyhaven could tell, which isn't much. I've never heard a Dunwarr speak of it. Is it truly connected to a Star of Timmoran?"

Raythen stayed silent. Astarra tried not to let the possibilities get the better of her. A Star of Timmoran was a shard of what had once been the Orb of the Sky, a conduit of magical power crafted by the greatest human sorcerer Mennara had ever known. It had been shattered into countless fragments when his friend and ally, the treacherous Waiqar, had betrayed and killed him. The Stars of Timmoran were the remains of the Orb, imbued with near-fathomless magical potential, in contrast to the runebound shards that traded potential for the focused power of the runes inscribed upon them. The Hydra Shard was one of the Stars, but with a crucial difference. Astarra pressed on.

"The Hydra is bound to a device that manipulates its

energies. Individually it would take decades, even centuries, to develop the skills necessary to harness a fraction of one of the Star's powers. With the device crafted by the runescribers though, summoning the full potential of the Hydra Shard becomes as simple as the flick of a dial on the mechanism. Even the least magically-adept librarium-clerks in Greyhaven could become a sorcerer of awesome potency."

"It allows the wielder to channel five forms of magic from the unbound shard," Raythen said, nodding. "The Runescribers' Guild worked for decades to fashion a device that could harness its potential without the need for laborious study."

Astarra had heard similar. She had always assumed much of it was exaggerated. The realization that the stories were true only increased the determination she now felt. Possessing such a relic would change everything.

"Where was it then, this device?" she went on. "In Thelgrim?"

"In the Hall of the Ancestors," Raythen said. "In the tomb of Deeplord Holburg. After the Third Darkness it was decreed to be too dangerous to use, except in times of greatest peril. Some even wanted to destroy it, but the runescribers feared what might happen if they tried, and the Guild Council was afraid they might someday need it, if a threat even greater than the dragons arose. It was sealed away in the tomb of the last of the Deeplords."

"Until now," Astarra said. "Is all this really because it's been stolen? The whole city, shut down on your father's orders?"

"On the orders of Korri and Zorri, more likely," Raythen said. "They've been his advisors for as long as I can remember.

But to do something as drastic as this, they would have to have won a vote before the Guild Council, probably with something like a two-to-one majority."

"I'm guessing that's not an easy thing to do?" Astarra asked.

"No, it's not. But it begs the question, if the city's been sealed, just who do they think has taken the Hydra? A Dunwarr? An outsider? And why?"

"It certainly sounds like something worth stealing," Astarra said.

"It does," Raythen said. "But it's no amateur's job, trust me. It's unlikely any but a Dunwarr could negotiate their way to it. Just the Hall of the Ancestors alone is lousy with traps and snares. The tomb of Deeplord Holburg itself is usually protected by a Null Stone, so no magics can be used to break it open. If the Hydra has really been taken, it would take a master thief, or an extremely capable group."

A cold sensation, quite separate from the Null Stone's, started to creep over Astarra. She sat down next to Raythen, staring at him.

"This isn't a coincidence, is it?" she asked.

"No," Raythen replied, his one eye fixing on her. "I think we were brought here to steal the Hydra. And I think some else has gotten to it first."

Demons.

They were all around him, their otherworldly, poisonous presence overwhelming. They stank like burned rock, like opened innards, like curdled milk. The air resounded with their yipping and snarling and the scrape of their claws on stone. Their misshapen bodies cast too many shadows.

Shiver retched, but nothing came up. He'd already voided his stomach. He was on his knees, shaking, shaking so hard the rune-etched chains that bound him rattled and clattered above the shrieking of the Ynfernael horde surging past him from the open portal. He felt the brush of their bodies, the buzzing of their ravenous, demented minds. He moaned aloud.

"Come now, my dear, it isn't so bad," said the voice behind him. It was melodious and soft, a cruelly ironic counterpoint to the cacophony of the monsters surrounding them.

"How many has that been?" it continued, right by his ear now, making him shudder all the harder. "Eighteen times? Twenty? Are you going to throw up every time?"

Shiver clenched his teeth. He wanted to lash out with every part of his being, to snatch her soul and seal it away for all eternity at the heart of a wall of ice. But he couldn't. As his mind railed, his manacles burned with ethereal light, nullifying his fury, leaving him utterly impotent.

"Such rage still," said the voice, as the press of demonic entities surrounding them finally began to ease. In the distance Shiver could hear the first screams as the leading edge of the newly-summoned swarm reached the nearest village.

"Your anger only makes this work more potent," said the voice. "It adds an extra edge to the hunger of our friends. Remember that, next time you attempt to strike your mistress. Remember that I want you to try."

Shiver screamed.

"It's happening again," Astarra shouted. She and Raythen had both bounded back to their feet as Shiver let out a hideous, mournful wail.

Etheric energies sparked and flared around his manacles, but this time they failed to fully materialize.

"The method he uses to regain his memories is magical," Astarra said, eyes wide. "How can he be using it with the Null Stone so close?"

"I don't think this is a new memory," Raythen responded. "I think it's an old one. And a bad one."

Shiver snarled and thrashed, an arm striking off the wall.

"He's going to injure himself," Astarra said, taking a half step towards the elf. She was surprised to realize the thought concerned her.

No sooner had she done so, Shiver's eyes snapped open. This time there was no copresence, no later Turning power. He looked at them, still shaking, but fully conscious.

"Can… can you feel that?" he stammered. The two stared at him.

"I'm not sure I want to ask," Raythen said. "But feel what?"

CHAPTER NINE

The nightmare-memory gave way, sloughing off like dead flesh from bone. It left Shiver tremoring in its wake, looking up at his companions.

It took him a moment to realize it wasn't just his own shivering that he could feel. There were tremors running through the stone underneath him, and they were growing stronger.

"What is it?" Astarra asked urgently, pushing past Raythen. "What can you sense?"

Shiver dragged himself to his feet, convinced now that he wasn't just suffering from the after-effects of the painful, unexpected memory-flare.

"Something's coming," he said to them.

The trembling grew worse. Raythen and Astarra appeared to sense it, looking at the walls and floor in apparent confusion. Shiver heard shouting outside, and the rattle of keys at the door.

"Get away from the wall," he told the other two. They looked at him, still confused. He pointed at the wall by the bench, struggling to find coherent words they could understand through the pain of the Null Stone.

"The vibrations are coming from the neighboring cell. Stand back."

"He's right," Raythen said, having to shout now over the thunder of shifting, churning rock. His Dunwarr senses seemed to have finally kicked in – he could feel what Shiver had already detected in the stone all around them.

"It's coming up from below!"

Together they snatched Astarra and hauled her away from the wall just as it caved in. With a whirr and a crash, dust and debris exploded through the cell. Shiver instinctively tried to conjure a ward made of ice, but his words rang hollow, rendered empty and meaningless by the cursed Null aura.

He shielded his face with a sleeve, coughing despite his best efforts not to inhale the surge of dust. When he looked again, he realized the whole far wall of the cell had collapsed. Jagged masonry had crushed the bench and partially blocked the doorway. He could hear the shouting of the guards outside as they fought to gain entry.

The whirring noise that had accompanied the wall's collapse began to die down. Shiver could make out a shape through the dust – something was still pushing its way into the wrecked space. It had clearly driven up through the floor of the neighboring cell, the angle of its entry leaving it jutting partially up. He could make out a heavy drill bit, as large as Raythen, that was only just ceasing its rotation, throwing dirt and pulverized rock across the room. Behind it was what appeared to be a small compartment or cabin, metallic in design but so befouled with dirt and grit that its shape was almost indiscernible.

In all his centuries wandering Mennara, he had never seen anything quite like it. As he stared there was a *thunk,* and a hatch in the cabin behind the drill levered open. Steam poured out, further clouding the cell. It was followed by the shape of a Dunwarr who pulled himself halfway out of the hole. He was coughing vigorously, the lower half of his face shaven but blackened with grime, the upper half shielded by a heavy set of goggles. Combined, the entire array looked like some sort of vast insectoid that had just burrowed its way up from the depths of the mountain.

"W- well don't just stand there," the dwarf blustered, waving furiously at the stunned trio. "Get in!"

He disappeared back into the hatch without another word. Shiver looked at Astarra, who looked at Raythen who, after a few wide-eyed seconds, shrugged.

"If either of you were praying to your favorite deity for a miracle, I suspect this might be it," Raythen said, before planting a boot on the deactivated drill head and clambering up into the hatch.

Shiver didn't pause to consider his options. Right now, all he wanted was to get as far away from the Null Stone and its baleful influence as possible. He followed Raythen as he dropped down into the hatch of the strange mechanism. Immediately his world was reduced to steam-choked darkness. The interior of the device was bare metal and painfully cramped. Raythen was crouched behind the Dunwarr with the goggles, who was sat at a cluster of brass valves, levers, dial gauges, and a single, large wheel. There was barely enough room for Shiver to kneel, let alone crouch. The only light came from a lone candle, set in an alcove above the forward mechanism and shielded by a small, grubby plate of glass.

Astarra came down on top of him, driving him forward into Raythen, who grunted as he was pushed against the strange Dunwarr.

"Fortuna's lucky dice," Raythen swore as Shiver and Astarra sought to right themselves. The human's staff was jabbing into the elf's flank, unable to properly fit in the packed hold.

"Sorry about the squeeze," the Dunwarr called out with a grin. "Sh- she wasn't built with transportation in mind. Or prison breaks, for that matter. In fact, I didn't think you'd all fit until just now!"

"We don't," Astarra snarled, clearly less than happy that she was practically hugging Shiver. Despite the desperate strangeness of the whole situation, he felt a pang of embarrassment.

"I'm going to need you to reach up and close the h- hatch," the Dunwarr said as he threw a heavy-looking lever. Shiver felt the metal hull around them start to vibrate.

"I'd also advise everyone, if you have a natural ability or a magical incantation that allows you to avoid breathing, I'd utilize it now," the dwarf added, grinning back at them again through the steam pouring from several of the valves. "By my calculations, we're going to run out of air several minutes before we reach our destination."

Raythen and Astarra both swore. Shiver simply started holding his breath.

Pistons on either side of them began to chug and squeal, moving slowly at first but rapidly gaining speed. Astarra reached up to bang the hatch shut, painfully jabbing Shiver again with her staff. There was a lurch, and the whirring sound picked up again. The Dunwarr threw another lever and gripped the wheel, hunched over his gauges.

Shiver assumed they were in motion, though it was difficult to tell. The interior of the contraption was infernally hot – he was soon drenched in cold, clammy sweat. Raythen was peering in apparent fascination over the shoulder of their would-be savior, the two bodies blocking Shiver's own view of the mass of controls directing the device.

He looked back at Astarra. He could sense her heart racing, and her eyes were wild and white as they returned his gaze. She was on the cusp of panicking, confined in a strange, heated metal tomb. Claustrophobia, an alien concept to both dwarfs and deep elves, was gripping the runewitch.

Shiver struggled to understand her fear. The bitter, suffocating pall of the Null Stone had lifted, like weights being removed from a drowning man's ankles. Being crammed into the boiling, dark, steam-choked metal hold of the burrower was an insignificant discomfort now that his soul could breathe again.

He reached out tentatively into the Turning, and felt a surge of relief when it responded to his immaterial touch. Being cut off from it had been worse than any wound or physical blow. It was as though a vital piece of his very existence had been carved out. Now, though, he was whole again, and able to think straight.

He closed his eyes and focused on easing the temperature in the oven-like hold. Raythen sensed it first and twisted awkwardly to look back at him, but said nothing. He felt Astarra's heartbeat easing slightly as the air became less choking.

He didn't know how long they spent in the burrower. He focused on his breathing, his own heart rate, keeping it slow and steady. He couldn't fathom just who this Dunwarr was, or why he'd turned his strange device to freeing them, but for now he was just thankful to be out.

At one point one of the valves seemed to break. The dwarf loosed a string of expletives in his own tongue as more steam seared through the packed hold.

"Keep a grip on that, would you?" the dwarf asked Raythen, indicating that he should hold the valve shut.

"For how long?" Raythen asked.

"Until we stop," came the reply.

Several thudding impacts shook the metalwork around them, making Astarra gasp and causing Shiver to grimace as her staff accidentally dug once more into his side. Shiver wondered if they'd hit an obstruction or were simply ploughing through particularly recalcitrant rock or Dunwarr-built walls. The burrower seemed to surge again though, overcoming whatever had been blocking it.

It would have thrown them around, had they not been so tightly packed. He focused on putting his mind elsewhere, overcoming the discomfort of the unnatural journey using the mantra that helped centre his thoughts. *Atali nametha ren. Nameth hatala.*

At last, he noted that the whirring, grinding sound he took to be the drill bit had started to decelerate once more. The Dunwarr was working the wheel and levers furiously, and the pistons slowly eased their frantic activity. Metal groaned and creaked around them, beginning to settle.

"Well, that was a record," the Dunwarr said, turning as much as he was able. "You can open the hatch again, lady sorcerer."

Astarra practically lunged into the space above, hauling herself feverishly up and out of the confined hold. Shiver followed her at a more measured pace, controlling the sense of relief he felt as he left behind the strange contraption. He looked out of the hatch before clambering through it.

The mechanism had tunneled its way out into what looked like another undercroft, or a long cellar. It was danker looking than the upper dungeon of the Dunwol Kenn Karnin, its walls consisting of exposed dirt and rock kept in place by iron beams. It was lit by lanterns, similar to the one inside the burrower, set into alcoves and covered by small glass screens. The illumination they gave off was dirty and flickering.

Shiver clambered from the hatch and dropped down to the ground just as Astarra was sick. She doubled over against the side of the mud-caked burrower, retching loudly. Unsure of how best to comfort her, Shiver tentatively placed a hand on her shoulder, which she batted away.

Raythen was clambering up out of the hatch just as a side panel on the burrower's grubby flank was hauled back, exposing the Dunwarr pilot. He dragged himself free of his contraption with some difficulty, ending up half in, half out, flailing on the floor. Flanked on one side by the struggling dwarf and on the other by the retching runewitch, Shiver looked up helplessly at Raythen.

The thief jumped down from the roof of the burrower. Shiver realized he had his short axe in his hand.

"Who in Fortuna's name are you, beardless one?" he

demanded, holding the edge against the neck of the Dunwarr pilot, who went abruptly still.

"I'm the d- dwarf who just saved your lives," he said.

"Why?" Raythen demanded.

"Because I've got a job for you," the dwarf said.

"We've already got a job," Raythen responded. "Do you know who I am?"

"I would hope so," the dwarf said, grinning despite the naked steel at his throat. "I'm the one who hired you."

CHAPTER TEN

The burrower pilot's name was Kayl Mavarin. He was short and lean, had a stutter, and laughed when Raythen called him beardless again.

"It gets in the way," he said as he led them up from the undercroft. "Gets set on fire, entangled, stained. Terrible for a Dunwarr who likes to experiment. So yes, I shaved it off."

Astarra hadn't encountered a Dunwarr who would do such a thing before, but the past few days had been revelatory for many reasons. The creation that had tunneled them out of the Dunwol Kenn Karnin alone was beyond her comprehension. Being inside it had been a panic-inducing nightmare. How it functioned, she had no idea – a part of her wanted to find out if runestones were involved in its locomotion, but every time she thought about the thing and its crushing, suffocating interior, her stomach clenched.

She tried to focus on Raythen's conversation with their apparent savior as he led them up a set of stairs from the buried basement they'd tunneled into.

"You knew the reason the city was sealed, but you brought us here anyway?" Raythen was exclaiming. "Didn't it cross your mind that the exiled son of King Ragnarson and two complete outsiders might end up being falsely accused of stealing the Hydra?"

"I hoped the great Raythen wouldn't just walk in through the front gates and into Ragnarson's open arms," Mavarin replied, his voice echoing back down to Astarra. "But I knew that if you did, I'd be able to get you out. I saw you in the street, with Captain Bradha. Truth is, I've always wanted to try out Garak Gaz on the citadel. I wasn't sure if she'd be able to drill her all the way through the foundations, and getting around the lake is no easy feat, but the League will be d- delighted with my findings!"

Raythen dropped into a series of Dunwarr words that Astarra took to be expletives. The stairway ended, opening up into a workshop. Benches and worktables lined the floor, heaped high with what, to Astarra, looked like junk. Strange metal devices, some of which wheezed and hissed and chugged with motion, competed for space with clear glass bottles of all shapes and sizes filled with curiously-colored liquids, and scattered mounds of books, papers and parchments. The room was dimly lit by a small, bright orb affixed to the ceiling, which Astarra took to be a miniature version of the brilliant globes that studded the roof of Thelgrim's cavern. The windows were closed and shuttered.

Mavarin strode into the room, raised his bulky goggles, and grinned through the grime befouling his lower face.

"Welcome, to the League of Invention," he exclaimed, spreading his arms wide.

Raythen, Shiver and Astarra stood at the entrance to the workshop, staring.

"This... is the League of Invention?" Astarra asked slowly. It looked every bit like the office of Professor Greysdon, one of her former tutors at Greyhaven, an infamously disorganized hoarder and collector of notes.

"Absolutely," Mavarin said, setting off once more, moving with a swift, purposeful stride. "Come, come! You all must be tired, and hungry!"

"Just follow my lead," Raythen growled to Astarra and Shiver. She rolled her eyes.

They trailed Mavarin through to a back room where a heavy-looking pot was bubbling away on an iron stove. The dwarf began to clear papers and more contraptions off the only table in the room, alternating between apologizing and swearing as one object – to Astarra it looked like a bowl with a twisted fork attached above it to a drill mechanism – tumbled off and broke.

He shoved the two rattling halves unceremoniously under the table with his boot before turning back to the trio, beaming again.

"Sit! Please, sit!"

Raythen slowly dragged out one of the chairs around the table and did so. Shiver and Astarra followed. She kept a tight grip on her staff. She could feel the energies of the Ignis responding to her touch, the unyielding barrier of the Null Stone now gone. As far as she was concerned, that was just about the only positive to come out of their new situation.

"So, are you maybe going to explain what in Fortuna's name we're doing here?" Raythen asked as Mavarin bustled about at the stove, beginning to pour what looked like thick stew and dumplings into clay bowls. The food's scent reached Astarra, and she realized just how badly her stomach ached. She'd just about recovered from throwing up over the giant burrower.

"Well, you already know the half of it," Mavarin said, as he ferried the full bowls to the table, stepping over and around the assorted books and scrap littering the floor without even glancing down at any of it. "The Hydra Shard and the device which controls it have been stolen. An act of untrammeled i-infamy! But we're going to get it back."

Raythen looked at Astarra. She didn't respond – she was now finding it difficult to think about anything other than the food being set before her.

"That's not what you hired us for," Raythen said, "if it actually was you. Which facilitator did you use?"

"Why Cayfern, of course," Mavarin said, placing the final bowl in front of Astarra. "He's the best at what he does in all of northern Terrinoth."

Astarra gazed at the stew, steaming gently in front of her. Poisoned? Worse? She realized she didn't care. She snatched up her spoon and dug in, only managing to regain a degree of control when she realized Shiver was staring at her.

The elf carefully picked up his own spoon and began to pick at his bowl, studiously avoiding the meat.

"We were hired by the League of Invention," Raythen said, ignoring his own food. "So where are they?"

"I told you, I'm the League of Invention," Mavarin said, looking nonplussed. "And this is my headquarters!"

"Where are the other members?" Raythen pressed. "You must have some sort of council or governing body?"

"Well, not really," Mavarin said, spooning a wad of stew into his mouth. "I have… two benefactors. But that's all."

Raythen appeared lost for words. It was Shiver who asked what Astarra was mustering her thoughts to say.

"You asked us here to retrieve a runestone and take it back to Frostgate," he said, easing his bowl away across the table. "This runestone doesn't exist, does it?"

"Well, not exactly," Mavarin said slowly. Astarra set her spoon down in her bowl.

"It doesn't exist?" she repeated coldly, glaring at him.

"Well, in a sense it does," the dwarf said, having the good sense to at least look shame-faced. "I mean, there are all m-manner of runestones in Thelgrim. The Runescribers' Guild have over a dozen, and King Ragnarson no fewer! I can guarantee that once we return the Hydra to him, he'll make a gift of at least one to you!"

"You can guarantee no such thing," Astarra growled, her chair scraping as she rose. She wasn't going to be taken for a fool by another dwarf, not after having been led on what now seemed like such a pointless, dangerous chase. She had come here to progress her abilities, not be led on by Dunwarr lies. Mavarin's eyes widened.

"Astarra…" Raythen started to say, a warning note in his voice, but she wasn't listening. She was reaching out, using the runebound shard to slide into the universal power of the Turning. She cracked the bottom of her staff off the stone floor. The volcanic shard lit up with the power of the runestone beneath it.

"Now just wait," Mavarin said, standing up so quickly he knocked his chair over with a clatter.

"You lied to us," Astarra hissed, striding around the table towards him. "You lured us here, into your trap. And now what? You want us to help you retrieve the Hydra? Why would we do that?"

She half expected the Dunwarr to quail before her, but he stood his ground, the fire from her staff glinting in his eyes.

"You'll help me because, without me, you'll never leave this city," he said, with a degree of determination she hadn't anticipated.

"I wouldn't threaten her if I were you," Raythen said softy. Astarra sensed Shiver rising behind her, but his ice magics remained untapped.

She let the fire run down her staff, her hands untouched by the flames.

"I could sear the flesh from your bones right here and now, you devious little Dunwarr," she said.

"You c- could," Mavarin said, standing his ground. "And then what? The whole of Thelgrim has been locked down until the thief is found. The Warriors' Guild patrol the streets. And something tells me you won't be trying to pilot Garak Gaz out from underneath their feet."

"Trust me, we'll think of something," Raythen said.

"Don't you want to return the Hydra to the tomb of Holburg?" Mavarin asked. "It's an object of near-unlimited p- potential. Whoever controls it could likely rule all of Terrinoth."

He looked directly at Astarra as he spoke. She let his insinuations burn up in the heat of her anger. It was taking a conscious effort not to engulf the Dunwarr in fire.

"Why are you so concerned with its whereabouts?" Shiver

asked, moving to stand alongside Astarra, hemming Mavarin in. She noticed that a rind of ice had started to form over his bony, clasped hands, steaming gently in the heat being generated by the Ignis.

"Everyone in Thelgrim is concerned about the loss of the Hydra," Mavarin said evasively.

"But not enough to defy their king and seek outside help," Raythen said, latching on to Shiver's line of questioning. "Not enough to lure a trio of adventurers here to help with its recovery. Ragnarson seems to have the whole city either shut away or bent to finding it, so what could we three, two of us outsiders, possibly offer in the way of help?"

He'd risen to his feet and joined the other two. Mavarin was surrounded, the stove to his back, his eyes darting from one to the other. He held his hands in the air.

"Fine. I want to be the one to find it! I know where it is. I just don't have the ability to get there and return with it alive."

"Did you take it?" Astarra demanded, her flames flaring with a crackling snarl. Mavarin's evasiveness reminded her of a less polished version of Raythen, and she had neither the will nor desire to entertain devious Dunwarr tricksters any longer. She had placed her faith in others for too long. From now on, she was taking matters into her own hands.

"No," Mavarin exclaimed, looking horrified. "But I have a d- device, an invention that can pinpoint runestones and unbound shards. I believe I've found it, in the deepling tunnels of the western wall, but I d- dare not go any further alone, and no one else will believe me!"

"What's stopping you from getting to it?" Raythen asked. Mavarin shot him a look, as though it was obvious.

"The deep elves," he said. "They're abroad in numbers unseen for generations. They're the ones who have taken the Hydra. They rove the deeper tunnels in daggerbands that will cut me to pieces if they find me."

"Why would deep elves steal this Star and its device?" Shiver demanded, his cool reserve seemingly strained by the accusation.

"Why are they roving the tunnels at all?" Mavarin responded. "They've even been attacking g- groups of Dunwarr who break the lockdown. Leaving no survivors."

Astarra sensed Raythen glance sideways at Shiver. Presumably he was thinking the same as her, recalling the deep elf ambush on the Hearth Road. That part of Mavarin's story, at least, seemed backed up by evidence, even if Shiver didn't like it.

"I need the Hydra," Mavarin went on, wringing his hands. "It calls to me! It's my destiny to recover it!"

"And use it for yourself?" Raythen asked sharply.

"To return it to its rightful resting place," Mavarin said. "The reward is what I seek. The recognition. Here I am Mavarin the Tinkerer, just an unhinged curiosity, a nuisance to the formal guilds. They deny the genius of my work and the potential it could unlock. But if my inventions and my initiative reclaim the mighty Hydra, despite the best efforts of the rest of the city to do the same, they will have to take notice. They'll approve the status of the League as its own guild! I'll have access to funds, a seat at the council, the respect of my peers!"

"And we get to walk out of Thelgrim alive?" Astarra asked fiercely, in no way enamored by the dwarf's suggestion. It reminded her too much of her own intentions of using the Hydra herself. It stung her anger. If the Dunwarr really thought she was going to help him out of kindness alone, he was mistaken. "Assuming we survive your little quest. It doesn't sound like a shared incentive."

"I have n- no doubt you'll be rewarded as well," Mavarin said. "The king is beside himself over the Hydra's loss. Its return will see you given whatever you desire from Thelgrim's wealth."

"You clearly don't know my father very well," Raythen said.

"I told you, go if you so wish," Mavarin said. "I leave tomorrow for the Western Deeps. In the meantime, you are welcome to rest here. It seems as though you all need the sleep."

He dared offer a small smile to the three.

Astarra glared down at the Dunwarr, but she couldn't deny what he said. She was running on anger and determination. None of them had had a moment's rest since reaching the Hearth Road.

"If you try and double-cross us, inventor, we'll burn you, freeze you, and deposit you into the Blackwater's depths in tiny little pieces," Raythen growled.

"If you double-cross us *again,*" Astarra corrected, not taking her eyes off Mavarin. He offered them a hasty bow.

"I'll do everything in my power to repair the trust I seem to have b- broken," he said grandly. "But in the meantime, maybe we can finish the stew?"

After they had consumed the entire contents of the pot, Mavarin took them up another flight of stairs and showed them into an attic room. The small, stone-cut area was as jumbled and littered with discarded objects as the rest of the inventor's property, but what floor space there was had at least been covered with straw. The Dunwarr provided several blankets, told them he would be downstairs, and bade them sleep well.

As soon as the door was shut, Raythen strode over to the room's only window, doing his best not to dislodge piles of junk as he went. The square opening had been cut into the natural rock of the wall, and while it was too small for any of them to fit through, it at least offered an indication of where they were. He stood on his tiptoes and peered through.

Mavarin's workshop appeared to have been dug into the base of one of the stalagmites facing onto the featureless expanse of the Blackwater. Across the lake from them stood the grandeur of the Guild Hall, but the curve of the rock formation hid the Dunwol Kenn Karnin from view. The workshop itself was the level below, facing onto the street that lay against the Blackwater's still banks.

The roadway was deserted, standing silent in the eternal, soft glitter that lit the subterranean city. Raythen had half expected to see troops of guild warriors tramping past, hunting for them. Wherever they were looking though, it didn't seem to be in such immediate proximity to the Dunwol Kenn Karnin. Hiding in almost plain sight was an old one, it would do for now. He closed his eyes and lent his head against the edge of the window.

He had panicked, back at the upper dungeon, and he was ashamed of it. He'd known it was possible he would encounter his father when he'd accepted the offer Cayfern had laid out in Frostgate, but somehow he hadn't imagined it would be this bad. He cursed himself for not picking up on the real risks. One last payoff, he'd told himself, knowing there was really no such thing in his line of work.

A part of him had wanted to see home, he now realized. To discover what had changed, drawn deeper by the mystery of the city's silence. He had behaved like a beardless youngling on his first contract, and this was where it had gotten him, shut up with two outsiders above the workshop of some radical tinkerer. He never wanted to see Thelgrim's gemstone-encrusted streets and arching cavern walls again.

"Anything out there?" Astarra asked, joining him at the window. He looked up at her and huffed.

"Nothing that can help us," he said, before leaving her to gaze down onto the street. He moved across the room, trying to work the ache from his limbs and shoulders. His body was stiff and sore, so he could only imagine how she felt. Dunwarr didn't tire easily, and hunger and fatigue were usually strangers to their hardy constitution. Deep elves, in their own way, needed little of either food or sleep – he'd heard it said that they could draw directly on the etheric energies their people were instinctively attuned to, using it to revitalize themselves in times of need. He didn't know how much of that was true, but Shiver seemed to have been able to match him so far. Astarra, however, looked bone-weary. Even the light of her staff had burned down to a dull, faint glow.

"We should rest," Raythen said, choosing a spot on the straw-scattered floor and picking up one of the blanket rolls Mavarin had left them. "Sleep. We can decide what to do about… all of this, tomorrow."

"Should one of us keep watch?" Astarra asked, turning away

from the window. "I don't trust that Dunwarr. He could have anything planned for us."

"I'll stay up first," Raythen said, grunting as he lowered himself to the floor. "Then Shiver, then you."

He glanced over at the deep elf for his assent, and was surprised to see him sat with his back propped against several stacks of books, slumped slightly to one side, eyes shut and mouth open. He was making a faint rasping noise which, after a moment, Raythen realized was snoring.

He caught Astarra's eye and couldn't help but chuckle.

"Looks like even cursed deep elves need their rest," he said. "I'll wake you when the time comes, runewitch."

CHAPTER ELEVEN

"Show me this device," Raythen said.

"F- Fine, fine," Mavarin exclaimed, delving into the rucksack he'd hefted up onto the table.

Shiver was only half listening. He'd picked up one of the pieces of erstwhile scrap lying on the floor around them. At first glance it was a large, dented copper pot with a closed lid, but closer inspection revealed something metallic coiled in its bottom. He sniffed at it and turned it over carefully in his long, pale fingers, trying to sense its purpose.

"I call it the tuner. You turn it like this, and it gives you a reading," Mavarin was saying. He'd produced a small, metallic box attached to what appeared to be a repurposed axe haft. Raythen was peering at the series of dials and switches on its face, clearly nonplussed.

"If this is supposed to be able to show us to runeshards, it should be sensing hers," he said, pointing to Astarra, who was sitting across the table from them eating a wedge of Dunwarr gritbread and goat's cheese.

"It is," Mavarin said, tapping one of the twitching dials.

"See? It's telling us this room has high dormant readings for the Turning. It's a sure indicator of runebound shards. A Star of Timmoran will be off the scale. That's how I was able to locate its presence from the edge of the city."

"It makes no sense to me," Raythen grumbled. "What happens if you're killed out there in the tunnels? How're we supposed to find the exact location of the Hydra without understanding this ticking metal box?"

"Well, the e- easiest solution would be to make sure I don't get killed," Mavarin said with a smile.

He smiled a lot. Shiver had noticed that. It was not the sort of false expression he had sometimes seen humans or dwarfs use to mask lies and hostility, but it was not warm and genuine either. It was a mask to cover what Shiver felt was uncertainty. To the elf, the supposed inventor seemed perpetually on the cusp of surging emotions, and few of them positive.

He placed the copper coil-pot gently back down on the floor where he'd found it.

"How far do you think the Hydra is then?" Astarra asked, washing down the last of the gritbread with a gulp of ale. She had recovered much of her spirit after the night's rest. The reserve that had wavered before the baleful power of the Null Stone was back in place, the fire beneath it rekindled. To Shiver's own surprise, it saddened him. He had found himself wondering what it was that drove the runewitch, what had really made her take up this task in the first place. Certainly, there was more to it than the simple desire for strength and power she had spoken of before.

"No more than half a day's journey into the deeps," Mavarin said, in answer to Astarra's question.

"More importantly, in which direction?" Raythen asked.

"Beyond the western cavern wall," Mavarin said, beginning to pack away the device he claimed would help them pinpoint the Hydra.

"Along the Running Deep, or up and into the old tin mine?" Raythen asked, clearly unimpressed with the incomplete answer.

"The latter," Mavarin said, settling his goggles on his head. "Then down, through the Wailing Gap and into the prospector tunnels beyond."

"I thought those tunnels had been sealed off?" Raythen said.

"The barriers are long broken down," Mavarin responded. "By who or what, I have no idea. All that matters is that's where I picked up traces of the Hydra."

Raythen said nothing more, though Shiver could sense his discomfort. They'd spoken that morning about the possibility of getting out, of abandoning both Mavarin and his self-centered quest. Shiver had concluded that there were no better options than their current course. None of them had any idea how to pilot the strange burrowing device, and that left only the northern and southern entrances to Thelgrim. The latter included the chasm bridge and its fortress, a riddle which even Raythen couldn't solve, while the former consisted of another fortress and, beyond it, a warren of tunnels called the Northern Deeps that were presumably as heavily patrolled by both Dunwarr and deep elves as the Hearth Road. Besides, that way would only take them deeper into the Dunwarrs.

They'd decided to follow Mavarin, for now. Shiver could read the discontent that option caused in his companions.

For his own part, he was considering departing when they reached the tunnels. It was clear Mavarin had lied about having more locks for him. He had little reason to stay, beyond the fact that he was curious about the activities of the local deep elf clans. He kept remembering the ambush on the Hearth Road, not only the death of the one who had come for him, but also the strange sense of connection he had felt with them all. It was almost akin to recognition, as though he'd known them before. It was an uncomfortable realization, but not one that was wholly alien to him. Many times, some buried part of his consciousness latched onto something that had been driven from his memories. Not everything had been cast out by the purging of his mind on the day he'd been freed.

He feared that, despite having no memory of it, he'd been here before.

Raythen was still pressing Mavarin.

"How are you intending to get to the western wall anyway?" he demanded. "We're still in the middle of Thelgrim. The streets are practically deserted, except for the Warriors' Guild. My father will have everyone out looking for us. I doubt it'll take them long to track us here."

"Simple, really," Mavarin said, casting a mischievous glance at Astarra. "We're leaving the same way we got in."

It almost took physical force to convince Astarra to get back into the burrower. In the end, she had called up a meditative trance she hadn't utilized since studying at Greyhaven. It just about made the crushing, shuddering, suffocating experience bearable.

This time, when she stumbled from the hatch, she wasn't sick. The stale air of the old mining tunnel they'd broken into could have been the freshness of her homestead's orchard as far as she was concerned.

"You'll get u- used to it," Mavarin said with his ready grin.

She didn't respond. A part of her hated the strange Dunwarr. She forced herself not to snap back as he drew his tuning device from his bag and started to consult it.

Raythen had lit a torch, and was now crouching by the burrower, priming his hand bow. Shiver stood, apparently as serene as ever, gazing at the mud-caked machine, as though trying to discern the mechanisms that gave it power and motion. Astarra made a point of not looking at it, instead lowering her staff and carefully unfixing the volcanic rock from its tip. She removed it and slipped it into her waist satchel, plucking out the Ignis after it. It was hot to the touch, and she almost shuddered as she freed it – it had been in there for too long. She found that if she used a single rune shard over an extended period – especially the Ignis – its essence began to seep into her soul. It was exactly the sort of risk her teachers had warned her about at Greyhaven. Contact with the Turning via it was a two-way process. After a while, the Ignis Shard would leave her feeling burned-out and hostile, her soul blackened and scorched like the rock shard that helped channel it, her throat parched, skin dry, soul blistered and angry.

Down here it was tempting to stick with the shard, to rely on the light it cast on the strange, dark realm she had found herself in. She knew she'd been relying on it for too long though. She had to break free. She needed the change, the regeneration, that her other runes offered her.

She pulled the Viridis Seed from the satchel. The size and shape of a small, smooth pebble, it was inscribed with a spiral marking. As soon as she slipped it into her palm, she felt its power, like the rush of a warm, summer breeze sweeping through the dank tunnel. It reminded her of home.

She slotted it into her staff, seeing how the inscribed tusker bone had become blackened and cracked from the constant heat of the Ignis. It would reknit and heal over time, just like the blackened edges of her soul.

She followed the Viridis with the small knot of heartoak root she kept in the satchel. It fitted above the pebble, slotting into the head of the staff. The warm wind blew again, invisible to her companions. She could breathe once more.

If the power of the runebound shard showed on Mavarin's tuning device, he didn't give any indication of it. He had paced a little way up the tunnel, bent over the metal box.

"Set?" Raythen asked, glancing up at Astarra. She nodded, even smiled.

"Being in that burrowing engine makes me appreciate open tunnels more," she said. Raythen chuckled and stood, throwing his cloak back over his shoulder and picking up his torch.

"What about you?" he asked, looking at Shiver. The elf said nothing, but inclined his head, his expression as serious as ever.

"I'm picking up strong readings," Mavarin called back down the tunnel, waving them forward. "We've b- broken through in the right place!"

"Well, that's a start," Astarra heard Raythen mutter under his breath. She hefted her staff, feeling the life energies flowing through her, and followed the Dunwarr as he tramped after his erstwhile kin, torch held high.

The tunnel the burrower had penetrated seemed to be an artery route for what Raythen had described as the western extent of Thelgrim's past mining activities. It was narrow, but just high enough for Astarra to walk straight, and Shiver if he maintained his slight, natural stoop. The walls were bare dirt, held in check by timber hoardings and occasional iron girders. It was musty and stale, as though it had been closed up for a long time. Cobwebs hung heavy from the struts that ribbed the ceiling, ghostly white in the torchlight. It was certainly a far cry from the splendor of the great cavern city they'd left behind, or the spacious, well-lit route of the Hearth Road. For the first time since leaving the crevasses that had brought them in from the valley, Astarra felt as though she was truly underground.

They traveled along the tunnel as it sloped, first up, then down. The sounds of their footfalls and their breathing felt unnaturally loud and intrusive. She found herself recalling the time she'd hunted for a Null Stone in the ancient ruins of Sudanya. It had been a city once, but at the time it had felt more like a tomb.

"Do you sense anything?" she found herself hissing back at Shiver. Just days ago, sharing the dilapidated tunnel with the gaunt elf sorcerer would have made her skin crawl. She still felt a twinge of discomfort with him following directly behind her, but the aura of darkness he seemed to have exuded when they'd first met no longer weighed quite as heavily. She supposed it was because she had seen him exposed, seen him vulnerable before the Null Stone. They'd shared that same trauma, an assault not only on their souls but upon their connection to the magics of Mennara, different though they may be. He was no longer quite the black-eyed, raggedy ghast she had seen before.

"There is something nearby, yes," the elf said, his voice a soft susurration in the passageway. "In the subsidiary tunnels, nearby."

"Something?" Raythen echoed. "What sort of something?"

"I'm not sure yet," Shiver responded.

They carried on. Mavarin would pause every so often and peer at the tuner. Astarra had been thinking about it since he'd showed it to them. As far as she was concerned the Dunwarr was insane, but despite the fact that his workshop appeared full of hundreds of useless, failed experiments, there was evidence he could craft strange wonders. The burrower, though horrifying, stifling and seemingly temperamental, was proof of success, as were the strange little orbs that lit his property's interior. If he really had invented a device that let him hunt down runestones, even unbound shards, then the possibilities were boundless. She'd been thinking of ways to acquire the device since he'd explained it to them.

"How close are we?" Raythen asked the inventor as he paused once more.

"Close," was all he said. They'd just passed several side-tunnels. Astarra had tapped into the power of the Viridis, the rune of growth making it seem as though the energy of every ancient, powerful forest in Mennara was transfusing her, making her senses keener, her reflexes sharper. She half expected death to come leaping from the shadows of those openings once more, daggers drawn and flesh pale in the torchlight.

"There's a crossroads up ahead," Mavarin said, setting off once more. "The Hydra Shard lies just b- beyond it."

The tunnel reached an end, branching out into a confluence of four. The passages to the left and the right were smaller than the one they had come through, only large enough for a crouched dwarf to easily navigate. The third, however, was much larger and included a set of rail lines that terminated at the crossroads. Astarra assumed it would once have been used to haul carts filled with ore up from one of the primary work shafts. It was nearly as wide as the Hearth Road, but its construction was as basic as the other tunnels around it.

They followed Mavarin to the center of the crossroads. He turned in a circle, looking down at his device, then seemed to decide on a direction. Astarra watched with guarded interest as he strode up to what appeared to be a solid wall.

"It's on the other side of this," he said, finally lowering the tuner and looking up at them.

"What, you mean buried?" Astarra asked. As tantalizing as the possibility of recovering a Shard of Timmoran was, she didn't much fancy going back for shovels and picks. "You think someone hid it here to retrieve it later?"

"Perhaps," Mavarin said evasively, placing his free hand on the bare earthen wall. "I think there's some sort of cavern or space beyond here."

He threw a questioning look back at Raythen, who joined him. Like Mavarin, he placed a hand against the rough wall, then leaned forward and pressed one ear against it.

"I think you're right," he murmured.

"How can you tell?" Astarra asked, feeling excluded.

"We're Dunwarr," Mavarin said.

"You're not miners though," Astarra went on, struggling to grasp just how innate their understanding of the rock and soil of the mountain was. She supposed it was built into their very being, the way old mister Dellin, who had collected apples from her family's orchard when she had been a child, had been able to predict the exact day the first southwing flocks would be sighted or when the gladeblossoms would flower.

"Miners are just Dunwarr who were never good at any real crafts," Raythen said. Mavarin chuckled, as though they'd just shared some sort of private dwarven jest.

"We need to split this open," the inventor declared, pulling off his pack and bending forward to rummage in it. Astarra watched as he drew out a trio of fist-sized orbs made from black metal. Each had a small hole at the top, through which Mavarin poured a strange, black powder from the nozzle of what Astarra had taken to be a drinking horn.

"What sort of mad devices are those?" she asked. Mavarin looked at her askance for a moment, then smiled.

"Oh, these aren't my inventions, sadly," he said, continuing to fill the black orbs. "They're blasting charges."

Astarra looked at Raythen, who nodded in confirmation.

"They're used by the Miners' Guild," he explained. "The black firedust combusts when lit."

"It explodes?" Astarra asked, trying to picture just what the dwarfs were cooking up. "But won't we be buried alive? What if it collapses the tunnels?"

"Not with three charges it won't, not if they're placed against an upper subsidiary wall like this one," Mavarin said, glancing up at Raythen. The thief had again pressed his head against the tunnel wall, as though listening to secrets being whispered by the rock.

"I'd say you're right," he said. "But no more than three, and we should head down that rail tunnel while you light the fuse. That'll offer us enough blast dispersal."

"Well, I only brought three anyway," Mavarin said with a shrug, fitting what seemed to be a length of match cord into one of the orb's holes.

Astarra looked towards Shiver, hoping he was as confounded by the dwarf activity as she was. To her surprise, she found him ignoring all of them. He was standing directly in front of the wide rail tunnel, staring ahead, framed by the darkness beyond it.

Astarra glanced back at Raythen and Mavarin, but they were both too busy fussing over the explosives. She took a step towards the elf.

"Shiver?" she said softly. He didn't move.

She realized that the temperature in the tunnels had started to drop.

It was down there, somewhere, waiting.

The darkness in front of Shiver was absolute. It wasn't merely the absence of light, the struggles of Raythen's torch to penetrate the rail tunnel. The shadows in there were hungry, and they consumed anything they touched. Deep elf or not, Shiver's eyes were unable to see more than a few feet. It was as though a thick, black shroud had been hung across the entranceway.

And worse, there was something whispering behind it. It was right on the cusp of his delicate hearing, the faintest murmur. He was sure he could hear it one moment, then doubted himself the next. It was all at once frustrating and unnerving.

He tried to turn away but found he could not. The darkness was all-consuming. Was it the darkness itself, and not those in it, that was whispering to him?

"*What are you waiting for*?" murmured the voice in his ear. Her voice, always there, always goading, taunting and, worst of all, commanding.

He shivered.

A hand clutched his shoulder and he turned, an arcane word locked on the edge of his lips, a moment away from reaching into the Sphere of Dreams. But it wasn't her. It was Astarra.

The runewitch let go and took a sharp step back, her staff raised in a defensive grip. Shiver realized his hand was rimed with frost. He let out a slow, shuddering breath, clouding in the cold air, and closed his eyes.

"What's going on?" Astarra demanded, her words shattering the stillness he was attempting to regain.

"Nothing," he snapped, feeling a sudden, vicious surge of anger as he opened his eyes once more. "It's nothing!"

She looked as though she'd been stung. Raythen and Mavarin both glanced up from their work. He felt an immediate stab of shame. His anger evaporated, gone as quickly as it had appeared.

"I'm sorry," he said, looking away from Astarra. "I… think I was having another memory."

"Of this place?" Astarra asked.

"That's not always how they work," Shiver said. "I told you, I haven't been here before."

She didn't look like she believed him. He knew he shouldn't be surprised – he wasn't sure he believed himself, not anymore. He kept his expression stoic, not wanting to hint at his rising concerns. It would do no good to burden the others with them.

"The deep elves, are they close?" Raythen asked from over by the wall. Shiver took a second to ensure his thoughts were steady and balanced once more before reaching out again into the Aenlong, sensing the other nearby souls touching it.

"Yes," he said.

"And getting closer?"

"Perhaps. This is… not a good place. We should hurry."

"That'll do," Mavarin said to Raythen, indicating the spacing of the black orbs they'd planted at the base of the tunnel wall. "Get back with the other two, I'll light the fuse."

Raythen handed Mavarin his torch and strode over to Astarra and Shiver.

"We should take shelter," he said. "Cover your ears with your hands, but leave your mouths open. You'll lose your hearing otherwise."

He didn't wait for a response but ushered them both towards the rail tunnel. Shiver froze.

"What is it?" Raythen asked, noticing his refusal to move. He glanced towards the tunnel. "Is there something down there?"

Shiver stared at it. He was looking for the hungry, whispering blackness, but it was gone. The tunnel lay before them, the rail track disappearing off into the shadows beyond the torchlight. He reached out into the Empyrean, carefully probing at it. There was nothing though. It was just an empty tunnel.

"It's fine," he said, trying to sound convincing, trying to convince himself.

"Well, come on then," Raythen snapped, hauling the pair along the tracks. Shiver could sense a new, nervous energy about the Dunwarr, an excitement that had overcome the gloom and dismay which seemed to have beset him in Thelgrim. He was back on familiar ground, doing what he did best and liked most – hunting for the next payout.

He hustled them into the rail tunnel and told them to stay back from the entrance. Shiver forced himself not to stare down into the darkness, looking back instead towards the junction. The wall where the blasting charges had been planted was now out of sight, as was Mavarin, but a serpentine hiss followed by the sound of running footsteps announced his return. He bolted in beside them, goggles down, as the others covered their ears.

Shiver didn't bother. He summoned up a frigid void, a sphere that encased him and momentarily dislocated him from the tunnel, shifting his essence into the Empyrean itself. He was aware of the blast in the same way that a sleeper, jolting upright, was aware of the dream that had awoken him. It was distant and ephemeral.

The spell lasted only for a few heartbeats. He dropped it, the cold evaporating. He was back in the midst of a tunnel now choked with smoke and dirt. All three of his companions were coughing and cursing around him. He looked down and brushed dislodged earth from the front of his robes.

"Did it work?" he asked.

It took some time for anyone to respond. Mavarin, his goggles raised once more, stumbled out into what remained of the crossroads and waved them out after him. Dirt and shattered stone covered the floor, and a steaming gap had been blasted in the wall. The neighboring timber supports had bent and splintered, and the ceiling over the gap was sagging, but holding.

Raythen approached the hole they had blown, still coughing, batting at the smoke and dust filling the space. Shiver glanced at Astarra. She was still clutching at one ear, her face creased with pain.

"Are you alright?" he asked her, considering offering her what healing energies she could draw from the Empyrean. She hesitated, looking at his lips, and he realized her ears were probably still ringing from the blast. She shook her head.

"There's a cavern back here," Raythen was saying, holding his hand out for Mavarin's torch. "Air's good enough. Come on."

CHAPTER TWELVE

Raythen stepped through the blast hole, torch aloft, peering through the settling dust.

They'd breached into a natural rock chamber. It was a little larger than Mavarin's workshop, its floor and ceiling uneven and jagged with geological disruption. At first Raythen thought it had been completely sealed off until the blast had opened it, but as he advanced, the light of the torch picked out a narrow passageway in the far wall, leading away into the dark.

Mavarin pushed past him, the inventor's eyes fixed on the center of the chamber, on a small plinth of natural rock. He strode up to it and bent over, staring.

"By the ancestors," Raythen heard him mutter. He hurried to the inventor's side, heart racing. He couldn't help himself – it was always the same on a big job. Being this close to success always left him jagged with excitement and nervousness. It was the sort of thing that, were it not for his experience, would've made him a bad thief, but it always kept him coming back for more. It was addictive.

"Where's the Star?" he demanded as Mavarin cast about the rock he'd pinpointed.

"I d- don't know," the inventor hissed, his movements becoming more frantic. "I- it should be here."

"What does the tuner say?" Raythen asked, feeling a pang of desperation. "You said it was close!"

"Hang the tuner," Mavarin shouted abruptly, his voice echoing through the craggy chamber. "I'm telling you, it's gone! It's not here!"

Raythen felt a sudden urge to draw his hand bow and point it at Mavarin. Anger and frustration burned inside him, the dark afterglow of the failure to land the score. He snatched Mavarin and pulled him eye-to-eye.

"Is this another of your little tricks?" he snarled. "Because I'm warning you, you don't double cross me. I'm the double crosser here, beardless one."

Mavarin roughly threw off Raythen's hand, uncowed and seemingly just as furious as the thief.

"I th- thought it was here," he said. "But if it was, it's gone now."

"Can't you track it?" Astarra demanded as she walked into the chamber. She appeared to have recovered from the shock of the breaching blast. Her expression was as dark as Raythen's. "Use that invention and follow where it went?"

"It isn't that simple," Mavarin said, his voice riven with exasperation. "The tuner can only follow something like the Hydra so far."

"You didn't tell us that before," Raythen said incredulously, resisting the urge to grab the tinkerer by the scruff of the neck and shake him.

"We're about to have companions," Shiver said before Astarra could respond. He was standing by the blast hole, looking back into the debris-littered junction. "Two separate daggerbands, closing fast. The explosion will have alerted more."

"Let's get out of here," Astarra suggested. "We can sort this mess out when we aren't trapped in a cavern surrounded by murderous elves."

Raythen wanted to argue, but he checked himself. He was in too deep, had been drawn on by the potential of one of the greatest finds of his career. Whatever was going on, the Hydra wasn't here. Now wasn't the time for desperate last stands in empty caverns.

Ignoring Mavarin, he strode for the blast hole.

No one spoke during the return to Thelgrim, and Astarra suspected it wasn't just because they were enduring the juddering, claustrophobic intensity of the burrower's interior. Her own frustration proved a powerful tonic to the discomfort generated by the strange mode of transport. Even the steady rhythms of the Turning being exuded by the Viridis couldn't calm her seething thoughts.

She was certain she'd been betrayed, though just how or by whom, she wasn't yet sure.

Mavarin hauled on his levers and brought the engine to an unsteady halt. He popped his side door as Astarra stood and opened the hatch. They were back in the workshop basement, the front half of the burrower extending through the entrance tunnel it re-ploughed whenever it left and returned. She dropped down, staff in hand, wincing at the cramp that had worked its way into her thighs while she'd been penned in the cursed machine.

Raythen had already followed Mavarin out of his hatch and was interrogating him again. He seemed even angrier than Astarra, though a part of her wondered if it was just for show. What if he'd made some sort of pact with his fellow Dunwarr in exchange for the Star, or had slipped it in the cavern amidst the dust and smoke?

"We're going to go upstairs, and you're going to tell me exactly what happened back there," Raythen was growling.

"You were with me, you saw exactly what happened," Mavarin said, throwing his hands. "The Hydra was gone!"

"Then why did you think it was there in the first place? Show me that cursed little box again."

"Now may not be the best time for this," Shiver said, dropping down lithely next to Astarra from the back of the mud-caked burrower.

"Why?" Raythen and Mavarin asked in unison, rounding on him.

They'd barely spoken before a shuddering report rang down the stairs leading up to the workshop.

"That's why," Shiver said.

Astarra saw an unguarded look of fear pass over Mavarin's face. Without another word, he turned and hurried up the stairs. Raythen followed, looking more like he was chasing the inventor than trying to gain the stairs himself.

"What is it?" Astarra asked Shiver.

"Dunwarr," the elf said. They both began to follow.

The main door out onto the street lay at the far end of the workshop. Its back was heavy with complex locking mechanisms, a fact Astarra was abruptly thankful for as the whole thing shuddered in its frame. Another booming impact rang through the room.

Mavarin had approached the door and eased open a small metal covering. He peered through it, then leapt back with a yelp just before the door shook again.

"They've found us," he hissed. "They've tracked us down. I didn't think they'd manage it so soon!"

"Ragnarson?" Raythen asked. Astarra noticed how pale he'd gone. She felt her own pulse quicken, memories of the bitter Dunwarr king and his grim fortress returning. She had no wish to fall into his clutches again.

"Even worse," Mavarin said. Before he could go on, a muffled voice called out from beyond the door.

"We know you're in there. Open this door, in the name of the king!"

Astarra recognized one of the twins that had accompanied Ragnarson in the citadel dungeon, his white-bearded advisors.

"Korri," Raythen growled, then looked at Mavarin. "There must be another way out."

"There's a passage through the neighboring block," the inventor said. "But what about my work? They'll destroy it, or worse, take it! Do you know how many people want to steal my ideas? There's a reason there are so many locks on that door! The Miners' Guild, the Runescribers, the Brewers' Guild–"

Raythen cuffed the rambling inventor round the ear, cutting him short.

"No one cares about your inventions," he snapped. "Where's the passage?" As though to underline his words, there was another booming impact against the door. One of the locks ruptured.

"I- It's behind the cooling block," he stammered, pointing at a large metallic box that Astarra had assumed was a safe or strongbox.

"The what?" Raythen asked, clearly confused. Mavarin had already dashed over to it and was straining at one corner.

"Help me shift it," he hissed. Astarra and Raythen hurried to his side. To her surprised, she found the box cold to the touch.

Together they heaved the block to one side, scraping it across the stone floor. Behind it lay a split in the wall, a crack in the natural bedrock the workshop had been carved into. It was just wide enough for them to fit into sideways.

"Where does it lead?" Raythen asked, urgency warring with suspicion.

"The Gundafs, they live next door," Mavarin said, glancing back as another blow shook the whole workshop, making the various piles of detritus rattle.

"You surely knew they'd come here sooner rather than later?" Raythen demanded, waving Astarra back round the other side of the cold, metal block. She made sure Shiver was following. "Who else has the ability to tunnel in under the Dunwol Kenn Karnin and break prisoners from the upper dungeon?"

"The Miners' Guild for a start," Mavarin said, squeezing his way into the crack. "And every other guild they trade with, which is all of them."

"They're going to know where we've gone when they break in," Astarra pointed out as she followed the two Dunwarr into the gap, holding her staff close to her body and trying not to think about how narrow the space was. The cooling block was still off to one side, leaving the hole in the wall uncovered.

"I knew I should have put it on runners," Mavarin said, peering past Raythen and Astarra at Shiver as he joined them. "Can your magics put it back in place?

"No," Shiver said, his voice amazingly – almost annoyingly – calm despite what was unfolding around him. "But I can create a different, temporary barrier."

"That might help," Mavarin said. Astarra could already see light at the end of the narrow passage – it was barely a dozen yards long.

A crash shook that stone around her, coating them in dust and making her ears ring. She flinched instinctively, remembering the terrible detonation that had occurred in the tunnels. She suspected the very same devices Raythen and Mavarin had deployed had just been used by those attempting to gain access to the workshop.

Shiver had raised both hands and was murmuring something under his breath. Astarra sensed the temperature drop just as she heard a banging sound from the opposite end of the passage. She shuffled along after Raythen and Mavarin as best she could, silently cursing herself for taking on a job that would obviously require a cool head in tight spaces. At the far end she found Mavarin kicking at a series of boardings covering the exit, light streaming through the cracks.

"What's Shiver doing?" Raythen demanded, trying to see past Astarra as she in turn tried to see past him at what Mavarin was contending with.

"Blocking the way," she answered, looking back. Shiver was covering the workshop end of the passage with a layer of ice, a heavy wedge of bristling shards that gleamed with the light refracting through it. She could hear voices beyond it, shouting, and abruptly the light was blocked out as a shape loomed at the opposite end. There was a cracking sound as a blow was struck against the conjured obstruction, splits running through the barrier.

At the same time, the boards covering the opposite end gave way. Mavarin fought his way through, Raythen shoving him from behind. Astarra went out after them, ducking under the remaining boards and raising her staff, snarling one of the words of power that awoke the Viridis.

That was before she was fully aware of what was waiting for them all on the other side. A trio of Dunwarr – a man, a woman, and a little, plump baby – were sitting around a table in a small but well-furnished room, eating what was presumably their breakfast. Mavarin had just led the charge into their home, bursting through a boarded-up section of wall. Confronted by the dusty, wild-looking four, the family simply sat and stared, cutlery poised, eyes wide. The baby let out a giggle.

"Sorry, Mister and Misses Gundaf," Mavarin said before hurrying across the living space and throwing the bolt on the far door. Raythen followed without so much as glancing at the family, but Astarra couldn't help but give a little, apologetic shrug as she crossed by after them. She made eye contact with Mister Gundaf as she passed, and saw shock giving way to anger.

"Mavarin!" the Dunwarr roared, rising to his feet. The inventor was too busy unlocking the Gundaf family front door to respond. Shiver hesitated, seemingly torn between walling up the breach with more ice, apologizing to the family they'd just burst in on, and following Mavarin. Astarra grabbed him by the collar of his robes and dragged him towards the now-open door.

Mavarin and Raythen lead the way out into the street. She noticed the latter had drawn his hand bow again. For her own part, Astarra's heart was racing. She could feel the energies of the Viridis stone responding, sharpening her thoughts, her strength, her speed. The ancient life-giver knew they were all in peril.

The street outside was almost full. The slight curve of the great stalagmite the Dunwarr houses had been tunneled into hid Mavarin's own front door, and whatever was happening there, but it seemed the king's twin advisers had been wise enough to leave a Warrior Guild reserve overlooking the street. There were half a dozen armored Dunwarr barely a dozen paces to their left.

They spotted the four. A shout went up, and Astarra began to speak, drawing forth the power of the runestone. She was interrupted by Raythen, who bundled her in the opposite direction from the group of warriors, shattering her concentration.

"Now's not the time for heroics," he said. "Just run!"

CHAPTER THIRTEEN

Mavarin had already set off along the street. Astarra followed, doing her best to ignore the unpleasant, draining sensation caused by the power she'd been drawing dissipating, unused, into the staff once more. She looked to one side to check Shiver was still with them and, almost amusingly, found the deep elf hiking up the tattered skirts of his robes so he could keep up.

There were shouts from behind them, followed by the clatter of armor and the pounding of boots. Astarra quickly gained on Mavarin and Raythen.

"Where are we going?" she shouted as they ran.

"Away from here," was all Mavarin said.

The roadway took them right, between two of the inhabited stalagmites. A single, elderly Dunwarr almost collided with them as they surged past, the sounds of their footfalls ringing back from the tiered buildings cut into the rock faces all around them.

They turned left, then right again. Mavarin came to an

abrupt halt, panting, one hand resting against the door of a shut-up alehouse.

"Why have we stopped?" Raythen demanded as the rest of them stumbled to a standstill. Astarra leant against her staff, trying to ease her breathing, her heart battering at the inside of her chest. It had been a while since she'd had to run before any pursuers – Sudanya, in fact. She was more used to standing and fighting.

"Bolt hole," Mavarin said, fumbling under his leather apron and drawing out a set of keys. He bent over the lock to the inn, cursing under his breath.

"Too late," Raythen growled, looking back. The pounding of iron-shod boots announced the Dunwarr patrol, rounding the corner.

"*Kagak*," Mavarin swore, and gave up. They started to run again.

Their path was taking them back towards what Astarra took to be the western wall of the vast city-cavern. The rocky mounts and outcrops that dominated the heart of Thelgrim were becoming smaller but more numerous, creating a rugged network of roads and pathways that wove between them. What few structures had been built into the jutting stone were smaller and poorer-looking.

"Are you really going to take us into the Cragwarren?" Raythen demanded of Mavarin as they went.

"No better place to lose an unwanted tail," Mavarin panted back.

"Or pick another one up," Raythen said.

They slowed to a trot. Astarra could still hear the sounds of pursuit, but the shouted voices of the Dunwarr were distant now, echoing strangely through the rock formations around them. Relief washed over her, bringing into sharp focus the heaviness of her breathing and the abrupt ache in her legs. She took in her new surroundings cautiously, half expecting a fresh pack of Dunwarr warriors to come charging at them from every corner.

She no longer felt as though she was in a city. The pillars and pedestals of stone around them were untouched, but for the odd, telltale sign of a small window or doorway, hacked roughly into the rock. Even the glimmer of the orbs and gems high above seemed weaker this far from the shining heart of the cavern.

"The Cragwarren runs around the edge of Thelgrim," Raythen said, apparently noticing her wary gaze. "The quality of the rock is poorer here. Only the desperate or the destitute tend to live this far out."

"Sounds like the sort of place we belong right now," Astarra said, with a hint of bitterness. Even when she'd been laying her plans on the road from Frostgate, she hadn't envisaged being hunted through Thelgrim's outskirts.

"Do either of you know where we're meant to be going?" she demanded, coming to a halt. Shiver almost collided with her back, manacles clanking as he side-stepped.

"She has a point," Raythen said, stopping too and looking at Mavarin. The beardless inventor was flushed and slick with sweat.

"The Plummets," he said, wheezing. "I have another bolt hole there, among the old mine shafts. One last refuge, in case of an emergency."

"Well, I think it's safe to say that's what this is," Raythen said. He nodded at Astarra. "Coming?"

She was almost tempted to say no. She barely trusted Raythen, let alone Mavarin. Allowing him to lead them into the tunnels surrounding Thelgrim simply sounded like switching one danger for another. But it was that or strike out alone. She knew nothing of the city. It was unlikely she could last half a day with the Warriors' Guild hunting her through the streets. Reluctantly, she gestured for the Dunwarr to lead on.

The western cavern wall was looming ahead now, curving up and over them like some great rock wave, frozen for eternity before it could come crashing down on the cavern floor. Astarra was no longer awed by the sheer scale of it. Her mind was bent wholly towards escape and survival, thoughts and possibilities racing through her mind as she ran, aided by the quickening magics of the Viridis.

"There's an old miners' entrance at the top of the next alley," Mavarin panted as they rounded another outcrop, boots scuffing on stone. "That'll take us down to the Plummets."

He'd barely finished speaking the words before he crashed headlong into a Dunwarr who'd been coming round the stalagmite in the opposite direction. They went down together with the clatter of armor.

"Oh Fortuna," Raythen exclaimed loudly, skidding to a halt. Astarra did likewise, snatching Shiver before he tripped on the hem of his robes.

Mavarin had run into a guild warrior. As they both tried to right themselves, a separate patrol of five more armored Dunwarr trooped round the rock and froze, staring.

Shiver and Astarra reacted at the same time. Each snapped a single, arcane word, Astarra's staff raised and Shiver's gaunt hands extended. A surge of wind and ice crystals pummeled the Dunwarr patrol, knocking them back and sending them sprawling, their armor rimed with frost.

Astarra looked at Shiver in surprise, and found the elf staring at her in turn. Raythen had snatched Mavarin and hauled him back to his feet.

"Looks like we're not going to the Plummets," Raythen grunted, shoving the inventor in the opposite direction.

"I don't have anywhere else," he complained desperately, as he was forced past Astarra. She lowered her staff, blocking both Mavarin and Raythen before they could pass.

"We can't go back," she said. She'd already picked up the sound of heavy boots beating at the cavern's bedrock. The patrol from before were closing in behind them, likely alerted by the ruckus ahead.

"Looks like we're fighting our way out after all," Raythen said darkly, throwing his cloak back to free his hand bow.

"We can break through," Astarra said. She felt confident, powerful, the vital energies of the Viridis lending her their potency. She advanced on the Dunwarr who had blocked her path as they righted themselves, calling upon the Turning, feeling the magical forces that surrounded them responding to her summons.

More winds surged from the ether, buffeting the dwarfs. They were better prepared this time though. At a barked command they locked together, shields overlapping in front and raised above their heads to form a protective wedge. Astarra grimaced, fighting to keep control of the gale that shrieked and whistled its fury as it knifed between the surrounding rock formations. The Dunwarr stood firm, as immovable now as the stones of the cavern floor.

"We need to split their formation," Shiver said, having to shout to be heard. He stepped up to Astarra's side once more, dark robes billowing, and raised his hands above his head, his manacled wrists crossed.

Grip white on her staff, Astarra let the winds bleed out, her mind still full of the keening screech of the arcane gust. Shiver had started to chant, the words alien to her. Had he been another rune practitioner the Verto Magica would have been churned into a maelstrom around them as they both tapped into its power together. His energies came from elsewhere though, from the Empyrean, the natural inheritance of his elven lineage. Astarra still felt its power, the vast potential of it, like fathomless oceanic depths compared to the swift-running river that was the magic of her runes.

The elf had called up the frigid void his soul seemed to be bound to. Ice crept across the cavern floor from where he was standing, running rapidly to the feet of the Dunwarr formation. It spread across their armor and over their shields, their breath clouding as the temperature plummeted.

"They weaken," the elf hissed through clenched teeth.

Astarra already knew what to do. She delved once more into the power running though her staff. The Viridis stone was the magic of the wilds of Mennara, from every root and branch and leaf, from every rushing stream, twittering birdsong and hatching egg. The stone of the mountain around them was cold and hard and dense, but it was not wholly without life of its own. Astarra sought it out, calling up the essence of the deeps and focusing it.

A boulder teetering on the edge of one of the outcrops around them responded first. It came clattering down between

Astarra and the Dunwarr, trailing dirt and grit. She felt the weight of its shadow in the magical plane, the unyielding force of it. With a roar of effort, she drew on the energies of the Viridis, an invisible surge of force – the flowing streams and rushing forest winds of the Aymhelin – and used it to redirect the fall of the stone into the midst of the cluster of Dunwarr.

The formation attempted to break, but Shiver's ice had fixed their feet to the cavern floor. There was a splintering crash as the boulder pounded through the center of the wedge. Shields, turned brittle by the magical chill, shattered into pieces, and helmets, weapons and bodies were hurled through the air as the rock forced its passage.

Astarra felt the energies she'd summoned peter out, the boulder coming to rest against another rock stack with a thump. She inhaled with a gasp, her body shaking. She felt as though she had picked up and flung the rock with her own bare hands.

"Go," she panted, looking at Shiver. The elf looked similarly drawn as he lowered his arms, though she noticed his hands and the manacles around his wrists were crusted with ice.

"We can't," the elf responded tersely. A bellow and the ringing clang of metal striking metal answered Astarra's question before she could ask it.

While the two of them had been breaking through the barrier, the other Dunwarr formation had caught up with them. Astarra turned in time to see Raythen's axe rebounding from the steel-shod shield of a guild warrior. Another two were grappling with Mavarin, who was wrestling with them in a desperate effort to break free.

Briefly, her mind baulked at the thought of tapping once

again into the power of the runestone at her disposal, afraid of the draining exhaustion that came with their excessive use. She overcame it with a grimace, closing her eyes and centering herself at the heart of the Turning energies in her grasp.

She reminded herself that she wasn't some Greyhaven novice or dusty old scholar intimidated by the power of the runebound shards. She was a runewitch, raw and primal, and her limits were far off yet.

The Dunwarr beat aside Raythen's axe with the rim of his shield, coming in with his own short sword and driving at the thief's stomach. Raythen gave ground, cursing his opponent and loudly questioning the legitimacy of the warrior's birth.

If he got a reaction, it was impossible to tell from the Dunwarr's expression – it was hidden behind a visor carved to resemble a dour, bearded face, an ancestor mask that would guard its descendants in a very literal sense. Raythen let the sword slide past and tangle in the fold of his cloak before coming back in swinging. The mask took a wicked dent, and blood from a crushed nose welled up brightly through the nose guard. The wounded Dunwarr stumbled back, clutching his helmet.

Raythen had a second before the other two who'd been trying to flank him rushed in. Mavarin was further to his left, and had been wrestled to the floor, his arms tied behind his back by one particularly burly Dunwarr with a fierce crimson beard. Right now, Raythen didn't care one bit what happened to the inventor. He turned, dropping his guard in order to snatch a glance back at Astarra and Shiver.

The runewitch was looking towards him, green energies

ensorceling her raised staff. Behind her something had broken and scattered the Dunwarr they had run into, but more were emerging from the narrow canyons around them, drawn by the melee.

Raythen had a few rapid heartbeats to make a decision. Not long enough to think, but long enough to go with the gut instinct he had trusted all his life. He locked eyes with Astarra.

"Find the Shard!" he shouted.

Something hit him with the force of an avalanche. He was slammed into the cavern floor, his right arm instantly numb from the impact, axe tumbling from his grip and clattering across the worn stone. He managed to roll onto his back, trying to sit. The studded sole of a boot met him on the way up, planted in his gut, driving him back down and forcing the air from his lungs.

He recognized Bradha standing over him, blocking out the light of the starglobes far above, just before the rim of her shield crashed down into his face.

CHAPTER FOURTEEN

Shiver shook. The power of the Empyrean was coursing through him, the manacles that had once bound his magical essence before the draining runestones embedded in them were shattered now, pulsing with power. Thin sheets of ice split and cracked across his robes as he moved, and pale blue energies played around his eyes and coiled across his quivering hands.

He was only half aware of what was happening around him, but Astarra brought him back.

"They've got Raythen, and the inventor," she said, her face close to his, forcing him to focus. "We have to go."

He dragged his mind back from the freezing precipice it had been teetering on. Dunwarr warriors were everywhere, spilling from the surrounding canyon-alleys. He could no longer see Raythen or Mavarin.

Two crossbow bolts slashed at them from one of the advancing knots. Fast as thought, Shiver reached out through the Empyrean and clenched an invisible, frigid fist around them. They were instantly encased in wedges of ice, the sudden weight causing them to plummet out of the air short of their targets and skitter across the ground, coming to rest at their feet.

"I don't think they're trying to take the two of us prisoner," Astarra said, moving so she was behind Shiver, standing back-to-back with him as the Dunwarr closed in. "Any suggestions?"

"The rock pillars," Shiver said.

"Already tried that. A boulder's one thing, a whole stack is something else."

"I wasn't talking about collapsing them," Shiver said. "Call upon the winds of your runestone one more time, and stay close behind me."

He was glad the runewitch seemed to have stopped questioning his every suggestion. As the ring of Dunwarr tightened like a glittering noose of shields, blades and grim helmet masks, Shiver clasped his shuddering hands together and drove them forward. The Empyrean responded, channeled in his mind's eye. More ice rushed up from the ether, forming at the base of the closest outcrop of the rugged, natural stone pillars that crowded around the edge of Thelgrim's cavern.

"Do it," he managed to say to Astarra.

The runewitch realized his intention. Shiver sensed her weary soul draw upon the well of energy that lay within her staff, calling once more upon the quickening energies that bent the power of the rune shard. He felt the ethereal wind return, and briefly imagined he heard the rustling of leaves and the creaking of ancient boughs.

The ice flurry Shiver had called up surged in the magical gale, forming a gleaming, jagged ramp up the side of the outcrop.

He didn't need to say anything. Side by side, the human and the elf ran at the frozen bridge. Astarra's footing slipped almost immediately, but Shiver grabbed her wrist and hauled her on, the ice reforming under his feet to better support him. More crossbow quarrels slashed past, cracking off the ice or sticking in it, leaving it crazed and cracked.

They reached the top of the jutting pillar of natural rock. The stone was rough and uneven, but was easier going for Astarra than the ice slope had been. Shiver let go of her as they scrambled atop the promontory.

"Keep going," he urged her, before looking back the way they had come. The canyon below was crowded with Dunwarr warriors now, with the nearest trying to mount the ice ramp after the duo. There was a clatter of armor as boots scraped and slipped and stout, heavy bodies went tumbling.

Shiver extended his arms and brought his palms smacking together. The ramp of ice exploded into a million shards, the cracking report echoing back like thunder from the nearby wall of the cavern. The Dunwarr were thrown from the base of the outcrop, battered by the hail of splintered shards, rebounding off armor and tinkling to the cavern floor sounding like a sudden deluge of hailstones.

Shiver turned and followed Astarra.

The outcrop didn't get them far, but the important thing was being momentarily out of sight of the Dunwarr beneath them. Astarra had already reached the far edge, where she'd come up short. There was another, lower rock stack ahead, but it was on the far side of the canyon-alley below. The gap was too great to jump, and Dunwarr warriors, aware they were now above them, had already started appearing beneath.

"Don't suppose you know any flying incantations," Astarra said to him as he joined her on the edge.

"No, but I can narrow the gap," he said, smiling for her benefit and immediately regretting it when a flash of alarm crossed her face. She was scared, he could tell, but trying to mask it with the confidence she so often led with. He empathized with that as best he could, though right now it was difficult – as was so often the case in matters of life and death, he found his thoughts cold and detached.

He knelt and planted his hands on the edge of the outcrop. His body was going numb, the shaking almost uncontrollable now. He was being drawn too far into the Empyrean, too deep, but he couldn't stop, not yet. His manacles were heavy with ice.

He dragged in a breath to steady himself and again summoned up the chill from the depths of his soul. Ice sprang up from beneath his fingers and spread, forming a jagged buttress that extended beyond the outcrop's edge, gleaming coldly in the cavern's light.

"Now we jump," he said, grimacing as he wrenched his hands free.

To her credit, Astarra didn't hesitate. She took a few steps back and lunged for the spur, flinging herself from its edge before she had the chance to slip. For a second it looked as though she wasn't going to make it, but Shiver felt the power of her runestone surge, his own robes billowing as the forest wind returned. She slammed down on the other side of the narrow canyon, rolling with the impact.

He followed her, almost vaulting over her. He hadn't needed the ice spur to make the jump, but he knew he couldn't have left her. Being the king's son, Shiver suspected Raythen could talk his way out of the worst of the punishment that was waiting for them. He very much doubted King Ragnarson could be convinced to show similar leniency to an outsider.

He landed lithely and helped Astarra to her feet.

"You're shaking," she said, as she took his frigid hand.

"All power comes at a price," he said. "We must keep going."

The Dunwarr below were out of sight again, but Shiver could still hear their angry voices ringing up from the canyons around them, barking in their own language. To his ears their words sounded like hammers clashing against anvils, full of anger and force. He led Astarra to the edge of their new outcrop.

"One more, and we can reach the cavern wall," he said. Thelgrim's western flank soared before them, a mighty cliff face of craggy stone that arched gradually towards the cavern roof overhead.

"What happens when we reach it?" Astarra asked, panting.

"We go beyond," Shiver said, kneeling and summoning forth another ice spur. He couldn't feel his hands or his forearms now, and the shaking in his legs was making standing difficult. Still, the ice responded. This time he barely made the jump – it was Astarra's hand which snatched out to steady him.

"Down," he managed to say, the words slurred on numb, blue lips.

"We can jump," Astarra assured him, pulling him to the edge of the last outcrop. It sloped slightly, and its top lay closer to the cavern floor than the ones they'd been traversing. Privately, he felt a surge of relief – he didn't think he could reach into the frigid ether anymore, not without his soul becoming permanently frozen.

They leapt down together, perhaps a dozen feet, both falling but managing to rise. Shiver cracked the ice from his fingers, looking up at the cavern wall that now lay directly before them. It was riddled with staired doorways and mining entrances, haulage rails and scaffolded walkways that formed a vertical network hundreds of meters up the rugged flank of the cavern. The immediate interior of the city's western edge, the area they had traveled beneath in Mavarin's burrower, was a honeycomb of tunnels and passageways, delved out, enlarged and connected over the centuries by the industrious Dunwarr.

"Mavarin said we have to reach the Plummets," Astarra said. "Which way are they?"

"I have no idea," Shiver said, taking in the array of entrances and shaft chutes that seemed to glare down at them. "I think we simply have to pick one."

They set off again, Astarra leading the way. Shiver could hear the Dunwarr in the narrow rock alleyways behind them. They were still in pursuit.

The runewitch appeared to pick one of the tunnel openings at random, leading them over a rail track and up a sloping boardwalk. Shiver assumed that the cavern edge would usually have been a hive of activity, but had been abandoned with the city's inhabitants curfewed until the Hydra was recovered. The entrance loomed ahead of them, an archway of hungry, impenetrable blackness.

Shiver drove off the sudden spike of dread. There was nothing in there, nothing but the same darkness he had known since birth.

He made it a few meters inside before he found himself on his knees. He tried to rise, but found he could not – strength had deserted his limbs. The shaking was wholly uncontrollable now.

Astarra came back for him. He looked up, feeling an unexpected pang of shame.

"The Empyrean… has drained me," he managed to admit between the trembling. "You should go on. I cannot."

Astarra knelt before him.

"Take hold of my staff," she said, the length of carved tusker bone planted in the ground between them. Shiver hesitated for a moment, wondering just why the runewitch was helping him.

"We don't have time for elven arrogance," she said, mistaking his reasoning. "Or I really will leave you. Trust my runestone and hold the staff."

With difficulty, Shiver reached out and locked his shaking fingers around the bone. The effect was instant. A vision of vast trees, dappled in sunlight and swaying heavily in a cool breeze, flooded his mind. He could smell honeyseed and fresh pine needles, and feel the warmth on his skin.

The aching chill of the ether retreated, little by little. He could feel his body again, his fingers, the life energies of the runestone surging through them. The shaking receded, and he found he could stand.

"You have my thanks," he told Astarra. "You could have left me. I believed you would."

"Like it or not, I could use a deep elf's senses just now," she said. "If I go in there alone, I'm not coming back out."

Shiver considered her words and nodded. He looked back

out of the tunnel entrance. Dunwarr were advancing from the canyons at the edge of the city, closing the ground up to the canyon wall.

"It seems there is no going back," he said, trying not to think about the darkness ahead. "So let us go forward."

Astarra did her best to map out the route they were taking in her head. After the sixth or seventh turn in the third new section of tunnels, she finally admitted to herself that she'd lost track.

She had swapped out the Viridis Seed for the Ignis. She hadn't wanted to so soon – hairline splits still marked her staff, and the tip where the volcanic shard slotted home was charred. She could feel the same charring on her soul, not yet fully healed by the powers of the Seed. Each of the shards demanded its own price – the Deeprune left her feeling numb after a while, and the Viridis sharpened her senses until they were achingly taut. The Ignis was the hungriest, the most aggressive. She had no choice but to call upon its light though. She couldn't have traversed the dark tunnels at Shiver's side without it, even if she'd wanted to.

Initially the runefire illuminated broad, wide work tunnels, their flanks still stacked high with barrels and sacking, the walkways on either side of the rail lines worn by generations of scuffing Dunwarr boots. It only took a few turns, however, for the spaces to grow rapidly lower, narrower, and less permanent-looking.

Astarra followed a step behind Shiver, not questioning the directions he chose while, at the same time, wondering if that was what she should be doing. The fact that she wouldn't have made it out of the city without him wasn't lost on her. He could easily have abandoned her. She was taking a risk and trusting him, just as she assumed Raythen had been taking a risk when he had called out for her to find the Hydra. The dwarf thief was the last person Astarra could imagine making a selfless stand to buy her and Shiver time to escape, so there had to be something more to it. He was gambling with odds that weren't yet clear to her. She had to try and figure out her own chances, but right now, it seemed as though staying with Shiver, and trusting him, was her best bet.

"Do you know where you're going?" she asked Shiver eventually, as they took a tunnel that passed a series of plunging, vertical mineshafts. The silence had become too much.

"I'm not sure," he said. She frowned.

"Do you make a conscious effort to be cryptic, or are you just unaware of how to interact with people?"

"A small amount of both," the elf replied without looking back at her. They walked a little further in silence before he spoke again.

"I'm trying to lose any pursuit. The Dunwarr know these mines intimately. They will be able to track us. Our only hope of evasion is if we reach less frequently excavated sections of the works. That means going deeper."

"I thought we were pretty deep already," Astarra said, trying to imagine a reality in which they could delve even further down than Thelgrim's shining, buried cavern.

"Oh, this is nothing," Shiver said, snatching a glance at her. If his smile was supposed to be reassuring, it didn't feel like it.

The elf took her along a sloping rail tunnel, then through a series of ever-smaller auxiliary excavation slips. The subterranean structures grew less and less permanent looking, the dirt walls supported by bare wooded struts and the low ceilings by uneven beam wedges. The air became staler. She found herself yearning for the soul-cleansing rush of the winds of Aymhelin, summoned up by the Viridis.

Shiver stopped abruptly. She halted behind him, looking back along the tunnel they'd taken. Nothing stirred beyond the flickering light of her staff.

"What is it?" she hissed.

"Nothing," Shiver said quietly. He began to walk again, more sharply than before. Astarra hurried to catch up.

"You sensed something," she pressed. "What?"

"My kin," the deep elf said.

Fear clenched up tightly in Astarra's stomach. Even during the chaos of the past few days, her mind had returned often to the initial ambush on the Hearth Road, to the sudden, desperate fury of the elven assault. She could have been dead before she had even realized it. A moment's hesitation, a misplaced incantation, a second's weakness, and they would all have ended with their throats slit, dragged off into the darkness or left for Bradha and her patrol to find.

Or perhaps not quite all of them. She'd seen the body at Shiver's feet. He'd killed one of them, but how much did that really count for? Had it even really been a corpse, or just frozen, dormant? Was it all part of a trick? Some wider plan?

But if so, why would Shiver be leading her on? He could probably have still escaped Thelgrim without her help. Perhaps the deep elves wished to claim her runestones, but if so, she couldn't fathom why. Their magic was wholly separate and, in truth, more potent than her runemagics.

That wouldn't be the case if she could claim the Hydra Shard. That was Shiver's ultimate aim, she'd decided. He wanted to capture a Star of Timmoran and its Dunwarr device before his fellow deep elves, perhaps to attain dominance among them. Astarra could at least understand that drive for power, the need for recognition.

"How far away are they?" she asked him.

"Far enough, for now," he said. "I don't believe they are yet aware of our presence."

"They're a different tribe from your own?" Astarra went on, wondering how much she could get out of him. "You've already claimed that you've never been to the Dunwarrs before. Where are you from originally?"

"Further south," he said.

"That makes two of us," Astarra said, thinking once more of the green pastures and the ripe apple trees of her home. It sat on the south-western borders of Forthyn, yet still it felt like a totally separate plane of existence from the dark, turgid, cramped world she now found herself in.

"Trast, upon the border of what you know as Lorimor," Shiver went on, to her surprise. "My people are the Aelthwael. I was born to the clan's high priestess. That was long ago now."

"You remember your childhood?" Astarra asked. "I thought your memories had been stolen from you."

"Some I have regained," he said. "My recollection of the times before these were put on are easier to recall." He raised an arm as they walked, the robe slipping back to reveal the heavy manacle around his wrist.

"And just why were those put on?" Astarra asked. She was wary of pressing the elven sorcerer, especially when he currently had her at his mercy, leading her blindly through the mountain's depths. She'd been turning his existence over in his mind constantly though, since the day they'd first met. She had been certain that her initial instincts, that he was sullied by a cruel and wicked darkness, were correct, but she had yet to see him act out on the shroud of evil that hung so heavy on him. His actions, both towards her and others, had been nothing but selfless thus far. She tried to remind herself that he had surely committed all manner of foul deeds in the past – he had barely denied as much – but she was finding it increasingly difficult to reconcile that concept with the person she had been interacting with now for weeks.

"The manacles were placed on me because I was a fool," Shiver said. "I sold everything. My birth right, my talents, my abilities, my hopes, my future. They remain on me because I am still buying it all back. One memory at a time."

"And the key, that's what unlocks your lost memories," Astarra surmised, once again finding the elf's dark description of himself at odds with how she had seen him act. She had wondered often about the key that hung around Shiver's waist. Even for elven magic, it was strange to her. She had wondered just what else it could unlock.

"Something like that," Shiver said. "We should be silent now. The Aethyn may hear us."

Astarra doubted very much that was the reason Shiver wished for silence, but she knew better than to keep up the questions. She was surprised he'd responded at all.

They carried on without speaking. At one point, Astarra

thought she heard a slight scuffling noise behind them. She turned and found nothing, though it seemed like, for the briefest second, the shadows that shrouded the length of the tunnel refused to retreat before the light of her staff.

Frowning, she hastened after Shiver.

CHAPTER FIFTEEN

They stopped to rest in an old crosscut branching off the stepped tunnel of an incline shaft. The effects of the Viridis Seed had started to wear off on Shiver. He felt hollow, drained. His concentration was at the point of wavering, and that was the last thing he wanted.

There was a small ventilation shaft intersecting with the tunnel. Shiver had left Astarra sitting beside it. He wasn't sure if the slightly clearer air was the help the human needed to stave off her exhaustion, but right then it was all he could offer. Neither of them had any food, and while Shiver, like most deep elves, could go days before feeling the ill effects from lack of sustenance, Astarra clearly did not possess a similar constitution. Though trying to hide it, she had clearly started to flag as they progressed deeper and deeper into the Dunwarr labyrinth.

"Sleep, if you can," he advised her as she settled with her back to a support beam, her staff propped against the dirt wall next to it, still lit. He saw doubt flash across her face. It was still there, the fear and distrust he had first seen in Frostgate. Then it had been so potent she had almost lashed out at him instinctively. Exposure seemed to have taken the edge off her loathing, but the wariness remained.

"Your kind need more sleep than mine," Shiver said, crouching in front of her, trying to be reassuring but fearing he was sounding condescending. He tried to change tack, aiming for something she might better understand.

"It makes no sense for me to betray you now," he said. "If I'd wanted to leave you behind, I could have."

"That doesn't mean you don't need me for something in the future," Astarra pointed out.

"Then trust me for now," Shiver said. "Down here, we only have each other."

Astarra said nothing, closing her eyes. Shiver felt a pang of sorrow as he looked away from her. He caught himself. He was seeking acceptance, he realized. Forgiveness. It was a trap he fell into so often. The desire to atone, even to those who knew nothing about him, knew nothing of his struggle.

There could be no forgiveness for him, no kindness from fellow travelers, not until his memories were complete and the last of his foul deeds had been atoned for in blood and ice.

Astarra was soon fast asleep, the light of her staff reduced to a dull glow.

Shiver sat beside her for a while, battling his own exhaustion. In truth, he needed to sleep as well, but he knew that to do so now would be unwise. There was always a chance the Dunwarr might still happen upon them, and the presence of groups of Aethyn clan deep elves still lingered on the edge of his senses. Besides, there were more dangerous things than elves and dwarfs in the Dunwarr Deeps. Of that he was becoming increasingly sure.

He roused himself a little way and walked to the edge of the cutting, looking down the rough timber stairs of the slope shaft. Nothing stirred below. He paced softly back to Astarra, whose lingering light was like a small firefly in the vast swathes of the night. He found himself strangely apprehensive about leaving the warm glow, weak though it was.

The thought was almost comical. Like all deep elves, he had grown up in the absolute darkness beneath the mountains. True enough, the shadows here were different to those he had known as a child, below the southern peaks of the Lorin's Gate Mountains, but the essential essence should be the same. Gloomy caverns and close, rocky tunnels held no fear for his kind.

Then why was he afraid? It was the first time he had acknowledged it since leaving Frostgate. A fear had been growing in him all the time, and now it was made manifest. Something was down here, something festering and hungry. Something that shouldn't be.

The fact that he was so certain of it was in itself a worry. He had reached out – tentatively – into the Aenlong, the land of dreams, seeking out what might be causing the sense of foreboding that had crept over him. The emotions of Thelgrim and its surroundings were busy and turbulent. The theft of the Hydra Shard had thrown the whole city into discord. That did not explain the shadow that had fallen across the Dunwarrs though. It did not explain darkness that refused to withdraw before the light.

"Not all darkness fears the light, Shiver," she said, that honeyed

voice worming in his ear, making him twitch. "You of all people should know that."

"I won't open another one for you," he mumbled, starting to shake. "I will die before I do."

She sighed, crouching in front of him. He kept his eyes down, seeing only her hand as it reached out to grasp the key tied to his waist. It was ridged with dark green scales, glittering in the torchlight, the nails long, black talons.

"You say that every time, my delicious little puppet," she said reproachfully. "Now look at me and take the key."

"No," he moaned, feeling the power being dragged from him to the surface of his consciousness, the Aenlong churning and soaring around him. "Please! Please, not again!"

The power surged. Energies ignited around his manacles, locking tight. There was a scream, ringing through the tunnels, the terrible wail of the utterly damned. His scream, he knew. Much as he tried, he couldn't stop it.

A blow struck him, sending him reeling. He reached out, elven reflexes responding, and felt something smack into his palm, held fast in his grip.

He realized he was holding Astarra's staff, stopping it from striking his head a second time. Upon contact, the energies of the runestone she was using roared through him, hot as a furnace, searing his soul and bringing him back to the moment. He let go, his palm singed, the icy magics he drew from the Turning cringing back with an audible hiss.

Astarra lowered the staff rather than strike him again. Her eyes were wide with fear.

"I- I'm sorry," he managed to say, voice trembling. His whole body was shaking. The power that had bound him moments before had snapped from existence, the ether-chains dissipated. He slumped back against the tunnel wall.

"Was that another memory?" Astarra asked quietly, staff held tight. "A new one?"

"Yes," Shiver said, his voice hoarse. Astarra was silent for a moment before speaking again.

"You said you needed the locks to access them. That, or you had to be somewhere of personal significance."

"Yes," Shiver said again, head still bowed.

"You've been here before," Astarra said. "Now you've seen it, you remember this place."

Shiver didn't answer. He reached down to the key at his waist and, after hesitating, grasped it and raised it before his eyes. It gleamed dully in the runelight. It was hot to the touch.

"We should go," he said, looking past it at Astarra. There was concern in her eyes, he realized. Not just fear. "Others will have heard that, or sensed it."

"You owe me an explanation," Astarra said, voice as hot as her runestone's flames as she strode after Shiver. They were descending along the slope shaft, going ever deeper into the mountain's roots.

He ignored her, but she carried on, her voice ringing after him.

"What did you do here? What did you see?"

"I don't know," he said, trying to keep a tight grip on the anger and confusion that threatened to overwhelm him. He hadn't anticipated this, not fully. He needed time to think, to collect himself, but that never seemed to be possible with Astarra.

"I don't believe you," she said. "Where are we even going right now? We're just wandering in the dark beneath the mountain. We have to find the Hydra!"

"There's something down here," Shiver said, his patience at an end. "Something other than the Shard. It's connected to me, to my memories. I have to find out what it is and, if need be, I have to banish it."

He realized Astarra had stopped behind him. He looked back up the stairs at her.

"I didn't sign up to this," she said, the flames of her runestone making her look fierce and untamable. "I left Frostgate intending to retrieve a runestone. I agreed to carry on because the Hydra Shard is a greater prize than anything I had anticipated. But this... this offers me nothing. Nothing but death."

"You came here intending to steal the very runestone you were asked to retrieve," Shiver said. It was an accusation, not a question. "Why else would you have agreed to journey all this way, other than to further your addiction to power? Now you wish to take the Hydra Shard instead. That even greater prize is what is keeping you here."

Astarra glared down at him before answering. "We are all here for our own reasons. I doubt very much that yours are any more just."

"My reasons are necessary ones," Shiver said. "I have been led here for a purpose. Justice is not a consideration."

"And what are your reasons then?" Astarra asked. "To claim the Hydra for yourself? Use it to subjugate the elves of these mountains?"

"No. You know not of what you speak."

"And I will take no lectures in morality from a *daewyl*," Astarra snapped.

Shiver reacted. He didn't mean to, but before he'd realized what was happening his hand was raised and icy crystals were surging towards Astarra. For a moment all he knew was anger, and the desire to strike.

She responded just as fast. Fire flared, lighting up the tunnel. The magical energies collided and dissolved, searing each other from existence with a loud, threatening hiss.

Shiver paused, his hand quivering.

"You do not call me that," he said, voice hoarse.

"That's what you are though, isn't it?" Astarra demanded, fire kindling in her eyes as well as atop her staff. "A fallen elf. A worshiper of demons. A servant of the Ynfernael."

Shiver felt suddenly weak. He leant against the sloping tunnel wall, his magics slipping through his fingers.

"I was," he said slowly, no longer looking at the runewitch. "A long time ago."

"Is it possible to stop being one?" Astarra asked. Her own fires had dimmed, though they still flickered dangerously.

"That's what I'm attempting to discover," he admitted. It hurt to say it aloud, but it was a truth he realized he could no longer deny. He didn't know if he could ever find repentance. Sometimes, even trying felt futile.

"And how does that fit into all this?" she went on. "You took this task for the locks. They bring back your memories. But why keep going when you discovered Mavarin doesn't have any?"

Shiver bit back an immediate answer. How much more could he tell her about the darkness he could sense, even now, all around them?

"I told you already, there's a shadow under Thelgrim," he said. "And I mean to banish it."

"How very noble," Astarra said. "So, you want me to believe that while myself and Raythen are here trying to steal a Star of Timmoran for ourselves, you're looking to battle the forces of darkness?"

"Perhaps those roles aren't as mutually exclusive as you seem to think," Shiver pointed out. "And perhaps you should ask yourself why Mavarin would hire someone like you or me to retrieve the Shard?"

"We have the required skills," she said, almost indignantly. "Raythen is a Dunwarr and a thief, you are a deep elf, and I am a master of runemagic."

"Adventurers and sellswords of every sort delve mountain depths and dungeons all the time," Shiver said, in no mood to indulge the human's shortsightedness any longer. The situation had grown far too serious for that. "Yet you think he needed we three in particular?"

"What are you trying to say?" Astarra asked.

"That there is more at work here than just a quest for a stolen Star," Shiver said. "I expect the threat I sense and the Shard are connected. How, I do not yet know."

"I should never have come down here with you," Astarra said. "I'm going back, and I'm doing whatever I can to leave these cursed mountains."

"I wouldn't advise that in the short term," Shiver said, as she began to climb up the shaft.

"Why?" she snapped without pausing. She only halted when she felt the temperature in the tunnel start to plummet, the telltale signature that went hand-in-hand with Shiver's magics.

"Because there's a deep elf daggerband currently on its way down to greet you."

"This is a trap," Astarra said.

"Not yet it isn't," Shiver replied. "But it will be if we don't hurry."

He urged her down the stairway. He could sense more Aethyn closing in, from both above and below. If they couldn't make it to the next level of the mine and its adjoining tunnels, they'd be cut off.

He could feel Astarra's hesitation. He'd lost his temper with her, and had damaged the fragile trust they'd been developing. There was no time to regret that – he had to steer them both clear.

He'd rarely heard of such aggressive encroachments by a deep elf clan into dwarven territory. Both peoples knew the high price that conflict between them brought. It was yet another part of the mystery that had enveloped the Dunwarrs, the one that Shiver felt as though he was being hauled inexorably towards.

"Hurry," he urged Astarra. He feared they weren't going to make it. The Aethyn were closing like a vice. He had no doubt they were aware of them. He slid into the Aenlong as they went, drawing up its power, made icy by the natural attuning of his soul. He was already tired, but he had to dig deep, perhaps now more than ever. He hoped he wouldn't need it, but the memory of the Hearth Road was still strong. Steel, striking for his throat, and an instinctive choice between life and death.

They reached the bottom of the slope shaft. It opened out into another level, the ceiling low and the walls narrow.

The deep elves were waiting for them. The darkness gleamed with black eyes and naked blades before the light of Astarra's staff, following Shiver down, lit the tunnel.

There were six of them, two with raised blowpipes. Shiver felt a surge of heat – both physical and magical – prick his skin as Astarra's fire surged the length of her staff.

"*Talqa*," he shouted, interposing himself between the runewitch and the pale elves. "Wait!"

The daggerband had hesitated. They could have hit them both with darts, and while they were clustered around the foot of the slope shaft, none had lunged immediately into the attack the way they had on the Hearth Road.

Shiver had already paused once when confronted by the Aethyn and had almost paid with his life. He could only hope he didn't regret the second chance. He could feel Astarra on the cusp of incinerating the elves, words of power straining at her lips. She hadn't sensed the second party descending the stairs at their back, almost atop them.

For a brief moment in time, Shiver thought he was going to be impaled from one side and incinerated from the other. He knew a slew of spells that would have protected him, but he didn't dare utter any of them for fear of eliciting a violent response.

The moment passed. An order was snapped, and the daggerband, slowly, lowered their weapons. Astarra's heat on his neck remained constant.

"*Telleth ahala*," Shiver said, and slowly brought his hand to his nose and mouth, making the greeting of the Aethyn clan.

None of the elves returned it. There was hatred in their eyes, and distrust, and something more – fear. They were expressions Shiver always told himself he'd grow used to, but knew he never would.

"Stand aside," said one, speaking in the Aethyn dialect. It always sounded firmer and more definite to his ears than his own tongue, influenced as it was with hints of the neighboring language of the Dunwarrs. The deep elves parted for one near the rear. She advanced towards Shiver, stepping into the shadow he was casting in front of Astarra's flames.

It was a woman, tall and raven-haired. Her face was like a bared knife, sharp-edged, dangerous and coldly beautiful. She looked at Shiver with something even worse than the fear and disgust being exhibited in her kindred's eyes. Recognition.

"After all these years," she said. "You dare come back?"

CHAPTER SIXTEEN

There was a scraping sound as the hatch in the door opened, followed by the crack of the dented metal bowl hitting the cell floor. Half of its contents, a thick, pale gruel made from mashed cavern mushrooms and deeproots, spattered across the stone slabs.

Raythen looked at the bowl for a moment, then stepped across the cell and stooped to pick it up. The chains binding him to the far wall pulled taut just as his fingers reached it. He edged it fully into his grasp, lifted it, and sniffed.

The temptation to eat all that remained in the bowl was there, a knot twisting tightly in his stomach. He took half a dozen mouthfuls, savoring its stodgy blandness, before moving so his chains were once more at their maximum extent. Straining, and trying not to make a sound, he scraped what remained from the bottom of the bowl and deposited it atop a small, congealed lump of gruel he'd been amassing in the grimy corner of the cell, to the right of the door. When it was scraped clean, he placed the bowl in front of the entrance and retreated to the far corner to the left of it.

Patience and misdirection, those were the only keys he needed.

They'd taken everything from him bar his boots, breeches, jerkin, eyepatch and cloak. He'd been thrown into the Dunwol Keg, the fortress pit, a single cell sunken at the bottom of a narrow shaft in the depths of the Dunwol Kenn Karnin. After the throne room and several tombs in the Hall of the Ancestors, it was the most secure place in Thelgrim.

It wasn't his first visit.

He settled down against the wall and waited. He'd been doing a lot of that. A lot of doubting too, though he tried to avoid it. He'd replayed the final moments in the Cragwarren over and over in his head. Should he have tried to follow Astarra and Shiver? Had they even made it into the deeps and, if they had, would they be able to find the Shard? If they did, would they come back for him?

He knew what would have happened if their roles had been reversed, and it wouldn't have involved him triumphantly returning to Thelgrim with evidence of their innocence. But they didn't think like him. Astarra was fueled by brashness and self-confidence, while Shiver seemed to be playing a game with very different rules and objectives from everyone else. As for Mavarin, he could only assume he'd been taken at the same time. He hadn't seen or heard him since being thrown in the Dunwol Keg.

He'd been mulling over how best to use his association with the inventor. If Astarra and Shiver didn't come through, then his options narrowed, but they didn't disappear completely. Trying to lay the greater part of the blame for everything that had happened on Mavarin's shoulders was a possibility, even more so considering that, really, all this was his fault in the first place. Raythen had scolded himself countless times over for the lack of due diligence before setting out from Frostgate. He'd expected better from Cayfern.

The other option was escape. Given the difficulties he'd encountered the last time he had attempted that, it was very much a last resort. It wasn't impossible though, even in a place like this.

Time was difficult to track in the cell. The isolation in itself wasn't wholly alien – he'd been confined alone for extended periods in prisons from Castle Artrast to Strangehaven. There were ways of coping, mind games, counting tricks, the compartmentalization of separate trains of thought. It was more difficult being here though. Things were always more difficult in Thelgrim. He bitterly regretted coming back.

At some point he heard the scuffing of boots descending the stairs towards the cell door. There was a rattle of keys. Raythen made sure he was positioned in the correct corner of the cell, but didn't look up. He expected it was his jailer, returning to take back his slop bowl.

It wasn't.

The hesitation at the door made Raythen look up. His father gazed back at him coldly. He was dressed in a leather doublet with gold trim, with his beard as heavily decorated as ever, though he'd dispensed with the circlet that marked him as the reigning King in the Deeps. From what he recalled from his childhood, Raythen knew that didn't bode well.

Ragnarson looked down at the battered, dirty bowl sitting on the floor in front of him. Then, to Raythen's surprise, he bent forward, picked it up, and handed it out to the jailer who had opened the door.

"Wait outside," he commanded. The Dunwarr bowed and swung the door shut behind the king.

"Hello, Father," Raythen said. He remained sitting. Ragnarson didn't approach, and he found himself praying silently to Fortuna that he didn't glance to the corner on his left and spot the small pile of congealed slop Raythen had collected.

"I should not be here," Ragnarson said. "I was advised against speaking to you before the trial."

"By those devious little twins?" Raythen asked. They had been constant companions to his father for as long as he could recall, always scheming, always watching, ready to report the slightest misdeed. He despised them more than any other Dunwarr he had ever met. "They were bad enough when I was growing up. Is there any part of the deeps they don't now control?"

"They serve me as they have served the last two kings of the Dunwarrs," Ragnarson said sternly. "I will not let your wily words detract from them."

"And yet you speak to me without their knowledge?" Raythen asked.

"I want the truth," Ragnarson said. "And I can't be certain that a formal trial will actually get to that."

"Is that what I'm to be subjected to?" Raythen said. "The ignominy of a 'formal trial.' The Guild Council will love that. A chance to mob the Dunwol Kenn Karnin and jeer you and your son."

"What else did you expect when you came here?" Ragnarson demanded. "Did you think I could shield you? That I would?"

"Well, it would certainly be a break from the norm if you tried," Raythen said.

He watched his father as he spoke, saw the anger in his eyes, flashing like sunlight from a newly drawn blade. He wanted to strike him. He could feel it. A part of him wanted to cringe, to flinch, but he didn't. He never had, even when his father had drawn blood with his blows.

"Just tell me the truth," the king said. "Did you take the Hydra Shard? Thelgrim's very own Star of Timmoran?"

"No," Raythen said. "But if I could have, I would. Whoever slipped it from the Hall of the Ancestors without being noticed has my deepest respect."

Ragnarson was silent. Raythen recognized the struggle to keep his temper in check. He'd known that same struggle many times.

The king turned abruptly and walked to the cell door, banging on it with one, scarred fist. Only when it creaked open did he look back at Raythen and speak.

"You know the punishment if the guilds find you guilty?"

Raythen returned his gaze, but said nothing.

Ragnarson turned and left.

Bradha came for him later that day.

"Get up," the fully armed and armored Dunwarr captain ordered.

"Why, are we going somewhere nice?" Raythen asked, not moving.

"Do you want me to bloody your nose again, thief?" Bradha demanded.

"I'd rather not have any more features rearranged by the

Shield's shield," Raythen admitted, pulling himself by his chains up onto his feet. His nose still ached dully from the blow that had incapacitated him in the Cragwarren.

Bradha stood aside for one of the guards, who advanced and unshackled Raythen from the wall. Hands still chained together, he was lead from the cell and out into the passageways and stairwells of the Dunwol Kenn Karnin.

He heard the Guild Council long before he saw it. Their voices rang through the halls and bastion chambers of Thelgrim's greatest fastness, at times as raucous as a king's ascension feast, at others grumbling and grating, like the slow sliding of rocks on a mountainside. They had been roused from their eternal squabbling in the Guild Hall and brought into the king's chamber, into the Dunwol Kenn Karnin, a fastness usually denied to them.

Their presence made Raythen afraid, though he did his best not to let it show to Bradha or the other guards who tramped on either side of him. He had been here before. He had known the ruthless examination of the Guild Masters, demanding he account for a crime he hadn't committed. He had trod this very route, decades before, when shame and ire had been new, unpleasant feelings. He still remembered the uproar when he had stepped out into the chamber. It had made his heart quail.

The thunder of outrage and disapproval was no less intense than he remembered it. He came in under the archway at the head of the hall and began to descend the long flight of stairs leading to its bottom. The throne room was shaped like an amphitheater, its sides composed of tiered stone seats. They were full, hundreds of Dunwarr rising to their feet as they caught sight of Raythen. Their jeering reverberated from the great vault of the buried chamber.

The throne itself sat upon a plinth of Dunwarr bedrock at the far end of the amphitheater's bowl. It was the ancient Throne of Tanngnoster, a mighty block of intricately carved granite, its flanks fashioned like great dragons that lay crushed beneath the weight of a Dunwarr keystone. King Ragnarson was seated upon it, as stony-faced and graven as the rock he rested above. Two of the three captains of the Warrior's Guild, Svensson and Svensdottir, stood resplendent in silver and gold ceremonial armor on either side of the pedestal.

Raythen was led by Bradha down into the bowl. He glared straight ahead, ignoring the barked insults and coarse laughter of the guild members crammed in on either side. They were all present, bedecked in the colors and bearing upon their chests the crests of the ten bodies that underpinned Dunwarr society. They jostled for the best tiers of the amphitheater, cursing and arguing amongst themselves, trading barbs and banter in equal measure.

It was rare for them all to be invited into the inner sanctum of the throne room. Normally their endless debates were confined to the Guild Hall, but a formal council allowed them to invade the Dunwol Kenn Karnin and remind the king, indirectly or not, that he ruled only by their consent. The thought that this was as difficult and shameful for his father as it was for him, restored a fraction of Raythen's spirit.

A series of stone slabs had been arrayed beneath the crag the throne was set upon. They were backed by a number of high-backed chairs, most of which were occupied by a collection of austere white-beards. Raythen spotted Korri and Zorri among the judges, looking down on him haughtily from their chairs. He forced himself to smile at them.

He was led to the slab facing directly towards the throne. There were no seats there, though one Dunwarr was already standing by it. It was Mavarin, his wrists shackled to the slab's flank. He glanced at Raythen, as he was brought up alongside him, and smiled.

"You got a much b- bigger cheer than when they brought me in," he said over the tumult.

"Lucky me," Raythen said dryly. He was already scanning the faces of the Dunwarr seated before the throne, trying to see if he remembered any, looking for anything at all that he could use to his advantage. There was fat old Galthi, the ruddy master of the Brewer's Guild, who had once caught Raythen when he'd been a child, siphoning from the great casks in the basement of the guild's headquarters. Considering the near-religious significance of ale to the Brewers, he'd been let off comparatively lightly that time. Then there was Krellen, the crag-faced master of the Miners' Guild. He embodied the ancient rivalry between the miners and the smiths, only enhanced by the fact that Ragnarson, before his election as king, had been the master of the Blacksmiths' Guild. Raythen's indiscretions had given Krellen a means to undermine the king's authority plenty of times before. Judging by the small, cold smile the old miner gave him, it seemed Raythen had done so again.

One of the guards who'd led him to the plinth shackled the chains binding his wrists to a thick iron ring in the stone's flank, securing him alongside Mavarin. Bradha offered a short bow towards the throne.

Ragnarson didn't wait any longer. He picked up a hammer that had been resting on the arm of his throne and struck a trio of ringing blows from a small anvil that sat alongside the great granite block.

"Silence!" Captain Svensdottir roared as the jarring reports of the hammer strikes resounded through the throne room. The volume of the assembled council dipped immediately, though it continued to rumble and roll, never properly quelled.

"Council Master Fellin, begin the proceedings," Ragnarson said, looking at the assembled Guild Masters seated before him. A scribe, occupying his own small block off to one side of the throne dais, began to scribble away at a long roll of parchment.

Master Fellin, the leader of the Artificers' Guild, rose and cleared his throat. There was a brief smattering of jeers from his rivals in the Smiths' Guild, swiftly quelled by the angry hissing of the dwarfs surrounding them.

"The Guild Council has hereby been summoned to meet on this, the Ninth Day past Runefire, in the eighty-second year of the Broken Dragon," Fellin said, the aged Dunwarr using a small optic lens to peer at the scroll laid out in front of him. "It has been called upon to sit in judgement before King Ragnarson Smithmaster, and act in its sworn capacity as questioners and as jury in the trial of Kayl Mavarin and Raythen Ragnarson. Do the chosen Guild Masters accept this duty, and swear to perform it to the best of their ability, before all the gods and ancestors and to the glory of the ancient city of Thelgrim?"

"Aye," the rest of the jury intoned loudly.

"And you, King Ragnarson Smithmaster," Fellin said, half-turning to address the throne while keeping his eyes on the parchment. "Do you recognize the authority of the assembled Guild Masters to act as questioners and jury, and to abide by and enforce their final, collective judgement over the assembled prisoners?"

"I do," Ragnarson said, without hesitation.

"Then I declare that the trial of Kayl Mavarin and Raythen Ragnarson has hereby begun."

CHAPTER SEVENTEEN

According to Shiver, the Aethyn leader's name was Maelwich. Astarra had listened to them conduct a terse conversation in elvish, before he had turned to her and done his best to convince her not to immolate them all.

She had grudgingly agreed not to. This was the trust Shiver had spoken of, laid bare. He had yet to deceive her, and Astarra had resolved to continue to give the elf his shot at repentance. Besides, now that the Aethyn had actually cornered them, he represented her best chance of parting company with them alive.

Exactly who Maelwich was remained unclear, but she certainly seemed to know Shiver. When the deep elves had cut off the bottom of the slope shaft, Astarra had feared the worst. The past hour hadn't provided a great deal in the way of reassurance.

The tunnels, passages and cuttings they were being led through had long become an indistinguishable warren, yet at some point she became aware that the spaces they were moving in no longer appeared to be dwarven in origin. When the miners of Thelgrim delved deeper into the mountain they did so using broad, straight lines. Even the most basic chutes appeared to have been cut inch-perfect through the bedrock, and some tunnels seemed more like feast halls than mining passages, their walls high and ceilings broad, lit by slow-burning oil candles and supported by row upon row upon row of timber and iron struts.

All the regularity, all the relentless, engineered precision, appeared to have been left behind now. Astarra's runefire revealed slender passages that wormed their way irregularly through the rock, as though tunneled by some great depths-dwelling creature. Distressingly, she could see no evidence of the supports or struts that were the foundation of many of the dwarven tunnels. Most of the time she couldn't even tell if the narrow crevices she was stepping through were the work of the elves, or simply natural fissures in the rock that they were exploiting. Whereas the dwarves of Thelgrim seemed to plough their way, firmly and unwaveringly, through the mountain's roots, the deep elves slipped over, under and around them, like rainwater sinking through soil.

They had paused momentarily in a small cavern with water trickling down one slick wall. Despite her caution, relief had filled Astarra, and she'd gorged herself at the bottom of the waterfall before refilling the water skin in her pouch. The elves had likewise taken turns drinking, albeit in a far more restrained manner, each one murmuring something in their strange, flowing tongue before sipping upon the blessing of the rocks. Shiver alone hadn't partaken. When Astarra had quietly asked him why, he'd simply said it was not his place.

Shortly afterwards, one of the elves approached her. Astarra met his black eyes unflinchingly. The voice of the Aethyn leader barked something in a tongue she didn't understand and, after staring her down for a moment more, the Aethyn made a gesture – two fingers brushed once, sideways, across his mouth – and withdrew.

She forced herself to let the flames of the Ignis gutter back to a dull glow. That was the second time one of the party that had intercepted them had approached her. She assumed they intended to take her staff. Just why Maelwich was stopping them she wasn't sure, unless it was simply the desire to avoid immolation. She had already instructed Shiver to tell them that she would die before giving up her runestones. Whether he had passed that resolve on in exactly the same words she had used wasn't obvious.

Maelwich issued another series of commands and the daggerband set off once more, Astarra and Shiver securely in their midst. Astarra had had few dealings with elves of any kind down the years, but even by their standards the Aethyn seemed strange. They spoke little – she'd barely heard a word uttered by any other than Maelwich, so much so that she found herself wondering if they were communicating by other means. All were lightly clad in leathers and dark, gossamer-like cloth, while their bodies were almost distressingly tall and aquiline, their large, black eyes seeming to dominate their jagged, white faces. Shiver actually appeared stocky and well-built by comparison, though Astarra wasn't sure if that was because he hailed from a different clan, or because he had spent so long away from the tunnels and passages of his birth.

The Aethyn led them on, traversing the twisting depths, through stalactite-studded chambers that the runeflames struggled to penetrate and along narrow, jagged cracks in vast cavern walls that stretched up into the surrounding dark. Astarra took in the mountain's core as they went, wondering whether light had ever disturbed its unknowable darkness. It was the opposite of Thelgrim, that sat like an unearthed jewel for all to see. These places were buried, secret still, the primordial roots of Mennara itself. It made the delving of the dwarfs, that had seemed so wondrous when Astarra had first beheld it, appear small and childish in comparison.

At one point, passing along a low passage, the daggerband came to a stop. The elves, all taller than Astarra, seemed to find no discomfort in remaining stooped. She crouched, realizing as she did so that there was a low, quiet conversation passing between the Aethyn. Tension hung in the air. Shiver tapped her on the side and murmured in her ear.

"Douse your flame."

Her instinctive response was to refuse, but she caught the gaze of the nearest deep elves, glancing back at her urgently. She closed her eyes, held her breath, and reached out into the Turning to snuff out the Ignis, wincing slightly as doing so singed her soul.

She opened her eyes to total darkness. Her heart began to race, her mind filled with horrible possibilities. They were afraid, she realized. What terrible thing had they disturbed down here? What could make these people of the Deeps pause and cower in a small rock cleft like this?

She felt something on her shoulder, and almost cried out before she realized it was Shiver's hand, gripping her. A warning? Reassurance? Could he sense her panic? She held her breath, trying to see in the darkness, trying to sense what had given the others pause.

"What was it?" she dared ask. Though her voice was hoarse and barely a whisper, it sounded painfully loud in the crushing, silent darkness that had enveloped them.

"*Latath kii*," one of the elves in front of her said. While she didn't understand the words, she recognized the warning tone.

"It's best not to question," Shiver said.

Finally, it seemed that whatever had brought the daggerband to a halt was gone. Astarra was allowed to reignite her staff. They carried on, slowly and quietly.

She realized after a while that she could hear the sound of running water, echoing gently along the passage they were taking. At first, she thought they'd reached another waterfall, before realizing that the tunnel ran over a subterranean stream, a dark flow that rushed by beneath them, visible beyond the ledge they were following.

She almost slipped into it several times. The rock underfoot was moist and thick with mushrooms and other fungal growths, blooming in the shadows by the waterway. She wondered if it was the same river that passed into Thelgrim and the lake via the artifice of the Dunwarr aqueduct.

The ledge led into a wider cavern where the water was more clearly visible, bubbling between rocks worn smooth by its passage over the millennia. They crossed to the other side along a spur of rock – again, Astarra couldn't tell if it was natural or had been formed as a bridge by the elves – before reaching a part of the cavern that she abruptly realized was already occupied.

They'd found an Aethyn encampment. Minimalistic structures of cloth and slender pieces of timber had been erected between the stalagmites at the far end, marking out an area where dozens of deep elves were congregated. Astarra saw young and old alike, gathered in small groups and staring at her as she passed. They were without the lean leathers that seemed to count for armor with the Aethyn warriors, but otherwise were similarly clad in light-wearing, dark-colored garb that appeared to have been woven, at least in part, from the rough fungal fibers of the countless blooms that clung to the rocks by the river. The women's hair was worn up, piled high on their crowns, and the menfolk had their hair pleated, while the children, universally, seemed to have theirs cropped.

Astarra took it all in as she was led into the encampment. She was surprised to see her runefire, which seemed to be the biggest source of interest among the elves, was not the only light illuminating this part of the cavern. Many of the Aethyn were clustered around what appeared to be particularly large, fluted fungal growths. The tips seemed to have been set alight, and were giving off a small, green-tinged flame.

She didn't have time to ponder the strange light source. The daggerband came to a stop, close to what appeared to be the cavern wall.

Maelwich said something to Shiver, who replied with a questioning tone. A short conversation ensued, before Shiver spoke to Astarra.

"They wish to question us both," he said.

"About what?" Astarra hissed back, trying and failing not to sound alarmed.

"I have spoken of the darkness I have sensed beneath Thelgrim," Shiver went on. "They wish to hear more of it."

"Perhaps you should tell them none of that has anything to do with me," Astarra pointed out.

"I would advise coming with me and saying little," Shiver said. "Because right now, it is only the will of Maelwich that is keeping us both alive."

Shiver stepped away before Astarra could respond and made a series of terse hand movements towards Maelwich that Astarra took to mean acquiescence. He nodded to her, then moved to the cavern wall.

There was a crack in the base of it. Shiver stooped and disappeared into the darkness beyond. Astarra hesitated just long enough to glance at Maelwich and the other deep elves, before deciding she'd rather risk the cavern depths.

She followed Shiver in, grimacing as she was forced to bend almost double. Her staff, held ahead of her, lit up a small chamber that lay off the main cavern, mercifully widening enough to allow her to stand once more.

Shiver was waiting, his face pale and unreadable in the runefire. She didn't have time to ask him anything more – Maelwich and three other elves slipped in after her, confronting both of them.

Maelwich spoke to Shiver in the elven tongue, and he responded in kind. Astarra endured the back-and-forth of the sharp-edged conversation for as long as she could before snapping.

"Enough," she said abruptly. Five sets of dark eyes turned towards her. She felt a surge of defiance as she looked from Shiver to Maelwich.

"They might not know the common tongue, but you do," she said to Shiver. "So, I'd appreciate at least some translation, especially as it seems like the outcome of this conversation might be more than a little important, for both of us. What's she saying?"

"I'm asking why a human sorceress is accompanying him along the roots of the *denwal far*," Maelwich said, catching her by surprise. Her voice was precise and cutting, though it never seemed to rise, even when giving orders.

"I was not aware I had to have a reason to walk beneath the mountain," Astarra said. Shiver shot her a warning glance.

"We were hired to come here, to seek an item stolen from the Dunwarr," Shiver said. "There is nothing more to it than that."

"And yet we find you fleeing from them," Maelwich said. "Implying you are the thief."

"There was a misunderstanding," Astarra said. "In fact, this entire venture feels like one great misunderstanding. I assure you, trapped in one of the caverns you call home is far from where I wish to be right now."

"Watch your tongue, runechild," said one of the other elves accompanying Maelwich. He was the tallest of them all, his plaited hair a dark auburn that turned fiery in the light of Astarra's staff. Talking to her seemed to disgust him.

"*Aro sar*, Talarin," Maelwich said sharply, before Astarra could summon a response. The elf smiled coldly, but said nothing more.

Maelwich and Shiver exchanged several more words Astarra didn't understand before the Aethyn addressed her again.

"You have seen the shadow?"

"The what?" Astarra asked, genuine confusion taking the sting out of her anger.

"The *tanab ru fél*, the shadow that hungers. Have you seen it, beneath the mountain?"

The words made little sense to her, but as Maelwich said them, Astarra found her mind drawn back to the darkness in the tunnel, the one that seemed to have stood and spited her runefire before reluctantly withdrawing. Despite the heat of the Ignis, she felt a chill run through her body.

"You have seen it," Shiver said, noticing her reaction. "Then it is as I feared. Not just some phantom memory which haunts me, but a living reality."

"This place is full of shadows," she said, trying to mask her uncertainty with further defiance. "I feel as though I have trod in nothing but darkness since being led down here. How can any of you tell one of these shadows from another?"

Maelwich and Shiver shared a glance, the meaning of which Astarra couldn't fathom.

"Darkness alone is nothing to my kind," Maelwich said, apparently for Astarra's benefit. "But this is something more. Something has escaped from beneath Thelgrim. It is hungry, and it is hunting my people. It will not stop until it has devoured us all, human, dwarf and deep elf alike."

Astarra tightened her grip on her staff, unconsciously casting a glance at the shadows beyond the light of her runefire. Too late, she was beginning to understand that she had strayed into something far more dangerous than a quest to retrieve a simple runeshard. And the worst thing was, she knew it was now far too late to turn back. She could only go on, deeper into the dark, and trust her unlikely companions to do the same with her.

The sound of hammer striking anvil rang once again through the throne room, battling with the wall of noise coming from the amphitheater sides.

"Lies and fabrication," Raythen barked above the tumult, raising his hands so all could see the chains that bound him. "I knew this fate awaited me should I return to Thelgrim. There is a reason I have not come home in twenty years. But to suggest I traveled here to assist in stealing the Hydra Shard, as Master Krellen insinuates, is an absolute fabrication!"

The jeers grew louder, and Ragnarson's strikes upon the anvil grew heavier. It took a long time for either to abate.

Krellen had been leading the questioning for over an hour now. At no point had he wavered from what seemed to be the council's main strategy – accuse Raythen in particular of either stealing the Hydra Shard or, at the very least, coming to Thelgrim with the intention of stealing it. He'd already pointed out that those constituted two very different claims, but Krellen was relentless. Ragnarson, the only member of the trial with the authority to change the line of questioning, had done nothing but demand silence every time the guild members jeered Raythen's protestations.

"Answer me this then, Master Ragnarson," Krellen called out as the tumult finally started to recede. He'd been calling Raythen 'Master Ragnarson' since the start of the trial, in an obvious attempt at insulting his father. "If you had no part in the scheme to steal the Hydra Shard, why did you join with this known reprobate and so strenuously resist the brave efforts of the Warrior Guild to return you to the Dunwol Kenn Karnin? It is only by the ancestor's mercy that there were no fatalities during your botched escape attempt!"

"I am no reprobate," Mavarin said loudly, before Raythen had a chance to respond. "I am the Master of the League of Invention, and you will address me as such!"

The throne room thundered with laughter, echoing and rebounding from the vaulted roof. Krellen smirked cruelly down at Mavarin.

"There is no such thing as the 'League of Invention', and you are certainly no master," he exclaimed. "Your antics belong in the Duldor Deeps with the rest of those disrespectful tinkerers. You are deluded, and your disrespectful antics have troubled the guilds of this fair city for far too long. We have humored you in the past, but no more. Even if you are nothing but a useful tool for Master Ragnarson, you are an accomplice to his heinous crimes, and you shall share in the verdict delivered by this jury."

"You speak as though the sentence has already been decided upon," Mavarin said, his tone at once bitter and angry. "Is this what has become of the great Guild Council of Thelgrim? That noble body that has steered our people's efforts for centuries? A sham trial?"

A squall of anger met Mavarin's accusation. Ragnarson beat upon his anvil angrily until the worst of it had subsided. Raythen rolled his eyes, silently damning Mavarin for goading their judges. He was leaving him with no choice, not if they wanted to regain the initiative and get out of this mess alive.

"Enough!" Ragnarson barked, glaring at the raucous assembly. "I have heard enough for now. The council will adjourn until this evening."

"No," Raythen said sharply, almost surprising himself. He had never heard silence settle over the Guild Council so rapidly.

"Adjourn if you wish," he said in the echoing stillness that followed. "But only for a while. I am calling upon my rights as a child of Thelgrim, and of the Dunwarrs. I am demanding I be allowed to sit the Trial of the Mountain."

CHAPTER EIGHTEEN

Shiver opened his eyes. He did not remember falling asleep. Exhaustion, it seemed, had finally caught up with him.

He looked around the small cavern where Maelwich had left them. Astarra was asleep too, curled up, still clutching her staff. Its light had gone out.

He sat for a moment, gathering his thoughts. A part of him was surprised their throats hadn't been slit while they slept. Maelwich's second, the fire-haired Talarin, had displayed nothing but loathing for both of them since they'd been taken. As for Maelwich herself, Shiver was less certain. She had, it seemed, only just been elected to the leadership of the Aethyn. She had tersely informed them both that she would seek the council of the rest of the clan before speaking any further.

More disconcerting was the fact that she remembered Shiver. She had known him from the time before, the dark time, when he had still been a slave to the terrible will of his mistress. It seemed he *had* visited this place before. It was no surprise that the daggerband that had happened across them on the Hearth Road had attacked out of hand, and little wonder that the one he had killed had snarled that word with his dying breath.

Daewyl. Fallen one. Slave-servant of the Ynfernael. That was what he had been, when last he had trod the deepling places of the Dunwarrs, the mountain roots known by the Aethyn as the *denwal far*.

Yet Maelwich had spared him. She had resisted the impulse to strike. Why, he didn't yet know. She had said little since he'd encountered her. He had no doubt there was more to their story, though just what he didn't know. Not for the first time, his memories mocked him. It embarrassed him, it frustrated him, and he knew that unless he found one of the locks or was graced with a vision of his past, there was nothing he could do about it. At the best of times he tried to remain calm and focused, to keep that anger locked away. Under stress though it became increasingly difficult. He had repeated his mantra so often in the past few days, trying to keep his thoughts under control, to not let fear and discord become the master of him. When that happened, dark things followed.

Atali nametha ren. The path is the purpose. *Nameth hatala.* The path goes on.

When they'd been caught at the foot of the slope shaft, Shiver had told her he was hunting the hungering dark. That seemed to have played a part in staying her hand. What little she'd said to them so far had been about the darkness. She had sensed it too, apparently. She said it had changed everything. He had heard fear in her voice.

He sat for a little while, considering Astarra. She had come this far with him. How much of that was due to self-preservation, greed, or a genuine, deeply buried desire to help, he wasn't sure. She was afraid, he knew, and far from anything she counted familiar. Her outward arrogance and fiery determination was more a mask than genuine. She was accustomed to self-reliance, but in these deep, stony, silent places she had found herself in the hands of those she neither knew nor trusted. Her fortitude impressed him, though he doubted she would have much cared for his opinion.

He rose silently, cast one more glance at Astarra's sleeping form, and ducked out of the small cave. Maelwich had said that neither of them were being forcibly confined before she'd departed, though obviously that was only half true. Beyond the cave lay the Aethyn camp, the cavern acting as their temporary home while they migrated through the Deeps. He knew the two of them would not be able to leave without Maelwich's permission.

Twin warrior-elves stood by the entrance to the cave, watching him as he ducked out. Neither made any move to stop him. Shiver greeted them in the manner of the Aethyn.

"Maelwich?" he asked. The two looked at each other before one spoke, neither returning his greeting-sign.

"I will take you."

The warrior led him through the encampment. Eyes followed him, lifted from fish skinning, weaving and pleating. Hushed conversation stopped altogether. Little ones hid themselves behind their parents.

Distrust and fear were Shiver's constant companions, but it was strange, being back amongst so many kin, even if the clan they hailed from was foreign to him. It made him feel uncomfortable in a way he hadn't known for some time. What had he done here, to earn this? What crimes had he committed within these very caverns, memories that now maddeningly eluded him? Why, if his return conjured up such dread, had he been spared in the first place, even allowed to walk with a modicum of freedom?

The warrior's path took them to the heart of the camp, where an open-sided covering had been erected between a trio of thick, fungus-encrusted stalagmites. Their twins in the cavern roof above dripped moisture down onto the shelter, the air damp and heavy, so close to the underground river.

There were six elves arrayed in council beneath the cover, sitting cross-legged around a small, lit jaela root. Their conversation ceased as the warrior led Shiver amongst them and introduced him.

"Leave us," Maelwich instructed her kin. They rose without complaint and departed, all bar Talarin.

"You should not be alone with this *daewyl*," he said, looking at Shiver as he spoke. He forced himself not to react to the insult. He was in no position to pick a fight, and besides, he felt responsible for Astarra. He had led her down here, and now she was in the midst of a place that was strange and dangerous to her. It was equally strange for him to have to consider the wellbeing of others, but he found it helping his control. He would get them both out of this.

"You know I do not repeat my instructions, Talarin," Maelwich told him. He made a parting gesture to her and left. Shiver felt the hostility crackling from his thoughts as he passed by.

"Sit," Maelwich said, nodding to the vacated space across

the jaela from her. Shiver did so, hitching his robes so he could cross his legs in imitation of the stance of the Aethyn leader.

"You have more questions," Maelwich surmised. "That is well enough, for I do too."

"Questions and answers make for the best of friends," Shiver said, quoting a common deep elf phrase. "Perhaps we might therefore find some form of friendship here."

"Perhaps," Maelwich said, the faint, green-tinged light of the jaela giving her sharp features a brooding under-glow. "The clan council are divided over what to do with you. Talarin believes you are the source of the darkness. He thinks you should be ritually slain."

"Talarin strikes me as someone who has been leading an Aethyn daggerband in the hunt for too long," Shiver said. "His soul is like a notched blade."

"You are perceptive," Maelwich said. "But Talarin is rarely wrong. He has helped guide us through many troubles."

"Yet he does not lead it?" Shiver asked. He was slowly trying to put together a picture of the Aethyn, and of the elf sitting opposite him. Right now, their goals, fears and needs seemed almost as opaque as his own memories.

"I was elected by the Aethyn," Maelwich said. "Not Talarin. A good leader knows when to heed advice, and when to spurn it."

"Is that the reason I'm still alive?" Shiver asked.

"In part."

"You knew me from the moment you saw me," Shiver went on, wondering out loud. "How?"

"We all know you, Shiver," Maelwich said. "Or we know the stories. They are not always the same thing."

"You know me through more than just stories," Shiver pointed out, seeking the truth of the matter. He had been shocked when Maelwich had first confronted him with recognition, and had been plagued by the potential ramifications ever since. Being recognized by someone he couldn't recall wasn't an unknown sensation – it occurred time and again during his travels. He hadn't expected it here though, in the darkness beneath mountains on the other side of Terrinoth from the place he called home.

"I know recognition when I see it," he went on.

"You really don't remember, do you?" Maelwich asked, her reserve momentarily giving way to surprise. "So that much of the legend is true, at least."

"My past was taken from me," Shiver said. "Taken and shattered into a thousand fragments. I have pieced together some of it, but none of the parts that belong to this place."

"Then perhaps you need this," Maelwich said. She reached into a pouch at her side and drew out a small object, carved from bone. It was a lock.

He felt an unexpected rush of fear. It was the same every time he found a new one. Yes, they were what he sought, a means to channel his memories. But he was never sure quite what the memories would be. All he was confident of was that they wouldn't be good.

"I was cautioned against giving you this," she said. "I am no sorceress, but I can feel its power. In the stories, you use locks like these to regain your memories of the Shadow Tear and the times surrounding it."

She hadn't moved to hand the lock to Shiver. He nodded. The time of the Shadow Tear had been the darkest for the deep elves, when the power of the Ynfernael had run rampant. It was the period of his enslavement, when he had been bound to the terrible will of his mistress. Just how much of a part he had played in the devastation was something he was still, tentatively piecing together. Those were the memories he sought most keenly, and also with greatest trepidation, for they revealed the darkest depths to which he had sunk.

"The memory is not contained within the lock itself, but the magical symbolism of it is vital. Echoes of my past are contained in the Empyrean, and the lock centers me, allows me to draw them back. That is what I believe, anyway."

"Who forges them, and why?" Maelwich asked, turning it over in her hand.

"That, I have not yet discovered," Shiver admitted. "It could be the spirits themselves."

"Or something worse," Maelwich said.

"Perhaps."

He had considered many different possibilities down the centuries. Perhaps they were conjured by his very own consciousness. Regardless, they were the surest means to discovering his past. They showed him all that he had done, and that knowledge, though repulsive, was precious. He had long ago decided that the only way he could absolve himself of the evil he had enabled, would be to piece together every vile misdeed.

"Where did you find this one?" he went on.

"It was discovered in one of the deepling tunnels beneath the Dunwarr city, not long after the shadow had started to grow. I felt its significance, and Kalwen, our storyteller, recalled the tales about you and the arcane locks of memory. I suspected there was a connection."

"This shadow, you have seen it too?" Shiver asked. Maelwich still hadn't given him the lock. He did his best not to focus on it, instead looking her in the eyes and silently repeating his mantra.

"I have," Maelwich said. "And it is more than just a shadow. It is death. The shadow-that-hungers. It has taken lives. Entire daggerbands. I fear it is stalking the clan. It means to consume us all."

"That is why the Aethyn are abroad?" Shiver wondered. Everything Maelwich had said seemed to have confirmed his own fears. The Ynfernael was at work here, beyond a doubt. That was bad enough, but he was now almost certain he was somehow bound to its presence as well. It filled him with fear and self-loathing, but that same self-loathing forced him to carry on. He would not falter, not when fate or the gods had delivered him into the heart of this struggle.

"The Dunwarr know you have been more active than normal," he went on. "Encroaching into their tunnels. They view it as an act of aggression."

"We are hunting," Maelwich said. "Hunting the shadow, and being hunted by it in turn. Some believe we have tracked it down to the caverns beneath the city itself. If that is the case, no tunnel-treaty or territorial claim will stop us from seeking it out."

"How do you know it has spawned from under Thelgrim?"

"That is where it is strongest, most impenetrable," Maelwich said. "That is where I saw it myself. The tunnels there are… not as they should be."

Shiver was silent for a while, considering Maelwich's

words. He had thought the shadow hailed from somewhere unknown, had crawled up from a lonely crack in the bowels of the earth or had slithered down from the far north. He had not anticipated its presence beneath Thelgrim itself.

"Why did you come here, Shiver?" Maelwich asked. The question was simple and honest, yet he found himself struggling to face it with an answer.

"We were seeking the Hydra," he said. "A Star of Timmoran."

"A fine prize for your human companion, no doubt," Maelwich said, her eyes discerning in the half light. "But not for you. What were you promised?"

"The locks," Shiver admitted, gesturing to the one in Maelwich's grasp.

"Were you lied to?" she asked.

"It seems so."

"Well, perhaps fortune wanted you to still have one," she said. She looked down, considering the device for a moment more, then stretched out her hand over the cold flame of the jaela. Shiver hesitated, then reached out and received it.

He felt the power as soon as it touched his palm, the redolent potency of the Empyrean confined into the carefully carved bone. He felt the fear he'd known before redouble, but twinned now with desire. It was always the same when he held one. The allure of the unknown would grow and grow, like an addiction, until he couldn't resist sliding in the key and seeing for himself what tortured fragment of his past had been dredged up from the ether.

"What made you stay?" Maelwich asked, watching him carefully as he stared down at the unassuming item. "When you realized your benefactor could not pay in the way you wanted. Why are you still here, wandering the *denwal far*?"

"The shadow," Shiver said. "I have… felt it before. I know its essence."

"I fear we all do," Maelwich said.

"It must be excised," Shiver continued. "Burned away, before it can grow any stronger. Before it can spread further."

"I will tell the council as much," Maelwich said. "They are not yet in agreement about what should be done with you."

"Does that matter?" Shiver asked. "As you said, it is your clan to lead."

"I said there are times to lead, and times to heed advice. I am not yet done listening."

Shiver inclined his head, looked for a moment more at the lock in his hand, and stood. He brushed his fingers over his eyes, an Aethyn parting gesture.

"How will finding your memories help?" Maelwich asked, returning the gesture, but not rising.

"They may contain knowledge about this darkness under the city," Shiver said. "A way to fight it."

"I didn't mean the shadow," Maelwich said, looking up into his eyes. "I meant you. The stories say you seek absolution for the crimes you were forced to commit. How does reclaiming your memories help your penance? How are you atoning by collecting them?"

Shiver smiled, a sorrowful expression.

"I'm not. But I cannot do penance before I first know everything that I need to be penitent for."

Shiver returned, without a guard, to the cave that lay off from the cavern. In the darkness within he found Astarra waking, her staff scraping against the bare stone floor as she remembered where she was. There was a hiss as the flames of her runestone ignited, illuminating her drawn, worried face.

"Rest easy," Shiver murmured. "I am here, and no one else."

"You left?" she asked hoarsely, sitting up.

"I needed to find where we stand," Shiver said, making no effort to conceal the lock in his hand. "I ended up with more than I anticipated."

"They had one of your locks?" Astarra wondered. "What did they want in exchange?"

"I'm not sure yet," Shiver admitted. "But hopefully, my help."

Astarra grunted something and fumbled in her pouch, drawing out her water skin and drinking from it heavily.

"You should change the runestone," Shiver suggested. "It is singeing our souls. The way you wield it, the power you dredge from it, you have borne its fire for too long."

He gestured at her staff, at the cracks that were visibly starting to split the dry bone.

"I need its light," she said between gulps, the flame atop her staff flickering every time she drank.

"Let us see if we can find a less costly source," Shiver said. He crossed the cave to the far corner, where a cluster of jaela were growing.

"Bring your fire here," he suggested. "And touch it to the top of the jaela."

"You'd have me burn a cave root?" Astarra wondered, as she found her feet and joined him.

"It is not the fungus itself that burns, only its spores," Shiver said. "See?"

He laid a hand on Astarra's staff and gently guided it down to the fluted crest of the largest of the fungi. There was a small hiss as the flame took, igniting not the plant itself but the air just above it. The greenish flame flickered and danced as it took.

Shiver felt the draining heat of the energies being given off by Astarra's runestone. He reached up and carefully removed the channeling focal, a share of igneous rock. It burned to the touch, its runebound fire-magics anathema to his own chill abilities. It made him want to snatch his hand away, but he made himself show no reaction, giving Astarra time to remove the runebound shard itself and, after the slightest hesitation, deposit it in her pouch. Only then did he hand her the rock.

"Are you going to open it?" Astarra said, glancing at the lock still in Shiver's other hand.

"Yes," he said.

"I want to see what you see," she replied as she removed another of her shards from her pouch. Shiver frowned despite himself.

"I do not know if that is possible."

"Have you ever tried with someone else?"

He hadn't. He'd never even considered it.

"Why?" he asked. "What could my memories mean to you?"

"They would let me see the world the way you do, if only for a moment," she said. "You speak often of trust. When we first met, my instincts told me that you were a creature of darkness."

"There are many kinds of darkness," Shiver said. "And not all of them evil."

"I know," Astarra continued. "And now I realize that my instincts towards you are telling me the opposite of what they did before. You have felt the touch of darkness, but you are no longer controlled by it. You walk in shadow no more. But instincts are one thing. Certain knowledge is another. I want to see."

Shiver held Astarra's gaze. His immediate reaction was to deny her, to lie about it being impossible or too dangerous. Both were valid reasons, but he knew they weren't the truth. He didn't want her to see his past. He didn't know what the lock would show them, and he was too afraid it would show the darkness that marred his soul.

She looked back at him unflinchingly. She had come far with him, further than most others. There was still distrust there, fear even, but it was now twinned with a stronger curiosity. He realized there was little he could do to deny it.

"You will have to relinquish your staff for the time being," he said. "I do not know what variance it could create."

Astarra considered the proposal, then removed another of her runestones, the Viridis, and slotted it home on the cracked staff's head. Then she moved to the wall of the cave, and propped it up, beside the smoldering jaela root.

"Is there an incantation?" she asked as she rejoined him.

"Not as such," Shiver said. "Empyrean magic often doesn't require any. It is more of an ... instinctual matter. But this one does require a degree of physical contact to trigger it."

"You hold the key," Astarra surmised. Shiver nodded, raising the ornate key that hung about his waist.

"If we use it together, you may be able to experience the power of the lock second hand," Shiver said. "This acts similarly to when you channel using your staff. Clear your mind, and use whatever incantation you normally would to bring forth the Verto Magica."

He held the key before the lock. Astarra grasped his hand with hers. It was warm on his icy skin. He hesitated, then fitted the key home, and turned it.

CHAPTER NINETEEN

Raythen looked up as the door to the Dunwol Keg creaked open. The jailer made way for not one figure, but two, the torchlight glinting in their dark eyes. They stepped in, watching Raythen the way wild beast tamers in the traveling carnival might watch an animal they suspected hadn't yet been fully broken. Raythen grinned up at them.

"Well, if it isn't my father's favorites," he said.

Neither Korri nor Zorri returned the expression. There was a shuddering thud as the cell door was closed and locked behind them.

"You are choosing death," Zorri said, his hands clasped over his long, white beard.

"Correction," Raythen said. "Death has already been chosen for me, by the Guild Council and, I suspect, by your good selves."

"That outcome is not set in stone," Korri said. He shifted to the left as he spoke, unconsciously almost squashing Raythen's mound of slop underfoot. He forced himself not to look at it as the advisor continued.

"All the king desires is the return of the Hydra. He does not wish to punish you, beyond formalizing your exile."

"A matter we advised him to make official decades ago," Zorri added, shifting to the other side of the cell, so that Raythen was forced to look from one to the other as they spoke, unable to keep them both in his vision at once. He realized he was instinctively glad that he had his back to the wall – he wouldn't have been able to concentrate with even the thought of one of them behind him. He'd known plenty of criminals he wouldn't turn his back to, but none came close to the feeling the twins gave him.

"I find it difficult to believe my dear father doesn't want to see me pulverized during the trial," he said, trying to keep a hold on the conversation. "If anything, the Hydra's loss is just a convenient excuse."

"The Hydra's loss vexes every soul in this city," Korri clarified. "But its safe recovery would go some way to healing the wounds caused by so heinous a crime."

Raythen scoffed. "You really think the guilds will forgive and forget if it turns up tomorrow in some Cragwarren gutter-channel? Once a full council has been removed from its box, it isn't easily put back in. My father knows that, yet still he allowed it. Hydra Shard or not, they will want blood for this. Nothing less will sate them."

"That much is true," Zorri said, the agreement catching Raythen by surprise. "But it doesn't have to be your blood."

"Your accomplice, the fool named Mavarin," Korri went on. "He has long plagued the guilds with his antics and accusations."

"If you were to tell us the Hydra's location, and swear upon all the ancestors that it was Mavarin who first stole it, we have no doubt the council would commute your own death sentence," Zorri said.

Raythen laughed dryly, not deigning to look at either of the advisors anymore, staring straight ahead instead. He was going to show them he wasn't afraid, of them or the Trial, even if that wasn't true. Those were the best odds, and he always played the odds.

"You two should know this isn't the first time I've sat in some dungeon cell, awaiting judgement," he said. "I can't count the number of times I've been asked to turn in an accomplice. Do you really think I don't know you've been offering the same to Mavarin? Telling him the council would do anything to see King Ragnarson's son on the executioner's block? Offering to pardon him?"

"True enough," Korri said, seemingly unfazed by Raythen's confidence. "But there is an important difference. Mavarin doesn't know where the Hydra is. He is, at best, an average liar. You, however, are a far more likely candidate when it comes to locating that Star of Timmoran."

"Mavarin has nothing to negotiate with," Zorri said, taking up his brother's words. "You do. Tell us where the Hydra Shard is, and your life will be spared."

"My life isn't in danger," Raythen said defiantly. "I will win the Trial of the Mountain."

That was a bluff, and a fairly obvious one. The Trial of the Mountain hadn't been seen in Thelgrim for decades for a good reason. It consisted of a series of progressively heavier weights being laid on top of the two suspects, until one confessed or was crushed to death. If either happened, the other was immediately absolved. To call upon it was usually a last act of desperation.

Raythen just hoped he was better at bluffing than Mavarin.

"You know your survival is far from certain," Korri said. "Even if Mavarin breaks before you, you may not survive. The mountain is indifferent when it comes to mercy, or restraint."

"I've no doubt he's content to see me executed in a more traditional manner," Raythen said. "Anything I can do to upset him is merely a bonus."

"Woe that our noble king bore so spiteful a child," Zorri snarled. Raythen merely smiled again. Inside he was quaking with fury. All his life, the twins had been at his father's elbow, poisoning him against his only son. They were devious creatures, the offspring of one of the old, noble houses who had fallen into disrepute and ruination when the guilds had risen to prominence and supplanted the ancient rulership of the Dunwarrs. They seemed to carry that bitterness in everything they did. His father, for whatever reason, never appeared to have realized that.

"Tell us the location of the Shard, and you will not have to risk the grim fate that awaits you," Korri insisted. Raythen fixed him with a glare.

"If I learned one thing growing up, it's that whatever you suggest, honest folk should probably do the opposite," he said. "You are two tips of the same forked tongue."

"Fortunate that you are not one of those honest folk then, isn't it, Raythen?" Zorri said, this time returning his smile. He laughed.

"I'll consider your wise advice, oh noble councilors," Raythen said. "But if it's all the same, I'd rather not spend my last few hours conversing with a pair of mountain snakes."

The advisors exchanged a glance, before Zorri beat his fist on the inside of the cell door.

"You don't deserve the mercy we offer, kingspawn," Korri said, as the rattle of keys announced the unlocking of the door.

"Do not leave your last chance too late," Zorri said.

Raythen offered them a light shrug. It wasn't until the door slammed shut and the echoes of their footsteps had receded up the Dunwol Keg's stairway that he finally managed to unclench his fists.

The tunnels stank of blood and darkness.

Shiver's senses were being assailed. He stood in the midst of carnage, of slaughter, of an atrocity that he knew he had unleashed.

The Aethyn were dying. The last of the daggerbands had made a stand in one of their sacred caverns. They were trying to buy time for those who could not fight to escape the darkness, and the avalanche of rending talons and wicked fangs that had come with it.

She knew that was the purpose of this final battle. The one who ruled Shiver, who controlled him, who had bound him to her dark purpose. She knew this was all a distraction. And Shiver knew how she hated distractions.

"Hurry," she hissed. The word was only partly meant for Shiver. It goaded the slaughter-beasts around them, claws scraping on stone as they bore down on the tunnel the remnants of the Aethyn were fleeing through. Hulks of the Ynfernael, redolent with demonic power, their bodies like slabs of molten rock bubbling with magma-heat, their great maws like fanged, blazing furnaces.

Shiver was driven before them. The tunnels beyond the cavern were narrow and winding, their bare rock walls amplifying the heat of the Ynfernael creatures. They swept round a corner and found the stragglers from the last of the Aethyn. A girl and her mother, too slow to keep up with the rest. The latter had fallen. The former was trying to help her back to her feet. She froze as she saw Shiver, framed by the terrible beasts he had unleashed.

Time seemed to stand still. The girl's eyes were wide in the terrible glow of the hulks. Shiver's gaze met hers, riven with fear and confusion and, in that fleeting instant, he made his choice.

He turned and stood before the oncoming Ynfernael creatures.

"No more," he snarled, the chains that bound him drawn taut as he spread his arms, blocking the tunnel.

His power surged, then stumbled, held in check by the enchanted manacles. They were rimed with ice, the air of the tunnel turned suddenly frigid. That was all though – since being shackled, Shiver had never been able to draw upon the Empyrean, never been able to unleash his magics in defiance of his fate. He didn't need magic right now though. He only needed that which he had been lacking for so long. Courage.

The hulks lunged, their terrible heat making the cold air shimmer. He faced them down without blinking, his heart pounding, his white flesh slicked with a cold sweat. He knew death in that moment, and welcomed it, welcomed the savage release of fangs and claws.

But it didn't come. A snarled command arrested the forward motion of the hulks, causing them to twist and writhe in agony just before they could collide with Shiver.

She stepped forward between them. The fires of the Ynfernael made her scales glimmer with a terrible, hypnotic beauty. Her eyes were beyond dark, a void born out of the shadow that had brought her to Mennara's plane. They doused Shiver's courage. Slowly, shaking, he lowered his arms.

"Stand aside," she commanded.

"No," he said, forcing the word out.

Her lipless maw curled back, exposing her fangs in an expression of disgust.

She lashed out, the blow catching Shiver in the abdomen. He grunted, but took it, straightening back up in front of her.

She struck him again, raking him with her talons. Bright blood streaked his skin. He cried out, but still he stood.

Blows fell in a rain. He raised his forearms to protect himself. Ironically, the manacles and their biting chains took the sting from the blows. He felt them pause as she realized she was in danger of shattering the very restraints she'd crafted for him.

To his surprise, she laughed. He dared lower his arms, his whole body shaking now, the sting from his fresh wounds making him hiss softly.

"You really do amuse me, Shiver," she said, her voice still riven with a dark, joyless mirth. "I have never known a child of the Deeps as stupid and cowardly. You've done my bidding across Mennara, been responsible for the deaths of thousands. You've unleashed the raw glory of the Ynfernael here today and doomed an entire clan of your kindred to extinction. Yet only now do you find the will to try and resist. After my objectives lie completed, after you have committed the greater evil, you try and stop the lesser from being carried out. Look at me."

He forced himself to meet the void where once her eyes had been.

"After all you've done, you'd die for one little girl and her mother?" she demanded.

"It's a start," he said.

He watched her face contort from amusement into rage. She snatched him by the throat and flung him against the tunnel wall, the Ynfernael beasts at her feet yelping as her anger was transmuted into them. Shiver grunted with pain as he hit the stone and slumped down, his chains rattling. He managed to look up, not at his tormentor as she towered over him, but past her, down the tunnel's length.

The girl and her mother had gone.

The crack of the master's cane against the side of the lectern made Astarra jump. She looked up in surprise before remembering to avert her eyes. Master Loach didn't like it when students held his gaze.

"Wrong again!" the fat old runemaster barked, knuckles white where he grasped his stick. "I despair, Astarra, I really do!"

"I'm trying, Master," she said, face flushed with embarrassment and anger. Her heart was racing and her palms were sweaty, making it difficult to turn the pages of the text arcanum laid out on the desk before her. The rest of the class had gone silent, most likely just happy Astarra was the current locus for Loach's wrath.

"That's what I'm afraid of," he growled. "I have been tutoring at the University of Greyhaven for thirty-three years now, Novice Astarra. Almost twice the length of time you've been alive! I can assure you, in all that lengthy period, I've never seen a student as rebellious and ungrateful as you. Never!"

"I'm sorry, Master Loach," Astarra mumbled, frantically searching across the page in an attempt to find where she'd misread the incantation. The words seemed to confound her, deliberately tripping her tongue, refusing to allow themselves to be uttered. The runeshard she'd been ordered to channel, the Deeprune, sat like a loadstone on the desk in front of her, gleaming with a deep, oceanic blue in the dusty light shafting through the lecture hall's high windows.

"When you first enrolled here, I held out some hopes for you," Loach was saying. She'd heard it all a dozen times before, and she

knew that if she didn't placate him soon, she'd spend the night scrubbing every crack between the hall's flagstones.

"To have already mastered a runeshard like the Viridis Stone at such a young age points to a degree of natural talent," he said. "Of course, I had misgivings about your lineage. Some Forthyn apple-picker's daughter. Still, I promised Grand Master Bellor that I would give you a fair chance. And I have, over and over."

"I'm sorry, Master Loach," she repeated, feeling her frustrations beginning to stir. She had been through this too many times. How often would she have to bow and scrape because some couldn't accept that someone who wasn't from wealth or power already possessed as much proficiency with the runes as they did? "I'll get it right this time, I swear by Kellos."

"Do not take his name in vain, young woman," Loach snarled, unhappy that his diatribe was being interrupted. "I have never known someone of your station to achieve anything of note, certainly in Greyhaven. You will be no different, I assure you."

Astarra realized abruptly that she'd snatched up the Deeprune. She could feel its energies flowing through her hand and arm, bitterly cold and crushing, like the depths of the Sea of Teallin. An audible gasp went up from the rest of the class. Loach had frozen.

"Novices are forbidden from touching a runestone, unless told to do so," he said. "The penalty for doing so is expulsion!"

Astarra gazed down at the small piece of marked stone in her palm, its size belying the fathoms of power it contained. It made her feel as though she could do anything, as though she need only think of something, and she would possess it. She looked up at Loach and met his gaze, feeling a potent surge of defiance as she held the eyes of the man who had so often spited her.

"I don't care," she said.

Fury gripped the runemaster. He hauled himself out from behind his lectern, spittle on his lips as he stormed towards her.

"You ungrateful little wretch! I'll teach you a lesson you won't forget!"

Astarra stood. Loach was bringing up his cane, face ruddy and twisted with fury.

She was faster. The words came to her now, unimpeded by stress or fear. As she said them, she raised the runestone in her right fist, calling on it, summoning up its power.

"Ataqua imedego!"

The runestone's energies surged, like water bursting through a dam. Invisible, it overturned Astarra's desk and slammed head-on into Loach. The runemaster was picked up and carried, hurled back into his own desk, sending books and papers flying.

Astarra gasped, feeling the phantom rush of cold water. She fought it, wrestled with it, feeling as though it was going to drag her under as well. Finally, she let go of the Deeprune. It clattered down like a lead weight, sinking heavily to the depths.

Loach gasped, slumped back against the remains of his desk. He was soaked from head to foot, his robes clinging to his fat frame, his hair lying lank over his shoulders.

"This… is an outrage…" he sputtered, staring up at Astarra. "You'll achieve nothing without the university! Nothing without the proper teaching!"

"I don't need runemagic to do this," she said, picking up his fallen cane and snapping it in half.

The lock exploded.

Astarra cried out. For a few racing heartbeats she didn't

know where she was. She could still feel the crushing force of the Deeprune, the rush of waters around her.

It was pain that brought her back. She raised her hand, and realized she had a long gash along her palm. Blood dripped slowly down her wrist to stain her baggy white sleeve, turning it black in the dim light of the smoldering fungal root.

The lock was no more. Seemingly overloaded by the confluence of energies and memories, it had burst apart in their hands. It was a shard of the split bone that had sliced across her.

Shiver seemed unhurt, though his black eyes were wide. He looked at Astarra, who returned his gaze with equal measurements of shock.

"You're hurt," he said slowly.

"Yes," she admitted. He reached out and carefully took her hand. His fingers were freezing to the touch, but he let her turn her palm over to inspect it.

"Relax," he ordered, before placing his own palm against hers. This time she did flinch, though the pain lasted only a moment. When Shiver removed his hand, her palm was still bloody – as were Shiver's long fingers – but beneath it the cut had healed.

"Thank you," she said softly.

"Did you see?" he asked her.

"Yes."

"Two visions?"

"Yes."

"We saw not only our own memories, but each other's. I did not know that was possible."

Astarra mustered up a shrug. Her thoughts had been thrown into turmoil. She understood now why Shiver had hesitated before agreeing to let her see a fragment of his past. It was intimate in a way she couldn't have comprehended before. To lay out not only a personal, private experience, but one that was redolent with pain and shame. She had never explained her past in detail to anyone before, let alone shared a recollection of it directly.

"I think it's because I forgot it," she said, forcing herself to admit to her thoughts. "That moment you saw. It was in Greyhaven, when I was still at the university. It was the night I left. I couldn't have told you anything about it before now. I think my memories blocked it out. It was too painful."

"It must have been very difficult," Shiver said. "The manner of teaching that seems to be employed at Greyhaven is far removed from the lessons my kind learn about the Empyrean, and the Turning."

"I should never have gone there," Astarra said. "It was only ever going to end that way."

"But if you had not, you would always have wondered," Shiver said. He was looking down at her blood on his hand. "You would have questioned whether or not a formal education could have unlocked the power you seek."

"It isn't power," Astarra said. "It's respect. I'm the daughter of an apple picker. There aren't many in Terrinoth who'd give me credit as a runemaster."

"There are many ways to earn respect," Shiver said, looking up at her.

"Have you found a better one than strength?" Astarra asked. "Than power?"

"Many," he said and, to her surprise, he smiled. "We would likely not still be alive had I not won Maelwich's respect."

"That was her, in the tunnel?" Astarra wondered. "With her mother?"

"I believe so. I had neither strength nor power that day, but found some degree of courage, at last."

"You were truly a slave then," Astarra said. "Bent to the will of the Ynfernael."

"No," Shiver said. "I was by then, but not at first. I flirted with its power. My essence was drawn to it by nature, it seems. For a little while, I embraced it. And by the time I realized the terrible consequences that came with it, I was already shackled."

"The one that did that to you," Astarra said, unable to hide a shiver as she recalled the terrible creature that had commanded him in the tunnel. "Who was she?"

"I do not speak her name," Shiver said. "Not yet. I... am not ready."

She knew better than to press him. Instead, she went and retrieved her staff. The cooling rush of the Viridis Seed was a welcome relief.

"We know that I have been here before," Shiver said, his gaze now on the key still in his hand, undamaged by the arcane lock's destruction. "We know that I was the one responsible for unleashing a terrible evil in this place. It can only be the same evil that now haunts the Deeps again."

"You're sure?" Astarra asked.

"No, but I will be soon," he said. "I am going to offer to lead Maelwich and her daggerbands to where I believe it emanates from. Once there, I will seal it away for all time. Another small step along the path of penance."

Astarra thought for a moment. The elf seemed set on his course. She didn't know what help she could offer him, didn't even know exactly how he expected to combat something as ethereal as a shadow. The one thing she was certain of was that she wouldn't be backing down now. She spoke.

"Thank you, for healing my hand."

Shiver blinked, as though he'd forgotten the deed.

"You are most welcome, Astarra."

"I'm coming with you," she told him, her tone brooking no argument. She was surprised to realize that there was no hesitation, even in her thoughts.

He nodded. "I thought you might. *Hoped* you might."

"You did?" she asked, genuinely surprised that the elf would want her alongside him after all her jibes and suspicions. She was even more surprised when she realized that he was smiling.

"There is a struggle ahead," he said. "Desperate and dire. I don't need to see your memories to know that you would never turn your back on a challenge like that."

CHAPTER TWENTY

The Dunwol Kenn Karnin resounded to the deepling drums. They had struck up about an hour before, and had been steadily rising in tempo ever since, their rhythm running through the stonework of the ancient citadel.

Raythen recognized the beat. It was a *mori barr*, the death march. It heralded the end of kings and the return of the fallen from war. It was called up from the Hall of the Ancestors to ring out through Thelgrim, through the very roots of the mountain itself. It was a statement of certainty. A dwarf would die this day.

Bradha led him from the Dunwol Keg. He didn't try to resist. He'd considered it. He could still make his play. But he knew he'd have been acting in panic and, in his experience, that never ended well. It wasn't time. Escape was the final option, and he still had other ones available.

As usual, he was gambling. On this occasion, it was on Mavarin breaking before he did. Mentally or physically, it no longer mattered. It had been up to him to raise the stakes. He couldn't blink first, not now.

There was no jeering this time as he was marched into the throne room. Instead, the Guild Council began to chant in time with the rising beat of the hidden drums, a wordless counterpoint that spoke of dark anticipation.

The beat grew faster as he was taken down into the bowl of the amphitheater, stamping boots reverberating back from the vault above and making the flagstones underfoot vibrate.

The blocks he, Mavarin and the jury had been gathered at had been removed, replaced by one large stone dais set before the throne crag. There were raised metal platforms on either side, both heaped with a series of carved stone slabs. Mavarin was already waiting under guard before the dais steps, while beyond it Ragnarson watched from his throne. His expression was as cold as ever.

"You really think this is a good idea, Raythen?" Mavarin demanded as he was led to his side.

"I think it's got potential, yes," he replied, mustering as casual a tone as he could. The inventor looked drawn, afraid.

"You d- didn't have to do this," he went on. Raythen ignored him. He was too busy trying to look unconcerned. His stomach was in knots and his mind was turning over in suppressed panic. He looked to his father, but there was no relief there, no comfort, only the chill indifference he'd grown up seeing every day.

The drumbeats and their accompanying chants were still ringing out. Ragnarson raised his voice to shout the appointed words over the din.

"The accused have called to be tried under the Law of the Mountain, and so have been brought to the base of the Judgement Stone. They will now bear up the weight of the mountain, rock by rock, until one admits to his crimes and recants, or one perishes. If either happens, the other shall be absolved of his transgression. We let the mountain decide!"

The chanting rose to a thundering crescendo. Mavarin and Raythen had their shackles removed and were marched by Bradha up the dais steps and onto the stone slab. Up close it was possible to see that the entire pieces were covered in Dunwarr runic script, as were the blocks on the platforms to their left and right. It spoke of the ancient rites of the Trial of the Mountain, a Dunwarr custom stretching back as far as the founding of Thelgrim itself. When two were accused and both protested their innocence, one could call upon the mountain to judge them both.

Nowadays it was considered a barbaric practice, and was rarely ever called upon. It was considered better to face a jury, or imprisonment, than risk so torturous an end. In Thelgrim, Raythen knew of a single trial involving it that had taken place when he had been growing up. Two thieves, accused of stealing the ancient and sacred recipes of the Brewers' Guild, had turned on one another. In desperation one had called upon the mountain. The other had eventually confessed, but it was too late to save either of them. Nevertheless, it seemed the law had not been struck entirely. Raythen had been hoping as much.

"Lie," Bradha instructed. Raythen did so, on one side of the dais, while Mavarin hesitated on the other, still standing. The drumming and the chanting had blended into one continuous thunder, a wall of sound that vibrated through him via the cold, unyielding stone at his back.

Two Dunwarr, faces covered by grim, black lacquered

ancestor masks, stepped off the neighboring platforms carrying a square, flat stone slab. The drumming cut off, followed immediately by the chants. It took a long time for the last echoes to fade away. The sudden silence was as painful as the anticipation churning up inside Raythen. He forced himself to look at Mavarin, who was still standing, refusing to lie upon the grim stone. He seemed to have frozen in the midst of that awful silence, shackled as surely by terror as he was by the irons he'd worn.

He said something, though even in the stillness it wasn't audible. Ragnarson had raised a hand to command that the trial begin, but he paused, looking pointedly at the prisoner.

"What did you just say?" he demanded.

Mavarin looked up, eyes darting from the king, to the nearer Dunwarr, then briefly looking over at Raythen who realized there were tears in the inventor's eyes, as he spoke again, louder than before.

"I said, I was the one who stole the Hydra Shard."

The tunnels took them down into the Deeps.

From what Astarra could gather, the elves of the Aethyn clan called the passages and caves they inhabited the *denwal far*. They seemed to migrate between them, but according to Shiver they rarely ventured this far down. These were the deepest and least hospitable parts of the southern Dunwarrs, ancient crevasses in the mountain's roots. They ran beneath the vast cavern where Thelgrim sat, undiscovered even by the dwarfs, known only to the elves in their legends and songs.

Maelwich was taking them into those legends, into the spaces between the rocks where no creature of flesh and blood should tread. The Aethyn had, it seemed, decided to trust their prisoners. That, or Maelwich wanted them where she could keep an eye on them. They were to accompany a daggerband to the deepest reaches of the mountains.

Astarra had made no complaint. She couldn't deny that there was something festering in the tunnels around Thelgrim. Even unattuned to the Empyrean, she'd seen it herself, and had felt it growing ever since. She believed in Shiver's desire to stop it. She had come too far anyway. What could she have done, begged the Aethyn to guide her back to the surface? She was too deep now, in every sense.

The party had set out from the cavern where the Aethyn had made their camp – herself, Shiver, Maelwich and fourteen warriors lead by the hatchet-faced Talarin. Most of them were carrying torches made from the fibers of the jaela root bound around the heads of long sticks. The sight of them surprised her.

"Why do you need torches when you can see well enough in the dark?" she had asked. Shiver had murmured his response as they'd started to descend through the narrow tunnels.

"What better way to fight a shadow?"

The arduous journey seemed to last an age. Astarra had to force herself along cracks in the rock barely wide enough for her to fit side-on, then crawl on all fours through tunnels she could barely fit her head and shoulders through. The elves didn't appear to be phased by any of it, their long, lean bodies seemingly ideal for finding passage through the tightest rock formations. On several occasions she began to panic, convinced she was going to be trapped in a narrow shaft and crushed to death or left to starve. Shiver stayed with her throughout though, murmuring words of advice and encouragement to her whenever she faltered.

The memory of his stand in the upper tunnels had stayed with her. The experience of the lock had been so visceral, so immediate. She'd felt his thoughts as much as witnessed his actions – pain, anger, an overwhelming, miserable shame. For a moment she'd shared in all of them. They'd been her feelings as much as his.

She wondered whether he had felt the same. Had he experienced the frustration, rage and embarrassment that had overtaken her the night she had left Greyhaven? Now that he'd experienced it firsthand, did he know the need that drove her, the determination to prove herself?

"Wait," Shiver whispered. Astarra came to a halt behind him, half-crouched in a low, narrow passage draped with mold lichens. She felt a spike of panic, recalling how they had stopped while first on the way to the Aethyn encampment. The fear then had been a palpable force, almost more than she could bear. Shiver seemed to sense her thoughts.

"The scout is just getting his bearings," he murmured.

She said nothing. She couldn't tell if he was speaking the truth, or trying to spare her.

They moved off again soon after, dropping down through a steep sloping shaft and then along a crevasse that was painfully narrow, but stretched up so far that the torchlight of the elves couldn't pick out its roof.

As they went, she found herself thinking about Raythen. The Dunwarr should still be with them. He'd sacrificed himself so they could get away. It was the last thing she would have expected from him, but just a few days ago she couldn't have imagined trusting Shiver either, let alone feeling empathy with him. It seemed as though she'd misjudged them both, believed in her own prejudices, or let herself be lulled by the personas they projected to guard their true selves. In that sense, she'd been as thoughtless and unthinking as Runemaster Loach when he'd scoffed at her own upbringing. The realization pained her.

What had become of Raythen? Was he even still alive? She had thought about going back to him, but she didn't even know how she'd reach Thelgrim, let alone find and free him from the heart of the city. She hoped the fact that he was a Dunwarr would see him treated fairly, with honor. A king's son no less. It was little wonder he'd played the careless, petty thief with them. Had he really come for the reward they'd initially been offered? Had he sensed they were walking into a trap?

Find the Shard. That was what he'd shouted as he'd been taken. Yet here she was, delving into the deepest, darkest corner of Mennara, hunting shadows. Shiver seemed to have forgotten the Hydra. She doubted he'd ever really cared about it. He'd been following visions and hunting memories. The Shard was just a convenient excuse.

They came to another abrupt stop. She looked at Shiver, who called out softly to Maelwich and the elf at the head of the group. She didn't understand the exchange, but she could hear the dismay in the scout's voice.

"He has trod these paths before," Shiver informed her. "But he does not remember this obstruction. The passage should not end here."

"You know what that sounds like to me?" Astarra asked quietly. Shiver nodded.

"A trap," he said.

He spoke to Maelwich again. They were ordered back along the narrow tunnel and up the rock slope, to an intersection they had taken earlier. The scout took them down another path. Astarra felt the hairs of her forearms and along the nape of her neck rise as they came to a stop once again.

"He says the tunnels have changed," Shiver murmured to her as he listened in on a terse conversation between the scout and Maelwich. "That they have… reformed since he was last down here."

"How is that possible?" Astarra hissed.

"It isn't," Shiver responded. She felt a chill come over her, and her heart began to race faster. This was almost exactly what she feared. To be trapped down in the dark, at a dead end, and shadows all around.

Before she could respond, one of the other elves standing near the head of the group cried out and pointed with his torch. Astarra followed his signal in time to see something emerging from a hairline crack in the rock face obstructing them. At first, she thought it was a serpent or some sort of great earthworm, but as it twisted and writhed, growing larger by the second, she realized it wasn't corporeal. It was a shadow, and it did not fear the light of the jaela.

It lunged before anyone else could react, snagging around the wrist of the scout next to Maelwich. He tried to haul against it, but was dragged off balance and pulled up against the rock wall.

"Ulthar," Maelwich shouted, a blade in each hand. She slashed at the coil of darkness snaring her kinsman, but the wicked, curved knives slipped straight through to strike off the uneven stone, drawing sparks.

Ulthar was shouting something. Astarra brought up her staff, drawing on the life-giving force of the Viridis, just as she felt Shiver tapping into his own powers, causing the temperature to plummet. Maelwich, however, was blocking the space between them and the hapless scout. She was striking in vain at the hairline split in the rock face where the darkness was pouring forth.

It billowed and surged, more exploding from cracks all along the stone. As Astarra watched, frozen with fear and horror, it took on the shape of clawed, black hands that gripped the screaming Ulthar, hauling him up off the tunnel floor and fully pinning him back on the stone.

He managed to rip one hand free, reaching out in desperation. Astarra reacted instinctively, lunging past Maelwich. She snatched hold of the elf, and found herself staring into his black eyes. They were wide with panic and terror, the whites showing.

He said a single word to her.

"Daewyl."

Then the darkness took him. The shadow hands closed over his mouth, then his whole face. His entire body was swallowed up, his hand torn from hers with such force she thought she heard his fingers break.

And then he was gone. The darkness disappeared back into the cracks it had bled from. There was simply no sign of the elf. The rock face stared back at them blankly, solid and immutable. Even the splits the shadows had bled from seemed to have disappeared.

Astarra stared in shock. It took Shiver's cold touch to bring her back.

"Step away from it," he whispered urgently.

She did the opposite. She raised her staff and snarled a channeling word, lunging out with the power of the Viridis. Its essence entered the rock face, seeking the life-force it could use to tear it down, either the shoots of rock moss and weeds or the stolid spirit of the stones themselves.

Instead, all she found was darkness. It engulfed her, trapping her in a void, invading her senses. It tasted bitter, and stank of burning rock. It was full of whispers and hatred and hunger. She tried to cry out, to scream, but it choked her.

"Astarra!"

The aching cold allowed her to resurface. She gasped, stumbling, and realized she was leaning into Shiver for support. After a second, he embraced her.

"Ulthar is gone," he murmured. "There's nothing beyond that wall but the shadow. You were right. It's a trap."

Astarra prised herself from Shiver. She was shaking. The darkness had released her, but its hunger lingered, inhuman and ravenous.

"It's down here," she managed to say. "It's down here, and it wants to consume us all."

CHAPTER TWENTY-ONE

Raythen and Mavarin were brought down from the dais, flanked by guards, as it was disassembled into its constituent blocks. The jury was summoned forth from the chattering crowd, and Ragnarson took up his hammer once more. If there had been any hint of relief when the stones had been hauled off earlier, there was no sign of it now.

"The council notes that the accused, Kayl Mavarin, has confessed to the crime of stealing the Hydra Shard from the Hall of the Ancestors," he declared. "He will now submit himself to further questioning. I call upon Haldar of the Masons' Guild."

Haldar stepped forward from where the jury had assembled on one side of the throne. She was as stocky and square-looking as the blocks of stone she so famously fashioned. She stayed silent for a moment, clearly enjoying the attention given to her by the now-silent council, before addressing Mavarin.

"Describe how you went about stealing the Hydra Shard."

Mavarin had gone deathly pale. Raythen had no doubt that

he was regretting blurting out his confession. For his own part, it was proving difficult to keep his expression neutral. He'd been certain since meeting him that Mavarin hadn't been telling them everything there was to know about the Hydra's disappearance. To have actually stolen it himself though – Raythen didn't think the beardless inventor had it in him. A part of him wondered if it was a false confession, a moment of raw panic brought on by the threat of the Trial. Fortuna knew, by the end he'd been considering it himself.

Mavarin looked from Haldar to Ragnarson, who met his gaze fiercely. He dropped his eyes and started to speak.

"I tunneled into the t- third undercroft, the family tomb of the Svenbaldars," he murmured.

"Speak up," Ragnarson snapped, his voice ringing back from the ceiling. A flash of anger crossed Mavarin's face, and he looked up at Haldar, his voice raised.

"I tunneled into the Svenbaldar crypt. The third undercroft hasn't been entered in decades. I waited there until the Hall of the Ancestors was empty, and went directly to the tomb of Holburg, where the Shard lay. I took it."

Voices surged among the crowd – shock, outrage, denial. Raythen tried to keep his expression guarded, to not let his dismay show through, but it was difficult. He'd considered the possibility that Mavarin was as much a thief and a con-artist as he was, and dismissed it. In a way, he'd been right. Perhaps Mavarin was *more* of a trickster than him.

Ragnarson was beating at the anvil once more, trying to quieten the guilds as Haldar shouted over it all.

"Every part of the Hall was searched afterwards, including the undercrofts! No evidence of tunnelling was found."

Mavarin shrugged. "I did my best to seal up the wall after me. Whoever was looking, perhaps they didn't look very hard."

"Are we really to believe you simply walked into the final resting place of Deeplord Holburg and plucked the Hydra from her treasure casket?" Fellin demanded. Haldar looked askance towards Ragnarson, angry that her line of questioning was being subverted, but the king was too busy bellowing for order from the rest of the council to reprimand the errant silversmith.

"There were n-no guards," Mavarin said. "The Hall of the Ancestors is not some musty, dead place of locked tombs. You know as well as I, Master Fellin, that the Dunwarr are free to visit the final resting places of their ancestors, to pay homage, seek guidance and hear the stories of yore. Or you would know that, if you honored the ancestors as I do. As all Dunwarr should!"

More outrage. Raythen was almost impressed. He still couldn't tell whether anything Mavarin was saying was the truth, but he'd certainly worked his crowd. Ragnarson had actually given up with his hammer and anvil and was sitting on his throne, glaring with unblinking, withering intensity at the inventor. The hall reverberated with the Guild Council's tumult, and Fellin had to be physically restrained by the rest of the jury.

Korri, standing amidst the accusers alongside his brother, made a curt gesture to the two captains, Svensson and Svensdottir, flanking the Throne of Tanngnoster. They began to beat their weapons against the rims of their shields, a battering rhythm that was taken up by the guards ringing the top level of the amphitheater. Slowly the uproar began to abate, until only the threat of sword and shield remained. That too was stilled by a sharp gesture by Ragnarson.

"Mistress Haldar has the floor," he growled. "And if any of you wish this trial to continue uninterrupted, she will keep it until I say otherwise. Continue."

Haldar, ruddy with anger, took a moment to compose herself before speaking again.

"Will the accused confirm he encountered no resistance during the perpetration of his heinous crime? While the Hall of the Ancestors is typically open to all, can he account for the absence of the Hall's wardens or the Tomb Master who oversees it?"

"I saw n-neither," Mavarin said. "And no, I cannot account for their absence at that particular time."

A murmur ran through the audience, checked by a furious look from Ragnarson.

"I find believing that a challenge," Haldar said. "It seems this jury needs to question the wardens and the Tomb Master to ascertain whether they were at their posts."

"They are not members of the guilds, and so were not summoned to this council," Ragnarson declared. "I will send for them at the next interlude."

"Might I make a suggestion as to their absence," Korri called out from the jury, looking towards Ragnarson. The king nodded, and both Korri and Zorri stepped forward together, ignoring Haldar's obvious frustration.

"I consider it highly improbable that the theft of the Shard was the work of a single criminal," Korri said. "And indeed, we have two accused standing before us right now. The Trial of the Mountain may have found in favor of Raythen, but that should not eliminate him from our understanding of the crime as a whole."

There it is, Raythen thought. The Trial had brought him a reprieve, but it seemed as though it was already up. He had refused to help the twins when they'd visited his cell. He had no doubt they wanted to pay him back for that.

"It seems likely to us that if Mavarin didn't have a hand in the apparent absence of the wardens, Raythen may well have," Zorri said, off the back of his brother's veiled accusation. "This Council might benefit from questioning him on the matter."

"As a victor in the Trial of the Mountain, I am not bound to answer this jury," Raythen said. "In fact, by law I could walk out of this hall right now, and none of you could stop me."

"That would be a point of debate," Zorri said, smiling at Raythen with all the charm of a rattlefang serpent. "And a hotly contested one at that. But I would certainly like to see you try."

Raythen shrugged. "Regardless, I will not answer, except to say that your accusations are baseless. I had no hand in any of this."

More growls from the audience. He snatched a glance at Mavarin – two could play a crowd.

"I wish to open a line of questioning regarding motive," Krellen, the master of the Miners Guild said, before the council could get out of hand again. "King Ragnarson, I request the floor."

"Granted," Ragnarson said, motioning for Haldar and the twins to step back. They did so with obvious reluctance as Krellen took their place.

"The question of *how* does not seem to be one we can answer immediately," he declared, his imperious tone immediately grating on Raythen. "It would seem wiser, instead, to try to establish the *why*. Can you explain your actions to the jury, Kayl Mavarin? Consider, as you do so, that your life surely depends on it."

Mavarin cleared his throat, then hesitated. It was clear to Raythen he was trying to put on a show of defiance, and was coming up short. He'd broken first, and he was still trying to work his way through the consequences. Whether he'd come up with a plan yet, whether these further admissions were all part of it, Raythen wasn't yet sure.

"I stole the Hydra Shard because I knew that whoever recovered it would be rewarded," he said. "I took it because I believed that once I claimed to have found it, the guilds would have little choice other than to admit the League of Invention."

A fresh surge of outrage gripped the throne room. Raythen caught himself feeling impressed. It was a drastic move, desperate, but it had almost paid off. Clearly Mavarin was obsessed with gaining official recognition.

"You really thought we would admit a lone madman onto this council?" Krellen demanded, caught somewhere between shock and anger.

"If I had been the one to find the Shard using my inventions, you would have," Mavarin said, voice filled with defiance. "And why not? My genius enabled me to steal it. Isn't that proof enough of my abilities, of the potential of my work?"

More rage. Ragnarson himself was barking something invective-laden at the inventor, his hammer and anvil forgotten. Raythen looked at Mavarin, catching his eye.

"You know, I'm almost impressed," he said above the uproar. Mavarin shrugged.

"Where is it?" Krellen was bellowing, pointing furiously at him. "Where have you hidden the Shard?"

"I don't know," Mavarin snapped back. "It's not where I left it. It's gone. I believe the deep elves took it."

It looked for a moment as though the guild council members were going to rush the two prisoners. Bradha signaled to the guards on the upper tiers, who formed a column that rapidly descended into the bowl and spread out around its edge, putting a barrier of burnished steel and iron-oak between the roaring crowd and the two prisoners.

Raythen could have laughed. It was all so obvious. The whole thing had been a charade, right up to the part where Mavarin had blasted his way into the cave off the tunnel junction. That was where he'd hidden the Shard after he'd stolen it, and that was where he had intended to triumphantly rediscover it. Instead, it had already disappeared, stolen, presumably, by another.

Only one part didn't make sense to Raythen.

"Why me?" he asked, ignoring the chaos unfolding around them. "Why did you hire three adventurers if the Hydra was never really missing?"

"It would have been too convenient if I'd rediscovered it alone," Mavarin replied, facing Raythen rather than the throne. "I couldn't trust anyone in Thelgrim, but if I hired outsiders, it would seem more legitimate when I rescued the Shard. Besides, those infernal deep elves are everywhere, and I didn't fancy having my throat slit traversing the last few tunnels. Planting the Shard the first time was more than enough."

"So, we were just hired muscle," Raythen said. "And an alibi. Don't insult my intelligence any further, Mavarin."

"What do you mean?"

"Come on. You specifically hired a traveling runewitch from the southern forests, the disgraced thief, son of the king of the Dunwarrs and a cursed deep elf who quite probably has the blood of thousands on his long, bony fingers. I couldn't imagine a trio more calculated to take the blame by this council for stealing the Shard."

"If I only intended to use you as a shield, wouldn't I have done that during this trial?" Mavarin said.

"I think you intended to," Raythen said. "I think you were caught off guard by the Trial of the Mountain. You panicked, and here you are. Full marks for planning, but execution leaves something to be desired… if you'll pardon the pun."

Mavarin looked away, clearly trying to master his anger. Raythen smirked, glad to be proven right by the tinkerer's expression, before the ringing report of the anvil drew him back to his father.

"The trial is adjourned!" Ragnarson was bellowing as he raised the hammer and pointed it at the two prisoners. "Captain Bradha, take them back to their cells. Both of them!"

"You can't do that!" Raythen shouted back. "The Trial of the Mountain is inviolable! I am a free Dunwarr!"

Ragnarson wasn't listening. In truth, Raythen had known winning the Trial guaranteed him little. At the very best, the jury would appeal his freedom and prevaricate over his release. Still, it felt good to be technically on the right side of the law, for once. He was going to make the most of it.

"Don't you dare lay a hand on me," he said to Bradha as she approached, one of the other guards grasping Mavarin.

To his surprise, she didn't grab him, but did point up the amphitheater stairs to the throne room doors.

"Free Dunwarr or not, if you want to leave this hall alive, I suggest you come quietly with me," the captain said. "Now."

"Point taken," Raythen replied, looking around at the pandemonium that had gripped the royal chamber. "We can discuss specific legalities later."

Maelwich helped lead them back up from the depths. News of Ulthar's unnatural demise spread rapidly through the encampment. The place seemed to grow even more quiet and somber.

"Thank you, for trying to save him," Maelwich said to Astarra and Shiver as the clan council prepared to meet once more. "Clearly the darkness below Thelgrim has grown more powerful than even we anticipated."

Astarra nodded, unable to bring herself to properly receive the thanks. She hadn't been able to save Ulthar's life. She felt as though the entire venture had been a failure.

"It has reformed the tunnels to confound any attempts at finding it before it is strong enough," Shiver said. "I believe it lies directly beneath the cavern lake the Dunwarr call the Blackwater."

"I am going to tell the council as much," Maelwich said. "I see no other option than to attempt to tunnel through. It's that, or abandon this place altogether."

The suggestion left Astarra aghast. She hadn't even considered the possibility of retreat. It didn't seem practical even when she did. It wasn't in her nature, she knew. It made no sense.

"You cannot abandon these mountains," she said "They're your home! And what about the dwarfs. They are completely unaware of what's coming. Once the shadow is strong enough, they won't stand a chance."

"We tried to warn them," Maelwich said. "Their mistrust and arrogance blinds them. They think we stole their worthless runeshard."

"And just who did?" Shiver asked. "Don't you think its disappearance is more than mere coincidence?"

"Even if we had it, there is little it would do to help us," Maelwich said. "You both felt the power in the darkness in those tunnels. It is of the Ynfernael, the hellish plane. It is the antithesis of the Empyrean. Petty runemagic will not stop it, even enhanced by a Dunwarr trinket."

"Runic magic is not petty," Astarra said, her anger goaded. She was trying to run through possibilities in her head, looking for a way forward that didn't involve abandoning the Dunwarrs to the Ynfernael. Maelwich gave her a withering look.

"You do not have the power to break open that stone," the elf said. "We will have to try by hand. I will speak to the council and call upon the rockshapers. If we can protect them, they may be able to delve through the rock and open a passage to the heart of this evil."

"It may take too long," Shiver said. "Every minute is vital."

"What if there's a way we can break through the rock?" Astarra said, her mind racing, the words struggling to keep up. There was one possibility, though she was almost loathed to admit to it. She had no wish to revisit that particular device. "A way to hit it so hard it doesn't have a chance to fight back?"

Shiver realized immediately what she meant. "Mavarin," he said.

"His device," she went on. "His burrower. We could reach the shadow before it has any more time to grow."

"What device?" Maelwich asked, adding something in the Aethyn tongue as she looked to Shiver.

"Mavarin is the Dunwarr inventor who brought us to Thelgrim," he said. "He has a large… contraption of his own design that seems capable of boring through the densest bedrock."

"We suspected the Dunwarr have some new, mechanical creation," Maelwich said. "We have been feeling strange vibrations in our passages for some time and uncovered unusual tunnels."

"It's perfect for reaching the space underneath the lake," Astarra said. "But we'll need him to pilot it. He was taken while Shiver and I were escaping Thelgrim. He and our other companion, Raythen."

"Why would the Dunwarr arrest two of their own?"

"King Ragnarson believes we had a hand in stealing the Hydra Shard," Shiver said.

"They were captured helping us escape," Astarra pointed out, looking sharply at him. "We abandoned them so we could get out. I want to repay that."

"I hadn't forgotten," Shiver said, his tone more defensive than she had anticipated. "But the threat of the shadow under Thelgrim cannot be ignored."

"You won't be ignoring it if we can get them out of Thelgrim," Astarra pointed out. "We need them."

"Are you suggesting breaking back into the fortress where

we were held?" Shiver asked. "Because that is likely where they'll be, under a full guard. We don't even know the tunneling device is still intact and can be reached once we have Mavarin."

"It's a safer gamble than trying to dig our way to the Ynfernael," Astarra said. "You said it yourself, we don't have time."

"I know nothing of gambling," Shiver admitted.

"Then consider it sound advice," Astarra said, looking to Maelwich. "If we can claim this device and its pilot, we can strike directly to the heart of the shadow. We just need a way of getting into Thelgrim's core."

"We have a way," Maelwich said, to Astarra's surprise. Apparently seeing her expression, the elf smiled.

"We have shared the mountain roots with the Dunwarr for many centuries. Not all of our interactions are peaceful. It would be remiss of me, as clan leader of the Aethyn, not to have a means of striking at the core of their fastness, should I need to."

"We do not seek war," Shiver said urgently. "If anything, the darkness below will feed off that. Every death will make it stronger."

"It wouldn't be a full assault," Maelwich said. "Merely an… expedition. I will inform the council as such and assemble the daggerbands."

CHAPTER TWENTY-TWO

"You can swim, can't you?" Shiver asked. He'd undone the upper half of his robes and secured them around his waist. The light of the jaela roots picked out his wiry, well-defined musculature, giving him a rangy, dangerous look.

"I can," Astarra said defensively, removing her short over-jacket and ensuring her long braid was properly bound. "I just haven't tried it underground before."

"The current is strong," Maelwich said. "Do not fight it. Let it carry you."

The deep elf daggerband, led by Maelwich and Talarin, had assembled on the edge of the river running through their encampment's cavern. The waters gurgled beneath Astarra, looking almost pitch-black as they wound their way over and around the smooth-worn rock. How she was supposed to navigate those lightless depths and avoid being dashed to pieces on slippery stone, she had no idea.

"What if I need to breathe?" she asked, only half joking.

"Raise your head," Maelwich said. "If it hits rock and you are still under water, keep swimming until you are not."

Astarra let out a little hiss of exasperation, and slung her staff over her shoulder. She really didn't want to do this. It had been her idea though, and there was no chance she was backing out of something she'd suggested, not when the Aethyn's council had agreed to it.

"Ready?" Talarin demanded impatiently. Astarra nodded. Maelwich had stepped up to the edge of the flow, long, swing daggers secured over her back. She looked to Shiver, who simply shrugged.

"*Atho alla,*" the leader of the Aethyn clan said, then stepped over the edge and dropped into the subterranean river.

The rest followed. Astarra hesitated. She realized Shiver was looking at her.

"I'm with you," he said. "Just follow the light."

"What li–" Astarra began to say, before Shiver pushed her. She just had time to drag in a huge breath before she hit the water.

The cold almost stole it from her. It was bitter and knifing, so overwhelming it momentarily shocked her into inaction.

The water around her shuddered as Shiver plunged in beside her. At first, she couldn't see anything, but she felt the current snatch her and pick her up. She struggled to hold onto her breath as she tried to right herself, thrown about in the black waters.

Just as she was about to panic, she saw what Shiver had meant. There was a light ahead, down in the river with her. She caught only a glimpse of it as the seething flow spun her around, but she was able to turn back towards it.

It was the green glow of the jaela root. One of the elves who had plunged into the river ahead had part of the fibrous fungi wrapped around a stick. It seemed to burn even underwater.

She held on just long enough to orient herself before the ache in her lungs grew too painful. She surfaced, dragging in a welcome surge of air. They hadn't even left the cavern yet. The current hauled her back under, like a living creature dragging down its prey.

Maelwich's words came back to her, amidst the broiling, frigid darkness. Don't fight the current. Let it carry you. She tried to relax, but it was difficult. The cold was all she could think about, that and the desperate desire to keep the light of the jaela in focus ahead of her. She struck out after it, and found, blessedly, that she was being swept along.

She didn't know how long she swam for. It became a nightmare of icy cold and surging, black currents. Several times her arms and legs struck painfully off unseen rocks, and once her staff snagged, arresting her and almost strangling her before she could free it from a submerged cleft. Countless times she struggled upwards, desperately seeking air, and found only the unyielding resistance of a flooded tunnel roof. She fought through the panic, kept going, until she reached even the smallest sliver of clear space between rock and water.

On and on it went, as the buried flood carried them along the twisting roots of the mountain. Then, suddenly, she realized that something had changed. The darkness was no longer absolute, no longer a crushing pressure around the tiny, wavering glow of the jaela being swept along ahead. Light had driven it off, had suffused the waters all around her. For the first time she could properly see the elves swimming alongside her, darting like sleek, aquatic hunters through the surge.

She surfaced again, struggling for air. The sight that greeted her stole the breath she'd been seeking.

The great ceiling arch of Thelgrim's cavern soared above her, a jagged sky of stalactites lit with the wonderous glow of a hundred starglobes and a million, million uncut gems and geodes. Their brilliance seemed to make the open air around her shimmer, and glittered back from the surface of what she realized now was Thelgrim's raised aqueduct. It felt as though she'd just passed through the darkest bowels of the Ynfernael and emerged into the glory of the celestial realms.

She laughed out loud, a sound of pure relief. They'd made it. They'd reached the aqueduct and were being carried above the city's rock-cut buildings. She wasn't going to drown in some watery tunnel or have her skull dashed by submerged stone.

She let the aqueduct's flow carry her back down, striking out with fresh purpose. The Aethyn were ahead of her, the glow that suffused the water making the bubbles that billowed from them gleam, like the knives strapped to their waists and backs. She caught up with them, locating Shiver amongst the pack. He glanced to the side and nodded to her.

They passed breaks in the stone on either side, tributaries that fed the aqueduct's water to other parts of the city. Astarra was forced to kick hard to avoid being hauled into one of them, staying with the elves as they followed the main artery.

Abruptly, the current surged. She no longer had to strike out – it hauled her along, a suctioning force she couldn't have resisted even if she tried. A roaring noise built amidst the pressure in her ears. She realized what was about to happen. She didn't get a chance to feel afraid.

The elves swimming directly ahead disappeared. She caught sight of the cavern roof through the water, and then she was plunging, her stomach turning over, and body buffeted by water as she fell. They'd reached the aqueduct's end and been swept out over its edge.

She managed to resist the urge to cry out. The freefall was over almost as swiftly as it had begun. She hit the surface of the Blackwater and was immediately forced under, battered and beaten by the roaring waterfall surging out over the aqueduct's edge.

A series of pounding blows hit her as she was driven down, down and down again by the weight of the water surging into the lake. She tried to struggle upwards, to find a current that would drag her out from under the waterfall, but there was none. The downpour forced her under and kept her there. She struggled with it, battling the deluge, panic starting to set in as she felt her strength waning.

Something snagged at her staff, followed by a sharp force. She lost the last air she'd been trying desperately to keep a hold of as she was hauled through the water, the horrendous, crushing pressure of the constant downpour finally relenting.

With a gasp she resurfaced, hauled up two-handed. Shiver had dragged her out. The elf was waist-deep, standing behind the flood of water cascading down from the aqueduct. The rest of the Aethyn had gathered beneath the structure's last, damp stone pillar, shielded from the view of anyone who might have been standing on the bank of the lake by the sheet of falling water.

"You are hurt," Shiver said. Astarra was too busy spitting out water and dragging air into her aching lungs to understand what he meant. She gained her footing in the shallows lapping around the aqueduct's final arch, barely able to stand, her body utterly drained of energy. Only when she doubled over with her hands on her knees did she realize what the elf meant.

At some point during the desperate, half-blind surge through the tunnels and caverns, her elbows and one knee had been scraped bloody. Between the surging currents and the bitter chill, she'd failed to notice at the time, but now the sting registered, making her hiss. The blood was running pink, staining her sleeves.

"Hold still," Shiver said, laying a hand gently on each graze in turn. She bit her lip at the sting of contact, but it lasted only a moment.

The grazes healed. She felt the power Shiver drew upon, the strange, unknowable reserves of the Empyrean, and momentarily thought she knew what it was like to be able to innately call up its energies. Then he withdrew his hand, and the sensation was gone. Her flesh was whole again. She stooped in the water to wash off the worst of the blood.

"We do not have time to pause here," Maelwich said. The daggerband had gathered itself in the lee of the aqueduct, checking blades and straps. They presented an even more fearsome visage when drenched, their skin appearing alabaster-white, their black hair hanging lank and glistening upon their shoulders, dark eyes seemingly full of threat. Astarra found herself thinking of the sharks she had once seen swimming in the Teallin Sea, their palled, sharp forms exuding predatory danger. She noted that none of them had suffered wounds or grazes the way she had, and none of them were shivering from the cold.

"I'm fine," she told Maelwich, trying to mask her own shaking. "Just tell me what's next."

"Next, we enter the lake," the elven leader said, nodding past the waterfall. "There is a submerged tunnel that leads to the fortress. The garrison is able to use it to access fresh water directly in the event of a siege."

"I'm assuming it's well guarded?" Astarra asked.

"There are guards, yes," Maelwich said. "And a sunken gate. But that's where you come in."

They struck out into the Blackwater, swimming downwards at first to avoid being seen on its surface.

In its stygian depths, Shiver tried to suppress his doubts. They'd been lingering with him since setting out into the river, their persistence frustrating. On one level, the plan was not without its merits. Astarra was correct, the burrowing device would be useful, and Maelwich seemed to be privately relishing the opportunity to strike at the Dunwarr in their most secure fastness. But still, he worried they had embarked upon a doomed venture. They were risking their ability to stop the shadow from spreading. What if he was unable to locate Mavarin and Raythen? What if they'd already been executed, or suffered some other debilitating Dunwarr punishment?

Astarra's claim that he had abandoned the two dwarfs stung, mainly because he now realized it was true. He'd become wholly preoccupied by the threat growing under Thelgrim, even more so after the realization that he likely had a hand in its creation. There were no longer any doubts – he had been led here for the purpose of expunging the evil that was taking root within the mountain. For a while, all other considerations had become secondary.

He chided himself for that. He had long ago come to

understand that pursuing a righteous end without restraint was a sure path to ruin. Was it not how he had fallen in the first place? At times, when the power of the Empyrean was coursing through him and the goal ahead seemed as though it was in plain sight, he had to catch himself, remind himself that the people and the places he encountered on his journey mattered too. If he betrayed them, if he abandoned them as he had abandoned Mavarin and Raythen, his penance would be hollow and meaningless.

He paused amidst the still waters of the lake, looking about for Astarra. She was still with them, her eyes full of determination as she swam. Privately, he had worried she wouldn't survive the journey to the aqueduct, though he understood her well enough by now to know that voicing his concerns would be a waste of breath. She was single-minded in her purpose. He supposed he wasn't one to judge.

He followed close to her, resisting the urge to outpace her. The light of the jaela root had been deemed too risky in the middle of Thelgrim, so her only guides were Shiver and the elves in front of her. His vision pierced the murky waters surrounding them, hunting for the submerged wall that would indicate the edge of the Dunwol Kenn Karnin.

He found his eyes drawn down, towards the depths of the lake. There was darkness there, the deeps that gave it its name in both Dunwarr and Aethyn – the Blackwater to the former, the Black Well to the latter. Even to the eyes of an elf it was impenetrable, seemingly fathomless and all-consuming. And as Shiver watched, it seemed to move.

The darkness shifted, and began to rise. It coiled slowly upwards, invading the surface waters where the glittering illumination of the far-off cavern ceiling dared penetrate. It drove the light back, spreading like a blot of ink.

Shiver recognized it too late, its hunger like a physical presence in the waters around him. It was a maw, a gigantic mouth of ravenous darkness, shadows coalescing to form vast, individual fangs as it yawned open beneath them. At the heart of it was a void, an utter absence of anything, a primordial nothingness that seemed to want to drag in everything around it – the light, the lake, the very essence of their souls.

It surged upwards with a howl that shuddered through the surrounding waters. Horror gripped Shiver. He lunged out, managing to grab onto Astarra, who turned, surprised and struggling. He ignored her efforts, kicking desperately for the surface and hauling her up with him. He could feel the darkness just below, coming for them both, its insatiable need to gorge itself on their bodies and souls overwhelming his thoughts.

He broke the surface gasping and panting. Astarra was with him, gulping down air, unable to speak. He found himself looking up at a sheer wall rising out of the lake before them, a cliff-face that was part natural rock, part artifice. It seemed to glare down at them both, its parapets and arrow slits laden with threat. He realized they'd surfaced directly beneath the lakeside bastion of the Dunwol Kenn Karnin.

The vision shattered, his fear of the ethereal shadow banished by the very real danger that they'd just been seen by someone.

He snatched Astarra's shoulder and hauled her back down under the water. They dove together, into its murky embrace, into the darkness that seconds earlier looked as though it was going to consume them all. It was gone now though, passed as if in a dream. The maddening hunger that had filled Shiver's mind was no more.

Silently, he cursed himself. He had no idea if they had been seen from the walls above. It didn't matter anyway. They had come too far. Regardless of what he thought of the plan, it was the one they were now committed to.

The rest of the daggerband were visible through the gloom ahead. They'd arrived at the waterside wall of the Dunwol Kenn Karnin, which plunged down beneath the surface. Tunneled into its flank was a large, circular port, an access point that admitted the waters of the lake into the lower part of the fortress. In times of siege, it was typically sealed off, as the water that flowed into the fortress was considered sufficient for the garrison, but without an enemy threatening the walls of the great citadel a heavy iron grate was considered enough.

Astarra surfaced again briefly when they reached the base of the wall, driven by the need for air. Shiver couldn't help but wonder again if they'd been spotted. He suspected if they had been, crossbow quarrels would already be slashing through the water around them. That, or they were now walking into a trap.

Astarra returned, her staff freed from her back. She had fastened the Deeprune in place. Shiver could feel its power radiating through the lake, drawing strength from it.

He worked his way down the wall until he was able to grasp the grate. It took only a moment of focus before he found the strength to reach into the Empyrean. Immediately, the bars beneath his fingers started to become covered in a thick rind of ice. It spread along the latticework of metal, the temperature of the water growing noticeably more chill. He heard, as though from far away, the crump and crack of metal starting to distort.

With a grunt of effort, he drew back his hands and kicked away, making space for Astarra. She took his place before the grate, uttered a word that was lost to the frigid depths, and thrust her staff forward. There was a concussive blast of pressure as the Deeprune channeled the crushing weight of the ocean bed in the direction Astarra had sent it, slamming it into the grate covering.

The Dunwarr-forged metal, which may otherwise have resisted the aquatic blast, had been made brittle by Shiver's ice. It burst inwards with a submerged pop that threatened to damage Shiver's eardrums.

Astarra pulled herself to Shiver's side as Maelwich surged through the opening, her daggerband following. Shiver nodded to the runewitch to go ahead of him. As she kicked after the Aethyn, he cast one more glance at the lake's darkness beneath him, then slipped past the twisted ends of the ruptured gate.

They were inside the Dunwol Kenn Karnin.

CHAPTER TWENTY-THREE

The sound of the horn reverberated through the halls of the Dunwol Kenn Karnin, echoing down the stairs to the depths of the Dunwol Keg. It had rung out six times since Raythen had been returned to his cell, two short notes then one long, drawn out, its echoes seemingly refusing to fade as they bounced through the vaulted, stone space of the Dunwarr citadel.

He knew what it meant. It was the *Kaz Nok,* the War Horn, and it was summoning the Warriors' Guild to battle.

He'd expected nothing less after Mavarin's admission. He'd claimed the deep elves had taken the Hydra from where he'd left it. Raythen knew the likes of the twins wouldn't need any further excuse to advise Ragnarson to muster Thelgrim's host. Conflict with the Aethyn seemed to have been brewing for a long time. The Dunwarr were marching to war, to reclaim their sorcerous relic.

Raythen wondered whether that was part of Mavarin's plan. On the face of it, the wily inventor was bound for the executioner's block. But if Ragnarson wanted to lead an army in pursuit of the Hydra, he'd likely need Mavarin to guide the host to the last known location of the Shard. Mavarin would have earned himself a stay of execution, and who knew what might happen if he was taken, even under guard, beyond the walls of the Dunwol Kenn Karnin?

He'd been dealt a new hand, while Raythen was down to his last card. He had sat and listened to the *Kaz Nok*'s warlike peals, and tried to weigh the odds. By rights, he was now a free Dunwarr, absolved by the Trial of the Mountain. Those laws hadn't been tested in Thelgrim for decades though, and he had no doubt Zorri and Korri were doing their very best to find a means to get him back on the block next to Mavarin. The mood of the guilds was certainly on their side, and he knew he couldn't count on his father to intercede.

He might yet walk out of the Dunwol Kenn Karnin, and Thelgrim, but his chances seemed increasingly slim. Perhaps if they could recover the Shard the guilds would feel placated, but he knew the realities of a Deepling War. Many Dunwarr would fall rooting the elves from their caverns and passageways, and the mood of the council would likely be even more bloody than it had been before.

Raythen had been reliant on the mercy of others for too long now, and that was never a good sign. It was time to take action. Time to do what he did best, and get well out, before it was too late.

He reached up, pulled back his eyepatch, and hooked a finger into the hollow socket beneath. A tiny slip of cloth, barely bigger than his fingernail, came loose in his hand. He carefully unfolded it, and then extended the sliver of metal within, before slotting it carefully into the lock of his manacles.

It took time – it always did, regardless of the stories most rogues told – but finally he heard the satisfying click of the manacle lock coming undone. The weight of the chains fell away, arrested by Raythen's grasp just before they could clatter to the floor.

He rubbed his raw wrists, stretched out his arms and legs, and silently approached the cell door. Manacles were one thing, the heavy lock on the entrance to the Dunwol Keg was quite another. He crouched in front of it and slipped the pick home, trying to do so in complete silence. The jailer was right outside.

He worked at it for what felt like an age, his limbs burning and sweat stinging his eye. Eventually, finally, he heard a series of dull clicks. He paused, breath held, heart racing as he waited to see if the jailer had noticed. There was a slight scuff of feet from beyond the door, but nothing more. Fractionally, he worked the pick from the lock.

Now he just had to wait, and hope. He stood and replaced both the pick and his eyepatch. Eventually, the first note of the *Kaz Nok* sounded again. He waited for the second, the echoes building, before grasping the door and hauling on it.

The jailer turned, a look of total shock on his face. Raythen struck, slamming one of the manacles he was carrying into the side of the Dunwarr's head. He dropped off the stool he'd been sitting on like a leaden weight, the clatter of his fall swallowed up by the reverberating peal of the War Horn.

Raythen knelt and swiftly relieved him of his keys, before grasping him under the arms and, teeth gritted, hauling him into the open cell. His heart was racing. In a way, it was a thrill to now be committed to the plan. And it had been an easy enough start too, but then again, he'd expected as much. The jailer was only really there to slide slop through the door hatch and open it for visitors. The real challenge would be the two fully armed and armored, veteran Warriors' Guild guards that protected the doorway at the head of the shaft.

He headed to the corner of the cell and retrieved the pile of stale slop he'd slowly been collecting since the start of his imprisonment. It had turned rock-solid, so he dipped it in the cell's drinking trough and worked at it with his fingers, until it had turned gelatinous and stodgy once more.

The jailer groaned and tried to roll over. Raythen hastily clamped the chained manacles around his wrists and patted one bloodied cheek as he came to.

"Sorry about this," he said. "Don't worry though, I'm going to find you some company."

He straightened up and strode out of the cell, using the helm of his shirt to cradle his old slop. Working quickly, he climbed a third of the way up the shaft's stairs and began to spread the paste across several of the steep stone steps, working his way back down. After coating four of them, he stopped and looked back through the cell doorway.

The jailer had come fully to. He sat up, groggy eyes fixing on Raythen. A hand tugged at his restraints, the chains rattling as he realized just what had happened. Fury replaced his dazed expression.

"Guards!" he bellowed, his voice ringing up the shaft. "Guards! The prisoner is escaping!"

"Oh no, what ever shall I do now?" Raythen muttered under his breath, looking up the stairs. There was a scraping sound as the hatch at the top of the shaft was unlocked and dragged open. Two Dunwarr appeared, both fully armored bar one missing a helmet. They spotted Raythen, hefted their axes and shields, and charged down the stairs.

Two veteran Dunwarr warriors, all-but fully equipped, and a single, narrow stairway, with a dead end and an angry jailer behind him – ostensibly, Raythen knew the odds were against him. But that was why he'd been on a diet.

The first of the guards hit the steps he'd covered in slop. The effect was immediate. The Dunwarr lost his footing and went flying. The second, following immediately behind, didn't do any better – he threw a hand out in an attempt to arrest his momentum, dropping his axe, but at the same time his iron-shod boot hit the paste and slipped through it. He went the way of his accomplice.

Raythen found himself faced with a cascading wall of metal, crashing down the steep set of stairs towards him. He threw himself down ahead of them and took cover in the open cell doorway as they clattered thunderously to the bottom of the shaft.

He was on them almost before they'd come to a halt. The one without the helmet was already unconscious, his brow bearing a nasty gash, but the other was trying to rise. His axe was attached to his wrist by a strap, which Raythen now relieved him of as he bore him back down against the steps, gripping the rim of his dented helmet with his other hand. He tore it off before the warrior could fully recover, and administered a crack to his head with the heavy, blunt back of the axe. The warrior slumped back, as unconscious as his partner.

Cursing the weight of their armor, Raythen started to drag first one, then the other into the open cell, their steel plate grating off the bare stone.

"Help!" the shackled jailer shouted, his voice echoing up the shaft stairs. "Somebody! The prisoner is free!"

"Hold your tongue, or I'll hack it out," Raythen grunted, waving the stolen axe in his face. "Be thankful I'm not dispatching all three of you."

The jailer went silent, then scoffed when he saw that Raythen had started to hastily unbuckle one of the comatose guards' armor.

"You're not really going to try and walk out of the Dunwol Kenn Karnin by dressing up as one of the Warriors' Guild?" he demanded. Raythen shot him a half-smile.

"You know, I laughed at that idea too. But sometimes the old tricks are the best."

"You'll never make it."

"Pray to the Ancestors I do," Raythen said, fastening the clasps of a breastplate over his jerkin. It was a little too big, and clattered and scraped against the pauldrons when he moved, but it would do for now. "Because if this works, you won't have to spend your days sitting at the bottom of this miserable pit, shoving slop through a hatch."

The jailer seemed to consider that for a moment, then shrugged.

"True enough."

Raythen retrieved the warrior's fallen helmet, shield, and the keys for the shaft's upper hatch. He paused to raise a single finger to his lips, looking pointedly at the jailer, then eased the cell door shut and locked it behind him.

CHAPTER TWENTY-FOUR

There were two guards watching over the Dunwol Kenn Karnin's water gate. They were sitting at a table in the small docking chamber, playing Skerei, an old Dunwarr board game. The first they knew of the Aethyn incursion was Talarin surging from the still waters beside them, his long daggers drawn.

They tried to resist, and died over their unfinished game, blood welling around the pieces. Talarin cleaned his blades as the rest of the daggerband pulled themselves up out of the water.

"Did you have to cut their throats?" Shiver asked, as he surveyed the slumped bodies. "I'd hoped we would be able to do this without killing."

"Yes," Talarin said coldly. Shiver looked at Maelwich, who shook her head.

"There are many times to show mercy," she said. "Leading a raid into the enemy's heartland isn't one of them."

"The Dunwarr aren't the enemy," Shiver said. "Not yet."

"Today they are," Maelwich replied. "Hopefully, tomorrow, they won't be."

Of that at least, Shiver was thankful. He had stayed beneath the mountain to try and stop the spread of death and darkness, but a full-blown war between the deep elves and the dwarfs would result in much the same thing. He only hoped the rest of the daggerband, including Talarin, shared their leader's attitude.

He turned back to help Astarra up onto the firm stone of the chamber's dock. She was shaking with cold and exhaustion. He felt a pang of concern, one that no longer surprised him when it came to his human companion.

"Now might be the time for your runefire," he said gently, as she rung water from her thick braid.

She nodded and retrieved the blackened little rock. Shiver could feel the heat of it as she slotted it home.

"Can you sense them?" she asked Shiver, the spark seeming to reignite inside her as she grasped her dripping staff. "Raythen and Mavarin?"

"Not clearly, no," Shiver said. "The fortress is large, and it is full of souls. More are coming throughout the city. Warriors, I think. We will need to make our way through the halls until I can get a better understanding of who resides here."

"I suspect the Dunwarr and their king might have something to say about that," Maelwich said. She pointed to a pair of great chains that dangled from the chamber's ceiling down into the water running in from the Blackwater. "That could help us. We'll be able to progress at least one level more without being detected."

"Possibly," Shiver allowed, looking up at the dark hatch

the chains passed through. They were for ferrying buckets from the lake up into the fortress proper, a simpler system than carrying them by hand up the stairways that riddled the structure. By climbing up they'd potentially be able to work their way deep into the Dunwol Kenn Karnin before having to take to the halls and passages.

The sonorous blast of a horn rang through the chamber, echoing down from the stairwell and from the bucket hatch. Two short notes and one long. He didn't know what the noise meant, but he doubted it was good. Concerned, he exchanged a glance with Astarra.

"Is that the alarm?" she wondered aloud. "Do they know we're here?"

Maelwich answered her question.

"No. But I've heard those notes before. They rang along the mountain roots years ago, during the last Deepling War."

"What do they mean?" Astarra asked.

"They mean that King Ragnarson is mustering the full strength of the Warriors' Guild," Maelwich said. "They mean the Dunwarrs are at war."

The last thing Astarra wanted was to return to the chill of the water. Only the heat of the Ignis had worked the cold out from the core of her being. She had to though – the Aethyn were already starting to scale the bucket chains, darting hand-over-hand with disconcerting dexterity up the twin lengths.

"What happened?" Astarra asked Shiver quietly, before he stepped in after them. "In the lake? Why did you drag me to the surface?"

He spent a moment considering his answer before replying.

"I had another vision. Of the darkness."

"In the lake?"

"Yes. I think it lies beneath it. And it's still growing stronger. It means to swallow this entire city, then the whole mountain."

Astarra had feared as much. It felt as though time was running through their fingers, like the darkness was taunting them, leading them on foolish quests while it coiled, about to be unleashed. She nodded, martialing her strength.

"Then we'd better hurry up and stop it."

Shiver dropped back down into the water, his glistening gray flesh a contrast to its murky blackness. Astarra slung her staff over her back and followed him in, almost moaning aloud as the bitter chill once more enveloped her. She grasped hold of one of the dangling chains and began to haul herself up, gripping it link by link as Shiver did the same with the opposite one.

It was hard going. Tiredness gnawed at her, dragged her down like a weight, stole the strength from her limbs. The chains were wet, and difficult to grasp. She tried to latch her legs around them, but that was even trickier. The rattling sound they made seemed painfully loud, echoing off the surface of the gently lapping water beneath.

She went a handhold at a time, blocking out her fatigue, letting her determination drive her. She wasn't going to falter now. She wasn't going to be left behind, not on a venture she'd suggested.

As Maelwich had anticipated, the shaft the chains hung from passed through a number of the Dunwol Kenn Karnin's levels. The wall contained hatches a dwarf could reach through to collect one of the buckets being hoisted on the pully system.

After passing the second one, in almost total darkness now, Shiver hissed something in elvish. Astarra just hoped he'd gotten a sense of where either Mavarin or Raythen were. She couldn't go much further.

Light spilled into the shaft as an elf higher up eased open one of the hatches. He pulled himself through it and kept it open for the rest to follow. Astarra silently thanked Kellos as she pulled herself up and threw a hand out, managing to grasp the hatch's edge as the chain, now devoid of weight further up, swung dangerously.

Pale hands hauled her through. She was about to curse out loud as she slumped awkwardly onto the stone floor on the other side, but Shiver's cold hand clamped abruptly over her mouth, stifling her. He caught her eye and shook his head once.

Astarra nodded, and the hand was removed. She crouched, looking around. It seemed as though they'd dropped out into the citadel's kitchens. A large chamber filled with heavy, black metal stoves and solid table-slabs stretched away from the huddled, dripping band of deep elves. Dried herbs hung from the ceiling, fresh cavern-root vegetables lay half-chopped on the workstations, and pots bubbled and hissed, suspended over the row of fire pits. The heat was a stifling contrast to the chill of the Blackwater, and the air was full of the scents of slow-cooked meat and spices. It made her empty stomach ache.

Thankfully, they appeared to have arrived during a prep break. There were no Dunwarr in immediate sight, though she could hear the clattering of pans and a carefree, disharmonious whistling coming from nearby. She risked a glance over the nearest bench and caught sight of a single dwarf in a stained white apron, working at scrubbing clean a vast stack of greasy plates and cutlery in a trough of soapy water. The racket he was making between his whistling and his clanging had masked the subtle sounds of the daggerband's entry.

She crouched back down and looked at Shiver, who nodded ahead, towards what appeared to be the kitchen's back door. The Aethyn were moving out, darting along the aisle towards it.

Astarra began to follow, crouched low, cringing with every step. How were they so accursedly quiet? She tried to time her movements with the clattering of the pans, making the final dash as the tuneless whistling reached its crescendo.

The deep elves were waiting. Maelwich motioned her and Shiver forward as they passed through the door. Astarra rose, and just had time to take in the sight of a stone-cut, fire-lit corridor and an open doorway immediately to her right before she realized she was standing face-to-face with a dwarf.

He stared at her, and she at him. He was portly and ruddy-faced, with a ginger beard and a crumpled cook's cap. He was carrying a platter in his arms heaped with soil-encrusted telle bulbs.

Maelwich reacted faster than either of them. She delivered an open-palmed chop to the Dunwarr's neck. He went down instantly, his tray about to tumble. With reflexes that Astarra was barely able to follow, Maelwich caught it before it could clatter and spill.

Astarra just stared, the series of events leaving her lagging. One of the Aethyn slipped past and grabbed the downed body of the Dunwarr, hauling him into the room he'd emerged from, to the right. She realized it was a pantry space, its shelves heavy with food.

"Just unconscious," Maelwich said quietly to Shiver, passing the platter to the other elf to leave in the pantry with the downed cook. "Happy?"

"Delighted," Shiver said, as the pantry door was shut. "But we need to be quick."

"You're sure one of them is on this level?"

"My certainty is relative. There's only one way to be sure."

He set off along the corridor, the wet robes around his waist trailing. Astarra hurried after him, her body flushed with belated adrenaline as the rest of the Aethyn followed.

They encountered their first proper resistance at the foot of a stairwell at the far end of the corridor. Two Dunwarr guards met Shiver. He reacted first, hissing a word of power. Almost instantly, the dwarfs were assailed by a wall of ice that froze their bodies and locked them in place, like silent, shocked statues that stared at the Aethyn as they passed. Not for the first time, Astarra felt a pang of alarm at the potency of Shiver's powers. She could not imagine facing him when he had been a slave to the Ynfernael.

The stairs took them to a lower ward. Shiver paused, apparently gathering his senses. As he did so, Astarra stole a glance through one of the arrow slits embedded in the thick wall.

Beyond it lay Thelgrim, in all its glittering glory. The Blackwater lay off to the left, the road to the citadel's main gate lying almost directly below. To her surprise, the route was almost full – serried blocks of dwarfs were marching down it towards the Dunwol Kenn Karnin, Dunwarr warriors arrayed for battle. She could hear the steady tramping of their boots.

"There's an army on its way here," she said.

"They are coming from their barracks across the city," Maelwich said, looking out of the neighboring slit. "Answering the call to war. Thelgrim's host is assembling, and I doubt it is the shadow they are readying to fight."

"Then all the more reason to hurry," Astarra said. She felt as though she had been locked into an unfolding tragedy, and the chance to avert it was slipping rapidly away. It made her angry and anxious at the same time.

"I have him," Shiver said. "The next chamber is the lower undercroft. He is being held there."

"Which one?" Astarra asked.

"Mavarin," Shiver replied. "But we must be quick. More and more Dunwarr are arriving here with every passing moment."

He led them down another short flight of torch-lit stairs and into a tunnel not unlike the one where they had been held when they'd first arrived. Astarra realized as soon as she stepped out that the time for stealth was over.

Six dwarfs occupied the undercroft, all warriors. Their shock at the sight of a band of deep elves and a human in the midst of their fastness lasted only a moment.

"*Azak ki*!" barked one, drawing a short sword. Astarra raised her staff, but the elves were quicker. Maelwich and the daggerband were darting forward, their knives flashing in the firelight. The barrel-shaped ceiling of the undercroft resounded with the clash of steel and a bellow of fury, followed by a cry of pain as the first of the Dunwarr went down.

It all happened before Astarra could reach within and summon up her runes. Dunwarr made for fearsome warriors, and the narrowness of the stony space worked in their favor, but they were too scattered along the corridor's length. Elvish steel took them, driving in at the weak points of their heavy armor – throats, armpits, hips. A single member of Maelwich's band found his knife lodged between the steel, and didn't manage to dodge the axe stroke that came back his way, cleaving into his shoulder. Blood burst across the stone wall and made one of the torches hiss and gutter.

That was the end of it. Maelwich knelt by the side of the one fallen elf, grasping his hand as his life slipped away. Talarin was doing the reverse to the dwarf, finishing the wounded warrior with a sharp thrust of his dagger. Shiver looked at him hard before walking down the corridor between the fallen bodies, like a specter come to collect the souls of the slain. His eyes were on the cell doors that ranked the undercroft's sides. He stopped abruptly at one, looked to Maelwich and gestured at it.

"He's in there."

One of the daggerband retrieved the keys from a Dunwarr body. Astarra joined Shiver as he unlocked the heavy door.

A single figure occupied the far corner of the cell beyond. He was crouching in terror, his face half hidden by his hands. It took a moment for Astarra to recognize Mavarin. She felt a rush of relief, twinned with a surge of fresh determination.

"Ancestors protect me," the disheveled inventor croaked.

"We're here to get you out," Astarra said brusquely, striding into the cell. Mavarin looked up at her. He'd grown a scraggy beard since she'd last seen him.

"How are you here?" he asked, seemingly doubting whether he was dreaming or not. "Some arcane sorcery?"

"No," said Maelwich from the doorway – she had joined Shiver, and she raised one of her daggers, glistening red in the firelight. "Something far simpler."

"More elves," Mavarin hissed, scrambling back against the cell wall. Astarra snatched his arm and dragged him to his feet.

"We've risked everything to break you out of here. You're coming with us. Where is Raythen?"

"I d- don't know," the inventor stammered. "I only saw him during the trial. They kept him somewhere else."

Maelwich came and started to unlock Mavarin's shackles. He looked up at the tall elf with undisguised fear.

"They're friends," Astarra told him.

"They want the Hydra, don't they?" Mavarin asked. "I've already told everyone, I don't know w- where it is!"

"This isn't about the Hydra," Astarra said, doing her best to reassure him. Time in the Dunwarr cell seemed to have gone some way towards breaking him. It made her wonder just what had happened to Raythen. Seeing his father's attitude towards him, she doubted separate treatment would mean preferential treatment. Was he even still alive?

"There's more at stake now," she told Mavarin, trying to focus on the objectives. "There's a darkness below Thelgrim. Something foul, and it is growing stronger. We have to stop it."

"I know," Mavarin said quietly. Astarra frowned, feeling surprised.

"What do you mean you know?"

"I've seen it in their eyes," he said, looking down at his feet. "Black, like the void."

There was a clatter as his manacles came undone. Maelwich pulled him from Astarra's grasp and marched him to the door.

"This is the one who commands the burrower?" she demanded of Shiver.

"It is," he said.

"Then he's all we need."

"What about Raythen?" Astarra demanded as the elves left the cell. She followed them out, her anger spiking. She'd come this far intending to free the thief, and that wasn't a part of the plan she intended to abandon. He couldn't be far. "We can't just leave him."

"If Raythen is not here, he can't be rescued," Shiver pointed out.

"Can't you sense him?" Astarra asked stubbornly. "He must be close, surely?"

"There are more Dunwarr souls entering this place every second," Shiver said. "It's becoming impossible to distinguish them, especially a being as used to hiding himself as Raythen. For all we know, he's not even here anymore. Perhaps he talked his way out. Or maybe he's escaped."

"Given how much his father seems to hate him, I doubt either of those things," Astarra said.

"True," Shiver admitted. "Regardless of his nature, we both owe him our lives. If I find any trace of him while we are here, I will make sure he leaves with us. I swear it."

Astarra took a second to compose herself. She supposed she couldn't hope for any better. There was no evidence of where the Dunwarr – or, specifically, the king's advisors – might have taken him. More than ever, she envied Shiver's ability to enter the Empyrean and sense the souls of those nearby.

The daggerband had assembled, one crouching over

the single elf to have fallen in the brief, vicious clash in the undercroft.

"Leave him," Maelwich said. "*Ilara leth.* We will mourn later."

"Where are you taking me?" Mavarin asked. He was now flanked by two members of the daggerband. He looked terrified. Astarra wondered just what had happened to him after he'd been taken. What had he seen? Whose eyes had he been talking about?

"We're getting you out of here," she told him, hoping she sounded reassuring. "We need your invention. The burrower. Is it still beneath your workshop?"

"N- no," Mavarin managed. "They took it. Said they could use it to finish the work. The Deeprun, the upper walls. They asked me to pilot it, but I refused."

"Who did?" Astarra said, trying to make sense of the inventor's rambling.

"The twins," he whispered.

Astarra remembered Mavarin's mention of eyes dark as the void, twinned with the darkness that had seemed so absolute in the tunnels. It sent a chill through her. If the king's advisors were really in league with the Ynfernael, the situation was even more perilous than any of them had imagined.

"We can discuss this later," Maelwich said sharply. "We need to move."

CHAPTER TWENTY-FIVE

Maelwich led them back to the stairwell. They'd just entered it when the sound of the Dunwol Kenn Karnin's horn rang out again, vibrating the stone underfoot. At first Astarra thought it was just another blast summoning the Warriors' Guild to the citadel, before realizing that the notes were different – shorter and sharper, more urgent.

"I doubt that's a good sign," Maelwich called out as their echoes faded.

They reached the floor where the kitchen was, and immediately encountered resistance beyond the stairway's door. A patrol of a dozen Dunwarr had emerged before them. Bellowed war cries went up, and Astarra found herself facing their charge.

This time, she reacted first. She brought her staff up, speaking the words of power. The Ignis roared in response, its flames bursting from the volcanic shard and surging into a conflagration. It created a curtain of fire along the entrance to the stairwell, a surge of heat that cooked the stonework and sent the Dunwarr reeling back.

"Go," she managed through gritted teeth, glancing back

at Shiver. He waved the rest of the daggerband past, further down the stairs. When the last was gone he put a hand on her shoulder.

She broke contact with some difficulty, the intensity of the blaze making a swift exit more challenging. Her hands were scorched, but she left the fire raging. She followed Shiver down, almost tripping on the steep, spiral stairs. Shouts of fury and alarm rang after them. The element of surprise was long gone.

The leading elves had reached the next level, but that was packed with oncoming Dunwarr too. Maelwich slammed the door to the stairwell in their faces and used one of the long blades proffered by one of her kin to lock it shut. It shivered in its frame, pounded by repeated blows from the other side.

"If the next floor is blocked, we fight our way through," she said fiercely. "We can't keep going down."

They carried on, Shiver taking the lead this time. Another corridor lay beyond the next door. At first Astarra thought it was empty, before realizing there was a Dunwarr guard right in front of Shiver.

Maelwich was past him in a flash, daggers darting for the warrior's throat and gut.

"No!" Shiver shouted. Astarra gasped as she felt his magics abruptly surge, seeming to drag every ounce of heat from the corridor. At the sweep of a hand a thin screen of ice materialized between Maelwich and the dwarf. Her daggers jarred off it, shattering it but checking her blows. The dwarf, though equipped with a shield and axe, raised neither.

"Oh, thank Fortuna," he said gruffly.

It was Raythen. He hauled his helmet off, his one eye

darting from Shiver to Astarra. She felt an outpouring of relief, so great she almost had to clutch harder onto her staff for support. Quickly, she tried to mask it from him, embarrassed by her instinctive response to seeing him.

"Took you long enough," Raythen said, offering her a grin.

"Are you… trying to escape dressed as a Dunwarr warrior?" she asked incredulously, still trying to disguise her relief. With the thief at their side, she suddenly felt a lot more confident about making it out of the fortress.

"Just thought I'd test out a terrible idea someone once suggested to me," he replied. His eye went to Mavarin, who was still being manhandled between two of the daggerband.

"I'd leave that one behind," he growled. "He's the one who stole the Hydra in the first place."

"We need him to pilot the burrower," Astarra said, unwilling to spend time taking in the concept of Mavarin being the one who'd taken the Hydra Shard. If that was the case, there would be a reckoning, but it didn't change their current circumstances. She had to keep them all on course, or the plan would still unravel.

"And there was me thinking you'd come to repay the debt you owed me," Raythen said. Astarra shrugged, trying to seem nonchalant.

"Enough of this," Maelwich snapped, shoving past Raythen and heading down the corridor.

"I wouldn't go that way," the dwarf called out after her. "There's nothing down there but the Dunwol Keg."

"There are two doors," Maelwich pointed out. Raythen frowned and followed her.

"I've no idea where that leads," he admitted, looking at an

archway set into the corridor wall. Darkness lay beyond it, seemingly impenetrable. "I've… never seen it before."

Astarra looked at Shiver, seeking an indication of what lay beyond. He seemed lost in thought for a moment, before taking a deep breath and nodding.

"Go," he said. "There is no other way."

"That doesn't sound very encouraging," Raythen said.

Maelwich took a second to count off the daggerband and then, as the crash of a splintering door echoed down towards them from the stairwell, she led them into the darkness.

The Ynfernael was here. Shiver could sense it on every surface, in every breath, inside every thought. Its evil made him want to retch and cry. Every instinct screamed at him to go back.

But he didn't. He went on, down, following Maelwich, trying not to think about how the darkness coiled and writhed around the lonely flame of Astarra's runestone, like a living thing, leering and insatiable.

He was not surprised that Raythen wasn't familiar with the tunnel. A glamor lay upon it, one that had been disrupted either by the presence of his magics and Astarra's, or by some other, deliberate design. Unlike the mines around Thelgrim or the corridors of the Dunwol Kenn Karnin, the passage didn't seem old or well-established. After the initial archway and a flight of stone stairs, it was all hacked rock and bare dirt. Loose stones cascaded from the ceiling at their passing. There was no obvious sign of just who, or what, had carved it. That in itself disturbed Shiver. He didn't dare run his hand along the walls to try and find out.

It seemed to twist and turn one way then another,

occasionally contracting, then widening again, like some vast, intestinal tract. Shiver tried to banish the idea as they went ever deeper.

He could no longer sense any hint of a pursuit from the fortress above. There was nothing, nothing beyond the cloying darkness.

"I do not like this," Talarin murmured. "This place is overrun with evil. I don't think we want to go any further."

"That is the very reason we have come this far," Maelwich said, shooting him a harsh glance. "We go on."

They came to an intersection in the tunnels, a circular space wide enough for the daggerband to gather and pause. Astarra had fed more light into the Ignis Shard, its flames illuminating no less than ten tunnels branching off from the junction and, strangest of all, a spherical hole in its bottom and another directly above, in the ceiling. For a moment, he thought he could hear a distant wail ringing through the winding dirt passages, though from which one it was coming he had no idea.

"We're not in the Dunwarr fortress anymore, are we?" Maelwich said softly. Mavarin let out a little, fearful groan.

"The shadow is here," Shiver replied, forcing himself to speak despite the fear gnawing at him, wondering all the while whether he was the only one who could truly sense its pervasive shadow. "This is where it will strike from."

"What shadow?" Raythen demanded gruffly.

"Something is rotting underneath Thelgrim," Astarra said. "We discovered it after we were separated from you. A shadow of the Ynfernael. The deep elves have been hunting it, while it hunts them."

"I didn't come here to chase literal shadows," Raythen said.

"What does any of this have to do with the Hydra Shard?"

"The twins are the shadow," Mavarin interrupted abruptly. Everyone looked at him. He was shaking, but he carried on, eyes fierce.

"The k- king's advisors. They summoned the darkness. They h- helped me steal the Hydra too. They ensured the wardens in the Hall of the Ancestors were occupied and told me about the chamber where I could hide it and claim I'd discovered it later on."

"You knew about this all along?" Astarra demanded dangerously.

"Not about the Ynfernael!" Mavarin insisted. "But it's clear now. There was a … a horror to the twins when they last visited my cell. They had taken the Garak Gaz, and they wanted me to pilot it. I tried to refuse. Their e- eyes … their eyes were like darkness. Pure, utter darkness."

The words brought back flitting memories of Shiver's mistress, unbidden, to his mind. She had possessed the same fathomless eyes, a terrible quality that had taken over whenever the power of the Ynfernael had gripped her. Just the thought made him want to quail. The idea that the king's advisors were the ones bearing the taint only made the current situation more perilous. The darkness had worked its way to the very core of Thelgrim.

He forced the fresh fear that surged within him back, focusing on the sound of Raythen's voice.

"What did they want with the burrower?" the dwarf was asking.

"They said they were digging at the Deeprun, where it branches out to the gates."

"The valley defenses," Raythen murmured, looking at Astarra and Shiver. "Fortuna's dice, they're going to collapse them. The Deeprun, it doesn't just feed the aqueduct. If the mountain is besieged, it can be rerouted to the crevasses I led you in through. It can flood the valley beyond the gates. If Korri and Zorri are opening a new tunnel there, they'll burst the dam mechanism and unleash it without Ragnarson's orders."

Shiver remembered the smooth rock of the narrow passageways Raythen had first taken them through, stone worn down by the passage of a vast flood. It suddenly all made sense. His vision, the refugees, Tiabette and Sarra. The rush of water, the crushing horror of it, plunging from the valley sides. A defense mechanism for Thelgrim, unleashed by treachery and deceit.

"They're trying to drown the refugees," he said. "The ones encamped in the valley. There must be thousands there by now. It would be… a vast sacrificial offering."

The closing of the gates made even more sense now. The twins had doubtless advised Ragnarson to do it in order to trap the Hydra's thief in Thelgrim, while their true purpose was to leave thousands of innocents at their mercy. He had known sacrifices before, far too many, and he feared even more remained hidden in thoughts that had been stolen from him. The idea of the valley being flooded sickened him.

"We have to stop them," Astarra was saying. "We need to destroy the burrower!"

"If it's drilling where I think it is, it'll take us over a day to journey to the Upper East levels of the cavern wall," Raythen said. "Assuming we can get out of this demon-cursed burrow anytime soon."

"There's no time to go up," Maelwich said. "The shadow is already too powerful. We need to uproot it at its source. We have to go down."

"I'm not part of your daggerband," Raythen said gruffly, squaring up to her. "You cannot command me as you please. I do not even know your name, elf."

"I am Maelwich," she replied, meeting the dwarf's glare and returning it with interest. "And down here my daggerband and I are your best hope of getting out of this place alive."

"She's right," Shiver said. He didn't want to admit it. Just now, he wanted nothing more than to get as far away as possible from the twisting, unnatural tunnels and the cloying evil that ran through them like rot. But this was what they had been seeking, a direct passage to the source of the darkness. They couldn't go back now, not after coming so close. Not with so many lives now clearly at stake.

As though in response to his thoughts, the shadows around them seemed to solidify slightly, encroaching a little further into the light thrown by the Ignis.

"It's trying to repel us," Maelwich hissed, looking at the surrounding tunnels. "It knows we seek it."

"I didn't come here to go hunting the Ynfernael in some accursed pit," Raythen said. "If I'd known that was on the cards, I'd have turned this whole venture down without a second thought."

"I would not ask any of you to go further," Shiver said. "Maelwich and the Aethyn will give their lives to stop this evil, as will I. Some part of it was my doing, I fear. But the three of you don't belong down here. You should go, before the darkness closes in completely."

"Why were we hired, Mavarin?" Astarra asked. "Did the twins pick us specifically?"

"No," Mavarin said hastily. "N- no, that was my decision. What I said during the trial was true, Raythen. I didn't dare venture after the Hydra without help, and it needed to come from the outside. I didn't trust the twins. I needed insurance."

"A fine three you picked," Raythen scoffed. "A thief, a university dropout, and a cursed elf. We're not exactly the saviors of Terrinoth reincarnate."

"But we're the three who are here," Astarra said. "How many of those who've triumphed over the Ynfernael down the centuries have thought themselves fit for the task? In the stories, it's never just a perfect band of heroes."

"I don't seek to be a hero," Shiver said. "I only wish to do my penance. And there will be a great deal of penance here."

"And the Hydra Shard, probably," Mavarin added. "If your deep elf friends didn't h- happen across where I hid it, the twins probably removed it before we got to it."

"So Korri and Zorri probably have the Shard as well," Raythen said. "Even better! A Star of Timmoran and the Ynfernael, working as one!"

"That's exactly why we have to stop them," Astarra exclaimed. "There are thousands of lives at stake now. Not just the refugees in the valley, but the whole of Thelgrim. If this darkness rises it will swallow the city whole!"

"Good!" Raythen barked. "That hidebound, oafish place deserves nothing less! I wouldn't lift a single finger nor spend a single penny, to save a single one of those braying fools in the Guild Council. They all wanted to see me crushed to death."

"Don't be such a coward," Mavarin said suddenly. "This is why your father disowned you! You shamed him before, and you're doing it again."

"You know nothing of my father," Raythen snarled, rounding on his fellow Dunwarr.

"The Ynfernael is doing this," Shiver said quietly. "I have seen it enough times before. It bends the will of those it touches to its purpose."

"I will waste no more time on arguments," Maelwich said tersely. "The Aethyn will strike down this evil, with or without your help."

"We're with you," Astarra said, before placing her hand on Raythen's shoulder and looking him in the eye.

"You risked your life so Shiver and I could escape from Thelgrim," she said. The Dunwarr scoffed.

"Only because it gave me the best odds at the time. If all of us had been taken I'd have been the first on the executioner's block."

"If the odds matter so much, then think about them here," Astarra pressed on, refusing to give up in the face of the dwarf's obstinacy. "The evil in this place has complete control. It can even shift and reshape the tunnels to its will. If you want to go back then fine, but you'll be going alone, and without my runefire."

Raythen did his best to appear unconcerned, but the fear was visible in his eye.

"And just what are you planning when you get back up to the fortress?" Astarra added. "You really think you're going to get out with the whole city on a war footing? What sort of odds would you get for that?"

Raythen glared at Astarra, then looked at Shiver, and finally, Maelwich.

"I want a weapon," he said.

"You have one," Maelwich replied, pointing to his commandeered axe.

"A dagger suits me just as well," he said. "Especially when it's of elvish make, and we're hunting demons. You seem to have plenty to spare."

Maelwich considered it for a moment, then issued a series of orders to her kin. Two daggers were reluctantly surrendered, one to Raythen and one to a relieved-looking Mavarin.

"Watch your backs with that one," Raythen added, giving the inventor a dark look. He glared back defiantly.

"I didn't know about any of this," he insisted. "And it's a mistake I'm willing to give my life to right."

"We'll see," Raythen said.

"Enough," Maelwich interjected, gesturing at one of her elves. "Plant the jaela here to guide us back."

The elf in question drew a jaela root from a pouch and knelt, burying it in the soil of the tunnel. He removed a flint and stone after, striking at it until it caught light.

"Now," Maelwich said, looking at Shiver. "Which way?"

He'd been afraid she was going to ask that. He didn't want to reach out into the dark, to seek it with the Empyrean. He took a breath and did so, tentatively. The response was immediate, a surge of hunger, a skin-crawling sense of wrongness. It permeated everything around them, but it was welling up strongest from a small tunnel directly across from the one they had entered through. The blackness there was absolute.

"That one," Shiver said, pointing it out. Maelwich nodded. "I will lead the way."

CHAPTER TWENTY-SIX

Raythen kept a tight grip on his commandeered elvish blade as Shiver led them down into the darkness. He was used to shadows – they were a thief's friend after all – but this was different somehow. It made him feel nauseous one moment, and squirming the next, like something cold was slithering along his skin, something he couldn't quite snatch at. There was something vile and wrong about the whole place.

This hadn't been part of the plan, not even close. Initially, when he had heard the alarm being sounded in the Dunwol Kenn Karnin, he'd feared his escape had already been discovered. That was when he'd run head-first into Shiver and Astarra, and a pack of deep elves no less. Being dragged into the depths with them was literally the opposite of what he wanted, especially as they had Mavarin with them. But Astarra had been persuasive – right now, he couldn't think of an alternative. He was damned if he was going to try and work his way through some Ynfernael-tainted labyrinth alone.

"This is unwise," one of the elves said as they went on, a

little too loudly for Raythen's comfort. "We do not know for sure that this tunnel is taking us beneath the Black Well. The evil there could be confounding us. Or it could take us the way it took Ulthar."

"He's right," Raythen added, wondering who Ulthar was. "We don't even know what we're going to find down here. It could be an infestation."

"Those are risks we must take, Talarin," the elven leader said to her kinsman, ignoring Raythen. "We were not expecting this opportunity, but the gods have provided. The Ynfernael must be purged wherever it is discovered, torn up like the vile cancer it is."

"We are with you," Astarra said firmly. There were murmurs of agreement from the rest of the daggerband, seemingly impressed by the human's resolve. Like all deep elves, they lived to combat the Ynfernael. It seemed Shiver wasn't the only one who could sense its presence, nor the only one repulsed by it.

They delved lower, the sound of their passage painfully loud in the confined space. He was sure he could hear whispers at the edge of his hearing, but whenever he focused on them they were swallowed by the dull scrape of his armor and the scuff of his boots. He cursed quietly, his heart racing. This really wasn't what he had left Frostgate for.

He realized the tunnel came to an end just ahead. Shiver had paused.

"It's here," he murmured back to the rest of the unlikely band, his voice tight with fear and pain. "Just ahead. The shadow."

Raythen found himself looking at Astarra, lit by the

wavering light of her runefire. Her expression was set, determined. There was a dull scrape as the elven leader drew her twin daggers.

"Then we kill it," she said, and without another word advanced into the cavern.

Astarra could feel the horror of the space beyond the tunnel even before she'd fully stepped into it. It was wide but low, the jagged ceiling seeming to close like a fang-filled jaw over them. It should have comprised of simple rock and dirt, like the myriad of other subterranean caves and passages she'd passed through, but there was something off about it, something not quite right. The stone seemed to twist and writhe at the corners of her vision, as though something foul and squirming had infested it just below the surface. When she tried to focus on it though it appeared sold and unmoving. Only around the edges of her consciousness was the vileness of the Ynfernael readily visible. It made her feel ill.

Even worse were the things already occupying the cavern, several dozen in number. Were it not for the skin-crawling unnaturalness surrounding them, she might have first mistaken some for feral animals. They were hunched over on all fours, their bodies a mixture of ridged, gleaming bone and red-raw musculature. The heads of many were distended like hellish canines, their thick jaws filled with row after row of fangs and a forked, barbed tongue.

Others among the bestial gathering were far larger. They looked like a nightmarish meld of some massive insect and a brute-armed southern simian. Like the hound-beasts, they were skinless, composed of horrific, bare musculature and jagged, bony spines that ran like a forest of blades along their backs and forearms. Their limbs ended in vast, snapping claws, with what appeared to be distended, slavering secondary jaws set within them. No two were exactly alike, each of them twisted and mishappen in their own way.

Everything about the gathering was loathsome and warped. They stank of fresh blood and burned stone, and the snarling of their throats and the scrape of their claws on the rock underneath filled the cavern with a cursed susurration. It almost sounded like a voice, whispering. It shook Astarra to her core. More than ever, she wanted to turn tail and run, to simply get as far from the cursed chamber and its diabolic denizens as possible. The nightmarish beasts were unlike anything she had seen before, unlike anything she'd even dared to imagine. All the stories told of the Ynfernael, in hushed tones around an Aymhelin campfire or whispered between the bunks in Greyhaven's dorms, had done nothing to prepare her for the creatures in person.

None of the twisted terrors were looking towards her or the daggerband as they stepped out into the cavern and illuminated its corners with her runelight. Their attention was on its center. There, a sphere of energy appeared to have split the air apart. It cascaded, about the size of a doorway, in the space just above a large mound that Astarra realized was comprised of piled bones. Light spilled from it, unwholesome and sickly, its colors alternating between purple, black and red. It seemed to vibrate the very air of the cavern, its shifting hues mesmerizing the swarm of monstrosities before it.

"Demons," Maelwich hissed beside her. "There is already a Ynfernael portal open!"

"Only partly open," Shiver said as he joined them. No sooner had he done so, than he doubled over with a hiss.

"No, not now," Astarra pleaded, grabbing the deep elf around the shoulders. This was the worst possible scenario, to lose him to a vision right on the cusp of a chamber filled with Ynfernael beasts. She tried not to panic, but she lost her grip on him as he threw her off. When he looked up at her, his eyes were burning with copresence.

"Get back," Astarra advised the others, just before Shiver's back arched, and ethereal chains blazed in to being around his throat and wrists.

He screamed.

"Welcome back, Shiver."

The voice twisted in his ear like a dagger, its ache running right through his entire body.

"I knew you'd come back. I knew you'd want to finish what you started for me, so long ago."

He was walking, walking towards the sphere of pulsating, foul luminescence. The cavern had receded into nothing. She was at his side, guiding him, her bittersweet words in his ear.

"Just a little further. A little more to give. Then it will all be over, I promise."

Memory or present? He couldn't tell. It was both, and neither. He tried to fight it, tried to throw off the cloying darkness, but it hurt to do so. He knew it was too late anyway. It had stained his soul when he'd been here last, sullied it forever. No amount of penance would be enough to make him clean again, not with the blood of thousands ingrained into his every pore. There was no point in going through the pain of resistance.

There were creatures ahead. Demons of the Ynfernael, a swarm in the making. He knew their kind, could tell their breeds apart, from snarling fleshrippers to the hulking spined threshers. All of them were filled with monstrous, insatiable hunger. All turned as he approached, the un-light of the portal rendering them as jagged, predatory silhouettes and leaving their crimson eyes glowing balefully in the darkness.

He was aware of a presence beside him. Astarra. He could sense her life-force rather than see her directly, attuned now to her essence after the trying weeks they'd spent together. She was attempting to drag him back. Crying out in a voice that didn't belong in his past.

"Shiver, stop! Come back to us!"

He couldn't. Doing so would be a betrayal of his very self. He had been born to do this, fated to serve the Ynfernael, to serve *her*. The darkness had always been there, gnawing away inside him. He had to accept that.

"The end is close, dear, sweet Shiver," murmured the voice.

The demons parted for him, just as they always did, slavering maws and eyes like burning coals averted. It was not reverence. It was the distain a lord would feel for his servant, a master for his slave. He did not merit their attention. He was a means to their hungry ends, nothing more.

But Astarra, they didn't ignore. As she tried desperately to reach out to Shiver, they rounded towards her, towards the unlikely band that had invaded the cavern. A howl went up from dozens of deformed, twisted throats.

Shiver didn't look back, even as he felt the stinking, chitin-plated bulk of the creatures leap into motion around him, surging past. His eyes were on the portal ahead, on the iridescent power bleeding from it. It was a raw wound, an opening into the Ynfernael, a gateway. It sang to him, reminding him of every foul deed and base killing he had overseen.

"Just a little further," she crooned, right beside him. "And it will all be over."

The demons came for them.

"*Ingatus*!" Astarra roared, summoning up the flames of her runestone, balling her fury and determination into a roiling burst of fire. It engulfed the leading creatures as they leapt past Shiver, who had started to walk blindly towards the center of the cavern, bound by ethereal energies and seemingly entranced by the portal pulsating there.

To Astarra's horror, her runefire seemed to wash over the oncoming monsters, doing nothing to slow their loping, gibbering charge.

"Not all fires can harm them," Maelwich shouted to her as the daggerband darted forwards to meet the surge. That was all she had time to say – with a crash the elves met the avalanche of bony claws and fangs, the impact clapping back from the cavern's low ceiling. The writhing of the stone had grown worse, driven into a frenzy as the bloodshed began.

Astarra stumbled back, cursing as she reached up and tried to switch the runes in her staff. Too slow. One of the skittering hound-demons had bypassed the elves who'd swept past her and was lunging for her, letting out a keening, hungry chitter.

With a bellow, Raythen launched her aside and met the thing's leap. Too late to change course, the demon's momentum carried it onto the dwarf's borrowed dagger, the wicked point of elf-forged steel punching through its open maw and up into whatever passed for its brain, driven home by its own momentum.

The thing let out an ugly shriek, spurting black ichor, and Astarra had to yank Raythen back in turn as she regained her own balance, the dwarf barely avoiding its thrashing, wicked claws. As it writhed, Mavarin came in from Astarra's other side and, with a courage and litheness she hadn't anticipated, darted in close and plunged his own dagger down vertically into the top of the thing's elongated skull, the two blades impaling its head from front and behind. It went abruptly still.

"Thanks," Astarra panted, not caring that the volcanic shard atop her staff singed her hand as she unslotted it.

"Why in Fortuna's name is Shiver just walking in amongst them?" Raythen demanded as he planted a boot on the demon's ridged back and, with a grunt of effort, twisted his knife free.

"His memories," Astarra said. "He must have been here before. He's lost control."

"Why aren't these things attacking him though?" Raythen went on, pointing after the elf. The demonic tide had parted for him as it swept past, the hulking, warped beasts closer to the rear of their charge making him seem small and frail next to them. He was still making for the portal, its iridescent energies seeming to drag him on, step by step.

"Perhaps he's betrayed us?" Mavarin suggested as he freed his dagger. "Maybe this was his plan all along? Lead us here as a sacrifice."

"I don't think he's the one orchestrating this," Astarra said, pointing past Shiver. She wanted desperately to reach him, to help him wrestle through whatever dark nightmare had taken hold of him. That would be impossible while he was surrounded by the Ynfernael however, and there were more threats materializing. The last of the demons had moved from around the portal's base, revealing two figures standing at the mound of bones it shimmered above. The twins.

"I told you!" Mavarin exclaimed. "I told you Korri and Zorri had the shadow."

"That's about the only truth you've spoken," Raythen said darkly, as he ripped his dagger free and glanced at Astarra. "Ready?"

She nodded, pushing home the smooth tanzanite atop the Deeprune. Its oceanic might filled her, the still, crushing power of the depths a counterpoint to the writhing madness of the cavern.

Together, they threw themselves into the melee.

Korri and Zorri stepped aside for Shiver as he made the final approach to the portal. He was only half aware of their presence. Their souls were like blots on the Empyrean, cancerous with Ynfernael energies. Their eyes were pits of impenetrable darkness. When they spoke, it was together, and more than two voices issued forth from their sneering lips.

"She has sent you as a gift."

Before him, the portal ignited, its multi-hued energies flaring like fire. Thick wisps of what Shiver first thought was smoke ran from the flickering colors, dark and coiling. It was the shadow, he realized, bleeding from the edges of the rift. It had seeped up from this point, infecting the darkness beneath the mountain, filling it with the hunger of the Ynfernael.

He felt that hunger now, dragging him on. It needed to be fed. It needed him.

He began to mount the bones piled thick beneath the tear, the remains of Dunwarr and Aethyn claimed by the insidious shadows. They were a sacrifice, an offering to draw the attention of those beyond the rift. He could feel them, close now, their sickening essence so familiar.

How many times had he done this before?

"She has sent you as a gift," the twins repeated from either side of him, though now it seemed as though their words issued from the portal itself, the bruised light pulsing with each syllable.

"A thousand and one souls it would have taken, but not with you. Not with one who has tread so long upon the Aenlong, who was once a master of the Sphere of Dreams."

CHAPTER TWENTY-SEVEN

Raythen never liked going against the odds, and right now that seemed to be exactly what was happening.

Maelwich's band of deep elves were outnumbered, but they'd met the demonic guardians of the twisted cavern head-on. And Raythen found himself in the thick of it. He went low for one of the hounds as it locked its multiple jaws around the arm of a Aethyn, grappling with the elf. His commandeered dagger found its throat, hissing black ichor jetting from the wound.

Even as it perished, it still savaged the screaming elf, bringing them both down. Raythen didn't have a chance to drag it off – there was another coming at him.

This time it was Mavarin who met it, grappling with it as its claws scraped the stone underfoot, drawing sparks. Raythen went for one of its three sets of eyes, punching the steel through its skull while fending off its snarling maw with the rim of his shield.

All around them was carnage. Almost half of Maelwich's

band seemed to have fallen already, their slender armor little match for the wicked talons and jaws of the chittering demons. Maelwich herself was like a force of nature, darting from one beast to the next, her daggers like quicksilver slashing through the air, leaving a mist of ichor behind them. She seemed to be the only thing holding back the tide.

"Watch out!" Mavarin shouted as a bellow ripped through the chamber. One of the larger, insect-like brutes had bullied its way into the melee, crushing several of the smaller hounds blocking its route. It had locked onto the two Dunwarr, its demented, hungry eyes blazing as it broke into a bull-like charge.

The thing lunged for Raythen. He brought his shield up, but found himself rooted to the spot, staring into the half a dozen yawning maws bearing down on him.

Just before they could snap shut, something arrested them. The creature shrieked from every mouth, then made an abrupt, ugly choking sound. Raythen watched in awe as it slowly began to rise up into the air, its many, twisted limbs thrashing, its orifices opening and closing, as though gasping for air.

He turned and saw Astarra, her staff raised, aquatic blue light pulsing from it. Her face was a rictus of concentration, her braided hair drenched with ethereal water as she reached out with her other hand and, with what looked like terrible effort, slowly clenched her fingers into a fist.

The demon crumpled. Black ichor burst from its maws as its insides were crushed, its spiny exoskeleton crunching and splitting as it was pulverized by the pressure of a fathomless depth, summoned up by Astarra's runestone. She released the invisible waters surrounding it, letting it flop to the cavern floor.

"By Fortuna," Raythen murmured, as Astarra bent double, panting.

There was no time to check she was alright. Several of the hound-beasts were already scrabbling to get over the obstruction caused by the broken body, their eyes wild, their huge jaws clacking and snapping. Mavarin slashed at one with his dagger, bellowing a Dunwarr war cry.

Raythen charged to his side, shield raised, and battered at the other beast, the heavy ironoak shuddering as it beat against the thing's jaw. He lunged at it with his dagger, holding it like a short sword, going for its eyes and throat. Talons from a second yipping horror scraped at his armor, gouging rents in the metal but failing to find flesh. He responded by hacking into its muzzle, sending it shrieking and reeling back.

As he brought his battered shield up again to receive another set of claws, he decided he was never going to try and escape from the Dunwol Keg ever again.

"This was what you were born to do, sweet Shiver," murmured the voice in Shiver's ear.

He'd started to shake uncontrollably, straining at the sorcerous chains that bound him. He could hear the sounds of battle all around, the terrible, yipping shrieks and howls of the demonic swarm and the screams of the elves as they were torn apart, one by one. He could sense Astarra's runemagic, the Turning responding to her demands. But it all felt so distant, completely separate from his current reality. It was like a memory, and nothing more.

"You know what you have to do," she urged him.

He collapsed to his knees, groaning. He could feel the Ynfernael coursing through him, like an infection gnawing at both body and soul, leaving him blackened and rotten like the twins. The portal blazed, its shadows full of whispers as they coiled thickly from its edges, filling the cavern, bleeding out into the surrounding tunnels and up, towards Thelgrim. It wasn't properly open yet, not quite, but it was achingly close.

"The runewitch," he heard one of the twins say in his warped voice, momentarily breaking through Shiver's horror. He looked at the corrupt dwarf, and realized he was holding a device in his hand – a dark green stone, its edges coarse, partially encased by a metallic band. As the twin raised it, Shiver felt its power flood his senses, its essence unmistakable.

It was a Star of Timmoran. The Hydra Shard.

"Go," said the other dwarf. The one holding the Shard turned and stepped down from the bone dais, entering the melee beyond.

"No," Shiver stammered, trying to get back up. An invisible hand – her hand – thrust him back down, black talons cutting deep into his pale shoulder. He still had the scars there from when it had happened.

"You will do as I command, slave," her voice snarled.

"You will do as we command, slave," snarled the remaining dwarf, the words spat from the portal.

"Open it."

"Open it."

He tried to answer, but there was blood in his mouth, forcing him to spit. In front of him, the heart of the rift had started to coalesce and solidify. In the middle of the churning confluence of Ynfernael power, something was a forming. A lock, made of pure darkness.

With trembling hands, Shiver raised his key.

"*Ataqua imedego,*" Astarra roared, slamming her staff forward. The surge of runepower flung a demon hound off the body of a deep elf before it could sink its fangs in, knocking it back into a knot of its braying kin.

She strode forward and helped the bloodied elf to his feet. The powers of the Deeprune were coursing through her. Her eyes glowed with aquatic luminescence, and her clothes and hair were floating, as though caught in an underwater current. She stood alongside the elf and smashed her staff's haft against the muzzle of another of the Ynfernael horrors, the invisible, localized pressure of the ocean crushing its skull with a gristly crack.

She'd lost sight of Raythen and Mavarin in the press. Shiver was still visible ahead, on his knees, framed by the terrible light of the portal. She had to reach him. She had to stop him, before he opened it.

"*Ataqua imedego,*" she snarled once more, and drove into the Ynfernael swarm. Her staff parted the writhing, warped creatures on either side of her, clearing a path towards the mound of bones and the hellish corona of light above it. Just before reaching it though, her power was checked. She gasped, her step faltering, a shockwave of Turning energies shivering through the whole cavern.

A wall of energy had met her runemagic and repelled it. She righted herself and focused ahead, along the channel the tides of the Deeprune had cleared through the Ynfernael swarm. There, at the end of it, stood Korri, his silver beard clasp glinting in the unnatural light of the portal. Shadows coiled like living creatures around the corrupt Dunwarr, but they could not obscure the power of the object held in his hand.

Astarra sensed it immediately. Its power was unmistakable. In a lifetime spent hunting runeshards, she'd experienced it only on a few, brief occasions. It made the energies she could call upon pale in comparison.

It was a Star of Timmoran, the Hydra Shard, and it was wholly under the Ynfernael's control.

Her heart quailed. She couldn't fight that. None of them could. A Star of Timmoran was everything her magics were not. The fragments inscribed with the runes were locked to a single form of magic, their potential only running so deep. The powers of a Star though, were almost limitless.

"You go no further, runewitch," hissed Korri, in a voice that was not his own. "Your power is worthless here."

"Release Shiver," she shouted, defiance flaring at the Dunwarr's words. "Stop this insanity before it's too late!"

"We are not the ones holding him," Korri cackled.

Astarra lunged forward a pace and summoned up another of the Deeprune's crushing waves, hoping to catch the Dunwarr off guard. She drove it at him, once more slamming aside the demons recovering on either side, snapping bones and shattering spines.

With a swipe of his hand and a snarl of effort, the dwarf cast the surge aside, sending it ploughing up into the cavern roof. The whole space shook, and dust and dirt cascaded down into the melee below.

Astarra's step faltered once again, and she was forced to clutch her staff to steady herself. Korri let loose an ugly laugh.

"I warned you, weakling sorceress. Let me show you true power."

The Dunwarr grasped the metal band that ran around the Shard and twisted it. Immediately its luminescence changed from a lustrous green to a smoldering, dark orange. Astarra felt the heat radiating from it.

Without even a word of power, Korri raised the stone towards her. Fire roared into being, jetting down the cleared channel as though blasted from the gullet of a great drake.

"*Salus darn,*" Astarra shouted in desperation, calling up a wall of unseen water in front of the tongue of flames. It evaporated in the searing heat, but not before it had taken the sting from the flames, the conflagration extinguished with a piercing hiss.

Astarra fought to stand upright, her limbs trembling with the effort. She realized Korri was laughing again.

"I thought I would make things simple for you at the start, and still you almost failed!"

The dwarf turned the Shard once more, its glimmer shifting to a searing white light. Astarra looked away with a growl, momentarily blinded. She sensed the power of the Star surge, followed by a sudden, sharp pain in her right leg, forcing her down onto one knee.

Korri was standing over her. The white brilliance had consumed him, and he had reappeared right before her, teleporting through the cavern.

He kicked her leg from under her, and was turning the band that controlled the Shard once more, changing the innate focus of its powers using the Dunwarr-made device. The white light turned a pale, cold blue.

She managed to get back onto her feet before the power of the Hydra surged again. This time it delved into bitter, icy depths, the twin of the chill magics commanded by Shiver. Swift as a racing heartbeat, a thick rind of ice materialized over her feet, lower legs and the bottom of her staff. She found herself fixed in place, pinned by the sorcerous cold.

She couldn't win this. In pure desperation she reached into the pouch at her waist and grasped the Ignis Shard.

"*Talatha ignis*," she cried out as she felt the heat ignite through her body. Fire surged down the length of her staff, and the ice around her feet evaporated in a searing flash, steam wreathing both her and the dwarf.

Korri simply laughed once more, an ugly, sick sound. He was toying with her.

"Are you sure you can handle two runestones at once, little sorceress?" the demons within him mocked. More ice surged from the ether, fashioned by demonic malice into a hundred wicked shards that hurtled at Astarra from all sides.

The first few sliced at her before she was able to fully marshal and control the energies of the Ignis, its power warring with the Deeprune in her staff. One shard cut her cheek bloody before the flames fully responded and melted the remainder from existence before they could impale her.

The rage of the Ignis was within her now, fully realized. She let it loose, feeding her exhaustion and her pain into it, channeling it into a raging firestorm that leapt into being all around her.

"Your power is built on a lie," she roared, flames licking from her eyes and throat, the fury of the runestone given voice. "It takes decades to master a Star of Timmoran, yet you think you can can control its abilities?"

For the briefest instant, she felt the power of the Ynfernael before her quail. She drove home her advantage, summoning the elements of the Deeprune and the Ignis Shard as one. The magical fires lit the swirling energies of the deeps, igniting like burning oil. She launched the pyroplasmic blaze at Korri, her whole body shaking and suffused with the twinned power of the runes.

The corrupt Dunwarr drew upon the power of the Star, but without true mastery of it he could only access so much. A wall of ice met the surge of burning energy Astarra had cast, but it wasn't enough to stop it, only checking it before it might reduce him to charred ash.

It gave him time though, time to twist the Hydra and summon its white light. Just as the last of the ice evaporated the brilliance consumed him, and suddenly he was there no longer.

Astarra roared with frustration. The lance of liquid fire surged over the nearest demons as they closed in on the bloodied remains of the daggerband, its flames searing away flesh and bone where before it had been unable to touch them. But Korri was no longer there. He had re-emerged in a blink of light back before the portal and its gristly mound.

She turned her rage towards him, fresh fires blazing, their roar drowning out even the howls of the burning demons surrounding her. The Dunwarr brought up the Hydra Shard once more, its light now gone, replaced by a void-like opacity.

Astarra unleashed her fire, slamming the channeled flames towards Korri. As she did so darkness rose from the Hydra

Shard, drawn forth by the Dunwarr. It was the blackness of the Ynfernael, twinned with the Star's energies, corrupting it. The shadows yawned into a maw that met Astarra's flames, consuming them. The two energies met with a thunderclap that shuddered through the cavern.

A scream of pain and effort ripped from Astarra's lips. It wasn't going to be enough. The darkness of the Ynfernael was driving towards her, eating up her flames as it went, pouring forth endlessly from the shard in Korri's hand. Behind him Shiver was still slumped before the portal, framed by it as it went into a psychedelic frenzy of colors. She could see shapes writhing behind it, trying to break through the final, thin skein protecting reality from their hellish dimension.

She couldn't beat it with two runestones. But she had three. She'd never tried channeling them all at once. It was madness, certain death. But it was certain death if she didn't. Worse even. She wasn't going to let their souls become playthings for these demonic horrors.

She delved into her pouch one more time and clutched the Viridis Seed, holding it in the same hand as the Ignis.

With a crack, the energies surrounding her redoubled. Her scream became a howl. Her staff was shaking, splitting in her grasp. The fire that had been surging around her began to burn her skin. Light blazed from her eyes, her mouth, from beneath her very skin. It was the power of the Turning unleashed, and it was not enough.

The shadows were checked, but they did not retreat. They fought with Astarra's magics, now a bolt of pure, crackling energy, consuming it, feasting on it. Their hunger was insatiable.

Astarra felt herself slipping away. Her very soul was being eroded by the unchecked power of the three runebound shards, hollowed out by the effort of trying to channel them. The pain had gone, her human senses overloaded. She couldn't remember her own name, or where she was. All she could see was directly ahead, to the clashing energies and Korri beyond them, the stolen shard held aloft.

Maelwich came from nowhere. The deep elf was a blur, darting between the writhing, embattled chaos surrounding her.

Elven steel flashed. For a second, Astarra thought she had opened the throat of the tainted Dunwarr. But she hadn't. She'd struck at the Hydra Shard and, more importantly, lashed out at the device controlling it.

The band of metal fell, scythed cleanly in two. Astarra saw it come apart as though in a dream.

The effect was instant. The black shadows recoiled, turning in on themselves and evaporating. A concussive blast ripped through the cavern, Astarra's own energies detonating like one of the Dunwarr blasting charges. She was thrown through the air, losing her grip on both her staff and the other two runestones.

Dropping them saved her life. The power that had been channeling through her evaporated in an instant, like a torch being plunged into icy waters. She landed on her back and arched her spine, gasping. Her whole body was in agony. Her skin was tender from the searing heat of the Ignis, and every muscle felt as though it had been ruptured and torn.

She moaned, trying to find the will to rise, even just to sit up. A shadow fell over, and for a second she feared she'd look up into the slavering, distended maws of one of the demon hounds, coming to avenge its master.

Instead, she found herself looking at Raythen. The one-eyed dwarf was practically dripping with foul, black ichor.

"It's Shiver," the Dunwarr thief panted. "He's still going to open the portal. We have to stop him."

CHAPTER TWENTY-EIGHT

"Get up," Raythen panted. He grasped Astarra under one arm, looking to Mavarin for help. The inventor was too busy driving back a snapping hound with wide, slashing sweeps of his dagger. He was grinning manically as he did so, as spattered with demonic viscera as Raythen.

"We have to reach him," Raythen added to Astarra. "We have to reach Shiver!"

The sorceress had managed to get onto her knees, clutching at her fallen staff and runestones. She looked dazed. Korri had been hurled back by the magical blast into the bone mound beneath the portal, but he was rising. There was no sign of the Star. Behind him Shiver was hunched over the heart of the portal, its shifting light now blinding.

"Shiver," Astarra murmured, her eyes finding a degree of focus.

"I'm going to try to get to him," Raythen said. "But if I don't make it, it's down to you. Understood?"

"Yes," she said more firmly, clutching at her staff. It was

close to splitting apart, but the light was still pulsing from its tip, however fitfully.

Raythen helped her to her feet and looked back towards the portal. The desperate struggle between the elves and the Ynfernael had spilled across the channel ploughed by Astarra and Korri's magics, blocking his route. Momentarily, he caught sight of the one the leader had called Talarin, the elf's auburn hair marking him out amidst the press, along with the glint of steel. His knives were unbloodied.

Raythen didn't have time to register his surprise. Behind him, he heard Astarra snarl a runeword.

Shiver felt the power of the Verto Magica in flux behind him, threatening to tear apart the entire cavern. He couldn't look though. As much as he tried, he couldn't rip his aching eyes from the portal, now right in front of him.

It was almost open. Malformed, writhing shapes, defying all the laws of nature, were half-visible squirming and writhing against the far side of the rift, making it pulse and shudder like a membrane that was a heartbeat away from rupturing. He could hear their whispering, the scratching of their claws. They were scraping at the inside of his skull.

"Still you fight," hissed her voice, her claws digging a little deeper. "You should know by now it will do you no good. Unlock it!"

Shiver's hand was shaking so badly he couldn't press the key home into the twisted, arcane lock that had formed at the heart of the portal, suspended by the churning Ynfernael energies. Her hand steadied him though. He groaned with horror and revulsion as, finally, the key slotted home.

•••

Astarra managed to stand. For a while it was all she could do. Her body was trembling and riven with pain. She had been utterly drained by the clash with the Hydra Shard, yet it was not over. Not even close.

She managed a runeword, bloodied lips spilling forth the arcane phrase as Raythen drove once more into the demons ahead. Every syllable made her ache. But still, the Deeprune responded, her ruined staff slick with water.

It called out to her, made her realize it wasn't the only stream in the cavern. The desperate fighting had riven the corrupted space, cracking both the floor and ceiling. There was water pouring from the rents overhead, drizzling down into the wild melee.

She remembered what Shiver and the other elves had said. The cavern was beneath the Blackwater, the lake at the heart of Thelgrim. There was a vast reservoir directly above them, untapped and full of potency.

Astarra reached within herself and drew upon the Deeprune once more. She let the power of the Turning quest upwards, beyond the slowly cracking layer of bedrock that lay between the bottom of the lake and the buried chamber. She could feel it there instantly, a crushing, powerful weight, the heart that gave the city above them life.

She tried to direct its pressure, to make it respond to the will of the Deeprune. It was sluggish at first, reluctant, its waters unused to taking commands. It had lain dormant for so long, still and undisturbed, while the evil beneath it had festered and taken root.

She swung her staff about her head, murmuring her

encouragement in the language of the runes, stirring it up and directing a portion of its power into the rock directly above the portal.

Now came the resistance. The stone of the cavern roof was tainted, rank with the corruption of the Ynfernael. It writhed and shook as Astarra tried to pierce it, to drive an opening in it.

She snarled with effort, pointing her staff directly above the portal, driving her will and her power via the Deeprune. The lake responded. There was a cracking sound, barely audible over the howls and screams all around. Water followed it, cascading in a sudden flow down, directly on top of where Shiver was crouched.

Shiver gasped. He was drenched, the sudden surge of water striking so hard he almost lost his grip on the key.

He felt the magics of the Turning in the downpour, the essence drawing from the great lake above. It shattered the memory that had been plaguing him, if only for a moment, clearing the Ynfernael fog brought on by the portal's presence.

The key was still fixed into the portal, unturned. His hand was upon it. He realized that his shaking had stopped completely.

"You must open it," snarled Zorri, reaching towards Shiver, ignoring the drenching flow of water from above. It was driving down on him, seeming to grow heavier and stronger, but he bore it up without question, his whole focus on the portal and the key.

"It is your destiny!" Zorri shouted.

He clutched Shiver's wrist, just above the manacle. It was

only then that he realized the ethereal chains that usually held him at bay when memories and visions assailed him, had gone.

He was bound no more.

He didn't even need to speak a word. Ice formed instantaneously beneath the flooding water, running from Zorri's grip on his arm up to the dwarf's shoulder. He tried to break free with an unnatural hiss, but the chill was relentless.

Shiver drove his mind into the Empyrean, sending ice surging up the downpour above him, freezing it solid in a matter of seconds. With a snarl he tore his arm free from Zorri and snapped a word of power. The ice overhead shattered, raining down around him in a blizzard of shards, those that struck him rebounding harmlessly from his hard, pale skin.

He snatched Zorri by the base of his beard and, with a roar of effort, flung the half-frozen Dunwarr straight at the portal.

It gave way behind him, the constituency of its surface now like thick, multi-hued oil. It seemed to haul him in, his strangled scream cut short.

Korri saw what had happened from the base of the mound of bones. He'd been thrown there by Astarra's magics and had only just managed to regain his feet, clearly shaken by the surge of energies. With a howl, he charged up the mound of bones at Shiver, fighting his way through the broken ice. The elf turned and with little more than a thought, drove a lance of ice into the Dunwarr's core, running him through. Infected black blood burst from the wound, the treacherous advisor stumbling, staring down in abject shock at the length impaling him. His eyes, Shiver realized, had lost the darkness that had been consuming them before.

"Go," Shiver said to him. "And account for your crimes."

He grasped the Dunwarr by the shoulders and drove him up, into the portal, after his vanished kinsman. It consumed him utterly, the black smoke broiling from its redoubling. Shiver stumbled back just in time, feeling its power trying to haul him in as well. He fought, broke free from it, and the darkness seemed to harden, its cursed light shrinking. He felt its strength draining, as though the power connecting it to the chamber had been cut.

He dared look away to survey the bloodshed beneath him. It was nearing an end – elves and Ynfernael alike, few were left fighting. Bodies covered the cavern floor in an indiscernible mess of blood.

Maelwich had forged a path through, helping Astarra. The runewitch was wounded, looking close to collapse.

Shiver felt a fresh surge of energies before he could call out to them. He turned back to the portal as a terrible shriek went up from the remaining demons, the unnatural sound echoing back over and over from the cracked, icy cavern roof.

Something was dragging itself through the portal. The lock at its center disintegrated into the ether as a bulbous, distorted shape broke the rip's sheen. An arm came first, a great trunk of melted flesh that bubbled and popped like running wax. Another followed, and then a head.

Shiver found himself looking into the faces of both Korri and Zorri. The twins had been melded together into a nightmarish, screaming visage, their left and right eyes fused to form one baleful, unblinking orb, their mouths, still separate, distended and filled with wicked fangs. Their beards were matted with protoplasmic filth, and their clothing had torn and ripped around the morass of their conjoined bodies. They howled with pain as, through willpower alone, they forced their way through the Ynfernael portal and back into the material plane.

Shiver felt the agony and horror of their minds as they reentered the cavern as one. It paralyzed him, filled him with equal parts terror and disgust. The monstrosity was halfway out of the opening and reaching for him with hands that, before his very eyes, were tearing open into secondary, screaming maws.

In that moment he felt utterly powerless, dwarfed by the raw, corrupting energy of the Ynfernael as it threatened to burst free. It would take him with it, he knew, soul and all, a plaything to be forever tormented with resurgent memories of all his misdeeds. He didn't have the power to stop this, he didn't even know how to close the portal.

And yet, amidst it all, five precious words came back to him.

Atali nametha ren. Nameth hatala.

The path is the purpose. The path goes on.

It would not end here.

No longer giving himself time to think, to fear, he lashed out once more with the Empyrean. It answered him, raising up a thick, glittering wall of ice to block the creature's passage from the portal. It began hammering at it, each strike sending jagged lines across the wall's surface, crazing the ice.

"That won't hold it," shouted Maelwich. "We have to destroy the portal!"

"I can't," Shiver admitted, momentarily losing focus. The sheet of ice started to come crashing down.

"I was only used to open them," he admitted, struggling

to rebuild the ice, both hands raised, channeling Empyrean power through his shuddering body.

"I can do it," said a new voice. Astarra had regained a fraction of her strength. She was leaning heavily on her split staff.

"I'll seal it," she went on. "But you have to get back."

"How?" Shiver asked. He had no idea how Astarra would know the dark speech necessary to bind the Ynfernael wound shut. He feared she was going to do something foolish, something that would cost her her life.

She didn't reply. The last of Shiver's ice binding the monstrosity that had once been the twins shattered apart. It hauled itself further through the splitting portal with a maddened bellow.

Maelwich lashed out before either Shiver or Astarra could react, her innate hatred of the Ynfernael driving her to strike. Launching herself up off the jutting bones of the sacrificed elves and dwarfs, she scissored her long, serrated blades on either side of the creature's trunk-like, bulging neck.

The deep elf steel bit home, clean and true. It scythed through the monstrous head of the thing that had once been Korri and Zorri, severing it completely. The deformed skull fell with a heavy thud, rolling down from the broken bone plinth.

Shiver experienced a moment of hope as he expected the bulbous bulk of the monstrosity's body to give way, but it barely even shook. The ichor was reduced to a pattering flow, and he watched in sickening horror as fresh spurs of bone and chitin formed a new maw set into the thing's shoulders. It let out a fresh, keening screech.

The sight of it made Shiver sick. Maelwich kept attacking, slashing long ribbons from its ever-shifting body with her knives, but it barely even seemed to notice. It was healing as fast as she could strike.

"It's still coming through," Shiver shouted, despairing. What more could any of them do? "I can't stop it!"

"I can," Astarra repeated with a snarl. "Get Maelwich back!"

There was no time to further question the runewitch's plan. All he could do was follow his own course, but that didn't mean abandoning her. Shiver snatched at Maelwich and hauled her away from the demonic monstrosity as it dragged more and more obscene bulk from the buckling, writhing portal.

"Get anyone still alive out," he urged her, trying to reach the elven leader through the killing frenzy that had gripped her. Maelwich managed to nod, looking back towards the cavern entrance. Only a few elves still fought on, and Mavarin. The Dunwarr was standing on top of a mound of slain demons, drenched in filth, waving his dagger and making a wild, keening noise.

"Go!" Astarra roared. Shiver could feel the energies of the Verto Magica responding once more to the runewitch's summons, her mastery of them now almost instinctive. He directed Maelwich towards the cavern entrance, but turned back rather than follow her.

"I won't leave you to face this alone," he shouted over the terrible wailing of the portal and its demonic spawn. But Astarra wasn't listening.

With a crack, the ceiling overhead began to split.

•••

"Aquatum vestra," Astarra chanted. *"Vestra naii destrus! Teo lasteth!"*

She was delving into power she had never known, driving both body and soul far beyond any limits she thought she had. The Deeprune, ever faithful, was still answering her call. It was directing the might of the Blackwater once again, driving the great pressure of the lake against the bedrock that supported it.

The ancient waters were obeying her. All across the cavern roof, cracks were beginning to appear, the twisting, corrupt stone being ripped apart by the weight bearing down on it. Water burst forth, first just a trickle, but growing and expanding as the splits spread.

The sudden springs cascaded down onto the carnage that had overrun the cavern. The surviving demons already on the material side of the portal had gone feral, tearing at one another amidst the littered bodies. Astarra was already drenched thanks to the power of the Deeprune, but she kept calling for more, the words taking on a life of their own. They surged and flowed from her lips like the ocean waves, summoning the Blackwater to lay claim to this undiscovered pit, this buried cavern that had existed, untouched by it, since the dawn of Mennara's creation.

The nightmare that had once been Korri and Zorri could not free itself in time. Great lumps of the cavern's ceiling were crashing down now along with the water, pulverizing the bodies beneath. A stalactite ploughed into the floor barely a dozen paces to Astarra's right, shards of stone whickering past her.

She barely noticed. It was almost complete. The whole cavern would come down, drowning and burying the horror of the Ynfernael before it could break through, fully formed. She would perish with it. The thought did not concern her. The power of the runes had burned away her fears, her doubts, every last unnecessary thought, sharpening and polishing the brilliance of her soul. She was as one with the Turning. She would not allow its purity to become befouled by the Ynfernael's cancer.

One of the falling rocks struck the mutated horror a glancing blow. Its shrieking redoubled as bones crunched and snapped. It was almost free though. She couldn't stop it getting out.

That was when she noticed Shiver. The deep elf hadn't left when she had told him to. Instead, he drove into the plunging water ahead, summoning his chill connection to the Empyrean. Ice formed rapidly over the lower bulk of the Ynfernael creature, welding it thickly to the crushed bones beneath. It twisted and writhed with a hideous, unnatural, disjointed motion, but Shiver was holding it fast, his hands extended, fingers splayed and shaking.

He managed to look back and make eye contact with Astarra as she clutched her sundered staff with both hands. A moment's recognition, an expression of understanding.

She broke contact with the Blackwater, hauling the energies of the Deeprune back into her staff. The great lake needed no more directing. Its wrath was in full flow, thundering down upon the cavern, crushing it and flooding it.

Shiver was running past her, snatching her hand as he went. Together they sprinted for the crack that marked the cavern entrance, vaulting bodies and dodging around the few remaining Ynfernael beasts as they ripped themselves apart.

Water and rock tumbled down ahead of them. Astarra bellowed with effort as they forged through it together, the thunder of the collapsing space filling their senses. Shiver lashed out one last time with the power of the Empyrean, freezing water in mid-flow above them, leaving splinters of rock lodged in them, locked in just above their heads. It lasted only a few seconds before the continuing flow from above melted and collapsed the ice and sent the pent-up mass of broken ceiling crashing down.

A few seconds was all they needed. They threw themselves out of the cavern, side-by-side.

Astarra hit the dirt and rolled, turning as soon as she'd regained her balance. She caught a final vision of the cavern and the portal at its heart. The twisted, bellowing monstrosity that had once been Korri and Zorri was being crushed, the collapse near-total. Behind it the light of the rift had gone into wild spasms, its unnatural energies unable to sustain it now that it had been abandoned beneath the pulverizing weight of the Blackwater.

She lost sight of it as the cavern entrance itself began to collapse, sealing off the surging flood that was threatening to burst through to the adjoining tunnel. She found the strength to rise and stumble with Shiver deeper into the warren that had led them to the portal cavern. Maelwich, Mavarin and two other deep elf survivors were just ahead. They urged them on as they reached the confluence of passageways where they'd paused before, the lone jaela root still burning, its green-tinted, fragile light dragging them up from the maddening depths. A last, shuddering crash ripped through the subterranean realm, setting the tunnels trembling and shaking dirt from the ceiling. Then, finally, all was still.

"By all the gods," Astarra managed to pant, before the pain and exhaustion finally caught up with her. She collapsed into the dirt, too drained to speak further, her vision swaying as she centered the last of her energies into staying conscious.

Shiver knelt by her side, concern on his face. He placed a single finger on her brow. It was cold to the touch, yet soothing, making her sigh as she grasped onto the enervating sensation.

The elf murmured something under his breath, words Astarra didn't understand. She felt their effect though. Her singed flesh grew gradually less sore, and she experienced the faintest sliver of strength returning to her limbs, drawn forth by the elf's innate link to the Empyrean. He was giving his own energy to her, his shaking returning as he in turn grew weaker.

"Can you stand?" he managed to ask. She gazed up into his eyes for a moment, then nodded. Her staff had fallen at her side, split down the middle. She reached out tentatively to pick it up, feeling only the faintest undercurrent of energy as she grasped it. The Deeprune was as drained as she was.

Mavarin joined Shiver, helping her to her feet. The frenzied warrior he had become in the cavern was gone, replaced by a tired, ichor-spattered rendering of the tinkerer that was somewhat more familiar. Astarra looked around, her thoughts still aching and slow. Maelwich and the last two elves were standing watching her guardedly, one cradling a badly bloodied arm. Everyone looked as exhausted as she felt, though there was still a cold steeliness to Maelwich's eyes.

"Are we all that's left?" she asked them. "No one else made it out?"

"I saw Talarin not long before the end," one of Maelwich's elves said. "He had retrieved the Star of Timmoran that the tainted Dunwarr dropped. I didn't see what became of him though. I saw no other survivors."

Astarra stared at him for a moment, then looked at the others.

"Then where's Raythen?"

CHAPTER TWENTY-NINE

"I can't sense him," Shiver admitted as Astarra looked back the way they had come. He didn't want to admit that the reason for his inability to feel the Dunwarr's presence was mostly down to his exhaustion. A cold, deadly fury had gripped him while he had been battling the Ynfernael, freed from his trance by Astarra's vision, but now the exertion of drawing so stridently on the Empyrean for aid was catching up with him. He'd almost lost consciousness while he'd been reviving Astarra, though he'd managed to shield his weakness from her. She had born enough of a burden in the fight already.

"There are markings here," Maelwich said, pointing at the floor of the confluence of tunnels. "It looks like some of the hound demons escaped the cavern during the melee. There are Dunwarr boots too, heading away from the cavern. There."

Shiver was no tracker – he could make little sense of the dirt and scuffed rock of the tunnel. His concern for Raythen ran counterpoint to the dangers that a number of the Ynfernael beasts had escaped. They couldn't be allowed to spread the corruption further. Maelwich at least seemed certain as she strode off into the darkness, gesturing to the others. "They can't have gotten far!"

One of the elves carefully pulled up the jaela root, the light of the smoldering spores providing the only illumination as he set off after Maelwich. The rest followed.

"Do you think Talarin made it out with the Hydra?" Astarra asked, grimacing as she was forced to lean on Shiver for support. He placed a hand around her shoulder, trying not to let her see how his own steps almost faltered.

"Why would he take it?" Maelwich said from ahead. She alone seemed unaffected by the desperate battle in the cavern. Her drive and energy was astounding.

"Why would anyone take it?" Mavarin spoke up. "Power."

Shiver glanced at him, trying to gauge the dwarf's thoughts. Raythen had claimed Mavarin had led them all here as part of an elaborate plan to steal and then 'rediscover' the Hydra Shard. He'd fought hard alongside them, but now he wondered whether the inventor still bore some ulterior motive.

"Talarin has power already," Maelwich said defensively, casting a sharp look back at Mavarin, her face lit by the jaela's glow. "He does not need more."

"Is that what he thinks, or what you think?" Mavarin asked. "I stole the Hydra from the Hall of the Ancestors and planted it where they told me. When I went back for it, it had gone. Who took it?"

"You've said it yourself, the twins," Astarra pointed out.

"But how?" Mavarin asked. "Do you really think even one of them could slink off to that section of the mines without being noticed?"

"They were rotten with Ynfernael power," Shiver said. "They could have retrieved it by all manner of dark means."

"Perhaps," Mavarin said. "But if the taint really runs that deep, it wouldn't surprise me if there were more helping them than just me."

Nobody had a chance to respond to the accusation. Maelwich cried out from up ahead, and raced off into the darkness. Shiver grimaced, trying to catch up without losing Astarra.

The leader of the Aethyn had come across another tunnel cross section. Four of them met at a central point, branching off into the unknown dark. Maelwich had halted between them, standing over her discovery.

A body lay at the center of the junction, slumped on its side. It was Talarin. The jaela light gave weak illumination to the slumped form.

Maelwich was staring at the body, seemingly frozen. Tentatively, Mavarin rolled it over onto its back, and recoiled.

Talarin's face, lit by the green glow, was twisted and deformed. Black veins formed a latticework all along his pale flesh, and his mouth had become distended with unnaturally long canines. His eyes, wide and staring, were glossy back.

"Talarin was a daewyl," Shiver said softly, looking down at the twisted body. Seeing its corruption laid bare filled him with loathing. There was concern too – he hadn't sensed the taint upon him, hadn't recognized him for what he was, despite the fact that he too had once born the same allegiance. "He hid it well."

"The Ynfernael hid it well," Maelwich corrected, her voice riven with equal parts sorrow and disgust. "From all of us."

"He must have taken the Hydra for the twins," Mavarin said. "They all serve the Ynfernael then. Demonic whispers and shared lies seem like their lot."

He knelt down to examine the pouch at the fallen elf's waist. It was empty.

"If that's the case, then who took the Hydra from him?" Astarra wondered out loud.

Maelwich bent over the corpse and grasped the elven dagger buried in its chest. She twisted the serrated blade roughly free.

"This was the dagger I gave your Dunwarr ally," she said, holding the dripping length of razor-edged steel up to the light.

"Raythen," Astarra murmured. Shiver felt a sense of dismay, quickly replaced by one of acceptance. Of course it would have been Raythen. He was a fool for not having predicted the dwarf's actions.

In the silence that followed, Mavarin began to laugh. Everyone looked at him, causing him to pause, then burst into even louder mirth.

"What is it?" Maelwich demanded, her pride stung. The dwarf took a moment to compose himself, still chuckling fitfully.

"Well, it looks like I was right to hire Raythen after all. He got the job done, even if it wasn't in the way I intended."

Shiver found little amusing about the situation. He felt Astarra's anger flare.

"He must have spotted Talarin picking it up after Korri dropped it," she said, a hint of bitterness in her voice. "Pursued him this far. I guess we shouldn't have trusted him after all."

"I'm amazed you ever did," Mavarin admitted. "I didn't

think for a moment any companionship between the three of you would last. In fact, I was hoping it wouldn't. It would make you all easier to direct if you didn't trust each other."

"Then that is your mistake, Dunwarr," Shiver said.

"Quiet," Maelwich interrupted, again raising the blade that had killed Talarin. "Do you hear that?"

Shiver paused and listened, instantly picking up what Maelwich had heard as Astarra and Mavarin fought to detect it.

"Fighting," he said. "Down that tunnel."

He pointed at one of the four leading to the junction.

"It sounds like Dunwarr."

They came across the last of the demons to have escaped the cavern before its collapse. They were attacking a band of Dunwarr at the end of one of the twisting tunnels, where it rose up towards another hidden entrance in the Dunwol Kenn Karnin's foundations. Astarra heard a roared battle cry as she arrived at it and saw Captain Bradha driving back one of the snarling hounds with wide swipes of her shortsword, a trio of her fellow Warriors' Guild members at her back. Two of their number already lay dead, savaged by beastly fangs, while a demon likewise lay hacked apart by Dunwarr axes, its limbs still spasming.

Maelwich leapt upon the remaining creature from behind, avoiding its spiny ridge as she plunged her daggers into either side of its neck. It tried to buck and gouge her with its chitinous back and wicked, barbed tail, but she darted lithely away from it, landing on all fours in front of Bradha and leaving it to die.

The dwarf captain raised her sword defensively, but did not strike. Astarra saw the eyes behind her helmet, darting from one member of their unlikely party to the next.

"By the Ancestors," she said gruffly. "You all look like you've been dragged through the Ynfernael backwards."

"I think we might have been," Astarra admitted, silently relieved the captain hadn't immediately lashed out at Maelwich. She knew she couldn't summon the power necessary to fight the four dwarf warriors, not even for a moment.

"There are demons loose beneath your city," Maelwich said, standing up, abruptly towering over Bradha. "My daggerband have ended their threat. An Ynfernael portal has been closed this day."

"A portal?" Bradha repeated. "Beneath Thelgrim?"

"Opened by your king's treasonous advisors," Maelwich went on, her words cutting and sharp. "Or did you think these creatures you have helped bring down are natural denizens of these tunnels?"

Bradha shared an uneasy glance with one of her warrior-kin.

"We were searching for him," she said, pointing her ichor-stained sword at Mavarin. "He recently absconded along with another criminal. Eight of my kindred are dead because of it, and I suspect you all had a hand in it."

"We mourn their deaths," Astarra said. "But there is more at work here than the feud between elf and dwarf. Evil has been uprooted from beneath Thelgrim, but it might yet triumph. Your king's advisors were seeking to break your city's defenses and flood the valley before the gates. They want to make a sacrifice of the thousands seeking shelter there."

Bradha stood considering the accusation, then gestured once more with her sword.

"You will be brought before King Ragnarson," she declared. "You can make your case to him."

"I'd rather not–" Mavarin began to say, but Bradha clattered her sword off the rim of her shield. The three Dunwarr brought their shields up, locking them together.

"We have all seen enough fighting this day," Shiver said, the weariness in his voice obvious. "We shall speak to your king, Dunwarr."

Silence lay heavy across the throne room of the Dunwol Kenn Karnin as Bradha finished conversing quietly with Ragnarson. The King in the Deeps was sitting atop his towering throne, looking almost small compared to its graven, stony bulk. Astarra did her best not to stare, taking in the sweeping majesty of the great amphitheater. Its tiers of seats were currently empty, cleared by order of the king as they had entered. Guards had forcibly ejected the members of the assembled Guild Council who had protested. Even the Guild Masters themselves had gone, ushered out by Dunwarr captains and Ragnarson's curses.

It seemed the king didn't want any to witness what was spoken of by Astarra, Mavarin and the elves.

Only the three captains of the Warriors' Guild, including Bradha, had remained behind, listening in stony silence to Astarra's story. She had marshalled what little strength she had left to tell them of the shadow beneath Thelgrim, of Korri and Zorri's manipulation and the desperate sacrifices made beneath their very feet. Afterwards Ragnarson had conferred privately with his captains, seemingly now the only Dunwarr he was willing to trust. They stepped away from the great throne's rocky perch as Ragnarson cleared his throat.

"Had Captain Bradha not brought me the head of one of these beasts, and were her testimony of what she has seen in the tunnels below this fortress not clear and certain, I would order you all to be cut down before me this very instant," he said, his voice as cold and hard as his expression. "As it is, there may be a modicum of truth to what you have just told me, runewitch."

"It's all true," Astarra said, too tired to feel anger at the Dunwarr king's accusing tone.

"What is true is that a number of my people are dead, slain by you and the elves you have thrown your lot in with," Ragnarson went on. "You broke into this very citadel, murdered eight guards and left with two criminals. That is all fact."

"One criminal, actually," Mavarin said bluntly. "M- Me. Raythen won his innocence in the Trial of the Mountain."

Astarra and Shiver both shot the inventor a withering look. Ragnarson carried on as though he hadn't heard the outburst.

"The blood of the slain demands justice. I would be derelict in my duties as king if I did not pursue it."

"The blood is on the hands of your fallen advisors, not ours," Maelwich said. Astarra had been worried that the proud deep elf would have little time for the Dunwarr king, but she had said nothing antagonistic since they had been led into the hall. Her words were calm and measured as she addressed Ragnarson.

"They twisted your will to their own ends. They were the

ones who instigated the theft of the Hydra Shard, and they likewise have now claimed this Dunwarr's invention, the burrowing device. They sought to start a war between our two peoples. They also hoped to kill thousands of innocents, and they may yet if you do not ensure the defenses above the valley are secured."

Ragnarson was silent, his grim expression unchanged. Maelwich went on.

"There is no dishonor in being taken in by the lies of demonkind. Deceit is the very essence of the Ynfernael. It has laid its roots slow and deep here. The corruption started many years ago. You could not have foreseen it – even we only sensed it as it bore fruit. Such mistakes cannot be undone. My people know that better than any."

Ragnarson looked at Maelwich, seeming to consider the words, then signaled abruptly to the trio of warriors by his side.

"Skirmish-Captain Svensdottir, you will take one hundred chosen warriors from the guild and march immediately to the Upper East defenses, where the Deeprun flows by the tributaries. Find the burrower device there and destroy it. Slay any who attempt to impede you. Be ever-vigilant for the spawn of the Ynfernael. Captain Svensson, take a dozen of your own warriors and issue a proclamation outside the Guild Hall. The curfew is now over. All restrictions in Thelgrim are at an end."

Svensdottir bowed and departed, calling up to the guards at the throne room's doors to send word ahead of her to the citadel barracks. Ragnarson turned his gaze back to the bedraggled outsiders who had been brought into his hall.

"You have sacrificed much to strike down the evil which

threatened this city," he told Maelwich. "That is obvious. I will consider the blood shed by your clan fair payment for the Dunwarr lives you have stolen. The same goes for your sorcerous kinsman, and the runewitch. As for Mavarin ..."

Astarra felt the inventor tense up beside her before Ragnarson went on.

"He may not have known of the greater evil he was committing, but he has still defiled this city and the halls of its ancestors with his crimes. He is my subject, and it is my place to render judgement on him."

Mavarin started to speak, but Astarra put a warning hand on his shoulder, stilling him while the king continued.

"The proper punishment for his transgressions is death. Nevertheless, there has been enough blood spilled in and around Thelgrim in recent times. I will not be responsible for any more. Instead, I call upon royal prerogative. He will be banished from this city. You will walk from here into exile, strange inventor. Go where you please, but never return, upon pain of death."

Mavarin seemed to consider the pronouncement, then nodded, a slow smile creeping across his dirty face.

"Funnily enough, I wasn't intending to stay anyway. Guild membership seems to have lost its allure lately."

"Your judgements are fair, King in the Deeps," Maelwich said, inclining her head. "And if all is thus settled, we shall take our leave. The clan will be anxious for news, and I wish to dispatch fresh daggerbands to ensure the *denwal far* true has been cleansed."

"Captain Bradha will escort you all from the city," Ragnarson said. Bradha stepped forward, indicating for them to join her.

"One last thing," Ragnarson said, his voice turning gruff for a moment. Astarra looked up at him, sitting alone on his cold, unyielding throne.

"Tell me again," he said to her. "When did you last see my son?"

EPILOGUE

Shiver felt the cool rush of the waters running over his face, slowly breaking down the filth that had defiled him for so long.

He stood in the shallows of the river running through the Aethyn's cavern, his robes hitched up around his waist, bending forward to splash more of the swift-running water over his face and torso. Astarra and Mavarin stood next to him, likewise crouching or stooped over, dousing themselves down.

They had returned to the Aethyn camp with Maelwich, where they had been greeted by the welcome sight of first rootbread and broiled silver fins, and then a short but deep sleep. Astarra had simply collapsed on a mat of woven cavern creepers beneath one of the clan's shelters, and Shiver slept on the stone beside her, too exhausted to even care about the dried ichor staining much of his body.

It was the first uninterrupted sleep he had known for months. There had been no dreams, no night terrors, and no memories. When he started awake, Maelwich and the two other Aethyn survivors of the battle in the cavern had already completed their ritual washing in the waters of the subterranean river. Now it was their turn.

Mavarin waded out into the current until it was almost up to his chest, scrubbing his battered leather apron clean before diving fully beneath the surface. Shiver was worried for a second that he had been caught up in the wicked current, but he re-emerged swiftly, spitting water, shaking his head and grinning like a dog. From fighting against Ynfernael horrors to bathing in a sacred deep elf cavern, nothing seemed to truly phase the dwarf.

"Where will you go, Dunwarr?" Shiver asked him, standing up and stretching aching back muscles. The inventor shrugged.

"I don't know yet. That's the good part."

"Don't the dwarfs of the Duldor Deeps value invention?" Astarra asked as she shook out her braid, her long, dark hair falling to her waist. Mavarin scoffed.

"Those tinkerers wished they were half as gifted as me! No, I think it's time to leave the mountains altogether. Perhaps I should become a rogue, like Raythen."

He chuckled at the thought, bringing a smile to Astarra's lips. Shiver waded up to the bank to where Maelwich was standing watching over them, murmuring the final blessings of the cleansing rite in the Aethyn tongue.

He'd wondered just what had become of the thief they had set out from Frostgate with. Had he really made it out of the warren beneath Thelgrim with the Hydra Shard? Had that truly been his goal all along? Shiver wondered whether he would ever know for sure. He doubted it.

"What about you, elf?" Mavarin called out from the river, seemingly reluctant to leave it. "Where will your wanderings take you next?"

"Wherever the gods will it," he replied, as Astarra came to

join him. She'd slotted the Viridis Seed into her staff, slowly reknitting its shattered bone. In the rushing waters of the river a spark had returned to her eyes, though her soul seemed a little sharper and a little harder to Shiver than it had been before they'd entered the cavern beneath Thelgrim together. She was a long way from the prickly runewitch who'd almost called arcane fury down on him in Frostgate.

"Will you seek out more memories?" she asked him, water pattering on the rocks beneath.

"I will," Shiver affirmed. "But I will be in no rush."

"I believe I'll come with you," Astarra said to his surprise, casting her hair back over her shoulder. "If my time in the Dunwarrs has taught me one thing, it's that I have more places to see and people to meet. The runes can wait, for a time. That's if you'll have me for company?"

"Yes," Shiver said with a slow smile. "I believe it will be good to have some company, for a little while longer."

Daylight. A part of Raythen had almost missed it. Strange for a Dunwarr, but then again, he was no ordinary Dunwarr. He was reminded of that as he stepped out onto the narrow, rocky ledge above the valley, leaving the cloying darkness of the mountains behind.

The valley lay beneath him, packed with people, Thelgrim's great gates glittering in the dawn light. The day was rising steadily, banishing the shadows, slowly driving them out of even the valley's squalid depths.

There were thousands down there, he estimated, a sprawling, miserable encampment that had quadrupled since he had first set eyes on it. The refugees had spilled out from the valley itself and now occupied the foothills beyond, the dispossessed of Terrinoth, washed up at the edge of the world and abandoned there.

Someone else's problem, at least for now. Raythen began to walk along the craggy pathway. He'd discarded most of his stolen armor in the tunnels behind him, though he'd kept the warrior's belt. The pouch strapped to it had been a perfect fit for the Hydra Shard, weighing heavily on his thigh as he picked his way along the mountainside. He could feel its energies, dormant for now, awaiting the touch of one who knew how to unlock its power. Raythen didn't know how to do that, but he was sure of one thing – those with the required arcane knowledge also tended to have an awful lot of silver.

Play the odds right, and nine times out of ten, you'd come out on top.

As he walked, he heard the sound of a horn ringing out through the valley. He paused, wondering if he'd been discovered. If so, he'd underestimated them. But no, he realized. He recognized the notes being sounded from above the great gates. They weren't for him.

He began to walk again, away from the mountains. As he went, he smiled.

It seemed as though someone had gotten through to his father after all.

The horn note woke Sarra. She began to cry.

Tiabette held her close. There was nothing more she could do. They had no food, no money, no possessions. For the past two days she had been forced to scavenge scraps from under a sutler's wagon to feed her daughter, remains even the stray hounds that seemed to have congregated around the camp wouldn't touch.

It had started out with hope, with cautious optimism, with a deep, powerful determination, but it had all ended here, beneath the cold, uncaring mountains, starving and shivering. She regretted leaving her home, regretted every moment of the long trek across Terrinoth. It had all been for nothing. She would die here, with her daughter in her arms, unremembered and uncared for.

A voice began to shout somewhere down the valley. Others joined it, a ripple of excitement. Tiabette could hardly bring herself to look up. When she did though, her heart nearly stopped.

Something was stirring, out beyond the wagons and the tents and the lean-tos, beyond the cooking fires and the laundry lines and the huddled masses. Movement. Motion.

Some force animated Tiabette, some spirit, long ago cowed but never quite killed off. She found her feet. She kept her daughter in her arms, despite how they shook. Sarra stirred against her shoulder, tearful and bleary-eyed, as her mother began to walk.

"Stay close," she murmured to her, her heart beating all the quicker. "Not much further now."

Ahead, the gates of Thelgrim were opening.

ACKNOWLEDGMENTS

A huge thank you to the whole team at Aconyte, without whom this book couldn't have been written. Especial praise goes to Lottie, my ever-patient editor. Thanks also to the Fantasy Flight Games team, especially Katrina, who helped make sure *Gates of Thelgrim* was worthy of their wonderful setting.

ABOUT THE AUTHOR

ROBBIE MacNIVEN is a Highlands-native History graduate from the University of Edinburgh. He is the author of several novels and many short stories for the *New York Times*-bestselling *Warhammer 40,000 Age of Sigmar* universe, and the narrative for HiRez Studio's *Smite Blitz RPG*. Outside of writing his hobbies include historical re-enacting and making eight-hour round trips every second weekend to watch Rangers FC.

robbiemacniven.wordpress.com
twitter.com/robbiemacniven

Legend of the Five Rings

At the edges of the Rokugani Empire, brave warriors defend its borders from demonic threats, while battle and political intrigue divide the Great Clans in their quest for glory and advantage.

Follow dilettante detective, Daidoji Shin, and his samurai bodyguard as they solve murders and mysteries amid the machinations of the Clans.

The Great Clan novellas of Rokugan return, collected in omnibus editions for the first time, with brand new tales of the Lion and Crane Clans.

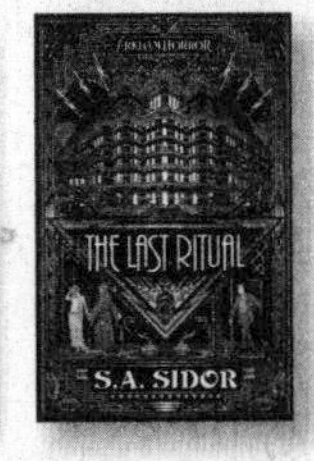

EXPLORE AMAZING WORLDS

WORLD EXPANDING FICTION

Do you have them all?

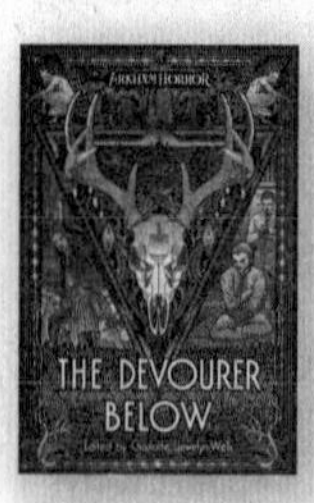

ARKHAM HORROR

- ☐ *Wrath of N'kai* by Josh Reynolds
- ☐ *The Last Ritual* by S A Sidor
- ☐ *Mask of Silver* by Rosemary Jones
- ☐ *Litany of Dreams* by Ari Marmell
- ☐ *The Devourer Below* edited by Charlotte Llewelyn-Wells
- ☐ *Dark Origins, The Collected Novellas Vol 1*
- ☐ *Cult of the Spider Queen* by S A Sidor *(coming soon)*

DESCENT

- ☐ *The Doom of Fallowhearth* by Robbie MacNiven
- ☐ *The Shield of Daqan* by David Guymer
- ☑ *The Gates of Thelgrim* by Robbie MacNiven
- ☐ *Zachareth* by Robbie MacNiven *(coming soon)*

KEYFORGE

- ☐ *Tales from the Crucible* edited by Charlotte Llewelyn-Wells
- ☐ *The Qubit Zirconium* by M Darusha Wehm

LEGEND OF THE FIVE RINGS

- ☐ *Curse of Honor* by David Annandale
- ☐ *Poison River* by Josh Reynolds
- ☐ *The Night Parade of 100 Demons* by Marie Brennan
- ☐ *Death's Kiss* by Josh Reynolds
- ☐ *The Great Clans of Rokugan, The Collected Novellas Vol 1 (coming soon)*

PANDEMIC

- ☐ *Patient Zero* by Amanda Bridgeman

TWILIGHT IMPERIUM

- ☐ *The Fractured Void* by Tim Pratt
- ☐ *The Necropolis Empire* by Tim Pratt

ZOMBICIDE

- ☐ *Last Resort* by Josh Reynolds
- ☐ *Planet Havoc* by Tim Waggoner *(coming soon)*

EXPLORE OUR WORLD EXPANDING FICTION

ACONYTEBOOKS.COM

@ACONYTEBOOKS

ACONYTEBOOKS.COM/NEWSLETTER